Bloom *books*

Dear reader,

I love every bit of this book. The character development was planned back from book one, but the way everyone connected on page just really set it off and made it so much more than I originally envisioned.

The relationships here, whether new or old, whether flourishing or failing, are what *Gleam* is all about. I love how it all unfolded.

Also, there's a particular scene in this book that I wrote before I even finished writing *Gild*. I think of it as the sundown scene and I rewrote it many times to make sure it was just right, because the build-up demanded it.

This book is all about triumph and heartbreak, desire and devastation. And the ending? It's one of my all-time favorites in the whole series.

I hope you enjoy!

GLEAM

RAVEN KENNEDY

Bloom books

Published by Bloom Books, an imprint of Sourcebooks
P.O. Box 4410, Naperville, Illinois 60567-4410
(630) 961-3900
sourcebooks.com

Originally self-published in 2021 by Raven Kennedy.

Cataloging-in-Publication data is on file with the Library of Congress.

Printed and bound in the United States of America.
VP 10 9 8 7 6 5 4 3 2 1

Oréa

SECOND KINGDOM

WALLMONT

GALLENREEF

ELLIMERY

FIRST KINGDOM

HIGHBELL

SIXTH KINGDOM

SEVENTH KINGDOM

To those who were kept in the dark.
May you smile at the sun.

About The Book

THE MYTH OF
KING MIDAS REIMAGINED.

This compelling and dark adult fantasy series is as addictive as it is unexpected. With romance, fae, and intrigue, the gilded world of Orea will grip you from the very first page. Be immersed in this journey of greed, love, and finding inner strength.

Please Note: This series will contain explicit content and dark elements that may be triggering to some. It will include explicit romance, mature language, violence, nonconsensual sex, emotional manipulation and abuse, sex trafficking and on-page sexual assault, and other dark and potentially triggering content. It is not intended for anyone under 18 years of age. This is book three in a series.

BRACKHILL

THIRD
KINGDOM

FOURTH
KINGDOM

CLIFFHELM

FIFTH
KINGDOM

RANHOLD

THE
BARRENS

PROLOGUE

AUREN
Ten years ago

The sky doesn't sing here.

It doesn't dance or play, it doesn't sink against my skin with a sweet perfume, or breeze through my hair with a fresh kiss.

Not like it did in Annwyn.

The rain weeps down, and water floods the ground, but even that doesn't sweep away the stench of this place. The sun dips and the moon crests, but there is no harmony with the goddesses slumbering in their eggshell stars. This horizon is tepid and lacking.

Nothing feels as alive here as it did at home. But then, maybe those are just the make-believe memories of a little girl. Maybe Annwyn wasn't like that at all, and I've forgotten.

If I have, I'd rather keep pretending. I like the way

it is in my mind—overflowing with a vivaciousness that saturated my every sense.

Here, my senses are saturated too, but not in a good way.

Derfort Harbor is still drenched from this morning's showers. Everything here is always waterlogged from either the sea or the sky. Sometimes both. There isn't a single wood-pitched roof that isn't sodden or a weathered door that isn't peeling from the oppressive moisture.

The clouds often pull in storms from the ocean and toss them here. There's nothing cleansing about the rain, though. It simply dumps back into the sea that fed it, reeking of fish while it floods the muddy streets.

The air is claggy today with a humidity that soaks through my dress and weighs down my lungs. I'll be lucky if my clothes dry once I hang them up tonight, lucky if my hair is anything other than damp and frizzed.

But no one looks at my hair or clothes anyway. Greedy eyes always fall against my gold-pinched cheeks, roam over my skin that's ten shades too gleaming to be real. That's why I'm known as the painted girl. The golden orphan of Derfort Harbor. No matter what rags I wear, there's absurd richness that sits beneath my sodden clothes. A worthless wealth of my skin that does nothing, yet has caused *everything*.

All along the market street, the vendor tarps are still dark, burlap sacks saturated, carts covered and dripping.

I close my eyes and breathe, trying to pretend that I'm not smelling the sharp iron from the anchor maker. I'm not smelling the drenched wooden planks on the moored ships. I'm not smelling the crates of flailing fish mixed with the brined sand from the shore.

My imagination isn't quite enough to stave off the stench.

Of course, the air would probably smell a little better if I weren't sitting on top of the pub's refuse bin. As terrible as the scent of old ale is, this spot is one of the driest and most shadowed, making it valuable real estate.

I shift my weight on the metal lid as I lean against the building at my back, gaze scanning the market alley. I shouldn't be here. I should keep moving, but even that's a major risk. Zakir has too many eyes in the city. It's just a matter of time before I'm caught, whether I stay in one spot or not. I'm hiding from him, from the duties he's placed upon me. I'm hiding from his thugs who roam the streets, keeping watch on the beggar children—not for their safety, but to make sure no one else encroaches on Zakir's territory or steals from his thieves.

I'm hiding in a place where there is no hope of staying hidden.

Like a tug against my eyes, my gaze lifts, going between two vendor tents to see the ocean beyond. I watch the sails of the docked ships, their shapes like tethered clouds that try to pull toward the sky. My stomach squeezes at the sight of them, at their taunt of escape. A bobbing temptation of freedom that's right there on the horizon.

It's a lie.

Stowaways are punished severely in Derfort, and I'd be a fool to try it. More than a handful of kids at Zakir's *have* tried it, and didn't live to tell the tale. I don't think I'll ever forget the way the gulls pecked at their flayed flesh from where they hung, their bodies left to sway in the tidal breeze and pucker beneath salted rain.

That smell, above all others, is by far the worst.

"What the bloody hell do you think you're doing?"

I flinch so badly that I scrape my arm on the rough limestone bricks at my back as Zakir appears in my shadowed spot, looming over me like a threat.

Brown eyes glare out of a ruddy face, his chin prickled with week-old hair like spines on a cactus. I can smell the alcohol on him, so strong it overpowers the trash beneath me. He's probably been into the cups for hours.

"Zakir." I can't keep the guilt out of my voice, am barely able to look him in the eye as I slide down from my spot to stand in front of him.

He puts his hands on his hips, making the sage-colored vest he's wearing gape at his hairy chest. "You got wax in your ears? I said what the hell are you doing?"

Hiding. Dreaming. Pretending. Avoiding.

As if he can hear the silent answer in my head, he

sneers at me, teeth stained from pipe smoke and pints of henade. Lips cracked from too many curses and verbal kicks and cruel deals.

Ever since the long moon came and marked the new year, Zakir's duties for me have changed. By his count, I'm fifteen years old. An Orean adult.

"I was just..." An excuse doesn't come to my tongue quick enough.

Zakir slaps me on the back of my head, making my neck snap forward. It's the only place he ever hits me now. My gold skin bruises a dark, burnished color rather easily, but no one can see the marks beneath my hair.

"You were supposed to be at *The Solitude* an hour ago!" he snarls, getting down close to my face. "Bastard came in hollering to me that you never showed, and the guy I had watching you said you must've snuck out the back door."

Wrong. I climbed out the broken window in the cellar. Easier for me to make my escape down the back street behind the inn. The other option would've been the side alley, and that's always full of feral dogs fighting for the scraps left in the bins.

"You fucking hearing me?"

I grab my dirty skirts and squeeze, as if I'm trying to pop the sound right out of his voice until it bursts like a grape. "I don't want to go to *The Solitude* again."

My voice trundles out like the roll of an uneven

15

marble across the ground. I don't even like to *think* about the inn, let alone talk about it. Despite its name, solitude is the last thing I'll find there. There, where my innocence was stolen like grubby fingers dipped into strangers' pockets on the street. All I'll find in *The Solitude* is the oppression of unwelcome gazes, the trappings of repulsive touch.

Zakir's face hardens, and I think he's going to smack my head again with his meaty, ringed fingers, but he doesn't. I wonder how much of my hard-earned coin went into buying him those encrusted gold gems.

"I don't give a fish-frying shit what you want. You work for *me*, Auren."

Desperation tightens my throat, cutting off my air with its grip. "Then send me back to the streets to beg on the corner or pickpocket the marketers," I plead. "Just don't send me there. I can't do *that* again." My eyes inadvertently fill up. Another thing in Derfort that floods.

Zakir sighs, but that hateful sneer doesn't loose from his face. "Ech, don't give me that weepy act. I kept you off your back for this long, which is more than I can say most flesh traders would've done. If I'm not making a profit off you, then I have no need to keep you," he warns. "You got it good with me. Remember that, girl."

Good.

That word trills through my head as I think of my life for the past ten years. Lots of other kids have come and gone, but I've stayed the longest because my strange golden skin attracts him the kind of attention that he's made profitable. But not once, in all of that time, would I ever say I've had it *good*.

Forced to beg on the streets all day and pickpocket at night, I had to learn to make my strange looks work for me while I roamed the port city. It was either that or I had to clean Zakir's house top to bottom, scrubbing surfaces until my fingers cracked and my knees hurt. Though, there was never really getting the cellar clean. It always dripped with cold and mildew and loneliness.

There are usually ten to thirty of us down there, crammed together beneath rotting blankets and old sacks. Kids sold and purchased and worked. Kids who never play or learn or laugh. We sleep and we earn coin, and that's pretty much it. Friendship is always squashed, nonexistent, while meanness and a competitive edge is constantly cultivated under Zakir's watchful eyes. Just dogs kept salivating to fight each other over a bone.

But I have to look on the bright side. Because even though it's not good...it could be worse.

"What'd you think was gonna happen?" he huffs out, like I'm a naive idiot. "You knew this was coming, because you've seen the other girls. You know the rule, Auren."

I look him steadily in the eye. "Earn my keep."

"That's right. You earn your keep." Zakir checks me

over, gaze stopping on my muddied hem as a frustrated cough puffs up from his pipe-burnt throat. "You're a damn mess, girl."

Normally, being a mess is part of the orphan beggar child act, but I've moved on from that. Being fifteen meant Zakir changed my clothes from patched up scraps to ladies' dresses.

When he brought me my first dress, I thought I looked pretty. I was actually stupid enough to think he'd given it to me as a birthday gift. There were real pink laces at the front and a bow at the back, and it was the most beautiful thing I'd ever seen since I've lived here.

But that was before I realized that pretty dress meant something ugly.

"Get to *The Solitude*," Zakir tells me, his tone elbowing aside any room for argument.

Dread settles in my stomach as his eyes drag back up. "But—"

A yellow-nailed finger points in my face. "The customer paid for you, and that's what he'll get. Locals have been waiting years for the painted gold girl to grow up. You're in high demand, Auren. A demand that *I've* grown even more by making them wait—another fact you should be grateful for."

Good. Grateful. Zakir uses these words, but I'm not sure he knows what they mean.

"Because of me, I've made you the most expensive

whore in Derfort, and you're not even in a brothel. The saddles are boiling with jealousy." He says this like it's something to be proud of, as if he's giddy that even other whores don't like me.

He scratches at a spot on his cheek, eyes gone greedy. "The gold-painted beggar girl of Derfort Harbor is finally old enough to buy for a night to get between her legs. I won't let you ruin my chance at earning those coins *or* ruin my reputation on the streets," he says, voice as rough as storm-chopped waters.

My fingernails prick into my palm as I fist my hands, and the space between my shoulder blades tingles, itching. If it would make any difference to scrape off my skin and pluck out my hair, I would do it. I would do anything to get rid of the gleam of my body.

There have been nights where I've tried to do just that while the other kids slept. But unlike the rumors that run rampant in Derfort, I'm not painted. This gold will never come off, no matter how many times I wash or scrub myself raw. The new skin and hair always grows in gleaming just like before.

My parents called me their little sun, and I used to be proud of the shine. Yet in this world full of gawking Oreans and a bereft sky, all I want to do is go dull. To finally find a hiding spot where no one can find me.

Zakir shakes his head at me, eyes bloodshot from late nights of gambling, a perpetual cloud of smoke

RAVEN KENNEDY

hovering around him like always. He seems to hesitate for a moment before he leans back with his arms crossed and says, "Barden East has his feelers out for you."

My eyes go wide. "Wh-what?" I ask, the fearful whisper puffing past my lips.

Barden is another flesh trader here at the port. He runs the eastside—thus the second name that he adopted—but unlike Zakir, who's somewhat tolerable, I've heard that Barden is...not.

Zakir had the decency to wait until I was considered an adult before he made me a saddle for passing sailors and townies. But word around Derfort is that Barden is the worst kind of flesh trader, who has no such decency. He doesn't deal in punitive child beggars and pickpockets. His wealth is made from cutthroats and pirates, from flesh trading and whoring. I've never traveled to the east side, but it's rumored that the way Barden runs his business makes Zakir look like a saint.

"Why?" I ask, though the word comes out garbled, throat too tight with a threatening noose that seems to be wrapped around my neck.

He gives me a dry look. "You know why. It's for the same reason the saddles in the brothel started painting their skin different colors. You have a certain...*appeal*, and now that you're a woman..."

Bile rises to my throat. Funny how it seems to taste of seawater. "Please don't sell me to him."

Zakir takes a step forward, crowding me against the side of the building. My neck prickles with his nearness, the skin along my spine jumping like my fear wants to sprout out.

"I've been lenient, because out of all the others, you've always made me the most on the streets," he tells me. "People loved giving coin to the painted girl. And if they didn't, you could distract them enough to pluck it from their pockets later."

Shame crawls up my throat. What would my parents think of me if they saw me now? What would they think of the begging, of the stealing, of the scrapping in fistfights with the other kids?

"But you're not a kid anymore." Zakir runs his tongue over his teeth before spitting a polluted glob onto the ground. "If you disobey me again, I'll wash my hands of you and sell you to Barden East. And I'm telling you now, if that happens, you'll *wish* you'd stayed with me and behaved."

Tears prickle in my eyes. My back muscles flinch so hard that my spine stiffens.

Zakir digs into the pocket of his vest and pulls out his wooden pipe. Once he puts it in his mouth and lights up, he levels me with a look. "So? What's it going to be, Auren?"

For a split second, my eyes move past him to look over his shoulder, to the ships at the harbor again. To those billowing sail clouds tied to the sea.

I was my parents' little sun.

I used to dance beneath a sky that sang.

Now, here I am, a painted whore in the slums of a sodden harbor, with filth in the air and a silent cry in my throat, and no amount of rain will ever wash the curse of my goldenness away.

Zakir sucks on his pipe, blue smoke wringing out through his teeth with a grunt. He's getting impatient now. "For fuck's sake. All you have to do is lie there."

My body shudders, tears threatening to spill. That's what the first man told me. *"Just lie down on the pallet, girl. This will be quick."* He dropped a coin on the mattress when he was done with me. I left it there, metal worn and tainted with the passing of too many hands, though it wasn't nearly as tarnished as I was.

Just lie there. Just lie there and chip away, little by little. Just lie there and feel yourself die from the inside out.

"Please, Zakir."

My plea makes his teeth grind on the tip of his pipe. "It's going to be Barden, then? You'd rather live on Eastside?"

I shake my head emphatically. "No."

Not even the people on Eastside want to live on Eastside, but most of them have no way of leaving. With trash at my back, puddles at my feet, and my owner blocking my way, I know the feeling. Nowhere to go, nowhere to hide.

He jerks his chin. "Then get to work. *Now*."

Hanging my head, I squeeze past him and start to walk down the street while my heart pounds in my throat and thrums down my spine. Two of Zakir's cronies step in front of me to lead the way, while he follows behind like an ominous shadow, steering me to my decrepit fate.

My shoes stick to the washed out gravel, but I barely notice when pebbles lodge inside, gritty pieces stabbing the soles of my feet. I barely notice the busy market either, full of shouting and haggling and arguing. I don't look at the ships again, because that taunt of freedom is just too much to bear. So, I search for that platitude of numbness inside of me and try to pretend that I'm anywhere but here.

I drag my feet, but it doesn't matter how slowly I walk to *The Solitude*. I still end up at its white-washed door, still see my bubbled reflection in the crude arrangement of bottom-cut bottles cemented in place like a window. The poor person's stained glass.

My heart hammers so hard that my feet waver, as if I were standing on one of those ships instead of solid ground.

Zakir steps up to my side, and I feel a breath of his blue smoke blown against my ear. It's the same color as those bottles. "Remember what I said. Earn your keep, or I'll let Barden East have you."

With a stern look, he walks off, a hand in his pocket

jangling the coins I've made him, while two more of his men materialize and follow like guard dogs. The others stay behind with me and take up stances by the door, herding Zakir's sheep. I already know without looking that there will be another man stationed at the back.

The spindly man on my left looks me up and down, the gray pallor of his face mismatched with his sallow eyes. "Hear Barden East likes to try out his whores first. Makes 'em go through tests before he lets 'em work," he says, causing the other man to trudge out a snort.

I stare at the door, stare at the blue glass bottoms that remind me of the circular eyes of a spider, knowing I'm going straight into its mouth, already trapped in the web Zakir threw me into.

I try to remember.

I try to remember the lyrical pitch of my mother's voice. The breeze through the wind chimes that hung outside my window. I try to remember the sound of my father's laugh. The way the horses nickered in their stalls.

But a blink goes by, and it's all drowned out with the sound of the men taunting me. With the market banging in my skull, pitched in shouts and clacking, just as the clouds crack and start to pour again, drenching us all with fetid water.

No, the sky doesn't sing here.

And every year that passes, the song of home gets drowned out from my memory just a little bit more, washed away to a polluted seashore rife with cragged cruelty.

Just lie down on the pallet, girl.

I shun the ships sailing away at my back, shun the choice that is no choice at all, between the East and the West, between Barden and Zakir. Between life and death. Then, with a raindrop on my cheek that might have spilled from my eye, I open the door and walk into the inn.

And I die, just a little bit more.

CHAPTER 1

AUREN

Truths are like spices.

When you add some in, it means you have more layers to digest. You get a taste of things you were missing before. But if you add too many, life can become unpalatable.

But when those truths are repressed for too long, when you realize you've grown accustomed to the bland lies, there's no hope of removing the overpowering taste from your tongue.

And right now, my mouth is charred with the revelation I have to somehow swallow down.

You're King Ravinger.

Yes, Goldfinch, I am. But you can call me Slade.

Rip, Ravinger—whoever he is—he watches me choke on his truth.

What do you do when someone isn't who you thought they were? In my head, Rip and the king were two very different males. King Ravinger was an evil I didn't want to face. Someone with a foul power that I wanted to stay far away from.

And Rip was...well, *Rip*. Complicated and dangerous, but someone I considered as a sort-of ally who taught me a lot in our short time together. Someone who both scared and irritated me, but who I came to care for.

But now I have to reconcile all of those previous thoughts. Because the person who pushed my buttons and forced me to admit what I am, the male who kissed me in his tent and stood on the snowy shore of an arctic sea to watch a mourning moon...he's someone else.

He's the king everyone fears. The ruler who delivers rotted corpses like they're bouquets of daisies. He's arguably the most powerful monarch that Orea has ever seen, because he's *fae*, and he's been hiding in plain sight.

I've been sleeping in his damn tent, just feet away from him every night, without knowing who he really is.

I'm unable to sift through all of the layers that this truth brings. I'm not sure I'm in a state of mind to properly pick it all apart and digest it, and I don't even know if I *want* to.

No, right now, I'm too pissed.

I glare at him. "You...you fucking *liar*." I can hear the scorching vehemence burning my words as surely as I can feel their flames light up my eyes. It consumes me in a second.

Rip—Ravinger, whoever he Divine-damned is— rears his head back, like my anger is a shock to him. His body tenses, the malevolent spikes of his arms reflecting off the dim light of the room. A room that feels entirely too small all of a sudden. "Excuse me?"

I stand in the doorway, and my fingers bunch into fists at my sides, as if I can take the reins of my anger and steer it galloping forward. I take a step into the cage room toward him, my exhausted ribbons trailing after me like sickly worms writhing on the floor.

"You're the king," I say, shaking my head like I can erase this fact. I *knew* his aura was strange. I knew I could feel an underlying power there, but I never would've guessed the depth of his trickery. "You tricked me."

Rip levels me with a glare. The black coal of his eyes looks like it wants to catch the flame of mine. He looks like he's ready to burn in my anger.

Let him.

"I could say the same," he retorts.

I bristle. "Don't you dare try to turn this around on me. You *lied*—"

"So did you." Ire bleeds through his expression, making the gray scales along his cheeks glint in the dark, the sharp face of a predator bearing down on me.

"I concealed my power. There's a difference."

He scoffs. "You hid your power, your ribbons, your *heritage*."

"Being fae has *nothing* to do with it," I snarl.

He eats up the remaining space between us in three long strides. "It has *everything* to do with it!" Rip seethes, looking like he wants to reach out and shake me.

I lift my chin, refusing to cower, imagining my ribbons rising to punch him in the gut. If only they weren't so limp and exhausted. "You're right," I reply with forced calmness. "I've had to hide in a world that wasn't my own for twenty years without seeing a single fae, until I met you."

Some of the hardness leaves his face for a split-second, but I'm not done. Not nearly.

"You pushed me relentlessly to admit what I was."

Irritation flashes through his features, lightning to strike the hollow ground. "Yes, to help you—"

My eyes narrow. "You forced truths out of me while concealing yourself. You don't think that's hypocritical?"

Rip's teeth grind together so hard I wonder if he'll break a tooth. I hope he does, the lying bastard.

"I couldn't trust you," he replies coolly.

A whip of a scoff comes out of my mouth, the sound of it punishing and unkind. "You self-centered ass. You stand there and talk about how *you* couldn't trust *me*?"

"Careful," he says, baring his teeth in a wicked smile. "There's a saying about rocks and glass houses."

"I don't live in glass, I live in gold. So I can throw whatever damn rocks I want," I snap.

"Right. I should probably expect nothing less from you."

My back goes rigid. "What's that supposed to mean?"

"Only that you're always so quick to judge me," Rip replies with cool indifference. "Tell me, did you call Midas a liar as well?" he challenges, his spiked brow lowering over his eyes. "How long has he been claiming your power as his own? How long have you been *lying* to everyone about him?"

"We're not talking about Midas."

A cruel laugh snakes out of him, ready to bite, to hurt. "Of course not, right? Your golden king can do no wrong," he says scathingly.

My nails dig into my bare palm so hard that I nearly break the skin. "You had no right to be angry when I chose to come back to him. Not when you've deceived me from the start."

A terrible growl escapes his chest, like he tried to hold it back and failed. "He's deceived you too!"

"Exactly!" I scream, and the sound of it, the utter emotion that comes barreling with it, makes him stagger back. "I am *so* damned tired of being deceived! The lies, the manipulations. You tried to pretend that

31

you were so much better than him, but you're exactly the same."

Rip's expression goes as dark as night, and my stomach clenches. "Am I?" His reply is a strike, but his eyes land the blow.

A hot, heavy quiet drops between us. The deadweight of a corpse smoldering at our feet. The smoke of our discretions clouds our sights of one another.

"Thank you for explaining exactly what you think of me." His aura slinks around him, and since I know now that it contains the repressed steam of his festering power, it makes me want to run and hide. "It's a good reminder of just how skewed your perceptions are."

I hate him. I hate him so much right now that my eyes burn. They burn until I can't hold back the lick of flame anymore. A scorching tear leaks down my cheek, and his eyes follow it until it drips off my jaw.

"Maybe my perceptions wouldn't be so *skewed* if the people I trusted didn't constantly trick and twist and lie," I retort, bashing away another stray tear.

Behind him, set in the shadows of the room, the broken cage mocks me. It's a reminder. Of exactly what can happen when someone I trust misleads me.

"Auren..." There's a sound there, in his voice, one that I can't bear to hear.

I look down, focusing instead on the puddled shadows that have formed at our feet, a breath shaking through my chest. "You stood there and kissed me and tried to make me choose you, when I didn't even know the real you at all," I say, voice gone flat as I look back up at him. "You made me feel like the worst person in the world for choosing him, even though I warned you over and over again that I had to."

Rip's head jerks at that last part, eyes narrowing in the dark. "You *had* to?"

I regret my slip of the tongue immediately.

Keeping a stoic expression, I say, "I want you to leave."

That dark, shadowy anger returns to his face, the lines of his power writhing against his bristled jaw. "No."

My heart squeezes tighter than my fists. I hate that part of me still feels relieved that he's here, as if I'm safe now, as if he's still my ally.

He's not.

I have no allies, and I need to remember that. Whatever I thought Rip was to me, that's gone now. I have no one.

Uncurling my fingers, I raise a hand and drag it down my face. I'm so tired. So damn tired of the lies. His. Midas's. *Mine.* I'm wrapped in deceit and molded in manipulation, stuffed full of everything I've done to survive.

I want it all to unravel. I want to come out of the tangles that have coiled around me before I become mummified with them.

The tension rolling off Rip's shoulders is so tight that he's practically vibrating with it, a cloud of thunder ready to roil. "So that's it? I'm to bear the brunt of your anger, while you continue to fall at Midas's feet?"

My eyes flash. "What I do is no concern of yours."

"*Dammit*, Auren—"

I cut him off. "What do you want, Rip? Why are you here?"

He crosses his arms, spikes sinking beneath his skin in a fluid, effortless motion. "Me? I was just going for a walk."

"Oh, good, another lie to add to the list," I say sardonically. "Should I grab a quill and paper to keep track?"

Rip sighs and scrubs his hands down his face in a rare crack of his stony facade. "You're overreacting."

My entire body goes still as I gape at him. "I just watched you change from the king to the commander as quickly as someone pulls on a coat," I say pointedly. "A few hours ago, you rotted Ranhold's front yard just by walking, and you threatened the city with war. Behind me right now, I'm fairly certain there's a roomful of guards that you killed. You just admitted to deceiving me the entire time I knew you, and yet...you think I'm *overreacting*?"

The muscle in his jaw jumps. "Tell me, which one of those things bothers you the most?"

"Oh, I don't know, I'm not a fan of lies, but mindless murder is pretty up there too."

"It wasn't mindless."

I swallow, trying to deal with the confirmation that there are definitely dead guards in the next room. "Did you rot them?"

"I'm far more interested in *your* power," Rip replies, and my stomach drops as he turns to look at the woman's statue inside the cage. "Is that the first person you've turned gold?"

"It was an accident," I blurt, because I'm *not* a mindless murderer.

His eyes flick back to me in victory, gaze sweeping my face, and I want to kick myself for just confirming his assumptions.

Realization dawns over his expression, making his eyes glint in curiosity. "An accident... Is it by touch, then? Is that why you always stay covered? Are you unable to control your own power?"

His condescending questions make shame pool in my stomach. Coming from the male who seems to have insurmountable control over his magic, I shouldn't be surprised that he picked up on my inadequacy, but it still stings.

"How does it work?" he presses when I don't answer.

"There you go again, trying to rip truths out of me that you have no right to," I say. "Is that why they call you Rip?"

"You let people call you the gold-touched saddle," he counters, making me see red. "For every thing you hate about me, it seems Midas has already done it a thousand times over."

He's right, and I hate him for that too.

The skin around my eyes tightens, but I can't say anything, because all that's caught in my throat is my own self-loathing.

Rip cocks his head and looks me over. "He plays it very well, to be a king without power. To use you with such clandestine forethought. No wonder he keeps you caged."

The last thing I want to do is talk about being caged. A cold sweat breaks out over my back at even hearing the word.

"How do you change the way you look?" I ask, changing the subject. "How the hell does no one realize that the two of you are actually the same damn person?"

As furious as I am with him for deceiving me, I'm even more furious with myself for not realizing the truth. Even with the rotted lines of power that crawled up his face, even with the green eyes and the shadows he was bathed in, I should've recognized him. I've been with Rip enough that I should have seen through it.

Ravinger has the same strong jaw, the same black hair. Rip is just more *fae* looking. Sharper. It's no wonder people say that the feared commander has been mutated by King Rot, because Rip looks so *other*. The bones of his face, the tips of his ears, the spikes on his back and arms, all sharp enough to cut glass and so different from anybody else I've ever seen.

In his Ravinger form, he looks strange because of those creeping dark roots that sway against his skin like shadows, so much of it hidden beneath the scruff of his jaw. I wonder just how far those lines stretch. I wonder what they *mean*.

Yet even with these deviances, Rip and Ravinger show enough likeness that I should've picked up on it. As soon as the king walked into the room, I should've sensed who he really was. Green eyes or black, spikes or smooth, tipped ears or curved, I should've known.

Both forms are drop-dead gorgeous and otherworldly, and no matter the eye color, he looks at me with the same intensity as always.

"A learned maneuver," he answers simply. "As far as other people, they see what they're told to see, believe what they're told to believe. But I don't have to explain that to you, do I? Midas has been reaping the benefits of that for years," Rip says with apparent disdain. "Why the hell would you let everyone believe that he's the one with gold-touch power, when it's been you all along?"

I nearly roll my eyes at his irritated bafflement.

"Are you kidding? I was *glad* to hide it. The first time gold started to drip down my fingers, I knew I was in trouble. Do you know what people would do to a girl

37

who can turn everything gold?" I shake my head at him, swiping a tired hand across my brow. "No. This world has used me enough."

Used, abused...and that was when I only *looked* gold. I don't even like to think about what would've happened if I hadn't run away when I did. If I'd still been there in Derfort Harbor when my power manifested, things would've become much worse for me, and I *never* would've gotten away. A tremor goes through me at the thought.

The spikes on Rip's back curl like fists, while unreadable expressions move over his face like shadows. "And now? Do you feel like you still need to hide, Auren?"

My golden eyes hold his gaze. "Don't ask me that."

"Why not?" he challenges.

"Because you want me to spill the truth for the wrong reasons." There's a sadness seeping through my skin, a disappointment that's settled over my shoulders like a cloak. "You want me to stop hiding so that I ruin Midas."

His silence, his inability to deny it, says everything.

First Midas, now him. I want to run far away from every damn king in Orea and hide where none of them can find me ever again. *How much more can I take?*

It's getting harder and harder to stand here, to look at his face and feel such crushing disappointment stabbing all the way through my heart.

"I want you to leave, Rip," I say again, hoping this time he'll listen.

"I told you, you can call me Slade."

"No, thanks," I reply curtly, enjoying the flash of frustration that goes through his eyes. "But I'll curtsy for you instead, Your Moldering Majesty."

He glowers at me. "Fine. I'll leave. If you tell me one thing."

"What?" I ask impatiently.

Rip leans in so our faces are right in front of each other, so close that I can feel the heat of his body. "Why were you screaming?"

I blink, caught off guard at his question. "I...I wasn't screaming."

The look on his face is wholly unconvinced, and my unprepared stammer didn't help. "Hmm. Maybe I should be the one to retrieve the paper and quill to keep track of the lies between us."

Bastard.

"You're mistaken. You didn't hear me scream," I lie, though my heart is pounding in my chest so hard that I hope he doesn't hear it.

In truth, I was like some caged animal, ready to tear down the door with my nails while the guards kept me locked in this room with no way out, but I'm not about to admit that now. Not to him.

Rip arches a condescending brow. "Really? So I imagined you shouting, begging to be let out?"

Shit.

It takes a lot of conscious effort not to reveal anything on my expression, especially with him so close. "Maybe you don't hear as well with that ugly branch crown around your head."

Much to my irritation, he smirks. I hate that the sight makes my stomach leap.

Even though there's barely a foot between us, Rip leans forward, making me suck in a breath. He steals all the air in the room, yanking the pulse in my veins like a dog on a leash.

Nearly chest to chest, he tilts his head down while I tip mine up. We look at each other with too many mixed emotions written in our locked eyes, with no hope of ever translating them.

What are the words in the silent, churning eyes of this male? Why is it that I feel like I'm being crushed from the inside out? He has a power over me that has nothing to do with his aura, and everything to do with the way my gaze strays down to his lips when he sucks in a breath.

He gives me that maddening smirk of his. "Mmm. I like your anger, Goldfinch. If only it weren't always directed at me."

I open my mouth to yell at him, but before I can get a word out, he reaches down and takes hold of one of my ribbons, freezing me in place as my heart stutters.

We both look down as he holds it, and when

he gently rubs the satiny gold length, I forget how to breathe.

As if it's purring, my ribbon vibrates slightly between the pads of his finger and thumb. A shudder travels through the rest of them, each one going languid in relief as if they can feel it too. Chills scatter over my arms as he continues to stroke, easing it in a way I've never felt before.

I should yank it away. I should back up. I should do anything to put space between us.

But I don't. I don't, and I can't even admit why.

His nearness, his gaze, it makes it too hard to think. I can't function properly with the feel of his exhale against my face, with his barely-there touch.

I need to remember who he is, what he's capable of. I need to keep my guard up now more than ever.

"You should always keep these out," he says quietly, and for some reason, another tear wants to spill out of me.

I don't like these feelings gathering around me. I want to hold onto my anger, to use it to help me push him away. The air between us has grown thicker, like we've passed the first line of trees and moved deeper into the woods. It's so congested with branches and brambles that I can't get through it without being scratched.

It takes effort, but I manage to clear my throat and whisper, "Go, Rip. Please."

His expression shutters, and whatever moment we were just stuck in dissipates. He drops my ribbon, and it immediately sags down, drooping like a flower, a silent sigh of regret bent to the ground.

When he steps back, I'm both relieved and bereft. I try to feel nothing instead.

Rip opens his mouth like he wants to say something else, but then he goes still, his head cocking as if he hears something.

My hackles immediately rise. "What?"

"Hmm, seems I can't leave just yet."

"And why not?"

His infuriating smirk returns, but it's not like before. This one is...mischievous, and it fills me with dread. "Because your golden king is coming. I think I'll stay and say hello."

CHAPTER 2

AUREN

My eyes flare wide. "*What?* Midas is coming back?"

Rip arches a brow. "What's wrong, are you distressed at that fact?"

I press my lips together as frustration washes over me. If Midas is nearly here, then I've lost my chance at trying to sneak out.

Although, honestly, that wasn't realistic anyway. I would have to know the ins and outs of this castle really well and be *very* lucky to make it out without Midas finding out. Even if by some stroke of luck, I *did* manage to flee, it would just be a matter of time before he tracked me down. He won't ever let me leave him.

I'm trapped. A saddle knotted in reins.

"You need to leave *now*," I insist.

Much to my aggravation, Rip just looks at me, not moving an inch. "Why?"

I blink incredulously. "Because if Midas finds you in here..."

"What's he going to do? Turn me gold?" Rip mocks with a vindictive gleam in his eye. Of course he's smug, why wouldn't he be? He holds Midas's greatest secret in his hands.

Tension wraps around me. "Don't—"

The smile he gives me is sly. "Excuse me while I slip on my other coat."

Before I can brace myself, his power lashes out, and nausea strikes my stomach. I slump against the door frame, nearly gagging at the turmoiled magic now clawing through the air.

Rip begins to transform again, and I watch as the sharpness of his features recede. His pointed fae ears soften, his cutting cheekbones smooth out, and his gray scales disappear. The row of short spikes above his brows are gone in a blink, just as quickly as the ones on his arms and back.

As Rip fades and King Ravinger settles in, his entire body quakes. He rolls his muscled shoulders, and dark, insidious lines appear beneath the skin of his neck. They crawl up, reaching his jaw like roots searching for better soil.

I inhale, breathing through the sick feeling in my

gut. But before it overwhelms me completely, his power pulls away, taking my nausea with it. Trembling, my body slumps in relief as I stare at him.

His transformation finishes, and when he opens his eyes again, the familiar black gaze is gone. Instead, I see the deep green of a rotten king's irises.

Look away, I tell myself.

I need to look away, because every time our gazes meet, my stomach twists and my chest aches, and I feel like I don't know him at all.

My heart is pounding hard again, but I don't know if that's from the effects of his power or if it's because he scares me in this form—*King Ravinger* scares me. Funny how he loses the scales and spikes yet somehow becomes far more terrifying.

I don't like seeing this version of him. No matter how much I try to remind myself that it's only Rip, he feels like a stranger to me. A stranger that I don't dare trust.

My trepidation tips over into fear, and I turn and stumble into Midas's bedroom, needing to put space between us, needing to *flee*.

But I only take a couple steps before I'm tripping over something on the floor. I manage to catch myself before I faceplant, only to realize that the thing I tripped over is a body.

"Great Divine..." My hand flies to my mouth as I look down in horror at the person sprawled at my feet.

The guard's eyes are closed, and his mouth is left gaping. The golden chest plate he's wearing gleams, but beneath it, his skin has gone wilted and gray. A grape picked off the stem and tossed on the ground for the sun to shrivel.

My gaze jumps from him to a second body, another guard in the same condition. And then another, and another, and another.

A strangled sound scrapes out of my throat, and my ears ring with chilling alarm. But I can't look away from the prone corpses, from the dried out eyes staring in shock. Can't turn away from the lips that have cracked and peeled, or the cheeks that have sunken in.

This...this is what Ravinger is capable of.

One second, all of these guards were alive, and the next, they're nothing but dehydrated husks.

I feel my chest rising and falling with rapid breaths, but no matter how quickly I seem to be breathing, I'm not getting enough air, because one thought blares through my head.

Would I have done the same thing?

If the sun hadn't gone down and my gold-touch power was still active, if I'd been able to break down that door, would *I* have been the one who'd killed them instead of Ravinger?

I feel tears burn my eyes. Maybe it's my body's only defense, attempting to blur the vision in front of me, though it doesn't work.

What does work though, is when Ravinger steps in front of me, blocking my view. My eyes trail up his body until I meet his gaze. Green eyes skate over my face like steam stroking over fevered water.

"You need to breathe, Auren."

"I *am* breathing," I snap.

"You're panting and going to hyperventilate if you keep it up," he replies calmly. "Have you only ever seen death gilt in your own power?"

I almost laugh bitterly. "I've seen plenty of death."

Old, creased memories tear open one after the other. I met death the night I was stolen from home, and it's been stalking me ever since.

"These men didn't deserve this," I say, dashing a tear away angrily when it falls from my lashes.

"I disagree. They were holding you against your will."

My eyes flash. "They were just following orders. Doing what they were told." My mind floods with the things *I've* been told to do. "I didn't want—" I hate that my voice breaks off. *"This."*

I'm choked with a guilt that seems to grow in the silence.

"Those golden eyes of yours, so expressive," Ravinger murmurs. "There's hate one second and heart the next."

With his forest-green gaze locked on me, he lifts a

hand, and I flinch on instinct. He pauses, face darkening at my reaction. "I won't hurt you, Goldfinch."

My expression tells him he already did.

With a tightening jaw, he turns his hand, as if he's turning an invisible handle. Slowly, the dark lines of his power swivel around the skin of his palm, wrapping around his fingers like creeping vines.

Like a breeze, I feel his power brush over me again. I brace myself for the nauseating impact, but it doesn't come. This time, there is no pulse of putrid wrongness. Magic tugs in the air like a wraith's grasp on an inhale, pulling breath into lungs.

Nothing makes me shudder or gag or keel over. I don't become sick. Instead, energy thrums around us, and the base of each of my ribbons stretches, my back prickling with goose bumps.

Coughing suddenly erupts in the room, and I jump in alarm, whirling around at the noise. "What—" All around me, the sprawled guards are rolling over or sitting up, hacking on dry coughs like sandpaper against their throats, gasping in breaths through flaking lips.

My wide eyes snap to Ravinger. "How did you—I thought they were dead!"

He lowers his hand again, the lines gone from his palm. "They would've been had I waited much longer. A rotting body can only be reversed after so long."

I blink, shaking my head while the soldiers get to

their feet. They're confused, looking like they just looked Death in the eye and aren't sure how they were able to cross the line back into living.

"You just...you...*why*?" I ask breathlessly, because I don't understand him at all.

Ravinger doesn't get a chance to answer me though. The bedroom door is suddenly tossed open, interrupting us.

Midas jerks to a stop in the doorway. His golden tunic and pants glimmer in the low light, somehow making his honey blond hair seem even lighter. The look on his face reveals his surprise as his gaze sweeps the room, his tanned, angular jaw tightening. He takes in the staggering guards still attempting to stand at attention, and then his eyes latch onto me. When he notices Ravinger standing next to me, his expression fills with rage.

"What is the meaning of this? What the *hell* do you think you're doing in my personal rooms?" I barely recognize Midas's voice with the fury currently running through it. He stalks forward and stops beside me, though his brown eyes lock onto the rotten king.

Ravinger doesn't seem bothered by Midas's anger. In fact, he's looking at Midas with bored amusement. It seems he hasn't just transformed his appearance, but in a split second, he's taken on another persona as well. Even his gestures look different. Ravinger appears cocky and relaxed, black brows arched with an expression that's somehow both aristocratic and mocking.

The spikes, scales, and glare are all gone. In their place is a derisive turn of his lips and lines vined into his skin, crown cocked on his head. No wonder other people don't suspect one for the other.

"Oh, are these not my guest chambers?" Ravinger replies with false innocence as he looks around the room. "My mistake."

"You damn well know it's not," Midas grits out. "And what the Divine hell did you do to my guards?"

The men are still coughing a little, but at least they managed to stay standing, even if they do look like death rolled over.

"Oh, them? I rotted them a little."

Midas blanches. "You...*you what*?"

I watch the two of them warily, stuck between two unyielding stones.

Ravinger shrugs. "They're fine now. A little food and rest, and they'll be right as rain."

I can feel Midas's anger as surely as I can see it simmering in his brown eyes. "This is an act of war."

Green eyes hook onto Midas, spearing him through. "If this was war, you'd know it," Ravinger says coldly, his disparaging expression replaced by something far crueler. My chest tightens, gaze shooting between them.

Midas seethes silently for a moment, and then his attention shifts to the open door of the cage room—the door that's now gleaming gold. "What is my favored doing out and vulnerable to a foreign king?" he demands of the guards.

I don't know how it's possible, since their pallor is already so terrible, but the armored men seem to pale even more. A couple of them steal nervous, quick looks in my direction, and my stomach sinks.

They saw. They saw the door to the cage room turn gold. In my anger, I slammed my palms against it, trying to break out, and I gilded the whole thing for them to witness.

Midas's brow gathers thunder, his eyes darkening as he realizes what they must've seen.

Shit.

"Foreign king?" Ravinger interrupts, seemingly oblivious. "Midas, we signed a treaty only a few hours ago, don't you remember? You and I are allies now," he says with a smirk.

"And yet, here you are, in *my* chambers, using your powers against my guards and standing beside my favored where you have no right to be!" Midas snaps. "You and I both know you didn't think these were your rooms."

Midas doesn't like to be caught off guard. Being the planner that he is, he's meticulous in the way things are supposed to play out. With Ravinger having infiltrated his personal chambers, it's leaving him threatened, like cornered prey.

Midas is dangerous when he feels cornered.

Ravinger looks around the room, noting the bed, the fireplace, the balcony—all of it with bored disinterest. "Perhaps you're wrong. Perhaps I truly did mistake these for my own chambers, and I rotted your guards because I thought you were attempting to ambush me."

A sound like a growl erupts from Midas's chest.

"Or..." Ravinger goes on. "Perhaps I simply wanted to see how the acting monarch of Fifth Kingdom lives." Green eyes slip over to me. "Interesting how one keeps a king's favored," he muses with a twist of his lips. "What does it say, do you think, about a male who keeps a woman in a cage?"

The breath in my throat catches. I can feel my heart pounding with the tension in the room. It's as thick as ropes, ready to coil around my neck and yank me off my feet.

Ravinger watches Midas, and Midas watches Ravinger.

I watch them both.

Ravinger wants to poke and prod, be a thorn in Midas's back. Midas, however, looks like he wants to pummel Ravinger to the ground.

But...he can't.

Of course, usually *I'm* the only person who knows that. Midas plays his part very, very well. He's had a decade of practice, after all. A sleight of hand here, purposely placing me there, bringing in gilded items

GLEAM

after the fact...he knows how to act like he's the one with power.

But Ravinger knows the truth now. Midas is ignorant of that—and I want to keep it that way. Yet maybe that's all about to be ruined, right here and now. Maybe Ravinger is about to call his bluff. Or maybe he'll simply rot Midas where he stands.

My nerves constrict, like a corset pulled too tight.

Midas's guards fidget on their feet. Maybe they feel the threat as easily as I can. The last thing they probably want to do is have to go up against Ravinger again. It didn't go so well for them the first time. But as guards, they don't really have much of a choice.

The silence in the room only makes the tension worse, and even my ribbons, as sore as they are, stiffen along my spine, like they expect a fight to break out. If there is a fight, it's one that Midas can't win. You can only get so far with threats.

He must come to the same conclusion as me, because I see it the moment Midas decides to back down. It takes effort, but his features smooth out, his fingers relax, and he forces his expression to go blank with a courtly visage, scrapping all traces of his true emotion.

Midas is no fool. He knows how to study his opponents, and right now, he sees that he doesn't have the upper hand. When you can't play to win with your power, then you play politics instead.

Which is why I'm not surprised when he clears his throat and says, "We are indeed allies, as you say. So I will forgive this *mistake*."

Ravinger tilts his head, mouth playing with a smirk. "Much obliged." His eyes slide to me again, and he tosses a wink in my direction before strolling out of the room.

As soon as the rotten king is gone, my eyes drag over to Midas, but he's busy watching the guards.

"You failed me," he tells them.

The men go tense, and some of them flinch when he strides past them into the hall, speaking words too low for me to hear. As soon as he pulls back in, ten new soldiers file inside, and they immediately grab hold of the guards who were charged with watching me.

The men don't fight as they're hauled away, and I know with sinking realization that Midas is going to have them killed for witnessing what I did to the door.

"Don't kill them." The plea sprouts up from my mouth like a reaching plant, though I know it will be fruitless. So many of my requests to Midas are.

"It's done," he replies, eyes pinched. "They sealed their own fate by seeing what they were not allowed to see."

My throat clogs with irrevocable guilt. Not only did I lose control and gild the woman who acted as my stand-in, but now these men are going to die because of my power too. Maybe not by my hand, but the end result is the same.

Like I told Ravinger, I've seen plenty of death.

Maybe the guards would have been better off as rotted heaps on the floor. Who knows what the kinder fate would have been? Which king's retribution would they have preferred?

I swallow hard, but this time, the nausea that rises in my stomach has nothing to do with Ravinger's power. Instead, it has everything to do with my own regret, and the man standing next to me.

CHAPTER 3

AUREN

With Ravinger gone, the room suddenly feels empty. I hadn't realized just how dominant his presence really was until he left.

I should feel relief that he's gone, but I don't.

My gaze locks onto Midas, bitterness breaking through the planes of my face like cracks in the glass. It's a wonder I'm not openly snarling. My entire body is tense, anticipating what he'll do.

For a moment, he does nothing but look at me. He's no longer wearing his crown or his robe, just a gold tunic and pants tucked into gleaming boots.

Ravinger mentioned that it's been hours since they made their treaty. Which means Midas was off doing who knows what, leaving me in here to pace like a savage animal. Anger simmers alongside the pain in my chest, both emotions bubbling beneath the surface.

I don't know what he sees in my face, but I see plenty in his. I'm reading him now, like everything he's ever spoken is a scrawl of lies across his lips. The pages he's taken up in my life are empty of anything real.

A knock at the door interrupts our silent regard. Midas strides over to the room where the cage is and closes the gilded door, shutting away what happened before he calls for whoever it is to enter.

Two maids walk in from the corridor, their golden dresses covering them from head to toe, with matching bonnets tied at the tops of their heads. One carries a pile of clothing, and the other holds a tray of food. They both dip into a curtsy before heading for the washroom.

I hear the clank of pipes and the screech of water.

Midas clears his throat, voice softer. "They'll get your bath ready, and you can clean up and eat."

I pause in surprise. I was expecting him to try and toss me back into the cage room. I was ready for him to berate me with questions about how I got out, about what Ravinger was doing in here, but instead, he holds his hand out like an olive branch.

"I don't want to take a bath," I grit out. What I really mean is, I don't want to take a bath just because he ordered it.

Midas lets out a breath. "Auren, the cage—"

"I will *not* go back into a Divine-damned cage!" I hiss in a vicious whisper. "You can bring in every blacksmith in the kingdom, and I swear to the goddesses above, I will break every single door. You can lock me in that room, set a hundred guards to keep me, but I will—"

I stop abruptly, aware of the two maids in the other room, both of us stealing looks toward the washroom.

Taking a deep breath to calm myself, I lean in closer to him, lowering my voice so that only he can hear. "If you try to shove me in there again, I will fight you every step of the way, and I won't *ever* turn another thing gold for you again."

The vitriol that spews from my mouth flares hotter than any fire. May it burn him as badly as he has burned me.

Midas goes stiff, his tanned face staining with twin spots of red anger on his cheeks. I've shocked him. I can see it in the way he's forgotten to breathe. He's not used to this version of me, this person who isn't bending over backwards and kneeling at his feet.

My chest heaves with the furious passion in my voice. I wouldn't be surprised if my golden eyes started to blaze.

Midas stares at me. I can see him calculating, can practically hear the thoughts spinning around in his head as he tries to think of how to handle me. I know this, because for all those years I was in love with him, I didn't just pine after him. I watched him, too. I *learned* him, as one learns a language.

It was necessary, because of his temper, because I never wanted to get on his bad side or set him off. It's because of my sensitivity to his emotions, because of my many years of studying him, that I know the way his mind works.

His expression softens, his carob pod eyes becoming tender, as if my words have gotten through to him.

Midas lifts a hand, letting the pad of his thumb brush along my jaw. I stiffen and move my head to pull away, but he brings up both palms to hold my cheeks, looking at me with tortured eyes. "I'm so sorry, Precious." His breath is at my lips, repentant voice in my ear.

Before, I would've melted at this. I would've leaned forward like a flower bending in his presence. But I don't curl into his touch, and my lips don't lift up in a forgiving smile. My lashes don't flutter closed, and a sigh doesn't pass my lips.

Because...it's too late.

The blindfold has been ripped from my sight. Now, my heart doesn't squeeze. My stomach doesn't flutter. He broke something inside of me far more than just my heart. He broke my will. My drive. My voice. He broke down my very spirit, and I let him.

The burden of love I held for him for so long has scraped off. Peeled away like dried, dead skin flaking in a scorching sun. Colorless, depleted strips that no longer feel a thing. Never again will I be the clay that he molds in his hold. I'm going to shape myself.

"I acted abominably. I was completely out of my head," he says, soft fingers caressing my cheeks as I stare at the gilded buttons on his shirt. "I was just so damned worried about you, and I needed to keep you safe after what happened. I only just got you back, and all this stress with Fourth Kingdom..." Midas trails off, hands dropping away from my face.

I say nothing, too busy seeing past his flowery words and digging into the gritty ground of what he's really doing.

He's changing tactics.

Midas is no fool. He knows that my threats would make his life difficult. After all, he needs me. His entire claim to the throne depends on it. The laws of Orea demand that only those with magic can reign, and Midas needs my power to uphold his deceit.

What would people say if he suddenly stopped turning things gold?

He needs me complacent. What better way to get me back under his control than to tug at my heartstrings?

He was always able to convince me to *behave* in the past. To do as he said, trust that he knew better, and let him do whatever the hell he wanted while I wasted away behind gilded bars.

But Midas can't keep me without my compliance, and that's a truth he never wanted me to see. He never wanted me to wake up and realize just how much power I actually have.

While we steep in silence, the sounds of the water cut off in the washroom, and the maids file out a moment later. They bob into a departing curtsy before letting themselves out of the room. Still, I say nothing.

"Come, I'll take care of you, and we can talk, just like you wanted to," he says beseechingly. He plays it so well—the remorse, the heartfelt acknowledgement.

I could fight him. I could spit in his face and tell him I know what he's trying to do. I could turn and run out of the room and try to get out of the castle. Even though those options sound wildly appealing, I hold myself back.

If I want to be free of him, *truly* free, I can't act impulsively. Like Midas, I have to plan. Because he will never let me go. Not ever. So if I'm going to do this, I have to be smart.

"Precious?" he prompts.

I have no allies, no connections. What's to say that, even if I could get out of Ranhold, someone else wouldn't capture me and use me for their benefit? No, I'm done being a prisoner. I'm done being owned.

I have to plan and do things right, flee where Midas can't get to me ever again. I have to become strong so that I can protect myself against the world that would use me.

So...I nod. It's time for me to play the game.

"Alright."

Midas's expression smooths in relief, the lines of worry around his eyes changing into the crinkling of a smile. How satisfied he must be, to think he's so easily hooked me again.

What a pushover I was.

He leads me into the bathroom, past a silver-framed mirror and the toilet, right over to a large iron tub at the back wall. It has clawed feet and a painted rim, with glass-covered stone carved into the shape of a lion, its mouth gaping in a roar that spews water instead of sound.

"Let's get the filth of Fourth's army off you," Midas says as I stop in front of the tub. It's already filled with steaming water, a thin layer of bubbles waiting along the surface like drifting lily pads.

"Did King Rot hurt you?" he asks, keeping his tone carefully even.

Yes. But not in the way you think.

"No. He only just walked in before you came."

Midas seems to be placated by that. "I don't like that ugly bastard being in the same room as you."

I blink in surprise. *Ugly?*

His power is ugly, sure, but the male himself? No. Far from it. Ravinger is achingly beautiful in the same way as when he's in his Rip form. There's an ethereal masculinity that doesn't quite fit in this world. Of course,

I suppose I shouldn't be surprised at Midas's evaluation of him. Midas abhors anything less than perfect. He probably looks at Ravinger and sees those strange marks of power that slither just under his skin, and he thinks that makes Ravinger grotesque.

Choosing not to reply, I turn away slightly while Midas busies himself with the tray of food that's been left on a stool beside the tub. Slowly, I begin to strip out of my clothes. Each piece is overworn, dirty, wrinkled. They feel heavy as I drop them into a heap on the floor.

For a moment, I just stare at them. So much happened in those clothes. I wasn't the same person before I wore them. It's like stripping off the armor that I'd worn during battle. The Red Raids, Sail, Captain Fane, Rip, Midas...all of it happened in that dress.

I don't know if Midas's eyes are on me, and I don't care. He's seen my naked body many times. I'm far more protective of what lies beneath my skin. What's inside of me—my mind, my heart, my spirit—those are the things I want to keep from his sight.

Taking a breath, I leave behind the pile of clothes and step into the tub. Sitting down, I'm immediately wrapped in warmth that seems to sink all the way into my cold-pressed bones. My ribbons slither to the bottom, their tired lengths soaking up this simple comfort.

I groan as I lean my head back against the curved rim, relishing in the heat. After weeks and weeks of nothing but rag baths in the snow, this is *heavenly*. I won't even let Midas's presence ruin it.

Eyes fluttering closed, I breathe in the scent of the floral oils the maids must've mixed in. But I flinch and spring them open again when Midas's hands suddenly begin to stroke my hair from behind. "Shh, it's alright, Precious. I'm going to make it all up to you."

"The only way you can make it up to me is by not trying to lock me away ever again," I tell him evenly, focusing on the bubbles as they float on the surface of the water.

I might need to play along, to act like I'm once more ensnared by his charm, but I won't go back to being a captive.

Midas hesitates for a moment, hands paused at my hair. "Of course," he says after a stunted breath. "Of course. The cage was only ever there for your protection. But if you don't need it anymore, then I'll keep you safe without it."

He backtracks beautifully.

I let a small smile play on my lips and turn to look at him over my shoulder. His handsome face is the epitome of adoration, but his shoulders are stiff, betraying the burden of his lingering anger. "Truly?"

"Yes," he replies vehemently, grasping onto my tentative hope as he reaches down to cup my face, as tendrils of blond hair fall across his forehead. "I'm so sorry for the way I behaved earlier, Precious. Forgive me."

"You hurt me," I say, and this time, I'm speaking true.

He leans down from where he's perched on the stool beside the tub and presses his cheek against my forehead. His skin is cold, while mine is dewy with the steam of the bath whispering between us. "I'll make it up to you. I'll earn your trust and forgiveness again."

"You said you didn't need my forgiveness," I remind him with a bite in my tone.

Midas winces before he reaches over and picks up a silver pitcher from the floor. He dunks it in the water and begins to wet my hair.

"I wasn't thinking straight." He rolls up his sleeves and drags the tray of food closer to me. Then he begins to lather soap in his hands and starts washing my oily, tangled strands. "I don't expect you to forgive me right away, but I only acted that way because I was worried about you."

I believe that Midas does care for me, in his own twisted way. But it's not healthy, and it's not enough. It's not what I deserve. I don't think I'll ever have the kind of love that I crave.

That thought makes my eyes blur as I stare at the ceiling, gaze locked onto the frosted window at the top of the wall. Grief clings to me as much as the beaded water against my skin.

As sadness overtakes my anger, I wonder what's wrong with me. Why couldn't he love me? *Truly* love me?

Midas loves my shimmering skin, my gleaming hair. He is undoubtedly in love with my *power*. I gave him my heart, and I was too young, too stupid to see that his adoration was for my gold, not *me*.

I must be defective in some way. Unworthy.

Or maybe this is simply what I'm destined for. Maybe this is all I'm allowed to have. The woman who can turn the world gold has to have a check on her own greed.

Perhaps love is the price of my power.

My thoughts droop down like a weight depressing at the edge of a petaled conscience. Midas continues to wash my hair, keeping up conversation in a steady cadence. He talks of how much he missed me, of the things he's been doing in Fifth Kingdom since we've been separated, of how much work we have to do now that we're together again.

I let him speak and he lets me stay quiet, using the food as my excuse not to talk. I eat everything on the tray without tasting it, too busy chewing my own quiet contemplation. I can't help but think about the last time he did this, took care of me, bathed me, right after the attack with King Fulke.

Automatically, my hand lifts to my throat, fingers stroking over the small scar that still resides there. It wasn't Midas who saved me that night, not really. It was Digby, and I lost him too.

Somehow, in some way, everyone I've ever loved has been taken from me. Even Midas, and he's sitting just inches away.

After I've scrubbed, rinsed, and polished off the last of the food, I get out of the tub and pull on a fresh night dress. It's thick white cotton, the hem reaching my toes, the sleeves wide and ending at points past my fingers. My ribbons wring themselves out before hanging loose in lazy strips against my back.

"There," Midas murmurs, looking me over from head to toe. "You're shiny and new again."

I offer him a tight smile. My body is as tired as my spirit, and all I want to do now is get away from him. "I need to sleep."

He quickly nods. "I've had the maids make up a room right across the hall," he says. "You can stay there. Have your own...space."

Wary surprise has me turning to face him. "My own room? *Without* bars?"

He tucks a damp strand of hair behind my ear. "No bars. Just your own room where you can relax and be safe," he says quietly. "I meant what I said. I was wrong, and I'll make it up to you, Auren. Now, come. You must be tired."

I let Midas take my hand, and he leads me out of his rooms and into the hall. Nodding to some guards, he opens the door across from his. I step inside with him and look around the dark room, though all I can see by the weak moonlight is a pillowy bed.

Letting go of me, Midas walks to the wall and closes the curtains, while I go lie down. I barely have the energy to pull back the covers before I slip onto the feathery mattress.

I stiffen when I feel the bed dip as Midas lies down beside me. He wastes no time pulling me in and arranging me so that my head rests on his chest. I'm like a block of ice against him, refusing to melt, wanting to slide away.

"Relax, Auren," he commands. "Rest now. I'll stay until you fall asleep."

A snort nearly escapes me. That's about as comforting as being told there's a monster under your bed, only, this one is lying down on it with me.

But my tiredness wins against stubbornness.

Inch by inch, I do settle in his hold. Yet when he starts to run a soft caress over my arm, I press my lips closed tight. Hate and sadness sweep through me, but I try to stave off the emotions that try to swell inside of me like a bloated cloud.

Numb. I need to stay numb. Unfeeling, uncaring, behind a thick wall where he can't affect me ever again.

"You're my precious girl." It's a murmur in the dark, a coax slipping through his shadowed lips.

I hate that he's so good at this. I don't want him to hold me, and yet, it was all I ever wanted for so damn long, and he knows it. Which is why a slow, cold tear drips down my cheek and lands on his tunic as he pets my hair.

"I love you, Auren."

Liar.

What a fake, conniving, devious liar.

"I missed this," he says through a yawn. Maybe that part is at least true for him, or maybe it's just another deceit to pull me in.

Either way, I give myself this moment. Just this one. For the innocent girl who lost the love she thought she had, I let her have this. Because this...this is her quiet goodbye.

Beneath my anger and the numbness are the bruised pieces of a broken heart. And that part of me, that girl who was doe-eyed and head over heels, she's in mourning beneath my bitter anger.

So for that part of me, I let out a shaky breath that vibrates like thunder. Then I press my ear against his chest one last time to hear a song that I thought played just for me.

I focus on the steady beat, and another tear falls with its rhythm as he strokes my hair, because it's not love I'm listening to. It's just possessive control. It's so loud, I can't believe I didn't hear it before.

"You're right back where you belong," he declares.

I close my eyes, wet lashes like drops of dew against my cheek.

If we shifted, if it were his head pressed against my chest, would he hear? Would he hear the sound of my heart and know what it means? Would he recognize the lyrical loathing?

I fall asleep listening to the constant thrum of our chests, to the two mismatched tunes that will never play in harmony. I let that girl in me break away beat by beat, saying goodbye in her own silent way.

When I wake up, I'll make sure my heart is hardened. Come morning, I'll make sure it only plays a song for *me*.

CHAPTER 4

KING MIDAS

*S*itting inside the iron gazebo, I'm pensive as I absently watch the men working throughout the courtyard. I find the cold air of Fifth Kingdom refreshing, the perfect sharpness to give one clarity.

The bench beneath me is cushioned with straw-stuffed leather that was probably comfortable at one point but has long since gone flat.

Set at my side, my ledger book is like a pair of eyes glaring at me. Inside are all my notes, all my plans, things needing to be done. It's written in code I only use for myself, even though I always keep it with me. You can't trust people, so one can never be too careful, and I have too much at stake.

The demands of running not just one kingdom but two weighs heavily on my shoulders. All the things I must do have become an incessant pressure that buzzes in my head during all my waking hours.

Now that Auren is back with me, I can focus more ardently on Ranhold. It needs the attention.

I've put off the grumblings easily enough, but I know it won't last. I brought enough gold with me for the transition, but people are growing restless. There are mutterings in the halls. They wonder why the Golden King hasn't turned anything gold yet. My excuse for respecting Ranhold and allowing time for mourning is nearly dried out, and my cache of coin right along with it.

I need Auren to get back to work. Yet I know I must handle her as delicately as I handle the politics here. I have dozens of strings that I'm tying simultaneously, all of which take concentration and finesse.

Which is why I keep coming out here to the gazebo, where the air stings just enough to collar my focus.

At the steady sound of a tapping hammer, my eyes skim over the sculptures outside. The courtyard is filled with them. Standing on stone pedestals every few feet, the blocks of ice are carved into elaborate likenesses.

From my vantage point, I can see one made into a willow tree, on another, a timberwing with its maw open in a fierce cry. Beside it, there's a sensual goddess with her arms outstretched toward the sky, a dress draped over hourglass curves. Each and every sculpture is incredibly detailed, some of them so tall that the artists need ladders to work on them.

With chisels, hammers, and buffing rags, the men painstakingly ensure that every piece is kept in pristine condition. The sculptors are always working, whether it be to create more carvings or to preserve what they've already made.

I can tell that they're uneasy being watched by me, but they keep their gazes pointedly away, working without pause. I'm just about to pick up my ledger again when a new worker comes out, purple uniform matching the others.

My eyes lock on him immediately, and for a moment, I have to blink to separate what I'm seeing from what I once saw.

With an artisan tool bag belted around his waist, he walks over to the sculpture of a sword standing on its point and begins to polish it with a rag, dusting off collected snow.

He's bald, and four prominent wrinkles run along the top of his head like a tiger's stripes. He has the gruff jaw of a man who could hide a sneering mouth behind his full white beard, though I'm too far away to see if it's true or not.

As he looks his piece over, he rummages in his tool belt before pulling out a pair of spectacles and propping them on his nose. Sharp air hisses through my teeth at the sight.

He looks like my father.

It's not him of course. Not unless he made a deal with the gods to be raised from the dead. But the beard, the bald head, the tanned skin, those Divine-damned *spectacles*, even the knuckled grip on his hammer, it's all very reminiscent of the one who sired me.

Silenus Midas.

Sile to everyone, father to me, though *father* is a term used *very* loosely. He was nothing but a village drunk who sometimes managed to stumble out of the house to do carpentry work in town.

As for me, I was just the bastard son he loathed. He hated that he had to sacrifice some of his money on food and clothes for me, when he'd rather spend it on ale.

I'm not sure if hate was in my own nature or if he nurtured it, but it was something we had in common for each other. I never knew my mother, but I loathed her too.

Apparently, she was flighty. A loose woman who went too far into the cups in a pub one night and ended up in Sile's bed, breeding me nine months later.

As soon as I was born, she dumped me on his doorstep with a jug of wine and six gold coins, and never looked back. Sile either couldn't track her down or didn't bother to.

I'm not sure what I detested most about him. His laziness, his drunkenness, or his tendency to beat the hell out of me.

Actually, maybe what I hated most was that he was such a joke to the village people. Everywhere he went, he was followed by sneers or mockery or pity.

They bestowed that same treatment onto me as well. I was nothing. Just the bastard son of a bastard drunk, too poor to rub two coppers together, and I was never going to escape that sorry excuse for a life.

Which is why the moment I became a legal Orean adult, I stole a jug of wine—in a mocking tribute of my mother—and left it for him on his soiled bed in our tiny, broken down cabin.

It didn't take long for him to drink himself into a blacked-out stupor. Took even less for me to spark the flint and set fire to the derelict shack of a house. It was always dry in First Kingdom.

"Sire?"

I pull my gaze away from the sculptor and find my main advisor standing just outside of the gazebo, between the iron balustrades.

"What is it, Odo?" I ask, reaching for the ledger before tucking it in the inside pocket of my vest.

"My King, we have a problem."

My eyes narrow. "Is it Prince Niven?"

Fulke's son is a whiny little prat who's proven to be difficult. Yet another delicate matter I've had to handle with care.

"It's not the prince," Odo says as he stands there

awkwardly, gaze darting around to ensure no one is close by. Aside from the sculptors, my guards were told to wait at the entrance of the castle where six of them stand sentry.

"Then what is it?" I ask, irritation coating my tone at being interrupted.

"It's your wife, Sire."

Tension tightens the line of my shoulders. "Hmm. Finally received a message?"

"Yes, but not from her."

My eyes bore into him as I wait for him to divulge.

Odo leans forward, bracing a hand on the railing so his words don't carry. Even ice sculptures have ears in Fifth Kingdom.

"Apparently, the pause in communications was not due to storms befalling Highbell. The queen has purposely stopped all correspondence going in and out of the castle. All the messenger hawks we sent finally returned, none of them bearing any letters."

I sit back, head turning forward again as my mind works, finger tapping on my thigh. "What is Malina up to?" I mutter to myself. I can't say I'm surprised that she's up to something, not after she tried to confront me about my plan to double-cross Fulke, but I *am* surprised at her daring.

Odo continues. "Your eyes in Highbell claim that the queen has made an appearance in the city. She was seen passing out goods to the people, though I heard there was some trouble with dissenters."

"She went to the city for *charity*?" I say incredulously. Malina would never concern herself with the people of Highbell unless for a specific purpose.

When some of the sculptors look over at the sound of my voice, I stand up and stride out of the gazebo. Odo hurries to catch up to my side while I stalk down the stone walkway, ignoring my guards at the door.

"There has been some talk amongst Highbell nobles as well," Odo tells me as we walk through the wide entryway of the palace. My footsteps are cushioned by a long purple runner, the glass and stone walls lit up from the ten-pointed-star window framed with wooden arches in the ceiling.

"What are they saying?" I ask as I turn sharply for the stairwell to head for my chambers. For now, I'm still staying in the guest wing. With Niven alive and Fulke's death fresh, it's best for appearances' sake. For now.

Odo's breathing becomes labored as he trails after my quick steps up the stairs. "That the queen is...well, she's wearing white, Sire."

I stop in my tracks, whirling around to face him with a frown. "What?"

Odo grips the banister of the stairway, panting out puffs of air before he answers. "She's not wearing gold in public, Your Majesty. None of the golden gowns. Not any of the crowns you've gold-touched, even her personal Queen's guards have had an armor change. I've had it confirmed from several sources."

Frustration has my teeth grinding. So *this* is how Malina thinks she can test me? It's not just a color she's refusing to wear; gold is a declaration of my power and reign. It's not a simple wardrobe change. It's a message.

"What would you like me to do, my king?"

I think for a moment before saying, "Nothing, yet. I want all the reports brought to my desk. I'll decide in the morning what to do with her."

"Very good, Majesty. And there is also the matter of the gold requests. We're still getting more and more every day."

"Remind our requestors that the kingdom is still in mourning. I do not need to flaunt my power while they just lost their king," I say with rigid chastisement. "Whatever debts this kingdom has, I'll pay them. As for the nobles looking to line their pockets, give them coin for now."

"We're out, my liege."

My face goes stony. "We're *out*? Of all we brought?"

Odo tries to suppress a wince but doesn't quite manage it. "Well, there were quite a lot of requests. Everyone wanted to have a token of your power. All of the gilded trinkets we brought are nearly gone as well."

My teeth gnash together so hard that my jaw bone pops. I'm running out of time. If I don't make a show of power soon, my grasp here might weaken, which can't happen.

I turn and walk up the steps again, but my pestering advisor follows me all the way to my private chambers. With a dark look, my guards hug the wall, making sure to leave us a wide berth as I enter my room.

"Sire, there's one more complication," Odo says quietly, his liver-spotted hands wringing in front of him after he shuts the door behind us.

A sharp sigh escapes me. "What now?" I need to read the reports about what's been going on in Highbell since I've been away. I need to deal with my cold bitch of a wife.

Once I know the details, I can plan. Then I can go check on Auren. She's been sleeping for two days now, clearly exhausted from whatever she endured with Fourth's army. I've let her be, while I've also had as many comforts delivered to her as I can think of. The softest of silks, the plushest of pillows. I've plied her with books and perfumes—I even had a brand new harp delivered to her.

Hopefully, once she rests, she will feel like herself again. I need her to get back on track since I can no longer delay on making changes to the castle and filling the coffers.

My tenuous grip on Ranhold depends on filling the nobles' palms with gold, on reminding everyone who I am and why it would be in their best interest to support my presence here. I've already done it once in Highbell, so I know how to take over a kingdom. You pour out wealth at first, fascinate the nobles and advisors with benevolence, be a shining presence to the commoners. And then you cinch it off little by little, making them dependent and wanting, fighting each other for the king's favor so that they might reap the benefits.

By the time I'm done, there will be no contest as to who they would rather keep. Me, who can make their kingdom dazzlingly rich, or the prig son of the dead king.

"As you know, the saddles were checked over by the mender once they returned, at your instruction," Odo informs me.

I cock a brow. "And?"

"The mender just confirmed it and sent word immediately." My advisor brushes down the ring of gray hair at the back of his head in a nervous gesture. "It... appears as though one of them is with child."

I freeze.

All thoughts screech to a halt as his words trickle down my spine. A second passes before I burst forward and grip him by the collar of his golden shirt. "What are you saying?"

Odo's milky blue eyes go wide, his entire body rigid as I yank him up on his toes. "Sh-she claims the child is yours, Your Majesty," he whispers quickly.

A bastard child...

I roughly release him and he stumbles, catching himself on the wall at his back. "The whore is lying, obviously. She wants to try to bribe me for gold or gain attention. She wants something, Odo, that's all this is. My saddles take herbs. It's never failed."

"Yes, Sire, it never has in the past, but the mender confirmed—"

I cut a hand through the air, making him flinch. "Then she fucked someone else. She was with Fourth's army, and the damn snow pirates before that," I point out. "Have her dismissed immediately from my service. I won't have an unfaithful saddle in my employ."

Odo runs a shaky hand down the wrinkled front of his shirt, watching me as I begin to pace. "The mender was disbelieving of her claims too, which is why he took longer than usual to alert me. He wanted to be sure, but he believes that she's nearly three months pregnant, which would mean that she was still in Highbell at the time she was bred."

My mind spins, pulse pounding in my head like the sculptor's hammer, a chisel to my skull as it chips down into aggravation. I don't like surprises.

My saddles were nearly as protected as Auren. I had a very strict rotation of guards. None of them would've dared to sneak in and fuck my saddles. I make a note to change out the guards too, just in case.

If the mender is correct about the timeline, if the babe is truly mine…

"Who else knows of this?"

"No one," he assures me. "The mender came directly to me, Your Majesty."

I nod absently.

Odo's hands fidget as he watches me think. "Would you like me to do anything?"

"Not yet," I say. "You're dismissed."

The man bows quickly and makes a hasty retreat, no doubt grateful to be gone from my presence.

Now that I'm alone, I go over to my desk and brace my hands onto the top, eyes locked on the neatly stacked papers, though not really seeing any of it. My mind is too busy navigating a plan like a sailor charting the stars.

My fingers flex over the wood, irritation locking my knuckles. Malina, Auren, the whore—*all* my problems are caused by Divine-damned women. This is exactly why you can't trust females. My mother taught me that.

I'm doing important work, and I can't allow anything to bring me off my path.

I was the one who pulled Highbell out of debt and made it into the symbol for gleaming wealth and prosperity. And now, Malina dares to test me? She is nothing but a bitter, useless woman, unable to even give me an heir. She's lucky I married her in the first place and allowed her to keep her crown.

Memories rush in—of my father, of the village children sneering at me, at the parish tossing me out for being unclean, at shopkeepers whispering "bastard" wherever I went.

After all these years of doing my duty and trying to breed that cold fish of a woman, and this is the thanks I get.

I *knew* Malina was the barren one.

Now, I've bred a saddle. My teeth grind again and again.

Yet, as my mind works through these strings that have been added to my grasp, I see possibilities of new knots. Knots that might be exactly what I need to tighten my reign.

A child can be a powerful thing. After all, there's nothing quite like a baby to endear the royal family to the public. It might even help solidify my rule here. If only it weren't a damn bastard.

I straighten up, hands falling at my sides as I smile.

No, what I need is an *heir*.

CHAPTER 5

AUREN

I jerk awake and sit up in a panicky rush.

For a moment, I'm not sure where I am. There isn't a black tent pulled taut above me, no golden ceiling gleaming. Instead, I stare up at lavender fabric draped over the four posters of the unfamiliar bed I'm lying in.

Everything rushes back to me. Where I am, who I was with. Luckily, the space beside me is cold, and the quiet of the room tells me that I'm alone. The only proof that someone has been in here is the gentle crackle of the fire at the opposite end of the room.

After being surrounded by Fourth's soldiers, the quiet privacy of the room is almost daunting. I'd grown used to Rip's steady breaths as he slept on his pallet. I'd become accustomed to the smell of the wet leather, of the coals smoldering between us.

I look around the richly adorned room, eyes settling on the pillow where Midas rested his head, and yet, all I can see is Rip's dark silhouette from across the tent, see the flash of his ink-stained eyes.

I rub a hand over my chest, because there's an ache in my heart that has nothing to do with Midas. I try to tell myself that the taste of betrayal isn't clogging my throat, that pain isn't stemming from a male with roots along his jaw and a stranger's green eyes. "Forget him," I murmur to myself.

Deal with Midas. Forget about Ravinger. That's what I need to do.

Taking a deep breath, I compose myself, forcefully shoving away all my emotions into a little box where I can slam the lid closed. There's no room for distractions. I have to cauterize the pieces of my bleeding heart, because I have plans to make.

I groan as I roll back my stiff shoulders, arms popping as I stretch them overhead. I have no idea how long I've been sleeping, but slices of light are cutting through the edges behind the thick curtains that hang over the glass balcony doors.

I yank back the golden blankets and stand up, but as soon as my bare feet hit the carpet, they grow wet, gold instantly soaking into the white. I should've slept with socks on, but I suppose it doesn't matter now. One good thing about being with Midas is that the evidence of my power is associated with him, so I don't have to hide it.

As groggy and sore as I feel, I luckily have the wherewithal to control my willful magic enough that I don't turn the rug solid. Finding a pair of slippers waiting for me, I slip them on before I go in search of clothes.

Somber sunlight greets me as I step through the doorway of the dressing room, my skin tingling faintly as I cross through the weak beams of light. All around, a new wardrobe waits for me, dozens of gowns hanging up in varying shades of purple.

I choose one with a low sewn back so that I'll be able to have my ribbons out. The moment I touch it, gold drips from my hands and soaks into the velvety fabric like ink to paper.

Inside the bureau, I snag some gloves and thick fleece stockings, but I can't find any shifts to go under my dress. Instead, I find piles and piles of frilly lace. I frown as I hold one pair up, and it takes me entirely too long to realize that these things are supposed to be underwear.

"Well, these can't possibly be comfortable," I mumble to myself. Unless I want to be bare beneath my dress, it's the only choice I have.

With a resigned sigh, I strip off my night dress before pulling on the tiny scraps. Walking over to the mirror, my brows rise as I turn to see myself, admiring the way the dainty lace hugs my curves.

"Well, bright side, it makes my ass look *amazing*."

Luckily, the softness of the leggings helps to counteract the lace, so it's not quite as uncomfortable as I thought it would be. The gown, however, is a different matter.

Apparently, the women in Fifth Kingdom don't have to breathe, because there's thick boning built into the bodice of the dress. It cinches so tightly that I'm out of breath just by pulling the damn thing on.

I look through the rest of the dresses to switch it out, but they all have the same thing. Glaring down at the bodice that's shoving my breasts up to my neck and holding my ribs captive, I act on impulse. My ribbons come out and snap the boning one after the other until I have enough give that I can actually inhale.

I look into the mirror again at the bodice that's now kinked, with broken lines of bones jutting out awkwardly, and I smile. "Much better," I say with a nod.

After slipping on my shoes and gloves, my ribbons tackle my hair by weaving it in a few braids that I pin up. Instead of hiding my ribbons completely, I loosely wrap them around my hips like a belt, shortening the length just enough so they won't drag on the floor, and then I'm ready.

To everyone else, I probably seem unchanged. I probably look like the same gilded saddle, the same gold-touched favored.

But if you look closer, you might see the gleam in my eye. You might catch the twist of my downturned lips that hints at the discontent lying just at the edge of my mouth.

Walking back into my bedroom, I head straight for the door and heave it open. I stride out without hesitation, and a little thrill travels up my spine.

The guards standing watch in the hall are so surprised by my sudden appearance that the two nearest jump, while the other four in the hall blink at me as I begin to walk down the corridor.

"Erm..."

Muttering ensues.

A pointed whisper. "Is she allowed to leave?"

"I don't know... Is she?"

"Why you lookin' at me?"

"My lady?" one of them calls.

I turn with a pleasant smile on my face, glancing at all six men staring at me. "Yes?"

The guard who called me has light brown hair cut short, thick sideburns on either side of his face. "Pardon me, my lady, but you're supposed to stay in your rooms."

I give him a look. "Is that so?"

All six of the guards exchange glances, and I can see their uncertainty as sure as I can see my reflection in their gleaming chest plates.

"Umm, yes?" he answers with uncertainty. "You've

been asleep for nearly three days. Perhaps you should... rest?"

I'm taken aback by that. *Three days?*

I tilt my head. "Well, if I slept for almost three days, then it seems to me I've rested plenty. What's your name?"

The man blushes, like I've asked him something scandalous. Maybe I have, since they've probably been told not to speak to me. He clears his throat. "Scofield, my lady."

"Scofield, am I a prisoner?" I ask.

His eyes go wide. "No, of course not."

"Good. Glad we got that cleared up," I say with a bright smile. "Now, if you'll excuse me."

I turn and walk away briskly, the guards stunned into momentary silence. One of them curses, and then a hissed argument breaks out between them, too low and rushed for me to hear. A few seconds later, two heavy footsteps hurry after me.

I look over my shoulder as I reach the stairwell. "You two drew the short straws, huh?"

I'm not surprised to find Scofield is one of them. "I don't know anything about straws, my lady, but I'm the only one here who's taken rounds at Highbell to guard you before. So the others, ahh, suggested I stay with you. And Lowe here served King Fulke, so he knows his way around the castle."

I glance at short, ginger-haired Lowe, who doesn't

seem very thrilled to be here. "Great, then you can help me by giving me a tour."

"A tour?" Lowe says, as if the idea tastes bad in his mouth.

"This is my first time at Ranhold, and I'd like to see more of it. Let's go to the kitchens first."

"My lady, if food is all you desire, surely we can have a servant send something up?" Lowe asks hopefully.

Scofield latches onto the suggestion. "Yes, we can have anything sent for you. There's no need to take a trip to the kitchens."

"Oh, I'm not going there for the food. I just want to walk around a bit," I say absently before I stop at the landing and turn. "Now, there's just one rule I want to make really clear to both of you. And it's a matter of life and death." The seriousness in my tone makes them pause. "Neither of you are to touch me. *Ever*."

Their eyes widen comically. My glare is probably a bit overboard, but I need to make sure they understand, because their lives depend on it.

I've been lucky so far that no one has touched my skin during the day, and I have to make sure it stays that way. Midas has already set the precedent that no one is to ever touch me, so all I need to do is drive that rule home.

"It doesn't matter if there's a wayward carriage about to run me down, or a viper in my soup bowl, or if you just want to offer your arm to help me down a broken

93

stairwell," I go on. "Never, under any circumstances, are you allowed to touch any part of me. King Midas will have you killed in an instant, even if your intentions were honorable. Do you understand?"

Lowe's throat bobs nervously, like he's even less pleased about escorting me than he was before. Scofield gives a wary nod. "I know the rules, my lady. The king made them *exceedingly* clear." He looks away, muttering, "Maybe not as colorful as you just did, but…"

I hold back a snort. "Okay, good. Just make sure you follow them." I take a deep breath and look around. "Now, which way to the kitchens?"

"To the left, my lady," Lowe answers.

I immediately turn and head in that direction and look around as I go, eyeing the jagged icicles insignia embroidered into the carpets. My gloved fingers itch to drag against the stone walls encased in the layer of glass, but I keep them at my sides. I shiver at the way it looks like ice, the effect helped by the chill in the air that seems to cling to the stunted ceilings and the crevices of every corner.

"Is King Ravinger staying on this level?" I ask curiously. As soon as I speak the question aloud, regret makes me bite my tongue. Whether he's on this level or about a thousand levels below in hell, it shouldn't matter, and I shouldn't care.

I *don't* care.

"I believe he's in another wing, my lady," Scofield answers.

A non-committal noise rises from my throat as I nod stiffly. *Forget about him*, I practically hiss at myself.

On the next floor down, we pass by a wide-eyed servant who stops dead in her tracks at the sight of me. She presses herself against the wall so tightly it's like she's worried I'll trip and fall into her and Midas will punish her for it. It's not a far-fetched scenario.

I give her a friendly wave but then stop when I notice the pile of rags in her arms. "May I have one of those?"

She blinks at me. "What?"

"The rags, may I please have one?"

A flabbergasted expression crosses her face before she manages to answer. "Sure, my lady. Take whatever you like."

"Thank you." I pluck one from the pile, pretending not to notice the way she winces.

As soon as I have the rag in my hand, she dips into a curtsy and hurries away. I try and fail to suppress a sigh. I'm well and truly back in a castle controlled by Midas. I know it's for the best that people are scared of me, because I don't want to hurt anyone accidentally, but at the same time, it was so nice not to endure that reaction for a while. In Fourth's army, no one flinched away from me, no one averted their eyes. It made me feel almost...normal.

When I look back at Scofield and Lowe, I notice

them frowning at the rag in my gloved hand. I quickly slip it into my pocket. "In case my nose runs," I say lamely. "It's...drafty in here."

I grimace at myself, but they simply nod, and I turn and keep walking. I follow Lowe's directions all the way to the palace kitchens, but once near enough, I could've found it by scent alone.

The smell of freshly baked bread greets me as I step inside the doorway. The space is large, with so much steam and smoke that it's like walking through a cloud. I take a moment to look around, noting the workers busy at their tasks.

I wasn't lying when I told the guards that I wanted to walk around. I want to get a feel for Ranhold on every level, and I figured the kitchens was an innocent place to start.

A cook with a sweaty face and a soiled apron finally seems to notice me even through the haze, and her eyes grow wide. "My lady?"

"Hello," I say with a smile.

The woman comes over while the rest of the kitchen staff go quiet and still, staring at me like they aren't sure if I'm real or not.

"Did you...did you need something, my lady?" she asks nervously, darting a look at the guards.

I glance around at all the stunned staff, wondering if maybe this hadn't seemed so innocent after all. "Oh, I was just wondering if I could have a piece of fruit?"

Behind me, I can almost feel Lowe glower.

"Of course, my lady."

She rushes over to a spot near the stove and grabs a basket of apples, bringing it over for me to choose. I pick out the largest one in the bunch. "Do you need anything else? Bread? Cheeses? Shall I send someone down for some wine...?"

I'm tempted by the wine, but I shake my head. "This is perfect, thank you." With a nod, I walk out, ears perking at the murmuring that erupts as soon as I leave.

"I thought you said you weren't hungry, my lady?" Lowe asks pointedly.

I shove the apple into my pocket right next to the rag and then give him a breezy look over my shoulder. "A lady is entitled to change her mind. Now, where should we go next?"

The guards look at each other, and their dread just makes it all so much more fun.

"We should really go speak with the king—"

I cut Scofield off. "King Midas is incredibly busy, and the last thing he would want is for you to interrupt him while he's working. It's just a castle tour," I say before turning on my heel and starting to walk again. "Oh, how about the library?"

"The...library, my lady?" Lowe repeats.

"Yep, you know, the place with historic tomes and the occasional romance novel?" When he still hesitates, I frown. "Does Ranhold frown upon reading or something?"

"It's just...well, the royal library is not open to the public. Unless you are royal, you must have an appointment with the scribes."

Wow, this palace is really particular about their books.

"Alright, then let's go make an appointment."

Lowe blinks at me. "Right now?"

"No time like the present. I didn't shove all my bits into this dress for nothing, gentlemen," I say, gesturing down my broken bodice. "Oh, and does the castle have a garden?"

Another long blink. Poor Lowe doesn't seem to like tours, or books, *or* plants. "Well, there's a greenhouse, my lady."

"Perfect, we can go there after."

I swear I hear Lowe sigh, which just makes a smirk tug at my lips. I probably shouldn't feel such a thrill at this, but I do.

It's a small thing, walking around, talking to staff, doing what I want to do when I want to do it. For nearly the entire time I've lived in Orea, I haven't been able to make my own decisions.

Everything has been dictated to me since I was a child, so this small piece of freedom is incredibly satisfying. My newfound rebellious streak has me practically skipping down the halls. I feel freer already, and this is just the beginning. This excitement reminds me of what I need to fight for.

Be quiet. Sit pretty. Play your silly music. Behave.

Those old orders play in my head like an overdone song that I have no desire to listen to anymore. I use every old order, every manipulation to stoke my fiery resentment, to keep me lit up with focus.

If Midas is going to keep up his remorseful and accommodating act to make me compliant, then I need to be on guard against everything he might throw at me. I can't let myself be tricked or swayed.

Which is why I start to recite every single controlling rule he ever imposed on me throughout the years. It's why I recall every time he pulled my strings, exploited me, used my feelings for his own machinations.

He made me suffer for years. He took away my control.

Now, it's time I take it back.

CHAPTER 6

AUREN

*M*y lady, can we please bring you back to your rooms now?"

I turn to look at Lowe over my shoulder as we walk across the castle's bailey. *Who knew trained soldiers could be such whiners?*

"Soon," I assure him.

He doesn't look appeased. "Forgive me, but that's what you said after the greenhouse."

"And the library," Scofield puts in unhelpfully.

I roll my eyes. None of the damn scribes would even come to the door when I knocked.

"The music hall as well," Lowe adds.

"Hmm, so I did."

My steps are unhurried, the hem of my dress sweeping the thin layer of powdery snow as I walk the grounds. Lowe and Scofield have taken me all around Ranhold Castle today, to as many places as I could think of to go.

And even though it's been hours, I'm still not ready to go back to my rooms. It seems I've developed a taste for freedom. Every time I take another bite, I want more. My spirit is ravenous for rampancy. Starving for wander. I want to go everywhere, see everything. For the first time, Midas isn't here to dictate to me.

It's so liberating not being told what to do. Not being a captive. Not being *kept*. It's an indulgence I've never had the opportunity to enjoy. It's a balm, cool and brisk, against a part of me that's been tepidly stagnant for far too long.

"My lady, you haven't got a coat. You could catch a chill," Lowe says, ginger hair blowing around in the breeze as he hurries to keep up with me.

"I've lived in Sixth for a decade and traveled through the Barrens to get here," I tell him. "I'll be fine. This place is nothing compared to those." It's true. The cold air of Fifth Kingdom is like an exhale across my cheeks. It's the gentle blow of a wintry breath, and I find it invigorating.

I pass a few loaded carts, watching the white birds peck at the snow for invisible bits of food. The guards and castle workers freeze in their tasks when they notice me, and soon, the outdoor bailey goes quiet. Gazes follow me, and whispers begin to hiss out like the curled tongues of curious snakes.

I ignore their stares, even as I feel them on the back of my neck. Although, their mutterings are harder to block out.

"That's her, King Midas's favored."

"That's the gilded saddle."

"Look at her face—gold-touched was right, wasn't it?"

"You think she's gold between her legs too?"

I'm unable to hold in my sigh. Different kingdom, same words. And therein lies the problem. Because wherever I go, words, attention, and recognition will follow me. Before Midas, I was simply an oddity. But he made me notorious, ensuring that I'm recognized throughout all of Orea.

I'll have to figure out what to do about that, since it's pivotal for my escape. For now though, I want to simply enjoy the fresh air.

I make my way across the square lot that's surrounded on all sides by the castle walls, gray and worn with cold. There's no layer of glass smoothed over the stone bricks here, no fancy filigree or snowflakes. This part of the castle grounds is not meant to be pretty, but functional.

At my back, there's a grain shed, the walls bleeding white paint in favor of the raw wood beneath. More birds peck at the ground in front of it where seeds and grain have spilled out, just to be shooed away by a worker. To my left, there are two tall towers at either corner of the wall, but I'm interested in the uncovered parapet.

I head for the coarse stone stairs at the front wall, gripping the front of my skirt so I don't trip.

"My lady, you're not allowed up there," Lowe calls from behind me.

"I just want to see."

There's no railing on these stairs, so I'm careful to keep my body close to the wall as I make my way up the steep steps. It's higher than it looks, and my breathing becomes labored before I've even made it halfway.

My ribbons loosen a bit so they can trail after me like the long train on a gown. The strands drag over the gray rock like trickles of gold water, as if they're enjoying the freedom too. It brings a smile to my face. Earlier in my life, I never would've thought they'd bring me happiness.

When they first sprouted from my back, I hated them for making me stand out even more, for causing me more pain. It was just another thing I needed to hide.

You're ashamed of them. You think of them as a weakness, but they are a strength, Auren. Use them.

Rip's previous words cling to me. He might've kept secrets about who he was, but he sure had a talent for making me face who *I* am. For admitting the limits and lies I've accepted.

I have hated, resented, and been ashamed of myself for long enough. I don't want to harbor thoughts like that anymore. By mentally breaking away from Midas, something else has shifted too. It's time to start embracing who I am and what I'm capable of.

By the time I make it to the top of the tall stairs, my legs are burning from the climb, but it's worth it for the height alone. The open parapet stretches a good hundred feet down the line, and there's an unobstructed view of the kingdom.

I stop in front of a notch in the wall that's probably meant for archers, but it gives me the perfect vantage point. The city below is an arch of buildings that surround the castle like a rainbow against a moon.

I'm high up enough that I can see all of Ranhold City laid out with its scattering of roads and rooftops, the buildings mashed together one on top of the other. The landscape is covered in snow and makes the ground glitter, and behind me, white-capped mountains stand like spires pointing to the bride-veiled sky.

Beautiful.

I turn my head slowly to take it all in, relishing in the fresh, stark air that ruffles my hair. It's not enough, though. Not nearly enough. So I lift my hands on either side of my little notch and heave myself up.

A strangled yelp of surprise escapes Lowe, while Scofield's face drains of color. "My lady! Come down from there!"

"She'll fall!" Lowe manages to squeak out.

"I won't fall," I say as I stand on the wall of the

parapet, making sure I have solid footing before I straighten up.

Lowe and Scofield are frozen, staring up at me with matching horrified expressions. Scofield reaches up like he's going to grab hold of me, but a glare from me has him snatching his hand back.

"My lady—" he begins.

I cut him off, facing the city again. "I'm alright. Let me look for a moment, and then I promise I'll go back to my rooms for the rest of the day."

He and Lowe go quiet at that, though I can feel the tension radiating off of them.

Maybe it's foolish to risk standing up here, but sometimes, you have to do foolish things just for the sake of doing them. I can look back one day and remember that I stood here, in the heart of an icicle kingdom, with a frosted city at my feet and a shivering sky at my cheeks.

This is so much better than a cage.

A smile plays about my lips as I breathe in the breeze. I think this is what it must be like for a bird before it lets out its wings and flies. I'm tempted to raise my arms, but it would probably send my nervous guards over the edge, so I keep my hands carefully balanced on the raised bricks at my sides.

My eyes scan the city again, but my attention is pulled like a magnet to a spot in the distance. There, where the darkened veins are spoiled into the snow, is where Ravinger walked and eked out his magic.

Jagged lines are slashed into the ground like torn paper, the edges singed brown against the snow. Even from here, I swear I can feel the sickly pulse of them, like they're rotted roots, waiting for their master to ground them.

Higher up, on a hill that overlooks the city, rows and rows of Fourth's army tents are set up in neat little lines. For some strange reason, my heart squeezes at the sight.

My fingertips drag against the rough stone beneath my palms as I tuck my fingers in. I stare and stare at those tents, at the dots I can see moving around, at the smoke lifting from burning campfires like a dark handshake with the air.

It takes another minute of staring before I can admit to myself that the feeling in my chest is longing.

I miss it.

A snort escapes me, because what kind of person misses the traveling camp of the enemy army that captured them?

And yet...they weren't the enemy. Not to me. I can't even say I was their captive, because in truth, they rescued me from the Red Raids. In fact, if things had been different, if I'd made the decision to stay, then maybe some of those soldiers down there would have been my friends. Lu, Osrik, Judd, Keg, Hojat.

Rip.

They weren't what I expected. But somehow, they ended up being exactly what I needed.

"My lady, I really must insist that you come down from there now," Scofield pleads.

I tear my stinging eyes away from the view to glance down at him. He's so nervous he looks about ready to pee in his uniform. Considering the cut of his trousers, that would probably make the poor guy chafe, so I take pity on him.

Turning back, I let myself indulge in one last deep breath of air before I hop down onto solid ground. Both of my guards let out a visible sigh of relief.

"Hey! What the hell are you three doing up here?" someone shouts.

I'm really glad I'm not still on top of the wall, because I flinch on instinct at the sudden sound. All three of us look over as a soldier stalks toward us. He's wearing Ranhold's armor and a purple cloak, but none of that is as well-tailored as the deep-cut scowl on his face.

Lowe tilts his chin practically down to his chest. "The Gilded Lady was just wanting to take in the view, Captain."

Displeasure rolls down my skin like beads of water and I shoot Lowe a look. Now all of a sudden I'm the *Gilded Lady*?

A stony gaze falls onto me as the man stops in front of us. "Well, she can take in the view through a window. The parapet is not a place for females to be carousing around."

"Of course, Captain," Lowe quickly says in deference. "We'll leave straight away."

Maybe I'm overreacting, but a wave of irritation rushes over me. Why is it so easy for everyone to boss me around and dictate my actions? Everyone always expects me to bend, to *behave*, and for some reason, right now it just rubs me the wrong way. It nudges at some perched temper inside of me until I feel a budding animosity flexing its wings, talons stretching out with ruffled ire.

I've realized that there are so many different kinds of cages, and if I want to stay out of them all, then I have a fight ahead of me. Because the world will keep on trying to leash me, men will continue trying to steer me in their grips of control. So I can't just roll over every time. I can't let that repressed temper of indignation sit stuck on that perch.

The goddesses made me a female. War made me an orphan. Midas made me a saddle. Up until now, those things have roped me. I've let myself be bridled, jerked around this way and that. But I'm sick and tired of gnawing on that bit at the back of my jaw with every tug of the reins.

Which is why I look the captain steadily in the eye and say, "We will *not* leave yet. I'll go when I'm ready."

The steel in my voice has the men looking at me with disbelief. They didn't expect me to do anything other than what I'm told. They don't have to say it, because it's there in their eyes.

The captain is the first to recover, giving me a scathing look that's so dry I'm surprised it doesn't peel right off his face. "You will leave *now*, madam. The wall is for soldiers only, not females, and quite frankly, you are not welcome here."

I'm not welcome *here*, as in the wall, or here as in Fifth Kingdom?

I give a cursory look around. "Are we so high up that your manners have evaporated, Captain?"

His expression is stony enough to rival the bricks we stand on. "You may be the golden girl of Sixth Kingdom, but here, you're just a female who's on my wall without permission. You need to leave," he says, eyes as hard as his tone. "You wouldn't want to get hurt out here, would you?"

My temper bristles, like feathers puffing up. "Are you *threatening* me?"

"You wouldn't be the first trespasser to fall off the wall."

I stare at the man in shock. His words might seem innocuous, but his eyes imply something much darker.

The unfurling temper of mine takes flight into full blown anger, gliding through me with a swoop, and it screeches the challenge of a sinister song. *Let it be a threat.*

"Fall? Or get escorted over the edge by a domineering wall captain?" I lob back.

Beside me, I feel my guards stiffen, feel the tension pull taut between all four of us. But I only have eyes for the arrogant captain whose mouth tightens, cold-chapped lips pressing together in a hard line of offense. "Of course not, and hysterics such as this are proof enough that you have no business up here where one needs to keep their wits about them."

Hysterics? I can show him hysterics.

"*Leave*, madam."

My spine snaps straight. "No."

The sudden standoff between this stranger and me calcifies, fusing my dug-in heels right where I stand. I should probably just go, since I was going to leave anyway, but because he's ordering me, because he's *sneering* at me, I just can't.

The captain scoffs, but the noise is stunted, the cockiness cut off at the knees with too much time passed between. "No more of this foolishness," he says dismissively. "You are interrupting my duty and taking up my valuable time."

I don't point out that he was the one who interrupted me. "By all means, go do your super important duty of wall-watching, Captain. You're blocking my view," I say with a fake smile.

He matches me, stubbornness to stubbornness. I don't know whether I'm more irritated or darkly glad.

His voice lowers. "Leave now, or I will remove you myself."

A polluted laugh fumes from my chest, and I lean in toward him before I can stop myself. "Go on. I *dare* you." My eyes burn with the flash of my challenge, my pupils taking on the heat of this airborne rage, and I want him to. I want him to try to grab me, to try to move me. Because right now, unaccountable violence is screeching through my veins and tightening the ribbons at my spine.

Do it, I chant wordlessly.

For the first time since his arrogant ass walked over here, the captain falters. His eyes sweep over my face like he's assessing an opponent and suddenly doesn't know if he brought the right weapon.

Then, his hand shifts, and my eyes snap down to the movement, my fingertips tingling. But before his palm even rises an inch, he stops himself, grip moving to the hilt of his sword.

My gaze lifts back up to his face. "That's what I thought," I chirp with smug vindication.

His face goes mottled with red-purple rage. "If you were my saddle, I'd have you flogged in the streets."

"Well, I'm not. And pity to the poor saddles who *do* service you. I hope you pay them well," I counter, eyes dragging over his less than appealing form.

For a second, he looks like he's debating if he can get away with that flogging he mentioned. I imagine it—him trying to punish me, the look on his face when he realizes his mistake as I pinch my bare fingers into his skin.

No one would be able to stop me. Not my guards, not the captain, not even Midas.

I could abandon my plan of waiting and gaining information, of escaping beneath the cover of secrecy. Instead of trying to slip between the knuckles of Midas's tight grasp, I could let myself fly into this budding tangent that's blooming in my chest. I could let gold drip from my fingers and solidify every obstacle that crosses my path.

This sudden realization of my true capability bites like the sharpest beak of a bird. I've never felt so powerful, or perhaps I've never really *comprehended* what I'm capable of, because I've been reined with fears and doubts, led with manipulations.

Punish him, a dark voice murmurs in my ear.

I barely feel it when my hand moves and tugs off my left glove. I don't feel it when my ribbons begin to slither down the backs of my legs like serpents ready to strike.

There's a small, strange smile tipping up the corners of my lips, and that's about all I *can* feel. That, and the echoing call of darkness screeching through my skull.

My hand lifts, bare finger pointed with purpose, and my blood trills even as my vision tunnels. I don't have time to stop and think, to consider what the hell I'm doing, because this Divine-damned darkness has taken flight inside of me, and it's all I know.

"What are you doing?" the captain asks, voice uneven, eyes wary.

I barely hear him over my pounding heart, pulse blaring at my temples. The beat strums in a challenge: *Do it. Do it. Do it.*

Just one touch. That's all it would take. My finger gets closer, ribbons tightening, and—

"I see you're awake, Goldfinch."

The dark, sensual voice snaps my devouring anger in half, yanking me from my trance-like state.

My sense of self trickles over me slowly, like the first drops of a rainfall. I blink, staring at my hand that's just inches away from the captain's frowning face.

"Toying with the wall watch?"

I jerk my head to look over at King Ravinger who's somehow now standing at my side, though I never sensed his approach. His voice slinks down my back, and my flushed skin erupts with chills.

"What?" My voice sounds dazed, and I quickly drop my hand, while warring emotions spin through me like a torrent.

Ravinger ignores the bowing captain and guards, his green eyes locked on me. Power coils around him like mist clinging to a dawn-lit field, and I lick my suddenly parched lips.

"Something I can help you with?" he asks in a teasing tone.

A blush rises to my cheeks for too many reasons to count. I almost...and then he...

What the hell was I about to do?

The captain seems to let out a sigh of relief at Ravinger's interruption, and he uses it to get away, clearly unsettled. "Excuse me, Your Majesty. I need to get back to my duties." He bows again stiffly before shooting a look my way. Then he turns and leaves, walking so fast I'm surprised he's not running.

Ravinger smirks at his retreating form before he turns back and levels that look on me. Great Divine, that *smirk*. The rough stubble on his face stretches in tandem with the paper-thin lines of power moving around his jaw, his obsidian hair tousled slightly in the wind. Dressed head to toe in black, his impeccably tailored pants and tunic do nothing to hide the muscles beneath.

He looks good. Way too damn good.

His gaze drops to his boots, and when I follow his line of sight, mortification flushes my skin when I see one of my ribbons curling around his leg.

With a frown, I make the ribbon release him and then shove it behind me. Ravinger's grin widens.

"Making friends?" he purrs.

I reach down to snag my dropped glove and pull it back on my shaking hand. "I've learned that any *friends* I could hope to make are wildly disappointing."

The smirk slides off his face at that. "And why have you come to such a pessimistic view?"

Even though my insides are a turbulent mess, I

meet his stare head-on. "Every person who has ever been friendly to me has done nothing but disappoint me."

Ravinger's expression sharpens. "That's unfortunate."

I lift a shoulder. "I'm used to it."

When his jaw muscle jumps, I know I've irritated him. Which is good, because then I can concentrate on that, on pissing him off, rather than what I almost just did.

My hands wring in front of me, and the movement betrays me, making his gaze flick down to my broken bodice. "Corset trouble?" His damn amusement has already rallied.

"Yeah, the *trouble is* corsets are stupid."

Ravinger chuckles, and the sound helps me let out the tight breath that was stuck in my throat. He lets a slow gaze drag over me, and I hate how it makes my skin heat, makes my heartbeat quicken. "Good to see you up and about, Lady Auren. I was worried that your return to your golden king was quite...restricting."

My eyes narrow on his choice of words. "Everything is well in hand, King Ravinger. I thank you for your benevolence in releasing me," I say with a sickly sweet tone.

He cocks his head, those mossy green eyes never leaving my face. "Does anyone need to release a goldfinch? Or does she do it herself?"

I open my mouth, but no words come out.

He arches a thick black brow, and I immediately see

Rip in that gesture, which just makes my stomach sour. Then he tips head ever so slightly in a gesture of respect. "Enjoy your day, Lady Auren."

Turning, he walks away with a confident stride, while I'm left to stare after him, grappling to make sense of everything that just happened.

"My lady."

I jump in surprise, whirling around at Scofield's voice. "Shit. I forgot you two were behind me."

He shifts on his feet at my curse, sharing a look with Lowe. "We really need to go back inside now."

His voice and the nervousness in his brown eyes makes me relent. I nod and begin to head back down the stairs, while sharp whispers are traded between my two guards.

The aftershocks of what just happened sway my steps and make my thoughts dizzy. Because that intensity of emotion, that dark desire to punish... I've never felt anything quite like that before.

Anger, I realize, tastes like a sugared flame. And after a lifetime of cold bitterness, a part of me wanted to indulge in it, wanted to bloom in its burning embrace.

I don't know when it happened exactly, but it seems a darkness has sprouted inside of me, nurtured from the cruel soil I was left to wither in.

I felt so powerful. So unstoppable.

And...*I liked it.*

The very person I accused of being a mindless murderer was the one to stop me from becoming one.

I see you're awake, Goldfinch.

Goddess, that cool, unruffled voice of his. I have a feeling he wasn't just talking about me getting up out of bed, either. One sentence, and he grounded me, like gravity to the earth. His voice cut through the sinister one in my own subconscious and drew me back down.

But all the way back to my rooms, one question follows me, like a ghost haunting my steps, dumping sickly cold water over my dampening spirit.

What would I have done if he hadn't interrupted?

I don't think I'm ready to face the answer.

CHAPTER 7

AUREN

I watch the falling snow through the glass panes of
my balcony doors as I hum a pub song that's stuck
in my head. It's an old tune from my time in Third
Kingdom, and I don't remember all the lyrics, but the
chorus always made me snort.

> *Dear John was a yawn*
> *But his trousers hung tight,*
> *So the frills would all smile*
> *And ask him home for a night,*
> *But poor frills, how they trilled—*
> *For it was only a pocket of pipe.*

I smirk as I reach into my pocket to feel the pipe
I nicked. I spotted its thin wooden length poking out of

a passing guard's holster on the way back to my rooms. It was almost *too* easy to take it. Seems some of those old pickpocketing skills I learned with Zakir can still be useful.

I release the pipe with a smile on my face, yet that smile slides right off again as I think of my interaction with the captain on the wall. I'd never felt such uncontrollable darkness surge up in me like that. Is that what happens when a caged pet finally breaks free?

Violence sang inside my chest, like a bird of prey lilting as it circled, ready to dive for the kill. It was a daunting lyric for a dark need. How tempting that wicked song sings.

If Ravinger hadn't shown up, would I have allowed the fury to manifest? Would I have another person's blood on my gold-clad hands?

And yet, even though that beast is once again silent, I can still feel it there, watching. Some untapped creature ready to rise up.

I go still at that thought, and an old memory slithers forward.

Shove down weakness, and strength will rise.

That long-ago advice has been cropping up in my head lately, but it comes back full force now, like it was always waiting for me to get right here, in this moment, so that I could remember.

My hair reeks of fish and perfume. The smell won't come out, and there's no point in trying. I'll be right back here tomorrow, caught beneath the trap of a straw mattress and the flesh of a man.

With my head turned to the right, I can see the harbor through The Solitude's speckle-stained window. The bed shifts, and straw crackles in a dry threat to poke through the wool sheets. A hairy arm blocks my view for a moment, but I keep looking, keep trying to see those floating ships, even when a metallic click sounds as the man drops a coin on the bedside table. "For you, pretty. I'll tell Zakir West what a good girl you've been."

A spot on my back pinches, the skin jumping right between my shoulder blades. I don't reach around to try and scratch at it though. I don't reply to him either. But my lips press into a thin line until he has the decency to stop blocking my view.

I hear him shuffle into his pants and shirt, all while my hair keeps tickling my nose where it's shoved between my cheek and the pillow. Fish and perfume come in with every inhale, so strong I can taste it.

He says something by way of a goodbye, but I don't hear what it is. I don't care. When I'm finally alone, the prickling on my back ceases, and I drag myself off the bed to pull on my dress.

It's a deep green color that reminds me of the moss that blanketed the rocks at the lagoon in Annwyn that I once snuck off to. It reminds me of the summer grass on the hills where my mother's horses grazed. It reminds me of the trees that stretched to the sky down the streets on Bryol.

It reminds me of home.

A tear slips down my cheek as I pull on my stockings and mud-caked boots. I walk over to the window and brace my hands on the rough wood of the sill just as the door behind me opens.

"Time to go. Got another renter for the night."

I turn to look at the buxom innkeeper as she goes straight over to the bed and starts to strip the sheets.

"Do you want help?"

Natia looks up at me from beneath a bun of thick black hair peppered with silver strands. She's a blunt woman, tells you her mind with a quick jab and no remorse, but has smile lines in the creases of her ochre face. "No, girl, this is my inn, and I see to it. Besides, you don't look like you know how to make up a proper bed."

I give her a shaky smile. "You're right," I say. I don't tell her that it's because I don't have one.

As she yanks up the sheets on the other side, Natia nods at the table. "There's a token there for you. Take it."

The skin at my back flinches, feeling tight. I don't even want to look at the money. "You keep it. I'm sorry the beds are always such a mess." My cheeks burn as I say it, and I'm forced to glance away.

Six weeks. It's been six weeks of coming here to The Solitude every day to meet whatever person Zakir sends. I never thought I'd actually miss begging on the streets. I never thought I'd miss being made to pickpocket all night from drunks and thieves, even when it meant I was caught and roughed up sometimes.

Can a person break in six weeks?

It feels like I am. It feels like I might be tearing at the seams, like a rag doll handled one too many times.

Maybe that's why my back keeps quivering, my skin constantly going tight with pinches and prods. Maybe it's because that's where my cracks are going to start to show.

It would be fitting, wouldn't it? For me to fracture down my back. Ironic, seeing as how I've bowed in submission at Zakir's feet.

I startle when Natia suddenly comes up to my side and grabs my hand, shoving the coin into my palm before giving it a squeeze. "Now you listen here, girl," she says sternly. "I've seen that look a thousand times."

"What look?"

"That look of giving up." Her fingers dig into my hand, the coin kept between us like a secret. "I've been around long enough to see it. You're not the first of Zakir's girls to use a room here."

If I thought my cheeks burned before, it's nothing to how hot my face feels now.

She nods toward the window. "You're always looking out at those ships, but I can tell you never think you'll be on one."

I blink in surprise that she noticed something like that. I've only seen her for a couple minutes every time... after.

"Well, I won't, will I?" I reply, tone tainted with bitterness.

"Why not?" she challenges.

I'm filled with new irritation at her question, and I pull my hand from her grasp, slamming the coin down on the sill. "What do you mean, why not? *Zakir would never let me leave, and you know what happens to stowaways."*

She leans in, her apron brushing against my dress as her brown eyes fill with defiance. "Who said anything about stowaways?"

For a moment, I just stare at her, not understanding. But then, her gaze falls down to the coin again. "Like I said, take your token, girl."

My fingers are a little shaky as I reach over and pick it up. It's not the first time I've been tipped, but I've left every single coin behind. I've been too ashamed, too loath to touch them. But when Natia reaches into the pocket of her dress and pulls out a small patchwork pouch, I already know what's inside.

"This isn't for Zakir West, you hear? These are yours. It's up to you how you use them." She tips her head toward the harbor again. "I hear the ships with the blue sails and yellow suns are from Second Kingdom where it doesn't rain for weeks on end, and the hot desert sand is as fine as powder."

Just the idea of being dry and warm in a desert instead of constantly soggy from the cold port rain makes me shiver.

"But that's not something a given-up girl thinks about, I guess," Natia finishes with a shrug. "Is that what you are? A given-up girl?"

I swallow hard, my eyes flitting back and forth between her and the trio of ships with the yellow sails floating in the distance.

This thing she's suggesting, this hope of escape, it's what I've been aching for. And yet, if I were caught, if I failed...

Tears spring to my eyes, and my body trembles. Zakir wouldn't just punish me, he might actually kill me if I tried to get away. Or he'd give me to Barden East once and for all, and then I'd wish I were dead.

"I can't."

"You could," the old woman retorts, glaring at me with her hands on her hips and a scowl beneath her thickly arched brows. "That's your fear talking, and it's a weakness that you have to shove down before it towers over you."

She's right, I am *weak. Her "given-up" nickname isn't far off.*

I'm weak and I'm alone, and in only six weeks, I've gotten the look of someone who's caved in on herself. There's just hollow spaces filled with broken walls and ragged pains, too much heaped in to ever be cleared out.

I hate that my bottom lip quivers, hate how small I feel. "I don't know if I can. I don't know if I'm strong enough to try."

Natia doesn't soften, doesn't give me a kindly pat on the shoulder or tell me it's all going to be okay. Instead, she shoves the pouch of coins at my chest so hard that it makes me stumble back a step as I quickly catch it.

"Either do it or don't. Makes no difference to me," *she says matter-of-factly.* "Though, it seems to me that trying and failing is better than giving up." *Her eyes scour mine like a soundless lecture.* "Shove down weakness, and strength will rise. You can't be strong without conquering those weaknesses first. That's what I think, anyway."

A chill travels down my spine as my fingers clutch onto the pouch, the edges of dirty money digging against my hold.

"Now go on and get out of here. I have customers waiting downstairs, and I still have to air this room out and get new bedding on. I can't be wagging jaws all hours of the day when there's work to do." *Giving one last stern look at me, Natia crosses the room and grabs the pile of soiled linens in her capable hands. Then she leaves without another word, while my ears pound with everything she already said.*

I stare and stare at the pouch of coins in my hand, wondering if I dare, wondering how much it would cost me to bribe a captain for passage. I loosen the ties and dip my fingers in, pulling out a single golden coin, the sides worn and grimy.

I twirl it around, asking myself if I really have it in me to try. Maybe Natia is right. Maybe it is better to try and fail than to be the given-up girl.

At hearing a sound in the hall, I quickly drop the coin back in and cinch the pouch tight before I bury it in my pocket for safekeeping. But...is it enough? Do I need more?

As I hurry out of the room, my skin pinches and jumps again, but this time, it isn't on my back.

It's on my fingertips.

I'm plucked out of the memory when my bedroom door slams closed.

My eyes fly over to where Midas stands, and I immediately tense up. The anger on his tanned face makes his handsomeness drain away, replaced with something ugly, something that makes my stomach ache. My mind falters for a moment under his glare. It's muscle memory, or maybe mind memory—something that makes me almost revert to old behaviors. The urge to placate, to please, is strong.

He's trained me very well.

Rather than give in, I call up on that anger, stoke the coals of its justified smolder, and I manage to get my shit together.

"Midas, how are you?" I ask with practiced pleasantness as I get to my feet and head over to the bed so I can keep space between us.

"*How am I?*" he repeats, throwing a hand in the direction of the door. "I was just informed that you've been traipsing around the castle grounds all day."

I gauge his anger and decide to play stupid. Acting oblivious, I begin to fluff the pillows on the bed. "I did," I say brightly. "It was great. I didn't get into the library, but I saw loads of other rooms, and Ranhold seems nice. Although, it seems to have a bit of a draft problem inside, don't you think? My guess would be porous wood used for the window frames. Bad planning."

Midas gets the most incredulous expression on his face while I continue to mess with the pillows. I shake one of the larger ones quite vigorously, and then—"Fluff this one for me, will you?" I chuck it at him as hard as I can before all the words even leave my mouth.

The golden satin slams into Midas's face, feathers bending around his head with a satisfying thump. Juvenile, sure. But it does wonders for my morale.

By the time he yanks it down and holds it at his side, I'm already busy straightening the blankets. I can see him in my peripheral as his grip tightens around the pillow.

"Auren."

I glance over at him. "Yes?"

"The cage—"

I immediately straighten up, all pretenses of my false brightness gone as furious fire flares in me. "*No.*" I won't stand to hear that word come out of his mouth. I'll play a part here because I need time and a plan, but if he tries anything with a Divine-damned cage again, I will rage.

Midas hesitates, brown eyes calculating as he assesses the snap-change of my demeanor. After a moment, he seems to decide on a different direction. "It's too dangerous for you to be out wandering the castle without me."

"I had two guards with me."

He shakes his head. "It doesn't matter. Everyone is a danger to you. You know this. You can't trust people. Especially when I hear that Ravinger went near you again," he grits out.

My spine stiffens. "He just happened to be on the wall when I was there," I defend.

Frustration makes his shoulders go tense. "I don't

like it. He and that commander of his are either infatuated with you or purposely taunting me."

It's on the tip of my tongue to point out that he's always made sure that people were, in fact, infatuated with me. He loves dangling me in front of others like I'm a gold carrot. King Fulke was a prime example. Midas just wants to control it.

"Aside from people being dangerous, you should remember that you're also a danger to *them*," he goes on, letting his words sink in. He watches to see how they tug at the expression on my face, even though I try hard to keep it blank. "One wrong move, one accident, and you could kill someone. Need I remind you that you just murdered your stand-in?"

This time, I can't stop from flinching. I can't stop the memory flash of how I shoved the woman back, my touch immediately lethal. She'll forever be entombed in a cage meant for me, dead by my hand. Guilt and regret cluster together like clouds, a humid pressure gathering in my chest.

"Think of Carnith, Auren. Think of what happens when you're reckless."

A drop falls, like a hiss of water against the smolder of my anger. I can see the manipulation for what it is. And still, it makes me waver for a moment. A drizzle of the old Auren sprinkling overhead, threatening to douse my fire.

The problem is, he's not wrong. One slip-up is all it

would take. If someone touches my skin, they *will* turn solid gold, and there's nothing I can do to stop it.

I don't know why, but people, animals, I can't just change their color. If I touch them, the gold takes over. A simple brush of my arm against theirs, and they're dead. Like the woman in my cage. Like Captain Fane of the Red Raids, whose statue lies somewhere in the frozen Barrens. Like the people in Carnith, when gold first dripped from my fingertips, and left me with blood on my hands.

"You need to stay inside during the day," Midas tells me, his eyes as rough as the bark of a tree. One touch, and I'd be sliced through with his splinters.

There's a lump the size of a peach pit in my throat that I struggle to swallow down while I work to control my overcast emotions. The idea of being locked in anywhere ever again makes bile twist in my gut. "You promised," I say vehemently.

"I'm trying to protect you from yourself."

I scoff and shake my head. I hate how much of an expert he is at this. He's trying to get me to bend, to defer, because that's how it's always worked between us. He knows how to pluck on the strings of my guilt and make me play his tune, so I have to play mine instead.

Shove down weakness.

Midas gestures around the room. "Don't be ungrateful for what I've already allowed."

I pin him with a look. "Don't be ungrateful for what *I've* allowed, Midas."

There's another stare-off between us. A clash of repellant wills. The tide and the shore, a forever battle between land and water, between give and take.

He may wear the crown, but *I* was the one who made it gold.

I can see the temper he's trying to hold in, but he never was good at compromising, and he *hates* it when I talk back. After a moment, he lets some of it leak out when he sighs and throws the pillow at the bed harder than he needs to, making it bounce right off onto the floor.

He takes another deep breath, hands bracketing his hips. "I agreed about you not going back into the ca— about you not being confined behind the protection of your bars," he amends. "But during the day, it's far too dangerous for you to be out on your own. For others, as well as for yourself. You can't control your power, Auren."

"I know that," I snap. He's trying to gain the upper hand, and I don't like it. "Just like everyone knows the rules. No one will touch me, and I'll be careful, just like I was with Fourth's army."

He looks at me with pitying disappointment. That look would've been like a kick to the gut before. It would've had me scrambling to fix it, to be *good*. "You're being irresponsible, Auren. Is it really worth it? Do you really want that on your conscience? I'm only thinking of you."

Bastard. What an emotional-string-pulling, puppeteering bastard.

And yet...*am I* being selfish? What if I do make a mistake, and someone else is killed because of it?

I bite my bottom lip, teeth sinking in as I nibble on the worry. A fight begins inside of me, a battle of thoughts, of warring wants.

Midas comes closer, like a shark scenting blood in the water. "Think, Auren. Are you truly okay with the risk of murdering someone? *Again*? Because that is what will happen. I'm just trying to protect you. You always trusted me before. I need you to trust me again."

My eyes begin to burn, and I want to spit in his face. I want to spit at my own damn face too.

I can feel him looping the strings around me, deft words trying to tie the knots. He's so damn good at manipulating me. How did I ever think I could beat him at his own game when he's such a master at it?

I feel utterly unequipped.

He needs me, I remind myself. I do have leverage here, because he wants me complacent, and I want him to think that all is well so that I can get the hell away. Of course, the last thing I want is to kill someone by accident, or gild the wrong thing at the wrong time and have everyone know my secret, but I can't be cooped up in this room day in and day out.

"No locks, Midas, or this room is no better than a

cage," I tell him. "I'll keep your guards with me at all times, I'll keep my hands and arms covered, and keep a distance, but I can't stay trapped in here," I say, tipping my chin up.

He watches me, and my heart pounds as I try not to fidget. Even though we're both standing still, I can feel the tug of war going on between us. Can feel splintering rope cutting into my palms as he pulls and pulls. If I let him, he'll drag me under.

So I don't back down. I don't let go. And finally, after another tense moment, he lets out a sigh. "I don't want to fight, Precious. I've had a long day. A long damn *month*." He looks tired all of a sudden, like this interaction has exhausted him as much as it's exhausted me.

Midas walks over and presses a kiss against my hair, safe now that night has fallen. "You should get some rest, okay? I'll send up some dinner for you, and we'll talk tomorrow." His eyes flick down to the bodice of my dress. "I'll have the seamstress fix your gown as well."

Not waiting for a reply, he turns and walks out of the room, and I'm left staring at the closed door. I know without a doubt, he's going to continue pecking against my resolve, trying to scratch me raw. If I don't come up with a plan soon, he'll sink his claws into me again, and I can't let that happen.

I have to slip through his fingers before he tightens his grip.

CHAPTER 8

QUEEN MALINA

*C*rickets. *That's what my advisors* remind me of.

Wilcox, Barthal, and Uwen, all noblemen from once flourishing Highbell houses. They're pests who hop at my feet, only daring to make noise when nothing else rises to challenge them.

"We cannot take away farming rights of House Bansgot," Barthal says, the frown fitting perfectly into his aging face, since it's one of his most-used expressions when he's in my presence.

"He's right, Your Majesty," Uwen agrees from my left. "They have had those rights for generations."

My fingers rise one after another, then my nails tap down in sequence on the table in front of me. It still smells of new paint. The palace carpenter looked at me like I was mad when I bid him to cover every gold piece of furniture in the meeting chamber, but he did as he was told.

It took five coats of white paint to completely cover the gaudy metal, and five days for it to fully dry.

Of course, that was the day my spies informed me that Fourth Kingdom did *not* wage war on Fifth like I hoped they would. Instead, it seems King Rot and Tyndall have struck some sort of tentative truce. That alone put me in a foul mood, but then I heard about *her*. The golden cunt is still alive, and back in Tyndall's possession.

My lips pull into a sneer.

I handed her and the other whores to the Red Raids on a silver platter, and the pirates ruined it, gave the saddles up and then fled like the cowards they are. Just thinking about it makes my temper frost over, ice burning in my gut.

Men ruin all of women's best laid plans.

Drawing myself back into the conversation, I give a terse shake of my head. "I don't care how long they've had it. House Bansgot declared that they will only pay their taxes directly to Tyndall, which is treason," I reply.

"The king—"

I cut Uwen off. "*Tyndall*," I stress pointedly, "is not ruling Sixth anymore. *I* am." Their chirping goes quiet, as it always does. "Taxes are due, and everyone will pay or reap the consequences. The Bansgots are three weeks late in their payment and have thus ignored all attempts at collection. So, they will lose their farming rights, and I will bestow it on a House who is loyal to their Colier queen."

All three men gape at me while I suppress an irritated sigh.

My grip on Highbell is tentative at best. Every day, I attempt to make strides, to solidify my rule and to vilify Tyndall, but the pushback only seems to worsen. The nobles are split down the middle. Houses that were once loyal to my father and his father before him now spit in their faces by rejecting me. All because Tyndall has dazzled them with wealth.

Which is why I have dried up their taps by cutting off their monthly gifts of gold.

Yet for every countermove I make, I seem to still lose ground, and it infuriates me. First the peasants, and now the nobles.

But I *will* bring them to heel. I must.

"Give the farming rights to House Shurin. They can hold the contract to supply Highbell with its crops, and we'll also send them a cart of gold to thank them for their loyalty," I say, fingers fiddling with the furred collar of my gown.

Uwen presses his lips together, though he writes it all down dutifully.

"Now—" I'm cut off when a knock sounds on the door. "Enter."

My guard pops his head inside. "Pardon, my queen, but a messenger has arrived for you."

"A messenger from where?"

"Fifth Kingdom."

I feel my advisors go tense, anxious air stilling in their throats. "Ah, Tyndall has at last come to the conclusion that I'm ignoring him," I say. "Show the messenger in. I'll receive him here."

A few tense minutes tick by while my nails continue to drum on the table. My dear husband has finally deigned to realize that his hold on Highbell is being challenged. I feel both excitement and anticipation to see what his response will be.

This is what I've been waiting for. The chess game of kings and queens is never dull, and I've been wanting to go up against Tyndall for a long time.

When footsteps sound down the hall, my thrumming fingers hit a little too hard. My eyes dart down to where the white paint has scraped off, now buried beneath my nail. Frustration blooms in my chest when I note the sliver of gold now showing through the scratch on the tabletop. One slip, and five coats of paint are ruined, just like that. The damning metal mocks me, a taunting crescent smile to meet my glare.

"Your Majesty?"

I look up at the open door, as two of my guards escort the messenger inside. He's dressed in gold armor and a heavy cloak with jagged tufts of snowfall stuck to it, like white-barbed brambles.

As soon as I look upon his wind-chapped face, recognition flares. "Ah, Gifford. Still delivering Tyndall's messages, I see. No promotion?"

The olive-toned man bows to me in greeting, ignoring my jab. "One doesn't need a promotion when doing the gods' bidding."

One of my snow-white brows arches up. "The *gods*? Goodness, first Tyndall rises above his station to become king, and now he's a god? How much gold did that cost him?" I ask with a wry pull of my lips. I feel Wilcox shoot me a disapproving look, but that only adds to my amusement.

Gifford shakes his head, brown eyes giving nothing away. "Not so much blasphemy as that, Your Majesty. Just that the gods ordain and bless the monarchs. By doing a king's bidding, I'm doing the gods' bidding as well."

My head tilts. "And what of queens and goddesses? Am I not ordained, Gifford?"

He hesitates, shooting my advisors a look before answering. "Of course, Your Majesty, I meant no offense."

"You've given none. I don't hold the sap accountable for its dribble. It's the tree that makes it, after all." I can tell by his furrowed brow that he has no idea what I'm saying. I wave a hand at him. "I assume you have a message from my dear estranged husband?"

Gifford shifts on his feet. "I do, Your Majesty. He sent me on a timberwing so I may arrive swiftly. He is concerned about you."

A corner of my mouth curves. "I'm sure."

"When all of his hawks went unanswered..." the man trails off.

"I'm on tenterhooks," I say blandly, holding out a hand.

He starts to come forward, but my guard holds up an arm to stop him. "*I'll* hand Her Majesty the message."

Gifford dips his head. "Of course." Digging into a pouch that's strung across his hip, he takes out a gold cylinder and passes it over.

My guard opens it, dipping the letter out, eyeing it suspiciously before he passes it to me. "Thank you," I murmur as he takes a step back.

The metallic wax seal of a bell—*my* bell—greets me.

The parchment is thick, though shorter than I expected. As I unroll it to read, my back stiffens with every scratched word, my lips pressing together so hard they probably turn white.

I've crumpled the letter in my fist before I even realize I'm doing it.

"Your Majesty?"

I don't know which of my chirping crickets speaks, and I don't care. I stand, shoving my chair back too hard.

The legs scrape against the painted floor, more white flaking up to leave behind a skid of gold.

My fist tightens harder around the letter.

"My queen?"

Still ignoring them all, I stalk out of the room, my guards hurrying to keep up with me as I leave behind a bewildered audience. The entire way upstairs, I keep my hand clenched, letting the thick, sharp edges of the paper dig into my palm.

It's not until I get into my rooms and slam the door behind me that I finally uncurl my fist and throw the damning letter into the burning fire. I hurl a yell of frustration along with it, a noise made through clenched teeth and a rigid neck.

Hands braced on the mantel, I glare into the flames, watch the words burn, wishing I could burn the hand that penned it.

"What's wrong?"

I don't turn away, don't blink. The heat of the flames blankets my eyes, but still I watch it all turn to ash.

Jeo steps up beside me and places a tentative hand on my back. "What happened, my love?"

"*Love*," I spit, jerking away from him as I turn. "You do not love me, Jeo. You are my royal saddle. A whore I pay to ride. Do not pander to me with pretty lies."

His arm drops and a look of hurt crosses his expression. I wish it would linger. I wish I could spread that hurt, make everyone suffer as much as *I* suffer this life.

"Fine," he says, copper hair flickering in the light of the fire, his freckled face red with both anger and embarrassment. "What's wrong, Queen Malina?" he asks pointedly.

"You want to know what's wrong?" I snap. "Every prick who ever prodded a maiden and stole her virtue. Every bastard who was ever born to taint bloodlines. Every man who rose up by standing on the bellies of women."

Jeo's thick red brows pull together. "I'm not following."

"He impregnated one of his *whores*!" I shout, the ice around my temper shattering.

He blinks in surprise. "Tyndall?"

"Of course, Tyndall," I seethe, eyes blazing. "Who else?"

My saddle opens his mouth, but then closes it before he can speak. Beside us, the fire continues to crackle, teeth gnashing on the letter I've fed it.

"Spit it out, Jeo."

"Well, it's just..." His hands run down the front of his white tunic, like he wants to smooth away what he's about to say. "I thought he was the impotent one."

I clench my teeth, my gaze turning so cold it could rival Sixth's storms. He's lucky. If I *did* have magic in my veins, I would strike him down where he stands for daring to say such a thing to me.

"So it's *my* fault I don't have a child, is that it?" My tone is so deathly low that surely it reaches the depths of the ground and seeps its way into hell.

Jeo's contrition does nothing for me. "My queen, I didn't mean it like that."

"Get out."

He rears back, blue eyes widening. "Malina..."

"I won't need your services tonight, Jeo. Leave."

Turning, I face the fire again and stare down at the demonic force, watching it lick and mangle everything into cinders. My ears follow the sound of Jeo's footsteps as he walks out and closes the door behind him, and only then do I let out a sigh.

I expected anger and a political move from Tyndall once he realized I was trying to take Sixth from him. I expected a Divine-damned response for all the hard work I've done to overthrow his rule right out from under him.

But no.

He's ignored all of it, as if I've done nothing. As if the quiet treason I've committed doesn't matter at all, and none of my moves are worth his attention. He didn't even deign to threaten me.

Instead, he instructs me to formally declare a pregnancy and then shut myself up in my chambers for the next six months. When I come out, it will be with a babe in my arms. With an infant that isn't my own. His whore's child, passed off as a prince or princess.

In his words:

You will do this so that you may finally do your duty to me as my wife, and I shall be able to claim a legitimate heir.

My eyes burn, but I don't blink. I let my irises become consumed with the reflection of the flames.

I know the true threat for what it is. There's no doubt that he knows what I'm doing here, but he plans to strap me with his bastard baby.

You will do this, or you will no longer be useful to me as a wife.

Useful. That's all that's ever mattered to him: whether or not I was *useful*.

I don't even notice that my hand drops down to my stomach, that my nails dig into the flesh there. The flatness that belies a barren womb.

If he truly believes I would *ever* take his whore's baby and pretend it was my own, then he doesn't know me at all. No, if I can't have children, then he can't either.

I'll rip Highbell from his grasp and crush his hopes of claiming an heir.

After all, he did it to me first.

CHAPTER 9

AUREN

*Yips and howls wak*e me up.

Peeling one eye open, I glance at the glass balcony doors. I forgot to close the curtains before I fell asleep last night, so the gentle dawn light is filtering in, the color like a dollop of cream over a tin cup horizon.

At the sound of more barking, I sit up and climb out of bed, shoving my feet into some slippers and pulling on the robe I left lying on the armchair. I make my way over to the balcony, my palms coating the knob in gold as I open it.

When I step outside, the cold morning breeze greets me, moving the loose strands of my hair. There's a light dusting of snow on the ground, my steps leaving a trail of footprints as I walk to the railing and look down.

The commotion is coming from a pack of excited

dogs racing around, nipping at each other in a wooden pen built against a small stone structure. A smile lifts my lips as I watch them roll in the snow, tongues lolling as they yip and spring.

Two men are down there with them, dressed in such thick furs that I'm surprised they aren't waddling. One of the men disappears into the building that I assume is the kennels, coming out a few seconds later dragging a dogsled behind him.

With a whistle, the shaggy haired dogs rush over to him, tails wagging while he hooks them up to the sled. I realize they're a hunting pack when I see the other man loading arrows and blades into the back.

Once the dogs are all strapped in, another shrill whistle pierces the air, and both handlers stand upright on the footrests as the dogs race off. The dogsled heads for the mountains standing sentry behind the castle, and I watch them until they disappear.

A pang of jealousy hits me while I watch them rush away. It must be so freeing, to ride off like that. With the wind blowing in your hair, the glittery snow at your feet. I bet it's even better than standing on the wall to feel the breeze.

Going back inside, I quickly go through my morning routine, getting dressed in yet another gown with a horrible boning bodice, snapping them all one by one. If females were meant to have their waists strangled and breasts shoved up all damn day, we would've been born with corset ribs.

With a coat on to ward off the chill, I make it halfway to my bedroom door before my footsteps slow and my conscience falters.

Are you truly okay with the risk of murdering someone? Again?

My fingers tingle beneath my gloves as my teeth worry my bottom lip. But this doubt, this is what he *wants*. He's getting in my head, and I can't let him.

Heading for the door with renewed vigor, I think of all the places I'm going to go today. Except when I grab the handle to leave, it doesn't turn.

I stare at the golden metal, noting the lack of a bolt on my side. *The bastard locked me in.* After I agreed to always keep guards with me, he still locked me up.

My back tingles. Sweat gathers on my neck.

I'm suddenly not here, in Fifth Kingdom's bedroom. I'm back in Highbell, inside my cage, palms wrapped around the bars like a prisoner in a cell.

Barred away. Locked in. *Kept.*

I'm frozen, an inhale stuck in my throat as that feeling of being trapped presses against my chest like a force of gravity.

But then my ribbons move, their lengths wrapping around my torso, squeezing until I remember to take a breath.

I hold all the power. Me.

With a shaky exhale, I dig down, brushing off the caged animal feeling and instead, I blow a breath against my anger to stoke it to life, using it as a shield. My anger makes me feel better, makes me feel more in control. It reminds me that I'm not the powerless favored he wants me to think I am.

Of course Midas locked me in. I should've expected nothing less. I should've been emotionally prepared. There might not be bars around me, but this is just another way for him to cage me in. My keeper has a new lock, but that doesn't mean I'm trapped.

Gritting my teeth, I raise a fist and knock on the door, knuckles rapping loudly. "Excuse me?"

I don't get a reply, which irritates me, because I know without a doubt that there are guards out there.

Pressing my lips together, I pound my fist this time and shout. "Excuse me!" I hear shuffling on the other side and then hurried whispers. "I know you're out there! Is that you, Scofield?"

There's another stretch of silence and then, "Yes, my lady." I don't have to see his face to hear his grimace.

"Scofield, my door seems to have jammed *accidentally.* Can you open it, please?"

"I can't do that, my lady." Yep, that's definitely a grimace I hear.

I stare daggers through the door. "Why not?"

"King Midas's orders. You're to stay in your rooms today for your safety."

"Is that so?" I ask through gritted teeth.

"Yes, my lady," his muffled response comes.

"Scofield, open the door so we don't have to talk through it."

"Sorry, my lady, I don't have the key."

Anger fumes in my chest. "That conniving prick," I hiss.

Scofield seems to make a choking noise. "What?"

"Not you," I say with a sigh as I swipe a hand across my forehead in frustration. "Listen, Scofield, I need you to go get Midas for me."

"I'm afraid I can't do that."

Goddess, he sure has this one trained well.

"Why not?" I ask.

"Because he said when you asked me to do that, that's how I was to respond," Scofield answers honestly.

My eye twitches.

"His Majesty also told me to inform you that this is necessary."

A scoff accompanies my rolling eyes. "I'm sure."

Turning, I pace around the room, hands fidgeting in front of me as I contemplate what to do. I could stay put until Midas lets me out, but that option leaves a disgusting taste in my mouth, one that makes me grow increasingly claustrophobic.

I could also try and see what kind of damage my ribbons can do to the door, but the guards would definitely alert Midas if I tried to break out.

My eyes cut over to the balcony. Maybe I can sneak out instead?

I'm across the room before I can second-guess myself, and I slam the door behind me. Walking over to the railing, I assess my situation, looking all around. I'm on the third floor. Not terrible. Not that great either.

There seems to be a couple of jutting stones on the wall that I might be able to use as a foothold if I can lower myself from the railing slowly. That is, if I don't slip on the iciness and plunge to my death. That wouldn't be ideal.

Even though I could get hurt, the thought of staying stuck in this room all day already has my pulse racing. I can't. I just *can't* be confined.

I lean further over the railing, trying to scout the best path, but then I lean too far without meaning to. My hands slip, and my center of gravity slips with it. Fear grapples my stomach as I go tipping right over, too fast to stop.

Shit!

A shriek rips out of me as I topple ass over head, and I curse at myself for my own carelessness. I squeeze my eyes closed against the plunge, but then faster than lightning, my ribbons act. They immediately thrust up and wrap around the iron railing, making my golden coat fly off as I fall.

My eyes fly open as my body jerks to a sudden halt, with another shout yanked out of my lungs. The skin at my back jolts in a painful tug as I'm left to dangle, my ribbons keeping me suspended in the air. Chest heaving, I stare at the ground beneath me—a ground that now seems much further away than I'd like.

Blood pounds in my ears from my short-lived plummet, and I swing lightly back and forth, hanging like a puppet by its strings.

The irony is not lost on me.

Straining, I try to reach up and grab my ribbons like a rope so I can pull myself back up, but on my first try, I immediately remember I have zero arm muscles because I became a lazy, complacent twit.

"Idiot," I hiss, arms shaking as I start to lose my grip.

"Funny, I called you the same thing."

I flinch in surprise at the voice, losing my hold on my ribbons in the process, and fall back down into my splayed puppet pose.

Not my finest hour.

My gaze immediately lands on the person standing on the ground beneath me. My favorite Wrath is smirking at me in amusement as I dangle. She has smooth ebony skin and a lithe form, hints of her strength buried beneath army leathers and a thick winter coat. She's got calf-high boots on and a sword hanging at her hip, and she looks up at me with her arms crossed and her booted feet planted shoulder-width apart, every bit the warrior.

"Uh. Hey, Lu," I say with a ridiculous wave. "What are you doing?"

She arches a black brow at me as I swing back and forth. "I think the more entertaining question is what are *you* doing?"

I cross my arms, but then realize that makes me look even more foolish, so I let them hang back down again. "Nothing."

Her lips twitch. "Uh-huh. Did you need help, Gildy Locks?"

"Nope. I, uh...I've got it handled. Don't try to catch me or anything, okay?"

A snort escapes her. "Wasn't going to. I want to enjoy watching you fall on your ass."

"Thanks," I say dryly.

With great difficulty, I crane my neck to look back at the wall. I search wildly for a solution, my eyes falling to the balcony railing below me that's about five feet away. I blow out a breath, trying to get my hair out of my face. "Dammit."

Lu starts laughing at my expense.

Sweat gathers on my forehead, and my spine is shooting in pain. It feels like my ribbons are going to rip right off my back if I don't hurry up. I grind my teeth and try to concentrate as I remove a few of the ribbons so they can grab the railing of the balcony below me instead.

Except, controlling just a couple at a time is *really* difficult to do when I have twenty-four of the damn things and I've kept them hidden for most of my life and only used them to do my stupid hair.

"Idiot," I curse myself again.

"Yep. Glad we've established that," Lu calls up.

Did I say she was my favorite Wrath? She's not. I prefer Osrik.

Slowly, I start to unravel three of them at once, but three more start to join in without permission. Then another three and another three and—

A scream tears out of my throat as I go falling again. This time, my ribbons are too tangled with one another to latch onto anything at all. A few of them attempt to go rigid and help break my fall, but I still end up face-first in a heap in the snow.

Great.

Stunned, all I can do is lie still for a second until I realize there's a telling metallic taste on my tongue. I've only been out of my room for about thirty seconds, and I've already made a Divine-damned mistake. I want to strangle myself with my own ribbons, but at this point, I'm not sure I'd even be able to manage *that* properly.

Shoving my arms beneath me, I scramble to sit up,

spitting out snow. My eyes widen when I see my golden faceprint on the ground.

"You alright, Gildy?" Lu asks as the sound of her footsteps draws nearer.

"Fine!" I rush to say as I feverishly wipe the gold away, burying it beneath a clumsy pile of unmarred snow and soaking my gloves in the process.

When her steps crunch closer, I leap up and whirl around at her nearness and try to back up a step, but my ribbons get tangled between my legs, and I almost fall. Again.

Luckily, I just manage to snatch the ribbons out from under my feet before I totter over.

Lu stops in front of me, eyes glittering with mirth. "Interesting way to leave your rooms."

"I was just practicing using my ribbons," I reply as I begin to dust the snow off my clothes. "You know. Trusting my instincts."

"...Right," she replies in a tone that says she doesn't believe me at all.

Around us, a gentle snowfall sends paper-thin flakes floating down from the scrawled clouds. The snow gathers on her shorn head, specks melting against the shapes of shaved daggers cut into her black hair, but she doesn't seem to mind the cold.

I quickly pick up my coat and yank it on, pulling up the hood so that snow won't gild against my face.

Out of the corner of my eye, I see a spot on the ground beside me where I missed some gold snow. I take a jerky step to the side, pulling the skirt of my dress to block it. Lu's brown eyes flick down before coming back up to my face.

My cheeks bloom with nervous heat, but I try to keep my face as impassive as possible. "What are you doing here?" I ask. "I'm surprised they allowed a Fourth army soldier inside the castle walls."

"They didn't." She shrugs her shoulders while lazily resting a hand on the twisted hilt of her sword. I wait for her to go on, but she doesn't. Not that Lu is exactly talkative, but she's usually more forthcoming than this.

An awkward silence shoulders its way between us like an unwelcome visitor. Now that the ridiculous moment of me hanging off the balcony has passed and she's no longer laughing at my expense, I can tell that the energy between us is different. There's something in her expression, something unsaid in her dark eyes as she looks at me. And then, with a jolt, I realize what it is.

Disappointment.

I clear my throat. "If you weren't allowed inside, then how did you get here?" I ask before looking around, but we're the only ones here. The dog kennel is the closest thing to us, and it sits quiet and empty.

"I walked."

My exhale comes out like a puff of smoke at her short response. "Lu..."

She tilts her head and looks me up and down. "I didn't think you'd actually do it, Gildy."

"Do what?" I ask with confusion.

"Come back to this," she says with a wrinkled nose as she looks over at the looming castle with distaste. "Doesn't seem like much of a trade-off."

All at once, I realize *that's* the reason for the stand-offish glare, the disappointment in her eyes. The longer she looks at me like this, the less I can stand it. She doesn't break the silence, doesn't back down. The expression on her face is like she wants something from me. An apology? I don't know.

"Look, I can see that you're mad at me."

"I'm not mad," she replies dismissively. "I just didn't expect you to rush back under Midas's thumb. I thought you were better than that."

I try not to flinch at her scathing tone. Attempt to dispel the hurt that inhales through my teeth and wriggles down my throat.

I like Lu—enormously. I lost a lot more than just my freedom when I chose to come back to Midas. I just didn't realize until right now that one of those things was her respect. Or how much it would bother me.

The tense silence stretches for too long, making me fidget beneath the judgment I see shining in her eyes. I don't know what to say. I have no idea if she knows that Rip is actually her king, or even if that would make a difference.

I want to ask about him, to ask if she knows we talked in the cage room, but I tamp down the desire immediately. I obviously severed any possibility of friendship with her as soon as I returned to Midas.

It's on the tip of my tongue to tell her that I'm not putting myself beneath Midas's rule again, that I'm going to figure out a way to leave, but I hold back. I'm not sure if that confession would even help, or if it would just endanger my plan.

The fact is, Lu and I aren't friends. She's loyal to Rip, not me.

I shift on my feet, unable to stand here under her scrutiny for another second. "I should go. Especially since you're not allowed inside the walls. I don't want you to get in trouble if you're seen with me."

Lu scoffs. "Ranhold's security is abysmal. I could break through the walls with my eyes closed and steal King Midas's crown right off his head if I wanted to."

My eyes widen. "Please don't do that."

"Don't worry your gilded head about it. I have things to do, but not *that*. At least, not unless I get bored."

"*Lu.*"

Rolling her eyes, she begins to walk away. "Don't worry about me. Go ahead and do whatever you snuck out to do."

My shoulders stiffen. "I didn't say I was sneaking out," I call at her back.

Turning, she continues to walk backwards as she taps the side of her nose and then points at me. "A sneak can always spot another sneak, Gildy."

Before I can come up with a response, she disappears around the side of the castle, leaving me alone.

With a sigh, I look up at where my balcony is high above me and shake my head. I'm lucky I didn't break my damn neck. Good thing there was a pile of plush snow to catch me. As it is, my back is aching and my face hurts from my graceful landing. All because Midas is a controlling, manipulative prick. And now, Lu hates me.

So far, my morning has not been great.

But like Lu, I turn and start walking away, because I do, in fact, have sneaking to do, starting with a layout of the castle grounds.

CHAPTER 10

AUREN

Sneaking, it turns out, is hard work.

Lu is right about the security though, because if *I'm* able to sneak around, then their patrols aren't the best. I don't exactly blend in. Not that I don't have to put in effort to not be seen—I do. But the fact that I'm able to get around without being caught is a bit concerning. I'm not exactly experienced at being covert.

I take my time scouting the castle grounds, making note of everything I see. After a while though, I start to just meander around, simply enjoying being outside by myself. It's peaceful here in a way that Highbell never was, no angry blizzards or wailing winds. There's just a gentle snowfall that comes and goes, white feather clouds to plume the sky.

Luckily for me, the grounds of Ranhold Castle are

vast, so I have plenty of places to wander. I see the kennels, ice sculptures, a courtyard, and rows of greenhouses. I'm able to build a map in my head, keeping particular note of every door that leads into the castle. It makes me feel better to get a layout of the exits, just in case.

Between the greenhouses, I watch my feet as I walk, my mind drifting back to Lu. My shoes crunch over the snowy walkway, the glass panes next to me frosted over in crystallized webs to trap my thoughts. I wonder what she's doing here and why she snuck into Ranhold. I also wonder if she or Judd or Osrik are doing anything... sinister.

The fact is, I don't really know much about them. I mean, Rip refers to them as his *Wrath*. That nickname doesn't exactly give the warm and fuzzies.

Yet, they treated me well while I was with them. Aside from my first encounter with Osrik, none of them were unkind to me. If anything, they went above and beyond any preconceived expectations.

But they have a lot of secrets. For one, they know Rip is fae, and now, they know I am too. I can't even begin to try and untangle the repercussions of that, the what-ifs. Are they going to use it against me? Do they also know that Rip is leading a double life?

It makes my head spin and keeps worry locked in my joints. The not knowing makes me feel vulnerable, open for anyone to take advantage of me.

Maybe that's why I reacted as strongly as I did when Rip revealed himself to me. For the first time in my life, I thought I'd found someone who knew the real me and wasn't put off. Someone who wasn't manipulating me.

I catch my reflection in the windowpane of the greenhouse, and even with the rippled glass, I can see the pain right there in my golden eyes. A pain I'm trying to deny.

My pride was hurt, sure, but my heart was hurt more. Because *Rip* felt like more. Almost.

He was my *almost more.*

An idea, a hope, a reach in the dark. It wasn't until my fist closed around emptiness that I realized I was grasping for him.

And that's what makes my eyes sting with regret. He pushed me to light, to *burn*, only to douse me with ashen deceit.

I've taken it personally, and I probably shouldn't have, but you can't reason with feelings. They do what they want, forcing you to endure. All you can do is grit your teeth and take it, hoping that time will dull it down.

Please let it dull down.

I wonder if Lu will tell Rip that she saw me today. I wonder if I *want* her to.

Just his name sends a sharp pang through my stomach. As much as I've been trying not to think about him, whether in his spiked form or his kingly one, it's almost impossible. Because every time my mind wanders, it saunters right back to him.

I pluck a piece of lifted ice off the glass wall next to me, like plucking a petal from a flower. A wish to garner from a fractioned shard.

As I'm looking down at it in my gloved palm, I hear voices in the distance. Dropping the ice on the ground, I peer around the corner of the greenhouse. A few hundred feet away, there's a stable. The stone structure is hitched with a large round pen, and inside, there's a thick-furred horse being lunged in circles by its handler.

I immediately spot the source of the voices, seeing two guards walking away from the stables and heading my way. Before I can turn away to avoid being spotted, my eyes lock onto the form standing just outside the pen, his forearms braced against the railing of the fence.

Even with his back to me, I'd know him anywhere.

Ravinger is dressed in dark brown, and his thick black hair is ruffled from the wind. From this distance, and even though I can't see the expression on his face, he looks relaxed, as cool as the snow at his feet. But that's him. He never looks ruffled, even here, in another kingdom, surrounded by potential enemies. Even when it's one against a thousand, *he's* the real threat.

My eyes skim down his form, gaze lingering. He's a scary, terrifying king. But bright side? He can sure wear a pair of pants.

Damn.

I'm still staring at his ass when I see his body stiffen. His shoulders go tense, and then he turns around, gaze landing *right on me*.

I jerk back and hide behind the greenhouse again, staying stock-still for a second. Maybe he didn't see me. He could've turned to look at something else, right?

Right.

I know I shouldn't do it, but against my better judgment, I slowly peek back around because apparently, I just can't help myself.

My heart leaps into my throat as soon as I look. He's leaning with his back against the fence now, arms crossed in front of him, and there's no doubt that his attention is locked on me.

When he sees me looking again, his lips turn up into a crooked smirk.

Shit.

I need to look away from him, but I can't. Our gazes are tied together, a line pulled taut, tugging on both sides. I don't even blink until a movement to his left breaks the connection.

My attention yanks away, and I finally notice the figure that's been standing next to him this entire time. Clad in full black armor and helmet, with wicked lines of spikes jutting out from the metal bracers on his forearms, and more of them lined down his spine…

Rip?

My mind stutters in confusion before grinding to a stop.

I let my eyes bounce back and forth between Ravinger and Rip, while my brow furrows.

In a baffled daze, I start to take a step forward like I'm going to march right over there and figure out this mystery, but Ravinger shakes his head sharply. Automatically, I stop, which is a good thing, because the two guards I'd completely forgotten about are now only several feet away from reaching the corner of the castle where they'll cross in front of me.

Cursing myself for not paying attention, I have about two seconds to figure out where I'm going to hide, because a see-through structure made of glass isn't going to cut it.

I can't run to the back of the greenhouse in time, since it's ridiculously long, but I latch onto the sight of the decrepit stairs against the castle. There's a door at the top that I've been eyeing. It's much closer than any other alternative, and I hope like hell that it'll open or that I can at least climb the steps and the guards won't think to look up.

I make the snap decision, picking up my skirts as I sprint toward them before the guards can reach the greenhouse. Darting across the walkway, I skid up to the bottom of the stairs and then start taking two steps at a time.

In my rush up the crumbling stone, I slip on a patch of ice just as I reach the top landing. I nearly go toppling right over the open stairway—*who's dumb idea was it to forgo a damn railing?*—but I manage to grab onto the door handle at the last second and keep myself from falling.

Without giving myself time to steady, I wrench it open, ecstatic when the knob actually turns. I rush inside and close the door behind me as quickly and as quietly as I can, my heart racing in my chest.

Phew, that was close.

Panting, I listen for a moment to make sure there are no shouts or hurried footsteps climbing up the stairs, but I hear nothing.

After waiting several seconds, I finally let out a breath of relief and turn to look around. I'm in some sort of empty antechamber, with pitiful light coming from a slitted window above the door. Unlike the rest of the castle, it's plain and drab, without any embellishments whatsoever. It looks unused and also appears to be a connecting room for several passages to spit into. It's also ridiculously cold.

Shivering beneath my coat, I cast another look at the door I rushed through. Even inside, with stone walls between us, I swear I can still feel Ravinger out there. How in the world did he know I was there?

The better question is, who was with him? That was

Rip's armor, Rip's helmet, boots, posture, height, even his damn spikes, but it obviously wasn't really him. This Fake Rip was too big to be Judd, too small to be Osrik. So who the hell was it?

Yet another trick, another deceit. My lips press together firmly, and I force myself to put him out of my mind.

Bright side? I got back inside the castle without any of the guards seeing me. Might as well make the most of it and start checking out the inside as well.

I make my way down the dreary antechamber, passing stone benches set against the walls. Why anyone would want to sit around in here is beyond me. I try to open a few doors, but each one is locked. No surprise there.

When I get to the last door—also locked—I unravel one of my ribbons and feed it through the crack between the floor and the door. It's a bit like trying to do up laces along your back, so I close my eyes and go for feel alone as I direct my ribbon to reach for the lock on the other side. It wraps around the old iron deadbolt, and with a rusty creak, it turns open.

No sooner does my ribbon slip back to this side and re-wrap around me than I'm pulling the door open with another protesting squeak of disuse. I creep inside the dark space, just as a familiar smell hits my nose, and my eyes widen as I look around and realize where I am.

The royal library.

The smell of books, old parchment and ink bound in leather, makes a smile spread across my face.

It takes a moment for my eyes to adjust to the dim lighting, because it doesn't look like there are any windows in here. The only lighting is coming from flickering sconces on the walls, but it's not nearly enough to keep the shadows at bay. Especially with the looming shelves towering over me that stretch further than I can see, some of them covered in chains to keep the books from being removed. It's about as inviting as a tomb in here.

Even though it's not exactly picturesque, a thought occurs to me, and I look around with new eyes. This place is quiet, dark, and *secret*. It's the perfect place to hide something.

With a new purpose in mind, I make my way down a row of shelves, careful to be as quiet as possible. I keep hold of my skirts so they don't swish too loudly over the floor, thankful that the soles of my shoes are supple enough not to echo my steps. It's so quiet that even my breaths sound loud.

Trying to move as silently as possible, I squint at the titles on the book spines I pass by. I note the requisite history of Fifth Kingdom, geography of Orea, tales of previous wars, genealogies of kings...boring, boring, boring. The more spines I read, the less I like my chances of finding any romances kept in this place.

But my trip isn't a complete waste. My eyes flit to a shelf ahead, one half swallowed by the dark. It's shorter than the others and covered in dust, looking like it hasn't been touched or even looked at in years.

Perfect.

I look around, but the only thing nearby is a single sconce several feet away. Turning, I quickly tug off my glove, and reach into my dress pocket. I pull out three things one after the other: the apple I got from the kitchens, the stolen pipe from the guard, and the rag from the servant. Three innocuous, random items, all taken from different places, from different people. Things Midas won't even know to miss.

As soon as my bare skin touches them, metallic liquid swarms from my palm. Each item is encased within seconds, their weight growing heavy as they turn solid gold. Looking up for a spot out of reach, I find two large tomes leaning against each other that make up the perfect little hidden nook. On tiptoes, I use my gloved hand to shove the rag and pipe between the books, hiding them from view.

Lowering myself back down, I slip the gold apple into my pocket, its weight heavy against my hip. I pull my glove back on and turn to leave, but a glint catches my eye on a lower shelf. I kneel down, swiping away a strip of dust, and my breath catches in my chest when a single word is uncovered.

Fae.

Beveled and black, imprinted into the leather beneath golden filigree, the word almost whispers to me, sending a chill down my spine.

There's a chain strapped to the front of the shelf, but it's drooping and loose. I glance around as if the shadows are watching me, but all is silent other than my thrumming pulse. Careful not to jostle the chains or leave tracks in the dust, I lift the small book out. The moment I hold it in my hands, my fingers tingle.

Barely longer than my palm, the cover is made of elderwood, with a delicate coating of red leather stitched around the tops of the boards, and thick thread pulled through the timeworn pages binds it.

For a moment, all I can do is stare at it. I have never, in all my time in Orea, seen a single book of the fae. To my knowledge, every piece of literature made by or about fae has been destroyed since the war. The only time fae are ever mentioned is in the history books, depicted as great betrayers and bloodthirsty murderers.

This book is forbidden. It should've been burned centuries ago, and yet here it is, stuffed between decrepit history books and rolled scrolls, on a dusty, chain-locked shelf.

Looking left and right again, I make sure I have no witnesses as I slip it beneath my coat and tuck it into the inside pocket against my chest. I stand up again, my heart pounding like stalking footsteps.

Wait. No. Those are *actual* footsteps.

Shit.

I dash to the right and take a sharp turn, pressing my back against the side of the shelf. A second later, I hear someone in the next aisle over walking with slow, sweeping steps.

Time to go.

Clutching my skirts with both hands, I lift the hem up completely, my ribbons coiling beneath my coat. I'm too nervous to even breathe, but I tip toe away past the shelves, cringing every time my shoes scrape too loudly against the stone floor.

I can't go back the way I came, not with that person so close. So I put as much distance between us as I can as I navigate through the cryptic room.

When I see more light ahead, I aim for it, hoping that it will lead to another way out. I cut down an aisle of shelves, and when I come out on the other side, I find tables with books and scrolls laid out and lanterns burning. But my eyes go right past them to the door directly ahead.

Thank Divine.

I rush forward, except in my hurry, I fail to notice the hunched over figure sitting at one of the tables, quill in hand. His head whips up just as I pass him, and the movement makes me jolt in surprise. "Oh, shit," I curse in alarm. "Sorry."

The old robed man is on his feet in an instant, his

chair screeching against the floor as he pushes up. "Who let you in here? You don't have permission to be here!" he seethes.

"Sorry," I say again, backing up with my hands held in front of me. "I, um, I wanted to make an appointment to visit the library," I say lamely.

The man's deep set eyes sweep over me with narrowed contempt. "I know who you are."

"Right," I say, not at all interested to hear an eighty-year-old man call me a gilded whore. "So...an appointment?"

"No."

I blink at him. Well, that wasn't what I was expecting. "No?" I ask.

"*Nobles* are allowed to make appointments," he informs me, his tone as stiff as his straw-colored hair. "All others are not welcome inside the royal library. Since you are clearly neither noble nor royal, you are not permitted entry."

"But—"

"We have scrolls in here that date back to dark years. We have books written by the first kings. I have *personally* been transcribing an account of Saint Bosef during the Poppy Plague," he informs me, chest puffed up with importance. "Now, this may come as a shock to you, but despite your nickname, this library is far more *precious* than you are," he says scathingly. "So kindly remove yourself from my presence and do not think of entering again, because you are not welcome here. Return yourself to the saddle wing where you belong."

I stare, stunned and still. I never imagined a scribe could make me feel as inferior and undeserving as a speck of dust.

His gaze drops to my coat, and instantly, the blood drains from my face. The stolen book in my pocket seems to grow heavier, tapping against my heart.

Is there an outline clearly visible? I don't dare look down, but when he raises a hand and points at me with an ink-stained finger, my stomach falls right through my feet. I'm not even allowed to *stand* in the library. What's going to happen to me for trying to steal a forbidden book?

"Do I need to call the guards to remove you?"

It takes me a moment to realize that he's not yelling "thief" or demanding I turn out my pockets. "I...What?"

His finger shifts to the side, pointing to the door behind me. "Are you daft? I said, do I need to call the guards, or are you capable of removing yourself?"

"No, no. I'll leave," I hastily reply.

I spin around to get the hell out as quickly as I can, yanking open the heavy door. I slip out of it as soon as the space is big enough for me to fit through. The door heaves shut with a thud behind me, and I lean back against it, hand over my chest to quell my racing heart.

I've met a lot of unpleasant people in my life, but that scribe was an ass.

With a shake of my head, I let out a breath. Beneath my fingertips, I feel the hard corners of the book like a badge of secrecy digging into my skin. I don't have any idea what's in it, but it *feels* furtive. As if the pages are whispers, and I'm leaning in to hear its secrets.

Once my breathing is back to normal, I let my hand drop and I straighten up from the door. Now that I'm no longer worried about being caught, irritation rises up at the contempt the old scribe showed. He looked at me like I wasn't good enough to even breathe the library's musty air, let alone read anything.

Do not think of entering again, because you are not welcome here.

He acts like my mere presence was a blot on the entire library, like I would've dog-eared a page or cracked a spine.

I mean, yes, I *did* just steal a book, but that's irrelevant. And yes, in the past, I *have* accidentally turned some pages solid gold when I wasn't careful. Also not relevant.

The scribe did have one good point though, even if it was meant to be an insult.

Return yourself to the saddle wing where you belong.

Funny, that's exactly where I wanted to go next.

CHAPTER 11

AUREN

F inding the saddle wing isn't easy. Not only because I don't know where it is, but also because I have to keep sneaking around. This means a lot of ducking inside rooms or doubling back whenever there's a servant or guard nearby, and it takes up a lot of time.

Yet searching and roaming around means I'm also able to map the floors, to get a feel for where everything is, which will be helpful for my plan of escape. A plan that's solidifying in my mind with every step I take.

A couple of hours later, I get lucky as I peek around a corner and find a pair of guards sitting outside a door.

"This post is a hell of a lot better than north wall. We don't have to freeze our asses off for once," one man says.

The other guard is leaning back on his stool, ear

pressed to the door. "Shit, I think I can hear one of 'em moanin'."

"Really?" That perks the other one up, and I roll my eyes as he presses his ear to the door too. "You think they just...fuck each other all day?"

A male groan echoes down. "Shit, I hope so."

"Midas has much better whores than Fulke did. Did you see the tits on that redhead?"

Well, I found the saddles.

I hesitate for a moment, trying to formulate a plan, but I know that I don't have all day lurking around this corner. Sooner or later, someone is going to walk by.

I don't recognize the guards, and obviously, they're new at this post, which may work in my favor. So, with a half-cocked idea, I take a deep breath and round the corner. I walk confidently down the ice-blue corridor, passing the decorative pillars that line the wall.

Since they're still trying to spy on the saddles, the gold-clad guards don't notice me until I'm two feet away. They immediately jump to their feet at my approach, looking flustered. One is older, with graying temples, while the other seems to be younger than me, with blond facial hair growing in sad little patches over his chin.

"Who are you?" Patch Beard asks.

The older one glances at him pointedly. "*Who is she*? Look at her. She's gold, you idiot. Who do you *think* it is?"

"Oh. Right." Twin dots of red appear on his cheeks.

I smile brightly. "Hello, I didn't mean to disturb you. I'm just going inside the saddle wing."

Gray Hair frowns in confusion. "Uh, that's not permitted, miss."

I adopt a haughty look. "Of course it's permitted." The best way to convince people that you're allowed to do something is to act offended when they assume otherwise. "You know who I am."

It's not really a question, but they nod anyway.

"So you know that I'm King Midas's gold-touched favored. His favorite *saddle*," I say slowly, my words punctuated with an arch of my brow to make them feel like idiots for not realizing this. "And this is the *saddle wing*, is it not?"

They hesitate.

"Well. Yes..." Patch Beard answers, that blush still on his cheeks.

"Right, so can you please move so I can go inside? I'd hate to have to tell the king that you barred his favored saddle from entering her own wing. I'm sure he wouldn't be too pleased about it."

The young guard blanches and whips his head toward Gray Hair. "You're insulting King Midas's favored," he says through his teeth.

"I am not," he argues. "I thought she—"

Patch Beard cuts him off, looking back at me. "Go

right on ahead, miss," he says as he reaches over and opens the door grandly.

I make sure to give him a sweet smile as I walk past. "Thank you."

When the door snicks shut behind me, I hear the two of them immediately start to bicker, making a snort rise in my throat. I didn't expect that to actually work, but I'm certainly going to take advantage of it.

I look around the small, empty entryway and hear a noise coming through the door to my right. Walking over, I peer inside from the doorway and find a large room. There are two white pillars standing along the back wall like bookends holding together the windows. The space is basked in the brooding light of frosted window panes, while icy blue paint and matching rugs makes it seem cold despite the fire burning in the hearth.

Egg-shaped chairs woven with straw are hanging from the ceiling, deep enough to fit a few saddles at once. Some of them are doing just that, lounging on plush pillows inside like the strange swinging seats are their shared cocoons.

My eyes dart from them to the decadent piles of more pillows on the floor in the corner, all white, blue, and purple. There's a skinny table filled with food platters and pitchers of drink on the opposite wall, and several chaises scattered around the middle of the room. All in all, it looks decadent, if a little messy.

I pick out most of the saddles I traveled here with, along with a few new faces, but none of them have noticed me yet. The ones in the swinging egg chairs seem to be dozing, lazy legs hanging out, the hems of silk dresses dragging against the carpeted floor.

They're all so...comfortable together that I have to tamp down a pang of jealousy. What would it have been like if I'd been included with them while we lived in Highbell? If I'd been allowed to visit the saddles, if they hadn't resented and hated me, my life would've been far less lonely. I know they argue and fight—I saw that while we were with Fourth's army—but they've formed friendships too. Even if some of them hate each other, at least they *have* each other. I had no one. *Have* no one.

A giggle to my right cuts off my pity party, and my gaze swings over to one of the chaises to find one person I do *not* want to be friends with.

Polly seems to notice me at the same exact time that I notice her, because her crystal blue eyes flash to me, the giggle dying on her lips. Beside her, the male saddle, Rosh, stiffens. Three more saddles sitting in the other lounger turn to look at me as I make my way over.

"Nice dress," Polly sneers, lips curling up in a malicious smile as she looks at my bent and awkward bodice.

A bit of heat rises into my cheeks at her scathing look, but I shrug it off. "My ribs aren't a fan of Fifth's clothing."

She snorts derisively, her body slumped against the purple cushions, blonde hair in disarray. "Pain is beauty. But I guess you wouldn't know."

The other saddles cackle. More heat blooms in my cheeks.

"Pain shouldn't be the requisite of beauty."

"Spoken like a true pampered whore," she lobs back, though her eyes are glassy, unfocused. "What are you even doing here? You're not welcome in our wing."

I glance warily at the other three women, who are watching me with a kind of bored interest. "I wanted to see how you were all settling in."

Polly rolls her eyes. "Liar."

"Fine," I concede with a shrug. I don't want to talk to her any more than she wants to talk to me. "I came to see Rissa. Do you know where she is?" I ask, looking around.

Her shrewd, albeit slightly bloodshot eyes, narrow on me. "Why do you always want to talk to her lately? You aren't friends."

It's like a kick to the gut, like she saw what I was thinking before I walked over here, and she wants to drive the knife in.

"How do you know we aren't friends?" I ask defensively.

"Because Rissa is *my* friend," Polly replies, her cheeks blooming with an angry blush that surprises me.

One of the other saddles laughs—Isis, the

statuesque one with black hair. "Are you jealous of the gilded cunt?"

I bristle at her words, but Polly does too. "Shut your fat mouth," she snaps.

Isis just laughs harder, so much so that she ends up falling into the saddle sitting beside her, making that woman erupt into laughter too. They flop onto the floor together in a heap of uncontrollable giggles, and then—

Okay, now they're kissing.

The petite, pixie-looking saddle named Gia—rolls her eyes and gets to her feet. She steps over the two women on the floor before plopping in Rosh's lap, and then she starts to kiss him.

There's a lot of kissing going on all of a sudden.

Polly takes one look at Gia and shoves her face away. "Go fuck someone else."

The girl pouts but begins to pepper kisses on Rosh's neck instead of sucking his mouth off. "Aw, come on, Polly. Let's all join. I feel so nice right now."

I stare wide-eyed as she starts to stroke Rosh's groin, who tips his head back with a groan.

Polly's mouth presses into a hard line, making her usual pink, plush lips go thin and white. An irritated sigh strangles through the tightly cinched gap of her lips. "I knew you bitches couldn't handle that much dew."

I frown. "Dew?"

Polly looks about as impressed with me as ever. "Yes,

dew," she says with an exaggerated eye roll. "You're not that stupid, are you?" When I just continue to look at her with confusion, she sighs. "You know, painted petal, the rouged maiden, dewdrops, cherry dew..."

A snort comes from Isis, still straddling the other saddle on the floor. "Cherry dew, because one lick and it makes even the most prudish maidens want to pop their cherries." She starts to laugh again until the girl beneath her gyrates, and then her amusement turns into a moan.

"Dew is...a drug?" I ask incredulously. Now, I'm looking at their glassy eyes and flushed faces in a different light, their lusty, languid behavior making me uneasy. "Won't you get in trouble?"

"From whom?" Polly asks with an arch of her brow.

"The king."

"Well, that would be strange, since he's the one who gave it to me."

My mind churns with a clunk. "*What*? Midas gave it to you?"

"Well, the mender gave it to us first. To help us cope after everything we endured with the Red Raids and the army. But Midas gave me my very own box because I pleased him," Polly replies proudly, shooting a vindictive smile my way, though she's still slouched against the cushions. "I pleased him *immensely*."

I swallow hard. "Recently?"

It's obvious she's enjoying this, because her eyes

sparkle and an impish smile curves her lips. "Just last night."

There should be a dagger that goes through my heart at her words, but I'm not hurt—not like that. Or if I am, it's an echo of past knee-jerk reactions to Midas's sexual exploits. I *always* had to suppress my jealousies. He made me think I was the one who was being unreasonable, unfair. But hearing that he left my bed to visit hers doesn't make me feel jealous right now. Instead, I'm just disgusted by him.

I was obviously very good at lying to myself, because there's no other way I could've convinced myself that he loved me.

We tell ourselves twisted lies to tangle around our wicked truths, all so that we can get caught up in the bind and not have to face bare regrets.

There were too many times that Midas had been with me, just to leave and visit one of them. Or make me watch him with them, like he got some perverse pleasure from the extent of his complete control over me. I should've busted his balls years ago, the saddle-riding snake.

And now, he's giving the saddles whatever this dew is to affect their behavior. The whole thing leaves a bad taste in my mouth.

"Maybe you shouldn't be taking that…" I say cautiously.

Polly stiffens. "There you go with your superiority

complex. You just can't help yourself from thinking that you're better than us, can you?" she challenges.

"That's not—"

"King Fulke's saddles have been taking it every day for years. They love the stuff. It makes everything so much more...enjoyable," she says, leaning over to drag a finger down Rosh's bare bicep as the man nuzzles into Gia's neck.

My brows fall down. "Fulke's saddles?"

Rosh lifts his head long enough to answer me. "Yep." He looks me up and down in a lust-fogged haze, his eyes more intense from the kohl that lines them. "Those ones over there," he says, gesturing behind me.

I turn to look, finding a group of women I hadn't noticed in a small alcove. Their bodies are slumped against the wall with pillows beneath them, hands between thighs. Unfocused eyes are staring at the walls like they aren't completely aware of where they are, even as their fingers move and their lips moan.

An unsettled feeling sifts through my chest, a sieve of grating sand to scrape at my worry. "What's wrong with them?"

"Fulke was a flesh trader," Rosh says with a shrug, voice slightly slurring as Gia rakes her fingers through his hair. "His royal saddles weren't permanent, so he switched them out a lot from what we've heard. They mostly keep to themselves, but they love their dew. King Midas has been making sure they still get it."

I drag my eyes away from their lax faces, their empty eyes. "I don't think you should take it."

"But feels *so good*," Isis says from the floor, her hand trailing up the other woman's dress. "You should try some."

"Like I would ever waste my gift on *her*," Polly snips.

I ignore that. "You don't want to end up like...like them," I say in a whisper, eyes darting over to Fulke's saddles. But even if I'd yelled it, I'm not sure that they're aware enough to care.

"They're happier this way," Rosh says absently, his gaze zeroing in on Gia's chest.

"Mmm, I want to be happier too," Gia croons. "Come on, Polly. Let us have some more."

"I can't even see your irises anymore, and you're dry humping Rosh. You've had enough," Polly retorts testily. She then reaches beneath the pillow at her back and pulls out a small glass box. As soon as she flips open the lid, all four of the saddles perk up, heads swinging her way, like dogs scenting a bone.

Isis tries to lean over and reach inside the box, but Polly yanks it out of her grasp and slaps her hand. "No, you've had enough, too."

Isis scowls and rubs her hand. "You're not the boss of us."

"King Midas gave *me* this extra dew. That means it's

mine. If you three bitches aren't careful, I'll cut you off. You'll have to try to get some from the Fulke phantoms over there," Polly says, waving a hand in their direction. I can't help but wince at her description of them. She's not wrong, they *are* like phantoms, listless and empty-eyed ghosts. "I said you've had plenty for now, and I meant it. Now go away. You're annoying me."

Isis shoots her another peeved look but obviously takes her threat to heart, because she gets up, offering a hand to the girl beneath her. The two of them stumble away toward the first swinging cocoon they reach and climb inside. Moans strike up soon after.

A throaty laugh pulls my gaze back. "That was mean, Polly," Rosh purrs. Gia is rocking on his lap now, the length of him noticeably growing beneath his velvet leggings as her small hips move up and down.

"You like it when I'm mean," Polly replies with a sultry look.

Rosh simply chuckles again before turning his head to lick a line down Gia's chest. She arches back in response, making an incredibly carnal noise that seems to rumble out of her.

"Can someone just tell me where to find Rissa?" I ask, growing impatient. I don't want to be here anymore. Uneasiness is crawling over my skin at how *wrong* this all feels.

"Nope," Polly says before flipping open the box

again. Inside, there's a stack of thick white petals with what looks like blood-red droplets on them.

"Polly…"

She ignores me and raises a petal to her lips, setting it on her tongue. She closes her mouth with sensual decadence, her eyes rolling into the back of her head as a look of euphoria crashes over her features.

She chews slowly, as if savoring every grind of her teeth and lap of her tongue. Rosh grabs Polly's face before she can swallow the petal, devouring her mouth, tongue thrusting greedily as if he's trying to lick away every essence she just ingested.

I'm still staring at them when a voice behind me says, "You should probably leave them to it. They're going to be at it for hours now."

I whirl around to find Rissa standing behind me, looking beautiful as always. "There you are," I say in relief. A loud moan erupts behind me, making me wince.

"Not a fan of dew?" she asks knowingly.

I shake my head.

"It's a popular commodity here in Fifth Kingdom, though I've heard it's quite expensive. King Fulke kept a stockpile of it, apparently. His old saddles don't seem to care about much of anything else. Well…that and fucking, since it enhances sexual desire. It's quite useful for saddles to be hooked on something like that, don't you think?"

Her words are bitter, biting. The snap of dainty teeth behind pretty lips.

I take in Rissa's coiffed blonde hair, her clear eyes, her lack of blushing skin. Unlike the rest of the saddles in the room, who I now realize are either doing something sexual or dozing in a stupor, she's completely put-together.

"You don't partake?" I ask curiously.

Her blue eyes go shuttered. "No. I don't want my problems to be shoved aside or to be forced into lust. I refuse to stay here and succumb." I don't say anything to that, and she finally drags her eyes away from Fulke's saddles and smooths a hand down her skin-tight dress. "I assume you came here to speak with me?"

"I did." Another breathy, sensual noise comes from behind me. "Can we talk somewhere that's more private and less...moany?"

Rissa snorts but turns and leads me through a doorway at the back. Inside, the space is stuffed full of unmade beds, though it's thankfully empty. Closing the door behind us, she takes her place by the far wall, leaning against it to face me. "I was wondering how long you'd make me wait until you came to visit."

"I'm not *making* you wait," I say. "I told you it would take time for me to get things in order."

"And? Are you getting things in order?" she asks, and I notice it then—the underlying desperation. She's hiding it well, but I see it in the way she stretches her tense fingers, the way her gaze fastens.

"I am."

"Are you?" she asks again with clear doubt in her tone. "Or maybe you're lying to me right now and instead, you've told the king and plan to double-cross me."

I don't point out that she's the one who's blackmailing *me*. "I gave you my word, Rissa," I tell her. "I said I'd get you the gold, and I meant it. But...I do need to make a new deal with you."

Rissa's eyes narrow in suspicion. "What is this *new* deal?"

I lick my lips and look around nervously before I whisper, "You said you needed enough gold to buy out your contract and to start a new life somewhere. But I know King Midas. He won't let you out of your arrangement until *he* decides. Trust me in this."

Her brows swoop in together tightly. "Is that so?"

"Yes," I answer matter-of-factly. "So we need a new plan. If you want to leave this place, it's going to have to be in secret."

"You mean *escape*?" she asks incredulously. "Are you an idiot? King Midas would hunt me down and drag me back to shove me in the dungeons."

"Not if he can't find you."

Rissa scoffs, like the very idea is ludicrous. "You're reneging on our deal."

"I'm not," I say adamantly. "But I *know* him, Rissa. I don't care that you're his best royal saddle. He won't believe for a second you've been given enough tips from other people to buy yourself out of your contract."

She holds herself very still, lips pinched together tight with anger, although there's a slight downturn to them that I don't miss. Now that I've planted doubt in her head, she either knows I'm right or doesn't want to risk it.

Since she's not outright threatening to spill my secret or storming away from me, I take it as a good sign. "You can still be free, and I'm going to do everything I can to make that happen, so long as you agree not to go through Midas, because we'll be caught in an instant."

Rissa chews on what I've said, though her hackles are still up, apparent by the stiff line of her shoulders. "I'm listening."

"I'll help you plan an escape out of here. I'll also make sure you have enough gold when you leave that you'll be a very wealthy woman."

"Getting out of Ranhold without anyone the wiser will be impossible."

"Not impossible," I argue. "Not if we plan it meticulously."

"And the gold?" she asks.

I hesitate. "I can't get you coin. Midas's power... "

Rissa runs a frustrated hand over her hair. "Gild me

some damn curtains for all I care. I told you before, there's a cost to your secret, Auren, and you *have* to pay. You were able to tap into Midas's power enough that you turned a man *solid gold*," she reminds me. "I want my due."

"I can get you gold, but what are you going to do with it?"

"I'll find a blacksmith here to melt it down in exchange for coin. Pay him off for his silence," she answers easily, propping her hands on her hips.

My head is already shaking before she's even finished. "Any blacksmith in Ranhold would know right away you're stealing from the king, and they'd sell you out quicker than you could blink. You know it's true."

Her mind seems to fumble, knuckles going white where they're braced at her sides. She drops her hands and walks away from me, pacing the empty room as if the shuffle of her steps will help her mind work out the new path I've laid down.

"I can get you gold," I say again, my eyes following her. "But you have to promise not to do anything with it until you're far away from Ranhold."

"Fine," she grudgingly relents as she comes to a stop. "I can see the merit of that. It would be a risk to pay off a blacksmith and try to trade for coin, and I don't have connections here like I did in Highbell. I don't want to risk being ratted out. I'm far too beautiful to waste away in a dungeon."

My lips twitch. "Definitely."

"You do realize that the saddles are always guarded, don't you? You're saying I can't buy out my contract, but then how do you expect me to leave without being caught?" Her tone is wary, rife with disbelief, but I'm one step ahead.

"I've found a way into the royal library," I tell her. "And every royal library always includes the blueprints of the city. Including the castle itself."

Understanding floods her ocean blue eyes.

"It might take some time for me to search, but I'll find the blueprints and chart a path out of Ranhold. Every castle has fail-safes and secret escape routes. It's just a matter of finding them. While I do that, you'll have to be the one to figure out a form of transportation. Something clandestine and inconspicuous."

She thinks for a moment. "The saddles are allowed trips into the city. I suppose I can try and find a way to arrange travel."

"Good."

Rissa's blue eyes scour me. "Just because I'm agreeing to this change of plan doesn't mean I completely trust you. I still want gold. At least a couple of pieces per week."

I open my mouth to argue, but she holds up her hand. "That's non-negotiable. Think of it as paying me for my continued silence."

"Fine," I say reluctantly. "But you need to have a good place to hide it. We can't be caught, Rissa, and if any gold is found, I'll be implicated as well as you."

"I have a spot," she assures me, tone tinged with confidence.

"You're sure?"

Irritation crosses her beautiful face. "Don't patronize me. I've lived with a gaggle of saddles nearly all my life, always sharing a space. I know how to keep things hidden that I don't want others to steal."

Fair enough.

My feet shift beneath me. "There's one more thing to our new deal."

Her teeth grind. "*What now*?"

This is the part I'm really worried about.

"I'm going with you when you leave."

Silence drops between us like a sudden rockslide, boulders landing at our feet in a heavy plummet. Rissa rears back with shock. "Are you out of your mind? You're the gold-touched favored. King Midas will *never* let you go. We couldn't possibly pull something like that off."

"We *can*," I argue, hoping like hell that I'm telling the truth, speaking with more conviction than I actually feel. "We go together. That's the deal," I say firmly, brooking no room for argument. "We get out of here together, and I'll make sure you never want for anything ever again. It won't matter if you run out of gold, because if I'm with you, I can get you more."

She doesn't look convinced, but I see the flash of rapaciousness in her gaze. "You can steal his power like that, even from a great distance?" she asks dubiously. "Because I assure you, I won't be staying anywhere near Sixth or Fifth Kingdom. When I leave, I'm getting on a ship and sailing as far away as it'll take me, where I never have to see a single speck of snow again."

"Let me worry about the gold-touch magic. All you have to do is stay quiet and get us transportation out of the city."

She looks me up and down. "You don't blend in, though. You'll give us away."

"I'll keep myself covered and figure something out," I promise her.

She stares at me long and hard, while I try not to bite my bottom lip or wring my hands. If she turns me down, if she sells my secret to the next highest bidder instead...

"Fine."

My eyes jerk to her face. "Fine?" I repeat back, unable to keep the surprise from my voice. "You're sure? Because this is a dangerous game, and we could both be punished severely."

"You think I don't know that?" she snaps. "I'm not a fool."

My heart leaps with hope. "Then we're in this together?"

She sighs. "I suppose."

I can't help but give her a tentative smile before I hold out a gloved hand for her to shake. "We're on the same side. You handle your end, I'll handle mine, and then we *will* get out of here. We'll be free, Rissa."

She hesitates for a second before taking my hand. Her hold is hard, fingers squeezing mine. "Don't double-cross me, or I'll make you regret it," she tells me, ruthlessness in her face.

Well, it's certainly not a *friends forever* promise, but it'll do.

Reaching into my pocket with my other hand, I pull out the gold apple and watch her eyes widen. "No betrayal. No double-crossing."

She releases my palm to snag the fruit, testing the weight of it before she stuffs it in the pocket of her dress. "Alright, Auren. We're on the same side."

She doesn't have to tag on the unsaid words of that sentence. The *or else* is implied.

But maybe, just maybe, the two of us can learn to trust each other enough to get the hell out of here and not have to do it alone.

Here's hoping.

CHAPTER 12

AUREN

As I *leave the saddl*e wing, I debate how to get back into my rooms without being seen, but the decision is ripped right out from under me when a worried looking Scofield comes barreling down the hall.

I freeze and glance left and right, which is stupid since there's nowhere to hide and he's already seen me anyway.

"My lady, how did you get here? I've been looking all over for you!" he exclaims, rushing forward.

"How did you know I wasn't in my room?"

He stops in front of me, brown hair disheveled. "I had a feeling you'd gone against the king's orders," he says as he fidgets with the golden buckles of his uniform. "Plus, I kept knocking on your door, and you didn't answer."

"I could've been sleeping," I say defensively.

"Honestly, Scofield, that's a little rude to jump to conclusions like that."

His brow furrows. "But you're *not* sleeping."

"Well, you know that *now*." I look around the empty hall. "Does anyone else know I'm here?"

Scofield shakes his head and scratches his sideburn. "Not that I know of. I had someone take my post so I could come looking for you, just in case. The others thought you were just ignoring me."

"See? That's a much more reasonable assumption. You should listen to them next time."

He gives me a pointed look. "They were *wrong*."

I just shrug, like that's beside the point. "Well, you found me now, so you can escort me back to my room if that makes you feel better. Lead the way." I gesture down the hall. "The sooner you get me back, the less of a chance King Midas has of finding out that I snuck out during your watch. He probably wouldn't be too happy with you."

I feel a bit guilty about the way the blood drains from Scofield's face as the weight of my words sink in, but I'm not above playing dirty.

Too bad Midas is already waiting in my room when we get there.

My stomach drops as soon as I open the door and find him standing inside. Scofield makes a choking noise next to me, while Lowe avoids eye contact in the hall.

As I pause in the doorway, Midas's unreadable gaze flicks over me. "Close the door," he orders.

Swallowing hard, I step in, swinging the door closed behind me before I face him. He has his arms crossed in front of him, and he's dressed impeccably. In formal pants and a long shirt, he's buttoned from collarbone to hips with elaborate filigree embroidered along the length of his tunic. I briefly wonder who he's dressed to impress today, but I'm more distracted by the set of his jaw and the cut of his glare.

To keep them from trembling, I clasp my hands in front of me.

I have the power. *Me.*

Those silent thoughts help me steel myself against the onslaught of temper I know I'm about to receive.

His brown eyes pin me in place, like a pair of needles to stick me against the door. "Where were you?"

I raise my chin. "I told you I wouldn't stay locked up."

All of the still silence bursts out of him at once. "I did it for your protection!" He takes a step toward me, hand slashing in the air like he wants to cut off my rebellion at its knees. "I let you out of your cage," Midas tells me, as if I should be grateful, as if he did any such thing.

"No. I let myself out."

Midas pauses at the look on my face, and for a moment, I know he's remembering the way my ribbons lashed out and ripped the iron door off its hinges and threw it at him. How he was slammed to the floor, stunned beneath its weight.

"I told you I didn't want you leaving this room." He pulls at the bottom of his tunic and lets out a firm breath, like his determination in the matter has settled it.

It hasn't.

"And *I* told *you* that I won't be locked away. I promised to keep guards with me and to be careful. I'm not your pet to be kept anymore."

Midas's eyes darken. "You are not allowed to wander around during daylight hours, and that's final."

The coals of my anger begin to glow, begin to build and heat. "It is *not* final!"

His regard over me is a cursory sweep that hooks onto my balled fists and knotted arms. "You're different since you came back."

My expression goes stony. "And you were different the moment you put on a crown."

He doesn't like that answer, not at all.

I shake my head. "What happened to you, Midas?" I don't mean to say it aloud, but it's a question I keep asking myself. Was he always this way? Or like a frog put into lukewarm water, did I just not notice the slow progression of the rising temperature of his greed until I was being boiled in it?

A storm gathers on his brow. "I grew up, Auren. I figured out what I wanted, and I *took* it."

"You got greedy."

He closes the space between us until that storm of his hovers over my air and threatens to douse everything light and warm.

"Greed is relative. I saw an opportunity to make my life better. *And* yours."

"You took advantage."

A bursting scoff escapes him. "Stop with the dramatics, Auren. Stop with this rebellion. It doesn't suit you."

"No, the problem is that it doesn't suit *you*."

That's the real truth of it. I'm a pet to be kept and a tool to be used, and if I do or say anything remotely individualistic, anything that he doesn't like or control, then he wants to squash it beneath his heel like a bug.

"Enough," he seethes, making me flinch. "You're acting like a brat."

I rear back at the insult. "A *brat*? Are you fucking kidding me?"

"Watch your tongue," he growls, finger raised to point at my face.

My spine stiffens. "I will say what I want, and I will leave this *fucking* room when I like, and you can't stop me."

You can't stop me
can't stop me
can't

The words palpitate between us, clogging in his ears and thrumming on my tongue, because there it is. The ugly truth that he never wanted me to know: that power doesn't just come from magic. It comes from your own grit. And I have both.

The look in his eye makes me want to turn away, but I manage to hold my ground. "Careful, Auren. Be very, very careful."

Every word is a lash of warning.

My breath heaves, that dark, coiled anger in my chest writhing and poking with feathers and beak like some unnamed beast. I'm trying to plan smart, to play the long game and disappear right out from under his nose, but he will *not* keep me captive. My soul can't take that again.

I hold the power.

Me.

I don't care how long he's tried to trick me into thinking it was the other way around.

"*Or what?*" I challenge, my voice cracking like a whip.

He wants to threaten me, and the creature that's bloomed under my skin wants to rise up and strike him down for it.

I'm not sure what I let through in my expression, but Midas's eyes narrow. "Hmm. I can see our time apart has done more damage to you than I first realized."

I let out a humorless laugh. "You think I'm damaged

because I refuse to be locked away like a mad person in an asylum?"

"Listen, I have plans in motion, and Third Kingdom is due to arrive soon, so I cannot have you acting out of line. A lot rides on this, and you need to do your part. That means gilding whatever I tell you to gild, and staying where I tell you to stay. You went through some traumatic events, and I am sorry for that, but I'm not your enemy. I'm your protector and your king."

My cager and betrayer.

"I'll gild whatever you want," I tell him, "*unless* you lock me away again."

The ultimatum lands like a star falling from the sky and exploding on the ground. The fire in the hearth burns low, a soft orange glow to compete with the shadows between us.

He watches me for a long time. Just the two of us staring at each other like strangers. I've never not given him everything he ever asked for or bent to his will. The bastard can't say the same for me.

Finally, he lets out a sigh and shakes his head. "Oh, Auren." His tanned hands come up to bracket his hips like he's bracing himself. Yet there's condescension on his face, and I wonder if he would look at me like that if it were still daytime. "I didn't want to have to do this, but you've left me no choice."

He digs into his pocket and then holds his palm out, revealing a small golden piece of grimy metal.

RAVEN KENNEDY

I frown down at the guard pin, eyes tracing over the bell emblem. "Why are you showing me that?"

"You don't recognize it?"

Wariness paints over my face. "It's the pin all the guards in Highbell wear."

Midas lifts it up, rolling it between his finger and thumb like a god holding the world in a threatening pinch. "You told me you thought your guard died with the Red Raids."

My mind races.

Stumbles.

Rolls down a cliff, scraped and scattered and left to fall.

For a moment, all I can see is a flash of red in the snow and sweet blue eyes. All I can hear is, *it's okay, it's okay, it's okay.*

His name yanks out of me like the dagger pulled from a chest. "Sail..."

But Midas shakes his head, and I tear my eyes away from the pin to look at him. "No. Digby."

My free-falling mind slams to a stop. Dots of black appear in my vision like a starless sky ready to swallow me whole. I physically stumble back, barely catching myself on the bedside table as my knees threaten to give out.

"*Digby?*" It's a whisper, a plea, a bewildered breath. "What...I don't...I don't understand."

Something glimmers behind the depths of his muddied eyes. "I have him, Auren."

The gut-wrenching gasp that rips out of my chest leaves my heart to gape out in the open. My lip quivers, ribs squeeze, fingers dig into the table to keep myself standing. "What are you talking about?"

He's cool and calm again. Calculated. Just that look alone fills me with dread.

"It was meant to be a gift, you see."

I squeeze my eyes closed for a moment, my head shaking as I try to comprehend through the shock. "Wait, wait. Are you...are you saying Digby is alive? He's *here*?"

"Like I said, he was going to be a gift for your return. I knew you were fond of the old man. Although, he had to be punished, of course."

Digby. Alive. He's actually *alive*? I can't—

"Wait," I rush to say, shaking my head. "What the hell do you mean *punished*?"

Midas shoots me an annoyed look at my curse word. "He allowed the Red Raids to capture you, and then subsequently, Fourth's army. I couldn't let that go unanswered."

Horror crashes over me like a sudden flood to knock me into its violent path. "He's *alive* and you've kept that from me this whole time? You've *punished* him?"

His eyes flicker knowingly. "He didn't do what he was ordered to."

My teeth gnash against the double meaning. The threat. That I'll be punished if I don't follow his orders too.

I cross my arms in front of me. "I want to see him."

Midas clicks his tongue. "Therein lies the problem. I was going to let you do just that, but in your current state of mind and overemotional hysterics, I simply can't allow it."

Can't *allow* it?

Fire flares in my chest and sears through my eyes. "Let me see him. Right. Now."

The dark warning in his face sharpens against an edge of satisfaction. "When you improve your behavior and your mood, I will."

My lips pull back in a sneer. "You son of a bitch."

Again, with his clicking tongue, a sweep of reprimand like I'm a child to be disciplined. "That's certainly not the way to go about it, Auren."

Hot tears fill my eyes, but I hold them back. "You're lying. You don't have him."

Midas looks at me with pity. "I do. But even if you think I'm lying, are you really willing to bet his life on it?"

I go still, like a fierce gale that suddenly died. Sucked away until every particle of air is depraved with stagnancy.

"Don't you dare hurt him."

Midas gives a shrug. "That's entirely up to you." He grips my hand and drops the pin into my palm.

I stare down at it and see it for what it is. His best bargaining chip to make me complacent. How can something so small feel so damn heavy?

When a tear drips into my cupped palm, Midas's eyes soften. That gesture probably would've fooled me before, would've made me doubt myself and had my emotions braided with confusion and heartache.

But the eyes of liars are tricky things. They can show you what you want to see without ever reflecting the truth. It's best not to look a liar in the eye. They're so good at their own compulsions that their gazes hold steady, and then *you're* the one who loses sight.

Midas pops a kiss on the top of my head, but I'm too numb in shock to jerk away. "I'm not trying to punish you, Auren," he says softly as he pets my hair, once more the benevolent master. "You need something to focus on so you can get back to being yourself. I'm giving you that."

He's betrayed me before, but this…

"As soon as you're better and behaving like yourself again, I'll reinstate Digby, and then everything will be alright." He gives me an encouraging smile. "I promise. Everything I do, I do for *you*. You see that now, don't you?"

My shaken eyes drag back up to his face. "Yes, Midas. I see."

I see.

"I'll have some food sent up. You'll have a clearer head in the morning after you get some rest, and then we will get to work on turning some things gold, alright?"

He's already tugging on his leash, testing to see if I'll heel.

"Okay, Midas."

A pleased, placating look crosses his face. "There's my precious girl. I knew this is what you needed. You'll be better soon." He taps my chin. "Don't worry about a thing. I always make sure you have what you need, don't I? I'll keep you safe," he says earnestly, hand once more stroking down my hair. "I'll even compromise with you. I'll allow you to wander in the castle after dusk *with* a guard. But during the day, when it's not safe, you stay put. More guards will always be posted outside your door. No one will get to you."

"Just you." The words slip out, unbidden.

His touch pauses on my head before falling away. "That's right. Just me," he murmurs.

It's a promise.

It's a threat.

It's a line in the sand that keeps dripping through the hourglass.

"Goodnight, Precious."

The moment he's gone, with my bedroom door snugly shut, my skirts crumple with my knees, the fabric fanning out like a rippling lake as I land on the floor.

Teardrops soak my lashes as I use my free hand to try and stifle the sobs that wrench out of me.

How could he?

How *could he*?

He knows that I've always had a soft spot for Digby. Felt comfortable with the gruff man who always watched over me. And all this time, I've been grieving him like I've grieved for Sail.

The thought of Digby being here at Ranhold this whole time and possibly hurt...

I have no idea how or when he would've arrived. No idea where he might be kept or if he's okay. But Midas could be lying too, and that's what's so agonizing about this. I don't know what the truth is.

My heart aches at the idea of him being punished, but I have to shove that thought away, or I'll never stop crying. I should've expected a counter move from Midas, though I didn't realize he'd stoop this low. It just solidifies everything for me. This is another barb in the collar that he wants wrapped around my neck.

Because Midas is right. Even if he is lying, I'm not willing to take that chance. So long as there's a possibility he has my guard, I will have to play nice. I will have to play smart. Digby is *my* guard. My only other constant I've ever had, and I want him back.

After another ragged sob, I make myself take a fortifying breath to help push away the panic and hatred, because I need to *think*. The feathered anger beneath my skin helps to steel my spine, and my ribbons give me a comforting squeeze.

The Golden King wants to pluck my strings and make me sing. So I'll sing. I'll do just enough to ensure that he doesn't hurt Digby.

Wiping my cheeks, I start to get to my feet, but pause when I feel the small book weighing down my pocket. I put the guard pin on the bedside table and then pull out the forbidden fae book. My eyes trace the elderwood, fingers running over the red leather that coats it, golden filigree and an ancient language meeting my touch.

The sound it makes when I open the front cover is the crack of a jaw yawning awake. It's the sigh of a breath kept inside for too long, closed beneath parchment ribs.

There are no words in this book, no lengthy explanations of my heritage, my people. It wasn't until this moment that I realized how desperate I was for that. Maybe I thought I was going to open this book and find all the answers to the questions I didn't even know I had.

Instead, there are only painstaking illustrations painted on each thick page, some cracked or dusted away, the paint given up in its battle with time. No words, no long-ago fae coming up through the pages to give me answers about who I am or about my home I've forgotten so much about.

Somehow, the silence is made up for by the apology

of paintings. As if the person who worked on this book couldn't give me words but gave me something else.

Annwyn.

My world looks up at me from forbidden pages of a forgotten land. Glittering rivers speckled with dawn light, flowers with smiles, and trees with grasping limbs. Hills that roll when you step on them, and sand made of glass.

Tears burn in my eyes with every picture I flip past, fingers tingling as if they can feel the echoes of something familiar. I come to a stop on the very last page, finding an Orean woman with flaxen hair and autumn eyes leaned against a fae male wearing an onyx crown. He has pointed ears, a dark complexion, and gossamer wings hanging like shadows against his back. They're tucked against a sunset sky, polka dot clouds brimming with oranges and pinks behind them.

The way they're looking at each other is as if nothing else exists. There's a subtle haze clinging around their embrace, love shining in their eyes. At the bottom of the page, a single word in the old fae language is painted in elaborate calligraphy.

Päyur

I stare at the pictures for a long time.

Flipping backwards and forwards, I use the light of the dying fire to feed my nostalgic craving. I look at the book until my eyes burn with tiredness while the thought of Digby drums in my veins.

I can't leave if Digby is here, so I'm going to find him. Even if that means I have to scour this castle from foundation to roof, I *will* find my guard. And then when I leave, because I *am* going to leave, I'm taking Digby with me.

Please be okay, Digby.

Please be alive.

I fall asleep with the secret book buried in the pocket of my dress, dreaming of that fae couple standing in the eventide, wrapped in a shared aura and whispering at me to come home.

If only I knew where home was.

CHAPTER 13

KING MIDAS

*T*hree levels below the ground floor of Ranhold Castle, and it's like being in an icebox. Even wearing my robe and thick gloves doesn't keep the cold from penetrating. I'm surprised I can't see my breath every time I exhale.

As I pass by cell after cell, some shadows behind the bars cringe away from me. I suppose the prisoners have been here too long in Fulke's dungeon to try and speak. Even if they do realize there's a new king ruling, they know better than to bother with pleas or to cry for mercy.

Based on the smell wafting from a few of the chambers, I'd say there's a good chance that some of them are already dead or have their foot in the door. Mercy won't do anything for them, and neither will I.

My steps echo down the gray stone passageway as

I pass beneath centuries-old arches built too low for my liking, its height meant to make the inhabitants feel even more trapped.

The ceiling drips with frosted condensation, a gift from the snow hundreds of feet above. The perpetually white-soaked ground seeps all the way down here, dripping with apathetic disdain for its inhabitants in the form of icy stalactites reaching down like frosted fingers pointing with accusation.

The dungeon guards on patrol give me a bow as I pass, and my steps take me up the narrow staircase to the level above. There's more light up here, given by double the amount of wall sconces, but the ceiling is still covered in frost.

My feet take me straight to the room off to the left where a guard swings open the door without me having to break my stride.

Warmth hits me as soon as I go into the antechamber, coming face-to-face with a thick canopy of leather hanging from the ceiling to split off the room from the outer door. I push past the heavy brown flap and duck inside the huge, steam-filled space.

There are several people hard at work, some of them scrubbing down the walls. In this room, instead of frost or dripping icicles, the stones are slick with hot moisture beading between every crevice. The workers tend to every inch, trying to deter any mold from growing. Others are amidst the long, straight rows of plants, tending to every leaf and bloom.

I look around, eyes bouncing from purple uniform to purple uniform, until I find the castle's mender at the far end, bustling around at the counter space built against the wall.

The gangly man doesn't notice I'm here until I'm standing right beside him. He nearly drops the bottle he's funneling when he does.

"Your Majesty, forgive me," he says with a quick bow. "I didn't know you would be coming down here."

"I had another matter to see to," I say, casting a glance at the row of blood-red bottles stacked and ready to go, complete with built-in droppers.

A worker comes up, apron wrinkling as she drops into a quick curtsy. She grabs one of the filled bottles, uncorking it as she goes. I watch as she pours the contents into the soil of the nearest potted plant until it's empty.

There are hundreds of these plants growing in here. They're fussy, apparently, since they wither in the sun but need moist heat to thrive.

Their branches point straight up like rows of picket fences. Growing from every limb are blossoms leeched of color, the petals white and ashen. The buds are useless and take a long time to bloom, but the mature ones, the ones nearly ready to fall off their stems, those are what the gardeners carefully collect.

If tended to correctly, those drooping petals bead with blood-red dewdrops. A powerful essence that, when ingested, causes you to relax and heightens pleasure. Dew makes quite a lot of coin in this kingdom.

"What can I help you with, Your Majesty?"

I turn back to the mender as he wipes his stained fingers on a rag before tossing it on the worktable. He has a fine sheen of sweat on his lined brow, ruddy cheeks from the warm humidity clogging the room.

"I wanted to ensure that all of the saddles have been given their contraceptive tonics."

"Of course, my king. I have been distributing them myself."

Nodding, I swipe at the back of my neck to get rid of the moisture beading there. "And the pregnant saddle?" I ask. "Has she been sequestered?"

"Yes, and I examined her this morning. I have her well in hand."

"I want reports for every checkup."

The man tilts his head in compliance and wipes his upper lip with a handkerchief. "It will be done, Sire."

"Good."

On my way out, I cast another appreciative gaze across the steam-filled room. Everyone is doing what they should be, everything inside precise and organized. This entire operation is put together like a perfectly tailored outfit.

Fulke might have been a fool, but when it comes to growing and supplying dew, he had enough sense to put the right people in charge.

Leaving the lower levels of the castle, my slicked skin goes uncomfortably cold within seconds, worsened by the moist sweat that's accumulated. The grime of the dungeon and the dampness of the grow room clings to my clothes enough to make my skin itch. A change of clothes is in order. Perhaps a bath too.

As soon as I make it to the upper levels and back into the public part of the castle, my guards peel away from the walls to follow me. Yet I've barely taken three steps when my head guard comes forward, holding out a missive. "A hawk just arrived for you, Sire."

I take it and keep walking, already planning which outfit to change into, but I pause on the stairs when I notice the white wax seal in the shape of a bell.

I tear it open, eyes quickly skimming left to right.

That cold, useless bitch.

I read through it again, and then a third time, while my teeth grind together to chew on my fury. When I get through it a fourth time, I already have a plan in mind.

Malina doesn't want to be useful anymore? Wants to deny her husband and king?

So be it.

I turn sharply, abandoning the route to my rooms completely.

The guards shadow my steps as I make my way out of the castle. Past the courtyard, past the ice sculptures, past the stables, my boots crunch on the powdery walkways until I come to an outdoor training ring.

Some soldiers are gathered around and running drills. From my peripheral, I see them stop to bow, but I ignore them and continue to stride forward to the building attached.

"Wait here and close the door," I order the guards.

Inside, the building is bare bones. Nothing but a small armory for training purposes. Wooden swords lie in piles, and there are stacks of padded chest armor for sword practice, as well as a litter of arrows and unstrung bows. It's messy and reeks of sweat, the floor made of nothing but dirt and straw to go with the rough stone walls.

Several soldiers look up in surprise at the sound of the door closing, but when they see me, they drop into stiff bows.

"Everyone out," I order sternly, sending the soldiers scattering before my eyes fall onto the older man. He's not a soldier anymore, not at his age, but he's been charged with keeping this place equipped and organized, though I see he's sorely lacking on the latter.

"Fetch Hood."

The man's brows lift in surprise, but he quickly leaves to do as I bid. I pace around the building while I wait, lip turning up in a grimace at the state of my shoes from the disgusting floor. I should have that man whipped for his severe lack of care at his duty.

Several minutes later, the door opens again and Hood steps into the room. I don't need to see his face to know it's him—the thick cloak and hood he always wears is telling enough. He never goes without it, face always shadowed beneath the cowl of material.

Even so, I can see the two-toned skin, both brown and pale, showing on his chin and neck. Vitiligo, they call it, a condition of the skin that leaches color in patches.

Some of the soldiers mock him, call him Cowhide, but the man never speaks, never snaps. He was wasted as a soldier for Fulke. It was lucky that I read some of the soldiers' reports and realized his potential.

I'm going to put that potential to the test.

"Hood," I say in greeting as he stops a few feet away, hand clasped around his wrist in a soldier's stance.

While his skin abnormalities may have made him a mocked outsider, his muteness ensured it. It took years for Fulke to realize that the man had magic.

I look at his cloaked form, eyes running over the patches on his hands as if I can somehow see why power chose to run through his veins.

Magic, *strong* magic, isn't as common as it once was in Orea. Without any more fae to mix with, it's slowly petering out of our world. It's held mostly in the royal lines, but that's only due to carefully arranged unions.

But the man in front of me is one who slipped through the cracks, who went unnoticed for too long. Just a common, albeit skilled, foot soldier. His secret was discovered only after a particularly bad fight, seven against one, and he disappeared in plain sight.

Luckily for me, Fulke kept good notes.

"I have a job for you."

Hood waits, unspeaking, just as I knew he would. Through the weeks of observing him, he hasn't spoken once. I view his silence as another asset.

"The cold queen has become a problem. I want you to take care of her for me."

Part of me is disappointed in Malina. I thought she'd be smarter than this, though I anticipated that she might react this way. Her bold refusal sits creased in my palm, her letter sealing her own fate.

That was the only chance I was willing to give her, and she just threw it away because she overestimated her own importance. With her pathetic scheming to try to keep Sixth, with her refusal to claim an heir, she's now become ineffectual.

Expendable.

"How quickly does your magic work?" I ask curiously as I walk closer.

In answer, he settles his arms at his sides, lifting his head slightly to reveal the patch around his mouth and nose as his eyelids drop closed in concentration.

The change happens slowly, like a roiling cloud high in the sky. His form builds and billows before it becomes a dark, translucent wisp inside the cover of smoke.

The man is stock-still silence and churning shadows.

I hum in approval at his wraithlike form, at the magic of a hidden phantom who can disappear into his own umbra and bend the light around him to make him disappear. I put my hand out to test these strange shadows, but my fingers pass right through, feeling nothing but cold smoke.

Fascinating. Effective. Perfect magic to put to use as an assassin.

Dropping my hand, I watch as Hood reappears, shadow and light coalescing around him until his body is solid and visible once more.

"I want you to leave tonight," I tell him. "Don't fail me."

Hood dips his chin in agreement at the order and then turns and slips away, leaving just as silently as he entered.

Malina will be sorry she ever refused me. I'm going to ruin her feeble efforts at holding my kingdom, and then, my shadow will extinguish her.

CHAPTER 14

AUREN

*Y*ou missed a spot on the floor, Auren."

I turn my head to look and see where Midas is indicating. My tired eyes land on a spot on the marble, gilded veins now running throughout every polished tile.

With weighted steps, I pad across the room to the offensive spot that didn't take. Beneath my bare feet, I will some of my gold to trickle through my heels and toes, but it's sluggish, drying up, my arches aching like someone's nails digging into the strained muscles.

As soon as I manage to gild the spot, I slump against the wall, limbs shaking with exhaustion. A layer of sweat pearls against my brow, and it takes all my willpower not to lie down right here in the middle of the throne room and pass out.

"It's nearly dusk," Midas says, as if I need the reminder.

He's sitting on the throne with a ledger in his lap that he's been going over for however many hours we've been in here. While he's been reading and making notes on who-knows-what, I've been systematically gold-touching everything in the room. Just as I've been doing in other various rooms for the past four days. Turning a castle gold is more draining than I remember.

When I did this at Highbell, my powers were still new. My gold-touch came in spurts and depleted quickly. Yet over the years, my magic has become stronger. I've been able to do more at one time for longer, but four days of draining my power again and again has caught up with me. So much so that the impending dusk makes me want to sigh in relief.

The fact that my power only works during the day means I'm limited, but it can also be a blessing. As soon as the sun sets, I can relax. I don't have to pay attention to every single movement, to be so aware of my skin and my touch. More importantly, I can have a break from Midas's incessant requests.

All I've done is work myself down to the bone, using my power again and again and again to please him. He's dangling Digby over me. Every time I want to tell him to shove it instead of turning another piece of clothing, plate, plant, or table gold, I've had to bite my tongue. I've had to fist my hands and do it anyway, because the threat of him hurting Digby looms over me like a dust storm ready to descend.

The only good thing about my constant work these past few days is that they've been enlightening. I've been able to see more of the main parts of the castle without having to sneak around, been able to make more of a map of everything around me. Now, I'm not just searching for ways out, but also trying to figure out where Digby might be held.

"I can't do any more today," I tell Midas honestly, shaking my head as I look down at my sticky hands. The liquid gold is claggy and clumped, half-drying against my palms like thickening paint. "I'm wiped out."

With a furrowed brow, he closes his ledger and tucks it beneath his vest before getting up from the throne. A throne, which, thanks to me, is now solid gold just like the raised dais beneath it. Gold-touch is immediate with whatever comes into contact with my bare skin, but the more I use it, the more difficult and exhausting it is. I don't know how many more days of this endless demand on my magic I can handle. Already, I feel like I've aged twenty years.

Midas walks toward me, gaze sweeping the throne room. He glances at the floors that now gleam, at the gilt window frames and the panes that are now tinged gold. I even managed to gild every inch of the walls, which took hours in this massive space since I had to do it in spurts so I didn't drain myself too quickly.

But now I'm tired, I'm cranky, and I've reached my daily limit with tolerating Midas's soft *suggestions* of what else needs to be gold-touched.

Midas's eyes lift as he takes in the ceiling with a frown. I wasn't able to get my power to stretch that far, so the ceiling and blue crystal chandeliers are untouched. Personally, I think the white and blue looks better.

The only other thing left in here is the viewing section to the left, the wooden banisters and benches intact. Although, considering the size of the room, I've done far more than I thought I could today.

"Shame about the chandeliers," Midas muses as he stops in front of me, head tipped up.

I have to hold my tongue to keep from cursing him. I've worked tirelessly all damn day, and *that's* what he has to say to me?

I can feel that earlier anger from the parapet wall peek its head up in the chasm of my spirit, an eye cracking open. I've tied my ribbons into simple bows at my back, but they tighten instinctively with my spark of temper.

While he's looking around the room, I look at him. "Sorry to disappoint you," I bite out.

"We'll get it done tomorrow," he says absently, not picking up on my tone.

Why he says *we*, as if he does anything other than sit there, is beyond me.

"Just in time too. I've received word from Third Kingdom. They were held up by their timberwings, but they're back on course and will be arriving soon." He looks at the gilded throne with pride, like he's already envisioning sitting in it while his new admirers look upon him.

The monster that's taken up residence in my chest trills out a warning, but I tamp her down.

Since I've been gold-touching every day, Midas has worked quietly, only offering a few words every so often, which means I've had plenty of time to think. I'm figuring out who I am outside of his control, but...I want to *like* who I become. I'm worried about what might happen if this dark beast that's taken root inside of me rears her ugly head.

Letting out a strangled breath, I suppress my temper once again, while my fingers come up to press against my aching temple. "I'd like to go lie down now."

Midas looks at me for the first time, a frown curving down as his brassy eyes skate over me. "Are you tired?"

"Of course I'm tired," I say snappishly.

Instead of the flash of anger or the pointed look that warns me to remember Digby, his frown only deepens. "You're right. You've done a lot of work for the past few days, and I should've ensured that you didn't tax yourself too much. Come, we'll go out the back door and I'll escort you to your rooms where you can rest."

Rest. Sounds heavenly.

He turns and starts walking, but I wince when I realize that before I can achieve said rest, I'm going to have to walk. Far.

I bribe my body with thoughts of my fluffy bed and feather pillows just waiting upstairs. The real tragedy of this throne room isn't that I didn't manage to gild the chandeliers, it's that there isn't a single pillow in here.

Since the softest thing present is now a solid gold throne, I give myself a pep talk.

I can do this.

I can walk the very long way to my rooms after hours of depleting my magic to the point of exhaustion. I can, because I don't want to show weakness in front of Midas. I'm a strong woman who's learning to be independent, dammit.

Ish. I'm a strong*ish* woman. That *ish* is going to have to be good enough for now.

With a determined breath that comes out a little bit like a whimper, I manage to peel myself off the wall and stand on two feet.

Bright side, I don't fall flat on my face.

But then I remember all the stairs I have to climb, and my *ish* falters a little bit. Stupid castles with their stupid multiple levels.

I snag my shoes and gloves where I left them on the dais, slipping both on, just as my skin prickles with the telltale sign that the day is ended.

I let out a shaky exhale as my gold-touch power evaporates like mist, going dormant for the night as the sun sets, and my aching palms twinge as the last of the gold soaks back into my skin.

Midas waits for me by the door, no doubt noting how long it's taking me to get there. My silk slippers drag, every step feeling heavier than the last.

His brow furrows as I finally reach the doorway. "I've overworked you. I apologize."

"It's fine."

"It's not," he replies as he leads me through the empty meeting room and then toward the door at the other end. "I've just been impatient to get started, and there's so much to do here...but it's no excuse. I shouldn't have pushed you for so long today." He stops before the second door and turns to me like he's actually concerned. And maybe he is, but it's not for *me*, not really. He can't have more gold if his spout drains dry. "Forgive me. I don't mean to be overbearing, you know that."

I know he's full of shit, and it's certainly not gilded.

"I just need to sleep, Midas," I say thickly, feeling like I'm about to topple right over. Stopping is not a good idea right now, because I might not be able to get going again, and the last thing I want is him touching me to help me along.

"Of course," he nods. "I can let you rest tomorrow as well. You've done so much already. If you're still too weak in the morning, we'll wait until the following day to do more of the castle."

Dizziness overwhelms me at just the thought of how much more he wants me to do.

He clears his throat. "*And*, if you continue on the way you've been behaving, until the celebratory ball, I'll let you visit Digby."

My stomach squeezes, chest leaping. "Really?"

"You'll have earned it by then," he says, flashing me a bright grin.

I'll have *earned* it...or I'll have found him myself.

I give Midas a shaky, desperate smile because it's what he wants. "Thank you."

With a nod, he opens the door, and we walk out into the empty hall. Every day this week as I've worked, he's locked the area down, not allowing anyone to come near the room we're in, guards included. Wouldn't want anyone to walk in and see who's really turning things gold, now would he?

As we walk down the hall together, I watch my dragging feet while Midas peppers the air with one-sided conversation. Telling me about which rooms we'll do next, which things I missed for my first go-around, how much gold the nobles need... Sometimes it feels like he's talking directly to my magic instead of to me. At least there's no need for me to reply.

By the time we spill out into the grand entrance, twin staircases curling up on the left and right, sweat is trickling down my back, and my legs are shaking.

I pause on the landing, gripping the railing to hold myself up as I catch my breath while Midas chatters on about some damn thing.

"King Midas."

Midas stops on the stairs above me and turns, while my own head swings to face the new voice. On the second staircase to our left, there's a boy descending the steps with three Ranhold guards trailing after him, purple cloaks hanging heavy at their backs.

"Prince Niven," Midas replies smoothly with a bow of his head. Only because I know him so well, I catch the hint of distaste in his polished voice. "I was told you were still unwell."

The boy is dressed in mourning black with silver icicles embroidered into his cuffs. Mourning for his father, the man who almost killed me.

My hand comes up, fingers sliding over the scar at my throat. It's not very noticeable anymore, just a small, jagged line, but when I touch it, it's almost like I can feel the edge of Fulke's blade digging in.

"I am having a better day today," the prince says, quick steps taking him down the rest of the stairway.

Niven is young. If I had to guess, I'd say he can't be older than twelve. And yet, he carries all the airs of a royal-born boy. A haughty chin, perfectly combed brown hair, and finely tailored clothes. When his eyes cut over to me, I'm glad to find that they're blue, not brown like Fulke's were.

He blinks at me in surprise, as if for a second, he thought I was a statue instead of a person. "So it's true," he says as he strides right up to me. "She's completely gilded."

I tense, but Midas is at my side in an instant to head him off. "Prince Niven, this is Auren. My gold-touched favored."

The boy's eyes rove over me. "Strange," he murmurs before glancing at Midas. "Why don't you turn all your saddles gold?"

"Because she's special."

I inwardly snort.

Based on the slight lift of his lip, Prince Niven doesn't seem very impressed with that answer either. "My father could duplicate everything one time, but his power didn't work on people or animals. But when *my* magic comes out, it's going to be even more powerful than his. Maybe even more powerful than yours," he says, tone as pompous as only a child prince's can be.

"I'm sure you'll be very impressive once your magic manifests," Midas replies placidly.

"Yes." Niven nods, casting his attention over me one last time before he seems to dismiss me completely. "I'm glad I caught you, King Midas. I would like to discuss some matters with you. Shall we go to the meeting room?"

I cut my glance over just in time to catch the irritated tap of Midas's finger at his hip, six consistent thrums against the golden fabric of his trousers.

Oh, he just hates this, doesn't he?

I have to keep myself from grinning like a loon. I might be a little slap happy right now from how drained I am, but this conversation has perked me right up. Midas must loathe dealing with the pompous little prince while he's busy playing ruler of Fifth Kingdom.

It almost makes my exhaustion worth it, just to see the look on Midas's face. I'm immensely pleased that I get to see how he has to force himself to swallow down every scathing thought he has and nod at the prince instead.

"Of course, Your Highness. I am here at your disposal to help in all matters."

"Excellent," Niven says, voice a little high-pitched and nasally. "Let's go."

"I'll meet you shortly, right after I walk my favored to her rooms," Midas tells him as he begins to motion for me to follow him up the stairs.

Prince Niven frowns. "Surely a king doesn't need to do something so trivial?" The boy looks around, spotting two of Midas's gold-clad guards on the landing above us. "You there! Come down here and escort King Midas's favored back to her rooms. Your King has very important business to attend and can't be bothered with such things."

Midas's face flushes red, and the sight makes a laugh bubble up in my throat. I staunch it before it can come out, but I make a choking sound that I have to cover up with a cough.

Both royals frown over at me.

"Sorry," I rasp. "Dust in my throat."

The guards from above quickly make their way down to us, while Midas steps up to my side. "Go straight up to your room."

I dip my chin, playing the part of his subservient saddle. "Yes, King Midas."

He pauses, eyes narrowing slightly, and it takes me a second to realize it's because I called him King Midas instead of *my king*. That should be telling enough for both of us. I don't consider him mine anymore.

The guards' arrival rips Midas's attention away from me so he can glare at them. "Escort her straight to her rooms," he commands before digging in his pocket and pulling out a key. He shoves it in one of the guards' hands.

"Yes, Your Majesty."

"Come along, King Midas. I have much to discuss," Niven says, impatience dripping off his pretentious tone as he begins to walk past us in the direction of the meeting room.

Midas's shoulders go tight, brow lowering with

irritation. I wonder what he'd really say to the prince if he weren't busy spinning a political web threaded with fake niceties.

With one last look at me, Midas turns on his heel and catches up with Niven. The prince's prattling voice carries up to me as he launches into conversation. Midas matches Niven's stride, so stiff that his arms don't even swing at his sides. They round the corner and disappear from view, and a tension I hadn't realized I carried immediately loosens its grip on me.

"Come, my lady."

I pull my attention to the guards. "Yeah. Okay," I say with a sigh. "Just...give me a second."

Still leaning on the railing, I look down at my feet, as if eyeing them will somehow offer encouragement. I manage a step, then two, but by the third, my legs are shaking again. When I lift my foot and pull myself up the stair, I realize there's a very good possibility I'll end up on the floor in a crumpled heap.

I stop again and lean against the railing, my palms throbbing where I grip the banister. Great Divine, four days of using my power nonstop is too much.

"My lady?"

"Just...gimme...a minute." I say a *minute* this time instead of a *second*, but really, I'm gonna need a few hours.

I try to breathe in and out, willing myself not to collapse. I pushed myself *way* further than I realized.

"We must escort you upstairs immediately," the guard insists.

I feel weaker than I have in a long time, and it pisses me off. This weakness is exactly what I need to eradicate. I need to get my mind, my body, my power stronger.

The guards share whispered conversation, but my mind is swimming, so they're just going to have to wait. I lay my head against the railing, trying to talk my body into not falling asleep standing up. I'm not sure it's working.

"Goldfinch? What's wrong?"

My eyes snap open.

Groggily, I swivel my head to the left without picking it up. *Since when is my head so damn heavy?*

"Rip?"

My vision tunnels as I watch him striding toward me, taking the stairs two at a time, his leather uniform practically molded against his muscled body. I can see it's the real him, not his body-double, because his helmet is off and his dark aura is clinging to his silhouette. His spikes are jutting out menacingly, and the look on his face makes the guards back up.

When Rip sees their retreating steps, a storm gathers on his thick brow, and his aura pierces the air like an off-key note, making me wince from the pitched tremor.

"You see a commander from another kingdom's army coming toward your king's favored, and your instinct is to *back the fuck up*?" he seethes.

Whoa.

A chill runs down my spine at the dark anger that bleeds out of his voice, and my breath catches in my chest.

He stops in front of the two men, a good half a foot taller than them both. The blazing black of his eyes make me glad I'm not the one who's catching the brunt of his glare.

"We...were just escorting her to her rooms."

"You were doing nothing but standing there being useless while she's practically falling over." His jaw is tight, expression filled with cutting disdain, and my pulse jumps at the ferocious protectiveness streaming from his words, like the warning growl of an alpha wolf.

Right now, he looks every bit the menacing monster that the rumors paint him as. Even *I'm* a little scared, and I know he won't hurt me. At least, not physically.

"I'm fine," I say, though my voice is throaty, quiet.

The prod of his aura reaching out toward me takes me by surprise, and I gasp at the feel of it caressing over my skin. "Oh?" Rip asks me with a cock of his brow that lifts the row of blunt spikes there. "Then stand up straight."

"Oh sure, I'll just lift a horse too while I'm at it. Maybe run all the way to the Barrens," I grumble.

"Mm-hmm," Rip says, clearly cocky about proving his point.

He turns back to the guards, who seem to have made his shit list. "You're lucky I'm not an enemy. You're lucky my king has signed an alliance with yours. Because you're both incompetent idiots who have no business guarding her," Rip growls, his voice the low boil of a brewing anger, and that anger seems to stoke my flushed skin, makes my chest tighten. "Leave, before I tell your king how you behaved."

The guards gape. "But the favored—"

"*I* will walk her to her rooms, and she'll be far more protected by me. Unlike you two, I would never back up if a threat approached."

My stomach does a flip, and a surge of emotions rises in me. I should be irritated that he's stepping in when it's none of his business, but instead, I'm...relieved. I'm relieved that he's here, relieved that he's defending me in his own way. Relieved that he's *Rip*.

"Commander—"

"If King Midas saw how useless you were just now, he would bolt your arms to golden beams. But I'll let you in on a secret." He leans in close to their faces, the spikes on his arms like talons ready to strike, while the scales on his cheeks glint beneath the waning light. "I'd punish you far, *far* worse."

I hear one of the guards gulp.

"Now go the fuck away." He jerks his chin up, and that's all it takes. The guard with the key thrusts it at Rip before the two of them turn and flee like their feet are on fire, steps rushing off until the noise fades completely.

I'm left alone with Rip, and as we regard one another, time seems to go still, flattening out between us like an iced-over lake.

I swallow, and his eyes trace down my throat, the skin at my neck flushing as if I can feel his gaze like the drag of a nail. Why does it all of a sudden seem as if my heart is a fawn picking her head up from behind a leafless shrub? Like I'm prey already entangled, not by teeth or claws, but by spikes. By the thorns hidden in the twist of the brambles I so willingly walked toward, my heart's blood coating each barb.

There's no mistaking it. Right now, at my weakest and my most vulnerable, the truth lies bare, like a maiden stripped down to nothing.

No matter how many times I try to lie to myself, no matter how many times I try to shove him out of my mind, the truth is in the blush of my skin and the ache of my chest.

This male with the bottomless eyes has already snared me.

CHAPTER 15

AUREN

*The ticking time between u*s is marked only by the beats in my chest, one that seems to match the thrum of the pulse in his neck.

Even though we're standing in this wide entry, white beams crisscrossing overhead like the leather straps over his chest, it feels as if we're in a tiny enclosure together, eating up every available space.

Rip assesses me where I'm slumped over the railing, and if I didn't feel so awful, I might care about how weak I look. Yet my mind is far too burned out, so all sorts of caring have gone straight out the frosted window.

"Are you alright?" he asks quietly. His tone is different. So very different from the one he used with the guards. The sound of his smooth voice somehow seems to coat my body, like mist over a starlit pond.

"Me? I'm great. Perfect. Never better," I reply sardonically, though my words are too sloppy, too slurred.

Rip narrows his eyes. "Are you *drunk*?"

"Drunk on power." Much to my embarrassment, an incredibly loud snort erupts out of me as I begin to laugh at my own bad joke. Then I just start laughing harder at the frown on Rip's face, until my entire body is shaking with mirth, making it even more difficult to stay upright. Yep. I've finally cracked. My senses drained right out along with my magic.

When the corner of Rip's mouth twitches with amusement, my stomach flips at the sight. My laughter ebbs away with the pull of the tide, my hysterics drying up like an abandoned shoreline.

Warring desires have me unsure of whether I want to get away from him...or get closer.

Bad idea. Bad, horrible, terrible idea.

Yet my tiredness has stripped me down, because I just want to *breathe*. To stop planning, stop pretending, stop worrying, and just *be* for a moment. Though this is treacherous water, and I never was a good swimmer.

Suddenly nervous, my eyes dart around with the need for a distraction, with the need to do...*something*, just so I don't take a step toward him, because I don't trust myself right now.

"I need to go to my room," I spout, voice belying my nervousness, my need to flee.

I jolt upright and move to take a step, but intense dizziness hits me, and my jellied legs give out. My feet slip from beneath me like the carpet is suddenly slick, and a bubble of alarm pops from my mouth as my legs buckle.

Before I can fall, Rip's strong arms go around me, one beneath my knees, the other behind my back, and I'm swept up before I can even lose my center of gravity.

I look up at him with wide eyes. "I slipped."

A soft laugh ripples out of him, as cool and refreshing as running water over timeworn rocks. "I noticed," he replies, echoing the same conversation we've had before. When it was just the two of us standing beneath a blue mourning moon at the edge of an arctic sea.

Things seemed simpler then.

The spikes on his arms are gone, sunk back into his skin faster than a blink so they didn't pierce me. I'm incredibly aware of his arms around me, of the way he doesn't falter as he holds me up, as if he could hold me for eternity and never let go.

Why does that make me want to cry?

"You caught me," I say, though my voice comes out in more of a whisper, the sound of an unsaid question drifting inside of it.

He tips his chin down, eyes coating me like shade against a scorched day. "I'll do that anytime you need catching, Goldfinch."

Now I'm dizzy for an entirely different reason. I peel

my gaze away from his, my chest capering like a flock of playful birds spinning together in the sky.

"Shit," I say, mind catching up as I realize how bad this is. "You shouldn't touch me."

The muscles in his arms tighten, but his face goes unreadable as he begins to walk me upstairs. "Because your golden king wouldn't like it?"

I shake my head. "No, it's not that, it's... Look, could you just put me down?"

"And let you fall? No."

I'm far too flustered now. Even my ribbons are wringing, tugging against the loosely tied bows. Feeling the planes of his chest against my arm and his strong grip on my body brings a sixth sense of awareness. How can I emotionally distance myself when he's holding me up?

"I could've golded you—I mean gilded. I could've *gilded* you," I stutter, face growing hot.

"You're sure you're not drunk?" he says with a teasing grin.

Great Divine, when he looks at me like that, when he flashes that subtle, secretive smile, it transforms his entire face. He's a smoldering, sexy warrior with transcendental beauty, and I like being in his arms far too much.

I lick my lips, and his eyes flick down to watch, making my stomach flutter. "Not drunk, but I'd really love to be right about now."

His smile widens, and I find my own lips twitching, corners tilting up like they want to join his for the dance.

"But I could've gilded you," I repeat. "Then you'd be a statue stuck right here on the stairwell, and I don't think gold's your color, Commander."

"I disagree. Gold has quickly become my favorite."

I gape at him, too dumbstruck to say a damn thing.

My gaping is so effective that my unblinking state of surprise sends my head into another exhausted dizzy spell. I slump further into him. "Ugh."

Rip adjusts his hold on me, and I have to work not to let my neck fall back. "You're very floppy."

I rest my head against his firm, muscled chest. "You're very hard," I counter.

A rich, dark laugh slips from his mouth. "You've no idea."

My face instantly flares as he smirks, the creases of his cheeks lifting the glint of his scales and making him look so damn gorgeous that all I can do is stare.

He's...*flirting* with me. And based on the giddy feeling in my chest, I can't even deny that I like it. *A lot.*

Feeling this forbidden *want* is a different sort of freedom, like crossing the border of a new land. I instantly find myself wishing that things were different, that we had met under other circumstances. That we didn't have King Ravinger and Midas and omissions jutting up between us in an impassable terrain...because I think I might've liked the trek.

How different would things be if he'd told me the truth about who he was? If I hadn't felt like he was following in Midas's footsteps with tricks and manipulations?

My anger rises up again, and not even entirely at him, but at the tangled web we're caught in, because I feel so *robbed*. Robbed of something...something that could've been mine.

A lump rises in my throat, and no matter how many times I try to gulp it down, I can't. "You shouldn't touch me," I confess, even as my gloved hands curve around his shoulders. "I'm dangerous."

His eyes sparkle with amusement, crinkling at the edges, making him look so much younger, so much less hindered and gruff. "You look it." I scowl at him, but that just seems to entertain him even more as he walks me up the stairs.

"I *am* dangerous," I insist, though maybe my declaration is a bit discredited at the moment. "Well... maybe not right now, since I'm depleted. And not at night, since my power doesn't work then, and not—"

"So your power *does* only work during the day? I thought so."

I press my lips together, internally kicking myself, but it's too late. I was right not to trust myself right now. Not just with my emotions, but apparently my secrets too.

Although, he already knows the main ones, and he hasn't revealed me. Yet.

A ball of worry rolls around in my gut. "Are you going to use that information against me?"

Rip looks down at me as he continues to walk, his aura thrumming around him like a syrupy murk.

His beard is thicker again like it was when I first met him, rather than the stubble that he goes back and forth with. The black hair over his pale jaw makes me want to reach up and touch it, just to see what it feels like. Is he sharp even there? Or is it softer, like the ruffled hair on his head seems to be?

Despite the fact that he's walking at a brisk pace, he's not jarring me in his arms. His movements are fluid and graceful, not at all what you'd expect by looking at him. But Rip has always been unexpected. Like when he replies, "My intention is never to use you, Goldfinch."

For a moment, I can't say anything. My hands tighten ever so slightly on his shoulders, a nervousness braced from my body to his. "You know, I think I believe you. Even though I shouldn't."

I feel the slightest bit of tension loosen from his bunched muscles. "Yes, you should."

One of my ribbons slips from its bow, the golden length looping around his arm, and an entirely too pleased look crosses his face. "Your ribbons seem to like me."

"Well, they don't have brains, so…"

The richest, deepest laugh I've ever heard lumbers through him and wraps around me. I almost lean toward the sound, like I want to bury myself beneath its bark.

Dangerous. I know this is dangerous, to be this close to him, especially in my current state. I'm not equipped, my walls not erected, and I *need* those walls to keep from toppling right into him.

So with a lot of willpower, I force myself to look away, breaking the heady connection with a tug on my ribbon.

As soon as I cut myself off from him, from the moment, I hear him sigh, chest rising and falling beneath my shoulder and carrying his breath of disappointment. "Which rooms are yours?"

Of course he needs to know that, but I feel suddenly shy to tell him.

Sensing my hesitation, he says, "Mine are on this level on the opposite side, with the snowflake door."

I pretend not to soak up that information. "Just down this hall and up one more flight of stairs. It's the door across from Midas's."

Almost there, and then I can shut myself away and hide from the way Rip affects me.

"Hmm."

My eyes cut up. "What does that *hmm* mean?"

He ignores my question as he turns in the direction of my rooms. "Why is your power depleted?" he asks instead.

Always this back and forth that we fall into, of flinging questions at each other and hardly catching answers.

He's tense beneath my ear, but the leather shirt he's wearing is supple, much softer than I would've guessed. "Because I used too much of it," I find myself saying quietly.

"And Midas drove you to this point?"

"He has a reputation to uphold as the *Golden King*," I say with far too much bitterness slipping off my tongue.

Rip seems to catch the taste, biting down so hard that I hear his teeth grind. "You shouldn't let him use your power anymore."

The judgment in his tone makes me go tense. "You don't understand," I say, my mind immediately snagging onto Digby. "I have to."

"You don't *have* to do anything," he retorts. His aura pulses again, but this time, it's erratic, irritated. Well, that makes two of us, because I know what I'm doing, and this playacting at obedience is necessary.

As he makes his way up the last staircase, I remember how this will look and what's at stake. "We're nearly there. You should put me down before the guards see."

Flared, brutal eyes snap to mine. "I don't give a flying fuck about Midas's guards."

His abrupt vitriol cuts my expression into a frown. "*Rip*."

"We've been over this. You couldn't even stand upright, Auren. I'm not putting you down," he tells me, his voice the rough scrape of rocks, hard and unyielding. "I don't care if Midas hears about me touching his *favored*. In fact, I hope he does."

I sigh at the stubborn bastard. "It's not just about Midas. I've made a mistake by making you think it's okay to touch me," I say quietly, unable to look at him. What if it hadn't been dusk? One touch. That's all it would take, and the implications of that terrify me. "It was selfish of me. But for your own good, you need to stop."

He stops abruptly at the top of the stairs and then swings me around, suddenly settling my bottom down on the flat railing on the landing, facing my body toward his. I grip the railing beneath me, centering myself before I go pitching backwards, but I don't need to, because his arms are already steadying me.

He boldly wraps his hand around the base of my head, fingers pressing against my nape with enough pressure to send tingles down my spine. Breath is locked in my chest as he angles my head toward his, lowering his face right in front of mine. He's all I see, blocking out everything else until he's all that exists.

"*My own good*?" The question is like a snarl, caught in the web of scales on his cheek. His voice is *right there*, felt against my lips like the sweep of a tongue, sinking past my ears and settling into my chest and making my entire body go on alert.

My ribbons are as frozen as the rest of me, snakes caught in the eyes of a charmer. "Y-yes."

The intensity of his gaze lights a fire in my belly. "*My own good* was stuck on a pirate ship, with an aura like a beacon that flared across the Barrens," he grits out, a thick spun voice meant to tie knots around me. "*My own good* was cowering before men who were nothing— *fucking nothing*—in comparison to her."

All of my ability to breathe is gone as I stare at him in shock.

"*My own good* hated me, fought me, argued with me, but I didn't care, because I watched her slowly come out of her shell, peeling back one layer at a time, and it was stunning." He raises a finger in front of my face. "I got one touch. One taste, and if it was an act of selfishness, then you should know, it certainly wasn't one-sided, Auren."

I can't blink.

I can't *think*.

"What...what are you saying?" My chest heaves with the breathless question, like undulating waves in an uncertain sea.

I might drown in the depths of his bottomless eyes.

His teeth snap together, as if my uncertainty sets him on edge. "I'm saying that *you* are *my own good*. And for you, I gave you a choice, but you chose *him*."

A storm rattles in my skull. A coiled collection of impregnated clouds billowing through my head, thundering through my pulse and threatening rain to fall at my cheeks.

But you chose him.

"Rip—"

"You will always choose him. That's what you told me."

I flinch at my own words that he tosses back in my face, a tumultuous deluge sluicing past the dam of my cracking walls.

"Is it still true?" he asks, like a desperate demand.

Water beads against my lids, a golden gaze hinged to pitch-black. The first drop trickles down my cheek, squeezing past my splintering resolve. But when I open my mouth to answer him, no words come.

Instead, Rip moves, and I move with him, wind and rain in harmonious tandem. My body turns, and he steps between my legs where I'm perched on the railing, one hand braced to my right, arm curled against my side to keep me from falling. That thumb against the nape of my neck holds firm, fingers dug into my loose hair.

When his mouth comes down, when it's against my cheek to soak up the tear, I forget how to breathe. His firm lips take in my riot, like he wants to sip from my soul.

And I want to let him.

Pressing closer and closer, we act like we aren't in Ranhold Castle where any number of people could be watching, but in a private void of our own making, a place where nothing else exists.

His mouth skims past my cheekbone, just below my ear, hot breath breezed against the sensitive skin. My hands tighten against the railing on either side of me, and I don't dare move, not with my thighs already squeezing his hips, not when all I want to do is turn my head and fuse my lips against his.

"Tell a truth for a truth," he murmurs, voice pebbling my skin.

"Or keep a secret for a secret," I finish.

A hot tongue darts out, brined with the salt of my tear, and I have to suppress a moan. The dangerous pinch of his teeth land against my neck, making my head tilt in precarious invitation.

His hand moves until he's cupping my jaw like he's ready to drink right from my lips.

"Tell me, Auren."

Fear widens my eyes, clearing some of the lusty haze. It hammers my heart, makes my mouth go dry. His words seem simple, but he's asking for *everything*. If I give in, if I speak out, there will be no going back.

He's a male. A king. Someone with secrets and plans. I don't want to repeat my mistakes, and I'm terrified of getting hurt again.

A tortured whisper drizzles out with the shake of my head. *"I can't."*

Disappointment drenches us both.

For a long moment, we just look at each other, soaking in dreary regret.

And then Rip pulls away, leaving me to sway, to roll without roots.

"Let's get you to your room," he says.

I can only nod, unable to look him in the eye for fear of what I'll see there.

In the span of a breath, his warmth, his intimate touch, it's gone. The openness, the softness, they're replaced by cold detachment, so remote that it's like we're suddenly a world apart.

The distance is agonizing.

CHAPTER 16

AUREN

*R*ip plucks me off the railing. His hold is different now, like he's mentally already let go. His touch withdrawn.

I hate it.

I hate that I hate it.

I hate that this is so *hard*. So confusing. So terrifying.

My bottom lip quivers, but I bite down on it. Regret blooms in the pit of my stomach, festering and weighty. Yet I'm too terrified of this constant pull between us, too scared of making the wrong call. His words and touches have left me with a clamor, the ruckus too deafening to think through.

Rip isn't Midas, I know that. So far, he's never used me, even when it would've benefited him. So maybe deep down I'm fighting that notion, that fear I have that he'll hurt me like Midas did. Which is why I hear myself admitting, "I don't choose him. Not anymore. I'm choosing *me*."

Rip's stride falters for a single footstep. Just a breadth of boot over the carpeted runner beneath his feet, but I feel it when my words stick to his soles. But then his steps resume, sure and steady, no reply forthcoming, and I wonder if maybe I imagined it.

All too soon, or maybe after way too long, we're outside my door. Scofield is there with another guard I don't recognize.

"My lady?" he asks, eyes going wide. "What—"

"Lady Auren fell on the stairs," Rip explains. "I'm taking her inside."

Scofield tries to address me again, but Rip fits the key into the lock and carries me inside without missing a beat or giving the guards a chance to do anything. With a kick to the door, he closes it behind us, eyes sweeping the darkening room, the fire nearly gone out.

"Where do you want me to set you?"

My throat squeezes at the indifference in his tone. "The balcony. Please." I need to feel the fresh air. I need to breathe in the night and let my lungs fill with something other than the warmth of Rip's chest. Maybe that will help to dissipate this swarm of emotions hopping beneath my skin.

With a terse nod, he crosses the room, grabbing a

pillow and blanket from the bed on his way. He opens the glass balcony door and drops the pillow onto the chair before setting me on it. The blanket is draped around me, but even that doesn't staunch the cold loss I feel as soon as he's no longer touching me.

My lips part to say something, *anything*, to try and lessen these miles between us. But he's already turned away, past the balcony and back into my room without so much as a goodbye. I suppose I don't deserve one, anyway.

With a shaky exhale, I turn from the doors and settle into the chair, wrapping the downy blanket tight around me as I try to tell myself this is for the best.

I feel my overheated body cool, feel the overtaxed sweat go dry against my burnished skin. But even in the quiet, stark air, my thoughts don't even out, my emotions don't stop swirling.

I keep replaying every wickedly exquisite second we shared as he held me braced on the railing. I keep feeling the scrape of his lips against my skin and the way his solid arms held me against his chest. How is it that I could feel so safe in his arms, and yet in such danger at the same time?

My body may be tired, but the interaction with Rip has left my mind buzzing.

Those things he said...

My own good. How in the world can I be anyone's *good* when I feel so bad?

Another tear makes the trek down my face, and I don't even bother swiping it away. I just lean back, head pillowed by the blanket against the high back chair, my eyes closed to the cold.

I've no idea how long I sit there while the night grows darker, but a blanket of black has covered the sky when the sound of footsteps jolts me from my agonized contemplation.

Looking over, I find Rip's silhouette lit up by the fire he must've coaxed back to life in my room. I hadn't even heard him moving around in there. I thought he'd left. There's a tray of food in his hand that he sets down on the small iron table next to me, the smell of sugared rolls immediately filling my nose.

"You brought me food?"

"A servant came to the door to deliver it," he tells me, tone carefully guarded. "You should eat. It might help with the power drain."

My mouth waters at the sight of it as I sit up, tucking the blanket around me so I can free my arms. "I'm starved." I cast him a quick look through my lashes. "Thank you."

He gives me a single nod and then turns to leave, but I find my hand shooting out to catch his arm before I even realize what I'm doing. We both stare down at my gloved fingers curled around his wrist, and I'm not sure which of us is more shocked that I grabbed him.

I quickly let go, a flush rising over my cooled face.

"Sorry, I didn't..." I clear my throat. "I mean… Do you want to stay and eat with me?"

Vulnerable. That quiet question is so very vulnerable.

Maybe all my good sense drained out through my palms right along with the gold, but I don't want him to go. There's this cavern split inside of me, a bleak loneliness that widened the moment I denied him the truth.

Rip stares down at me but says nothing, and shame crawls over me like creeping ants, making me want to itch. What I'm doing isn't fair to either of us.

I should've hardened myself against him just like I did with Midas. I want to. I've tried to. So why can't I hate him, like I hate Midas? It would make everything so much easier.

I can see in his conflicted face that he's going to deny me, shut me down just like I did to him on the railing. So I beat him to it.

"Never mind. Thank you for carrying me upstairs."

He just stares down at me, expression unreadable in the dark.

"Really," I say nervously. "Don't feel obligated to stay with me just because I asked. It's probably a bad idea, anyway. I have a power hangover, and after that moment on the railing..." I trail off, like my blush has stolen my voice. "Anyway. I'm still furious with you for lying to me, you know, and it's obvious you're angry with me now too, so it's probably better that you don't stay anyway."

He shakes his head, looking up at the sky for a moment as if he's trying to see if he can find some patience tucked away with the budding stars. Maybe he finds some after all, because he lets out a breath and says, "Well, with an invitation like that, how could I resist?"

To my surprise, he sits down in the chair next to me, and I'm not sure if I'm more freaked out or relieved.

I watch him from the corner of my eye as we begin to eat the food on the tray together, always careful that our hands don't touch, not even letting them get within an inch of each other. My nerves are extra aware of him, and I swear I see his gaze keep landing on the side of my neck, following the path where his mouth traveled.

This was *definitely* a bad idea.

For a few minutes, the silence between us is a burden. It's carried on our tense shoulders, groped by stiff hands. But slowly, the weight of it comes off, slipping into something easier, something familiar. For a moment, I can almost pretend we're back with his army, sharing the quiet of the tent.

I devour two sugared rolls, some honeyed ham, and fruit dipped in cherry-red syrup. I've found that the food here is always sweet and sticky, though I don't really mind right now, since every time I lick my fingers, I feel Rip's eyes cut over to me.

When we've cleared the entire tray, I feel better, no longer like I might topple over any second. With a mug of steamed mead cradled in my palms, I lean back with a sigh just as it begins to snow. The flakes tear off from the clouds, falling like confetti paper ripped off onto a parchment ground.

Soft, slow, comforting.

I look up, letting snow fall onto my lashes, and when I turn to glance at Rip, I find he's already looking at me.

"So, still angry at me?" he asks with a wry tinge to his tone. I leap at it, relieved to end the silence, to move past the rebuttal on the stairwell.

"Furious."

Rip tips his head down, as if he expected nothing less.

"You?" I ask him.

"Livid."

Our mouths twitch in synchronicity, shared smirks tipping up at the corners.

He leans back in his chair, the spikes along his back disappearing beneath his leathers. "We're quite the pair, you and I."

At his words, chills scatter over my arms, even though I'm wrapped beneath the blanket. "What do you mean?"

There's an enigmatic look on his face that I can't decipher, and he opens his mouth to answer, but appears to reconsider, going silent once more. Flakes of snow land on his black hair, soaking into the inky locks while he considers me with that intensity I've grown so accustomed to.

"It's remarkable, you know."

"What is?" I ask.

"We might be the last two fae in the entire world, and somehow, our paths crossed that night."

His words from before, about how my aura was a beacon that he followed, make a lump appear in my throat. "Fate does funny things."

"It does," he murmurs, thumb brushing against his bottom lip as he regards me.

"Can I ask you a question?"

He arches a brow. "You know the rules."

"You know enough of my secrets," I reply with exasperation. "I want to know how you're tricking everyone. I saw you outside the stables, with Fake Rip."

His eyes dance. "You mean when you were checking me out."

My face immediately grows hot, and my mouth pops open. "I was *not* checking you out!"

His white teeth gleam in the night. "Little liar."

I cross my arms. "Well?" I demand, trying my best not to look flustered.

"Well what?" he deflects with a grin.

"Figures," I grumble. "Alright, then tell me this, why do they really call you Rip?" The question has been plucking at me, an itch I can't find to scratch.

He crosses his ankles in front of him as he stretches out, and my eyes fall to his strong thighs before lifting back up again. "Now *that* is an interesting answer."

I can't stop myself from leaning forward more, like a dog being teased with a bone. "*And*?"

"And...I'll tell you one day."

The prick.

I roll my eyes and sit back. "When?"

His lips tilt up, making him look entirely too sexy for his own good. "When you're no longer furious with me."

Taking a sip of my drink, I enjoy the warmth that blooms in my chest as it travels down. "Fine, keep your secrets."

"I do. As I keep yours."

His reply makes my stomach tie in knots. I know I'm sitting here in the night, pretending. Pretending that he's not King Ravinger, pretending that he doesn't have his own plots and ploys.

"And *why* are you keeping my secrets?" I ask carefully.

We're already so far down this gully, I figure why not go a little further? This might be the only chance we have at such open honesty, while our walls are splintered beneath a paper torn night.

"Because it suits me to do so." I'm pinned with the pierce of his eyes just like a needle to a moth's wings, and the sting is the same.

Like pebbles on an ocean floor, disappointment settles in the bottom of my gut. A warning, then. That just because it suits him for *now*, it doesn't mean it will suit him always. If it were Midas, he'd wait to use the information until exactly the right moment. It's what most kings would do.

I suppose the flutters of stomachs and squeezes of hearts just can't be trusted. Everything that happened tonight—him carrying me, his words, the heat of his hips caught between my thighs as his lips grazed my cheek—they were stolen moments. Moments that we can't afford to have. Not with our goals so misaligned. Maybe as Rip and Goldfinch, but as Ravinger and Auren? Never.

As much as I wish that things were simpler, different...they're not, and I can't pretend otherwise.

Rip straightens up. "And there it is."

"There *what* is?"

He gestures at my face, as if he's read some secret from it. "You just remembered I'm King Slade Ravinger and not just...this."

I don't deny it. I can't. Part of me feels guilty about that, but it's the truth. If he were just Rip, this wouldn't be so hard.

"I can't trust kings." It's impossible to keep the sound of regret from my voice. To keep the silent wish from weighing down the words.

He leans forward, bent elbows braced against his knees. "You can trust me."

The desperation shows. I know it does, because I can't help the way my eyes flare, the way my body bends toward him. "*Prove it.*" Not dismissive. Not filled with doubt. My words are pleading with him, *demanding* for him to do just that.

Please, prove it.

As if he can hear my imploring, Rip unwinds from the chair. His powerful body stands up straight, spikes slowly rising from his arms and back like claws extending from a predator's paw.

Slowly, that predator in him brings his body closer to mine, one deliberate step at a time. His hands come down on either armrest at my sides, and I plaster my head against the back of the chair as he leans in and steals up all the air.

"I will," he murmurs, and I let out a puff of a gasp.

Right in front of my eyes, Rip morphs, magic swirling around him like wisps of steam. I'm held immobilized by the waves of his power that gently pulse out. Onyx eyes turn mossy green, scales disappear along with the spikes, ears and bones soften, and tiny fissures reach up his neck to root beneath the scruff of his beard.

My heart pounds uncontrollably as I look at the face of King Ravinger, my hands going slick where they're bunched in the blanket. Pale skin, forest-green eyes, so masculine and gorgeous that it almost hurts to look at him.

"I'm glad you're choosing you," he says quietly, and my lips part, like I want to swallow the rumble of his cadence.

"You are?"

I go completely still as he moves his hand and grips my chin, like he wants to make sure I'm paying attention.

I am.

"Yes, Goldfinch. Because I'm choosing you, too."

Like a ribbon caught on a wind-bent branch, he lowers, and I lift.

My lips land on his, his tongue sweeps against mine, and then we're suddenly kissing like we're *starved*.

We kiss like two stars colliding, our heat flaring with the threat to burn, while the cold world around us fades in our light. We kiss like we need the taste of one another or we'll never be able to emerge from the dark.

My entire body bends toward him, every ribbon unwinding, stretching, reaching for him like wings reach for a breeze.

His hand moves to encase my jaw, angling me right where he wants me, and just that—the dominance of him, the strength but utter care—it makes me feel like I could burn forever.

The fire beneath my skin has nothing to do with anger or vendettas. This is pure, hungry, aching *want* that thrums in the pulse of my veins, refusing to be ignored.

When I nibble on his tongue, he bites down on my bottom lip with an erotic twinge that sweeps a moan from my mouth. He drinks in the sound, calloused hands cradling my face firmly, like he doesn't want me to slip from his grip.

My ribbons trail out like vines, slinking up his body, wrapping around his arms to pull him closer. A guttural groan thunders from his chest at that, and he deepens the kiss even more, until it's not just my skin that's hot, but a needy fire that's ignited between my legs. He stokes that need even higher when one hand skims down to stroke my ribbons, making a delicious shiver trickle along my back.

Just a kiss. One kiss, and I'm wrecked, because I never want this to stop.

I never realized that a kiss could be like this.

My hands brace against his shoulders again, like I need the reminder that he'll hold me up, fingers digging into the strong muscles beneath the leather. I resent my gloves. I want to feel him, skin to skin, but I can't stop to pull them off.

Flakes fall from the sky, dusting us with their chill, but the cold has no hope of touching us. I'm hot all over, passion kindled with an aching temptation of more. I think I'd come right out of my seat if he weren't bowing over me, his body the lure I'm trying to hook to.

But just when I'm ready to drag him down with me, his lips leave mine.

Our breaths are quickened, the blanket a forgotten pile pooling at my waist. I stare at him as my chest heaves in a rapid pitch, lips tingling with the echo of his hold.

His gaze caresses over my face, and mine does the same, my finger coming up to trace the lines of his rooting power, noting the faint shifting beneath my touch.

He pulls away, or...he *tries* to. We both look down at my mess of ribbons wrapped around him, like they've decided to make him their own personal present.

"Sorry..." I say, suddenly embarrassed, moving to quickly tug them off, though they come away begrudgingly.

Ravinger gives me a crooked smile and tucks a strand of hair behind my ear with such gentleness that my throat constricts. "Hopefully that clears things up."

He straightens up, and even though the sight of him still has my pulse racing, it's not in fear. Not anymore. His timing of that transformation was deliberate. Because his form might change, his eyes, his stance, his name, but those lips, his hands, his words, his *heat*...they're the same.

Rip and Ravinger are the same, and it took a kiss for that to really sink in.

As he turns away, he's already changing again, bringing back the spikes, the scales, the unforgiving stride of a warrior, but it's still him.

He stops at the balcony door and looks back at me, the last of his green eyes ebbing away. "Goodnight, Auren."

It's still him.

Which is why I murmur, "Goodnight...Slade."

His eyes widen for an infinitesimal moment, belying his shock that I've called him by his first name. Then his lips curl up, my ribbons curling too, as if we're sharing something private, intimate. Something poignant between us.

Maybe we are.

When he's gone, I sit back in my chair, blanket forgotten, unnecessary after the heat we invoked. In the silent snowfall, I whisper his name again, just a few more times, a single-word plea to the cluster of hidden stars above.

Please, let him prove it.

CHAPTER 17

QUEEN MALINA

What *used to be old,* frostbitten stone is now weathered gold bricks that nip at my hands as I lean against the yawning mouth of the tower's archway.

A rare peek of sun has hammered through split-apart clouds, the waning daylight brightening the bell behind me. The golden reflection beats from its surface, engulfing my back in a judgmental glare.

Highbell's bell tower is so high up, I'm told over a hundred workers lost their lives during its construction, though that didn't stop my ancestors from seeing it through to the end.

We Coliers don't give in.

Which is why the sight far below me, in the heart of the city, grates against my nerves like a plow scouring the surface and churning up what lies beneath.

Riots.

Everywhere.

From the filthy shanties to the upscale boutiques, the city has risen against me.

Looting is rampant, and desecration of royal property is nonstop in the square. The constabulary is being attacked every time they try to step in and make arrests. I watch it all from the tower, the bell at my back, gleaming with disgust as its people revolt beneath.

I had them.

For a moment, I *had* them. I was on the throne, ruling as I always should have. I was winning nobles, reviving Highbell to its former glory, repositioning myself—a true Colier—as the rightful ruler.

Everything was falling into place.

Until it all started falling apart.

The mobs are nothing but speckles in the city proper, clumps moving together. They're burning, pillaging, and just generally breaking laws, until the city's constabulary can cut them off. The problem is, when one rampage is subdued, it seems two more crop up.

My fingers curve in like claws, fingernails scraping the frost that's gathered on the gilded sill, the cold air soaking into my skin. Three days, this has been going on, and every minute that passes in which these people do not come to heel, is another tick mark against them. I tried to be the kind queen. Benevolent with offerings, reminding them that it was *Midas* who let them starve, let them despair and ebb into poverty.

Yet, they've turned on *me*.

The muscle in my jaw kinks, a dull ache shooting through my ground teeth.

When another fire blazes to life in the city, I turn away with disgust. All four of my Queen's guards are silent as I turn for the spiral stairs, its golden steps gone black from too many trodden heels.

It's a dizzying way down as my pale hand grips the railing, curving walls mocking me with the staircase's endless corkscrew.

When I finally reach the bottom, I'm berated by a biting wind while I walk through the open-walled walkway to yet another set of stairs and then finally back into the castle.

Inside, the air is thick with the scent of paint.

The walls are thick with it, too.

Two dozen carpenters. That's how many workers have been hired to paint over every gaudy surface or build around them to hide it.

And yet everywhere I look, there are blemishes. Where the walls are painted white, nicks have appeared. Where floors have been covered, the rugs have slipped. Where wood has been nailed over table tops and window frames, gaps loom, like slitted smirks meant to mock me.

Highbell has become a living, breathing castle that

sneers at me through every gilded surface. If I don't get it all covered, if I don't erase every last inch that's been polluted, I'm going to go mad.

This is all his fault.

He took my home from me, turned it into a mockery of itself. Turned *me* into a mockery of myself.

As I walk past the main hall, Tyndall's message thrums in my head. He thinks he can make me perform by dangling a bastard child in front of my face? I'd rather kiss his feet, and *that* will be a cold day in hell.

I will never claim his bastard, and without me doing so, that child can never be an heir, can never have Highbell.

Neither of them can, because it's *mine*.

I look into doorways as I pass. "Where are my advisors?" I ask no one in particular.

"I'm not sure, my queen." The answer comes from my head guard, his answer hesitant.

"Well, send someone to find them," I snap impatiently.

He jerks his head at one of the other guards, the man slipping away to go locate them.

A frown pulls at my lips as I glance around the empty hall again, hearing no noise, seeing no one at work. "Where are the carpenters? Shouldn't I be hearing hammers and seeing ladders braced on the walls?"

He shifts on his feet, silver chest plate showing my mottled reflection. I can see my pale face scrunched up in irritation, white hair swept up at the top of my head.

"The carpenters have not come since the riots began, Your Majesty."

My nostrils flare. Those lazy, insufferable fools. They're probably in the city, getting drunk and using the riots as an excuse not to work. "Fine. Then their contracts are hereby terminated, *without* pay. I want people willing to work here by tomorrow morning."

The guards share a look, but I don't care. I won't tolerate such a lack of respect. During my father's reign, no one would *dare* skip out on a day's work in the palace. It was considered an honor to do the bidding of the Coliers.

"Am I clear?"

"Yes, Your Majesty."

Turning my back on him, I decide to go up to my rooms. My temples are beginning to ache, and I could do with some food.

Yet before I can get to the stairs, a servant rushes forward. "Your Majesty, you have a guest in the drawing room."

My lips nearly lift into a sneer. "*Who?*"

"Sir Loth Pruinn."

An impatient sigh scratches up my throat. The charlatan. The silver-eyed merchant who fancies himself a fortune teller. Ever since his cart blocked my carriage that day in the city, he's been dropping in unannounced.

I nearly threw him out the first time he did it, except he came with the one thing I couldn't resist, and it had nothing to do with a trick map claiming to show the way to achieve my greatest desire.

He came with baubles to sell, sure, but what he was *really* peddling was information. Sir Pruinn quickly realized how to make himself worth my time, and he's been feeding me information about the city and the people ever since.

It's why I knew the unrest was spreading. Why I wasn't surprised when the riots broke out days ago. Unfortunately, once a rebellion lights, it can catch as easily as a spark on dry grass.

"Fine," I say, spinning on my heel.

I enter the drawing room, finding Pruinn lounging on the cushioned chair, an overflowing shoulder bag resting on his lap like a lumpy pet.

Entering the room, I greet him coolly. "Pruinn."

The blond man stands regally, his bag clinking when he rolls into a bow. As always, his clothes are impeccable, an ice-blue tunic heavy with furred trappings, his jaw clean-shaven, the hair on his head only an inch above his scalp.

"Queen Malina, you look indefectible, as always."

I give him an unimpressed look before flicking my hand behind me. "Leave us."

The guards file out, door closing behind them as I take a seat across from Pruinn. The room is cold, the windows along the outer wall cracked open in hopes of airing out the paint fumes. It's been days since the walls were covered, but it takes ages to dry with such cold leaching through.

"I'm not interested in your trinkets and clutter today, Pruinn, so that better not be why you're here."

He sits down, tucking that knapsack back onto his lap, arching a darker brow up high. "Are you sure? I've a very exotic perfume from a merchant you can only find in the sand dunes of Second Kingdom."

I don't even dignify that with a response.

Pruinn's expression gleams with amusement. "Right then. Well, the city is rioting."

"I can see that," I snipe. "Do you have *real* information, or are you trying to wear my patience? Because I can assure you, I'm not to be trifled with today."

Instead of looking chastised, he leans forward, elbows braced on his knees. "Do you know someone by the name of Gifford?"

My blink is the only thing that gives away my surprise at hearing that name. "Yes, he's Tyndall's messenger. He came from Fifth to deliver me a letter," I say sharply.

"Well, he's not *just* a messenger."

One of my hands folds over the armrest of the chair. "Explain."

His gray eyes practically glint with an eagerness to divulge. I never knew traveling merchants could be such insufferable gossips, but I'll reap the benefits regardless.

"Apparently, when you gave your answer, King Midas ordered the man to act accordingly. He sent off the hawk and stayed behind."

Unease slithers up my back. "For what purpose?"

"He's been meandering throughout the city. Pub to pub, inn to inn, storefront to storefront," Pruinn leans forward. "Everywhere he goes, he's been rousing the unrest. Ruffling up the grumblers. Making it spread. He's the drip that has caused the ripple of riots."

My fingers dig into the painted wood armrest, the claggy white color stuffing full beneath my nails. "Are you telling me that Midas ordered this messenger to escalate the unrest?"

Pruinn gives a resolute nod. "Yes."

A hiss pours from between tight teeth, and I spring to my feet, pacing toward the window to peer outside. I can see nothing but the side of the mountain and an edge of surrounding castle walls, but I glare out of it anyway. I stare as if I can look straight into the city, right to that scoundrel Gifford as he spins his messages, leading the people like frenzied sheep with a sudden taste for blood.

"I want him killed."

"No doubt," he replies, completely unruffled by my declaration. "Unfortunately, he's already gone. Flown away on his timberwing yesterday."

The brisk wind feeds in through the crack of the open

window and bites into my stomach, but it has nothing on my gnawing fury.

Tyndall's fault.

All of it.

After a moment of icy anger crystallizing in my chest, I turn around. "I gather you're capable of seeing yourself out, Sir Pruinn," I say coolly before I start to walk away.

"Of course, Your Majesty," he replies easily, unfolding from the chair to dip into another bow. "Have you given more thought to the map?"

I stop at the door, shooting him a look over my shoulder. "There is nothing to gain in Seventh Kingdom, Sir Pruinn, least of all my greatest desire," I snip. "Good day." My dismissal has me yanking open the door, and if he says anything in reply, I don't hear it. Not over the raucous lividity that's playing in my head.

My guards are quick to shadow me when I pass the hall, determined steps taking me upstairs while my headache twinges with a newfound furor.

Just as I reach my doors, the fourth guard rushes up, his breath coming in quick pants.

"Well?" I prompt. "Did you find my advisors?"

"No, Your Majesty, but when I went to ask the patrol outside, I was informed that the rioters have taken to the road, and the constabulary was unable to keep them blocked off. They're heading for the walls."

My very veins seethe. "What do they want?"

He shifts nervously on his feet. "Well...it appears they're coming with makeshift weapons. I think they mean to try and storm the castle."

"I want them stopped," I grit out, pale eyes pinning each and every man standing at attention. "Do you hear me?"

My head guard nods immediately. "At once, my queen. We will set up the blockades. No one will get—"

"No." I shake my head. "We need to make an example of them. Remind the people that an attack like this is not tolerated." I take a step closer, uncaring that I'm a foot shorter than him, because *I* wear the crown. "I want them all *slaughtered*. Anyone comes within two hundred feet of the walls, I want them cut down like the ungrateful animals they are."

I turn and go into my room, slamming the door behind me, leaving behind four grim-faced guards.

These people want to rise up and threaten their queen? Want to rampage their city and defy my laws? Then I'll have every last rebel killed, and ring the bell in the tower as the frost covers their thankless corpses.

I'll remind them that there's a reason I'm the Cold Queen.

CHAPTER 18

AUREN

My power burnout must've been really bad, because I sleep right through the next day. When I finally drag myself awake, dusk isn't far off, the last hours of day burning through the windows.

I stretch and yawn as I get up, rubbing at my eyes. I strip out of my wrinkled dress and pull on a silk robe and a pair of gloves, though I'm just going through the motions. My mind is full of the man who haunted my dreams, his words a heartbreaking melody that won't stop replaying.

I'm saying that you are my own good.

And for you, I gave you a choice.

But you chose him.

My tongue drags against my lips, like I might still get a lingering taste. I don't know if I'll ever forget the feel of him or ever lose the thrill I felt when he looked me in the eye and told me that he was choosing me. It makes my heart feel so hopeful and yet so damn terrified too.

With an anxious sigh, I run my hands through my tangled hair and grab the fae book I stuffed under my mattress, before I take a seat on the gilded chair in front of the fireplace. I was woken up earlier when the servant came in to build up the flames and bring new wood, though I groaned at the unwelcome presence of the two guards monitoring her. Luckily, they were all out again before I even cracked open both eyes, and none of them said a word.

Digby would've grunted at me, telling me in that wordless way of his to stop moping around, but that thought just makes my stomach twist with a hurt I can't ease.

Tucking my feet underneath me, I stare off into the fire and look through the book absentmindedly when a knock sounds on the door. For a second, my heart beats wildly, like it might be Slade on the other side, though I know that's a stupid thought. Setting the book down, I wander over to the door, cracking it open to find Scofield.

I'm careful to keep my body mostly hidden, since the robe only reaches my knees. "Yes?"

"My lady, King Midas has summoned you," Scofield tells me, though his tone is formal, and he's not quite looking me in the eye, probably because of my state of undress. "You're to meet him in the formal dining room in an hour."

"Alright...did he say why?" Up until now, he's preferred that I stay shut away in my rooms during the day unless I'm gilding the damn castle. This summons is reminiscent of when I'd be called to formal meals in Highbell...and not in a good way.

"Her Majesty the Queen of Third Kingdom arrived last night. King Midas and Prince Niven are hosting a welcome meal in her honor."

"Is that so," I say under my breath, my mind already working. It won't be dusk for a while yet, so I'll have to be careful. "Thanks for the heads-up, Scofield."

I move to shut the door, but he raises a hand, stopping me. My brows pull together. "Is something wrong?"

Scofield looks just over my shoulder. "No, but...we are also to assess your rooms."

I look between him and the other unfamiliar guard, and irritation roots my bare feet right into the ground. "*Now?*"

"Yes, my lady."

For a second, I envision slamming the door in his face, but that would really only be satisfying if it were Midas standing here.

Instead, I spin on my heel and walk away, leaving the door ajar behind me, letting Scofield and *three* more guards file inside.

None of them will look at me.

Systematically, they all start checking the entire space. I'd forgotten how much I hated Midas's random room checks. Back in Highbell, they were often. But no matter how many times it happened, I never stopped hating them. They always feel like such an invasion of privacy, reminding me that even though these are my rooms, they aren't really *mine*.

Midas could've had this done while I was gone, but he purposely has me in here while they're doing it. As a warning, maybe, to remember that everything belongs to him.

My eyes fly to the book I haphazardly left on the chair. I look back at the guards, but so far, they're all near the bed. I hold back the urge to run and take measured steps instead. The second I'm sitting down, I stuff the book beneath my thighs and fix my robe to make sure it's hidden.

Body tense, I watch the guards sweep the room with meticulous attention. One of them even has a little piece of parchment in his hand that he keeps referring to, and based on the way he's counting my pillows, I know it's a tally mark of all the possessions I should have.

The sheets and blankets on my bed are scrutinized. The rugs and curtains are checked, the chairs and walls examined. I wonder if they know why they're doing this or if they count it as another one of Midas's controlling tendencies.

My eyes follow them as they turn over everything in my bedroom before moving on to the dressing room and bathroom.

The sound of fabric shuffling around and shoe boxes being opened comes from one door, while quieter scrutiny happens in the other. By the time they all come filing back out, I'm simmering in both irritation and anxiousness, though I try not to show it. I braid my hair and keep my legs still, the forbidden book digging into my skin like the pinch of a lie.

The men are just about to leave when Scofield walks over to me. "Sorry, my lady. The chair. Could you…?"

My heart slams against my chest so hard I worry it's going to crash right through. I grip the reins of my panic and shove them down, reminding myself that none of them have permission to physically move me.

"Scofield, do you really expect me to get up in my current state? It's not appropriate. I'm not properly *dressed*," I say with as much indignation as I can muster, my hand sweeping down my body. "Midas wouldn't like it."

His cheeks redden, and he immediately backs up. "I—apologies, my lady. Of course you should stay there."

With fire in my eyes, I nod and then watch as he spins on his heel. The men do another cursory look around for any unapproved paraphernalia, checking the list every two seconds like a cook with a recipe to make sure nothing is missing.

Finally, all of them leave, Scofield unable to even look at me as he goes and shuts the door behind him. I let out a relieved breath and pull the book out from under me.

I was too careless, and that's one thing I can't afford to be. I need to return this book the first chance I get. I don't know if Midas would care that I had it or not, but he'd certainly question it. He might know a lot of things about me, but being fae is one secret I've never told him, thank the Divine. To him, I'm just a very powerful Orean, my ancestors' fae magic not as diluted.

This room sweep is also precisely why I can't turn anything gold in my room and sneak it to Rissa. Everything I have, everything I use, is accounted for. Evaluated. Checked.

Midas is always making sure that not a single piece is missing, whether by my hand or someone else's. He used to say the checks were to ensure that nothing had been stolen or broken. But really, he likes to make sure I'm not doing anything secret with the things I've gold-touched. As if it all belongs to him. As if it's *his* power that's made anything of worth.

I need to take another trip to the library soon, but for now, I have a dinner to get to. Spurred into action, I force myself to head into the dressing room to get ready. The evidence of the search is very apparent in here, dresses scrunched together on the hanging racks, hat and shoe boxes opened and shoved against the wall. Every drawer in the bureau is open too, gloves and undergarments in counted piles while perfume bottles lie knocked over.

With a gritted sigh, I hide the book inside one of the hanging dresses, cinching up the bodice ties to hold it in place. When I'm satisfied it won't fall out, I strip off my robe and look through the gowns with an assessing eye so I can choose what to wear.

I'm not sure what I'm walking into in that dining room, but I know that whenever royalty is involved, there are always plots and plans. Midas will have his schemes, and I'm sure the queen will have hers.

I rack my mind, trying to remember exactly what I know about Third's Queen. I know she's a young widow. She married someone much older than her, and he died not long after. Since she has power and the legacy, she kept the throne, but I can't for the life of me remember what her power is, and that leaves me feeling uneasy.

In my defense, I've tried blocking out everything about Third Kingdom. That land brings up memories I want no part of. I was stuck in Derfort Harbor for *ten years*, owned by a flesh trader whose only stake in life was acquiring wealth on the backs of children.

This queen wasn't ruling during that time, but I'm still wary. Whenever I think of Third Kingdom, my mind irrevocably puts me right back there as the painted beggar girl. The girl who almost didn't get away.

Shoving aside those thoughts, I shuffle through the

dresses, snagging one that's already been turned gold by my touch. The corset on this one is visible, the stiff fabric stitched around the outside.

I get dressed, harden the edge of one ribbon, then cut a short line down the back. This way, my ribbons won't be squished uncomfortably against my spine, and the corset will stay up, but not squeeze the life out of me. Win-win.

Once I get my top secured, I have my ribbons drape around the gauzy skirt in wide hanging arcs before tucking the ends behind me in a loose bow. I grab a pair of silk slippers and gloves appropriate for dinner, and then set the task of taming my hair in a long braid that I wrap around my head like my very own version of a crown.

When I'm done, I leave my room and step out into the corridor. Scofield leads the way, while two more guards follow behind me. I should probably feel nervous that I'm about to be shoved into a royal welcome dinner, but I'm not.

I've spent far too many years being nervous. Being timid and worried. Always trying to make the first impression that Midas wanted me to make, whether that was shy or seductive, adoring or proud. He always had an angle to play.

With King Fulke, it was the lure of having me visible but not accessible. Teasing the man with me present in the background but always in my cage. There for him to covet, but unattainable.

I don't know what Midas's angle will be with the queen, but whatever it is, I hold no stake in it anymore. I'm not on Midas's side. It's not my goal to please him other than behaving enough to keep Digby safe.

Once downstairs and past the main hall, I walk through the doors into the formal dining room. The focal point of the space is the long glass table in the middle of the floor. It's at least six inches thick, with bluish veins running through it to make it look glacial. Stretching along the top, the glass has been blown to spike up in jagged crystals like upside down icicles jutting from the center.

All around the table are high back chairs with plush purple cushions, enough seats for three dozen people. Unfortunately, nearly all of them are occupied.

I recognize a few of them: Midas's advisors, Fulke's advisors who used to visit with him in Highbell, but there are new faces too, I'm assuming from the queen's kingdom.

The royals are congregated in the middle, looking across at each other between spires of fake icicles that are lit up between flickering candles. Midas sits with the prince at his left, their advisors sprinkled off to the side. With her back to me sits the woman who must be the queen. There's really no question, not with the glittering crown resting on her head, thick sable hair securing it in place with pins of pearls and sea stars.

When I'm halfway across the room, Midas looks up from his discussion and raises a hand to beckon me over. Keeping my steps unhurried and even, I let my eyes sweep across the faces that turn to track my arrival.

Above me, the chandeliers throw off crystalline light, and there's a harp in front of the windows behind the table. A fireplace is roaring off to the left, big enough that I could walk inside and sleep on its logs.

I round the table, murmured voices lifting to my ears as people sip from wine goblets, waiting for dinner to arrive. At least I'll be able to stuff my face, because I suddenly realize that I'm starved.

As I reach his chair, Midas's assessing gaze roves up my form, not with appreciation, but with appraisal, like he's checking to make sure I'm suitable for his fancy supper. His eyes snag on the torn strip at the back of my dress, and a tic appears in his jaw. "Auren."

I nod and give him the same sort of evaluating look, just to irritate him. "King Midas."

Across the table, the queen of Third Kingdom arches a brow at my exchange. At the very least, a full curtsy would've been proper, but I won't bow to him anymore. The only reason I'll be bending the knee for him again is to jerk it right back up to hit him in the groin.

"So this is your golden girl..." The queen regards me with her attentive umber eyes, and I use the moment to do the same to her.

Her tawny complexion goes beautifully with the gown she's wearing, the buttermilk fabric molding to her curves, with wide buttons down the bodice that shine like diamonds.

"Yes, this is her." Midas's hand reaches over to run a knuckle up my sleeved forearm.

My ribbons tighten around my hips, the silken strips going hard like they want to lash out and smack his touch away. A creepy crawly feeling tapers down my skin as he continues to stroke me, and it takes everything in me to school my features and not yank my arm away.

"Auren, meet Queen Kaila Ioana of Third Kingdom."

I dip into a curtsy. "Your Majesty," I murmur. "I hope your travels to Fifth Kingdom weren't too taxing."

Her lush lips pull up at the corners. "Not nearly as taxing as I've heard *your* travels were," she replies. "Captured by the snow pirates, then taken by Fourth's army, all while traveling across the Barrens into Fifth." She makes a clicking noise. "It's a wonder you've made it in one piece."

"I was lucky that Fourth was there to intervene."

Midas stiffens and drops his hand, though he says nothing to dispute my words. He and I both know it's true. If I'd gone with the Red Raids, there's a good chance I'd be dead right now. So much has happened since then. If Fourth's army hadn't been there, I would still be that girl pining after her captor.

"Well, isn't she just a golden doll?"

My attention goes to the man sitting to the queen's right, and I immediately see the family resemblance.

"My most trusted advisor and brother, Manu," the queen introduces.

He has thick black hair pulled back tight at the nape of his neck, and he's wearing a yellow vest beneath his dress jacket, a tuft of silken fabric pooling out across the neckline. With one hand holding his goblet and the other flung across the back of the chair of the man sitting next to him, he gives me a look that I can only describe as delighted.

"Keon, don't you think she's a doll?" he asks, leaning into the man at his side.

Keon runs dark brown eyes over me, the shine from his bald head gleaming beneath the chandeliers and highlighting the dangling necklaces roped down his front. "She's taller than I thought she'd be," the slight man responds.

Manu nods. "And look at that *hair*." He leans in, the collared frills gaping down to reveal his tawny chest beneath. "Doll, you could sell that for barrels of coin."

"Umm...thank you?"

Queen Kaila shoots him a look. "Don't fluster King Midas's favored, brother. It's bad manners."

A dazzling smile encroaches over Manu's handsome face. "But being bad is so much more *fun*, dear sister."

She gives him a deadpan look, though it's impossible to miss the affection sparkling in her eyes.

"Ah, dinner is served."

Midas's announcement pulls everyone's attention to the dozen servants filing in from a doorway at the back and carrying platters of food.

"Auren."

I look over at Midas, who gestures to the empty seat at his right. My brows notch up in surprise. He's *never* had me sit beside him at a formal dinner, especially not at a table full of royals. I take a tentative seat, though my hackles are up, wheels churning. Because this isn't a boon. This isn't him showing me favor. I just don't know what his play is yet.

The servants begin to place heaping platters of food along the table, the scent of syrups and sugars immediately engulfing the air, while I silently hurry along the setting sun so I can eat and, more importantly, drink.

Picking up my goblet, I find it empty. That just won't do. "Excuse me, may I have some wine?" I ask the servant nearest me.

The girl dips her head and retreats as soon as her platter is set down. Up and down the table, voices are lobbed back and forth, everything boring and political. Since it's not night yet, I can't eat. Well...I *could*, but the moment it touched my lips, I'd be chewing on metallic gruel.

So instead, I pretend and make myself look busy. I drown out the talk by serving myself from the platter nearest me. Unfortunately, it doesn't look very appetizing, but it'll have to do. With my spoon held in my gloved hand, I stir around the coagulated sugary oats.

I'm really going to need some wine to wash this stuff down.

"So, Doll, I heard you got captured by the Fourth Commander hunk."

Startled, my eyes rise to Manu between two cerulean blue icicles of the table's glass centerpiece, finding his features lit up with mischievous intent.

I shoot Midas a look out of the corner of my eye, but he and Niven are talking about something. "Yes, I was."

"Now *there's* a story ripe for the dinner table." Eager eyes stay riveted on mine as one brow arches up. "I wouldn't mind being captured by him. All those *hard* spikes and *thick*...muscles."

I practically choke on my tongue, feeling my cheeks flaming with heat.

Beside him, Keon reaches over and stabs a hunk of meat right off Manu's plate and shoves it into his glowering mouth as he gives him a glare. Manu just laughs and smacks a kiss on his cheek. "Don't pretend you wouldn't jilt me in a second for that monster man."

Keon points his fork at him. "You jilt me, and I swear to the Divines, you will regret it."

"Ooh," Manu purrs. "How positively titillating."

Keon snorts.

My lips tilt up, their banter making this dinner seem not so awful after all. "How long have you two been married?"

"Three months," Manu chirps.

"Three *years*," Keon corrects with a roll of his eyes before he steals more food off his husband's plate.

"Ah, that's right," Manu says, plopping a grape in his mouth. "Time flies when you're riding good c—"

"*Carriages*," Keon quickly intervenes, cutting him off with an elbow to the arm, stealing hurried looks at the frowning advisors.

Manu grins at him, rubbing the spot where his husband jabbed him, and I think these are my two new favorite people ever.

"Do you guys play drinking games?" I ask, perking up.

Manu snaps his fingers and points at me. "See? I knew I liked you. I can always spot the fun ones."

With a smile, I try to find the damn serving girl, but she and my wine are still nowhere in sight. My mouth is watering from all the smells of the food. The very second the sun sets, I'll be stuffing my face and downing a cup.

"I've told the servants you're not to drink wine tonight."

Midas's words startle me, jerking my head in his direction. "Why not?"

He looks at me coolly, and there's something there, some flicker that I hadn't noticed until right now. "Because I said so."

The curled up creature inside of me yawns, the stretch of anger waiting to see if it wants to awaken. Midas is wound up tonight, either because of Third's presence or something else.

And then it hits me.

He *knows*. Of course Scofield and the others would've reported to him that Rip carried me to my room. My stomach ties into knots, and worry flares in my head. Did he do something to Digby because of it?

Or...would he prefer to punish *me*?

I can feel eyes on me, loaded gazes watching us, and it makes my anger flush with a wave of embarrassment. Yet I keep my attention on Midas, on the critical glaze in his eyes.

"I don't want you getting obnoxious on wine, Precious," he says with scathing politeness, making heat hit my cheeks at implying in front of everyone that I'm some sort of lush unfit for company.

"Am I allowed to have water, Your Majesty?" My tone is on the bad side of saccharine, too smarmy to be sincere, and I know I've gone too far.

Beneath the table, his hand comes down hard on my thigh, and I tense as he pinches the skin hard between his finger and thumb. Even though he's doing it over my skirt, it still hurts, the fabric barrier doing nothing to block the sharp pain.

Harder and harder, he squeezes, but I school my face. I don't let myself flinch. I don't even *blink*. He can pop off the skin for all I care, and I'll still sit rooted here like a damned daisy, because I won't give him the satisfaction of wilting.

The table has grown quiet beneath mine and Midas's stare down, his attention on me just a few seconds too long, his face just a few degrees too harsh with his supposed *favored*.

"My father didn't trade with Thirders, and I can't imagine why we'd start now with how high your trade tax is," Prince Niven drawls, his young, nasally voice distracting Midas. "Can Third's resources truly justify their worth for that kind of fee?"

Everyone looks at the queen now instead of me, her fork pausing on its way to her mouth. Niven sure has his princely pompousness down, but when it comes to tact, he's severely lacking.

Midas's hand thankfully drops away from my leg, leaving the spot throbbing in pain. My skin prickles as blood rushes up to it, but I ignore it in favor of the political drama.

Before Midas can smooth things over, the queen looks at the prince with an edge of provocation. "We *Thirders* don't need to trade with your ice people, Prince

Niven," she says coolly, tone as sharp as the spires on her glittering crown. "Third Kingdom flourishes, with ten times more resources than your slab of snow. King Midas invited us here to strengthen our alliance, and we are here because it could be beneficial to our people. But make no mistake, you need us more than we need you."

Prince Niven blushes furiously in a patchwork of raggedy reds across his cheeks and neck, but Midas intervenes before the boy can shove his foot in his mouth again. "Sixth *and* Fifth Kingdoms are grateful for your presence, Queen Kaila. Any new trade agreements we can come to will surely benefit all those involved."

She gives a terse nod, while her brother Manu, no longer looking so jovial, leans in and whispers something into her ear.

When Manu settles back, the queen takes a drink, seeming to gather herself and dissipate the tension in her face. "I forget how young you are, Prince Niven, and still mourning your father. You are indeed lucky that King Midas has come to aid you in this time of transition for rule."

In other words, *you're an idiot, kid.*

Niven sits up in his chair, as if to make himself look taller, older, though his baby face and the cowlick at the back of mussy brown hair kind of kills it. "My thirteenth year is only two months away."

Kaila smirks. "Ah, thirteen," she says reflectively.

"That's when my powers manifested. You remember, Manu?" she asks, turning toward her brother.

"How could I not?" he replies, letting the smile hang on his mouth in a clear play of realigning the conversation. "You used to make me mute so I couldn't tell on you to Mother and Father."

Her lips twist. "You deserved it."

"Probably," he concedes.

The prince frowns. "I thought you had the power to pull voices toward you? To hear every whisper in the room?"

Well, shit. I need to remember never to speak secrets anywhere near her.

Midas cuts him a sharp look, but the prince is so oblivious he only shoves a spoonful of stew into his mouth.

"My magic can do many things," Kaila says cryptically. "Some people who annoy me enough with the abuse of their voice lose the privilege of having it."

My gaze cuts over to a red-faced Niven. Beside me, Midas's foot taps on the floor six times in tense aggravation.

Niven nods. "My power will develop soon, and it will benefit Fifth Kingdom. My advisors estimate that I'll have stronger magic than even my father. Perhaps even more than anyone in this room."

I nearly snort aloud. If the prince notices the steam

coming from Midas's and Kaila's ears, he pretends not to notice as he keeps going, obviously trying to win Most Pretentious Little Prick Prince prize in all of Orea. He's a shoe-in.

"Now, King Ravinger...there's *power*," Niven goes on, looking up and down the table to see who agrees with him. Nobody meets his eye. "Too much, if you ask me. His rotting magic leeched into Fifth's lands when he got here. You probably saw it on your way in. That, and his loitering army," he says before slurping another sip of stew. "We were forced to give over a piece of land or face his army's attack."

As if on cue, Slade strides into the room right then, dark voice whipping out without pause. "I think you got the better end of the deal, don't you?"

CHAPTER 19

AUREN

Every single person at the table stiffens at Slade's sudden appearance. But me...my body seems to relax for the first time since I came in here. My ribbons loosen, their lengths slipping out of their drapery, ends slinking beneath the table like they want to slither right over to him.

I get a bit of tunnel vision as my attention locks onto him, and my lips go warm, once again remembering the press of his mouth and the nip of his teeth.

Great Divine, that kiss.

His green eyes sweep the room, onyx hair perfectly disheveled and body encased head-to-toe in black tailored clothes with a simple brown leather strap around his waist. His gaze doesn't land on me exactly, but I swear I see the slightest twitch of his lips curve up.

Slade walks into the room with all of the swagger befitting his uncompromising confidence. Behind him is his Wrath, each of them in full armor, including helmets. The only reason I can tell it's them is because Osrik's hulking form can't be missed, and neither can Lu's featherlight tread. Judd walks just behind her with a relaxed swing of his arms, while the fourth in the group...

My eyes flick back and forth from Slade to the Rip look-alike. Slade swaggers, but Fake Rip *stalks*. With booted steps striding forward, curved spikes protruding from the arms and back of his armor, he looks every bit the army commander I've come to know.

Except for one thing. No aura pulses around him. No inky presence of his essence hovers in the air. This person is definitely an impersonation. The question is...who the hell is he?

"King Ravinger," Midas declares, watching as the four Wrath take up spots against the wall of the dining room, Ranhold's guards shuffling out of the way to accommodate them. "When you didn't arrive at the stated dining time, I assumed you had other obligations."

A verbal jab, letting it be known that Midas doesn't appreciate Slade's tardiness.

"Pardon," Slade replies as he sits down across from the prince and begins helping himself to the platters of food. "I didn't intend to *leech* off of Fifth Kingdom's dining niceties, but time got away from me."

Niven goes as pale as his chowder, but for once, the prince has the good sense to keep his mouth shut.

The passing minutes are so thick with tension that it would take a knife sharper than the one at my place setting to cut through it. Everyone eats and talks while I push around my food and bob my head politely whenever someone says something, while my internal clock ticks.

The monarchs are all sliding looks at each other when one isn't looking, their words nothing more than riddles fluent in derision or rife with fake flattery. The only one as quiet as me is Slade.

My eyes lift of their own volition to steal a look at his profile. I glance over the cut of his jaw, the reaching power barely visible behind the high collar of his shirt. Like he feels my attention, deep green eyes flash over to me, and I snatch my gaze away, trying to keep still as I stir my food around.

I shouldn't look at him. Not with the way my heart is pounding, not with the observant eyes at this table.

And yet, the moment I look away, I swear I feel a brush of his gaze against my cheek again, as if he feels the pull too, the crave to collide. Instead of falling into that trap, I let my eyes rove over his Wrath.

Osrik stands like part-giant against the wall, more pillar than man, like he could hold up the entire ceiling if it came down. To be honest, he probably could.

Judd is next to him, head scanning left and right, while Lu stands perfectly still, hand resting on the sword at her hip, perhaps to remind people that she might be the smallest of the four, but she's just as deadly.

If any of them notice me sitting here, they don't let on.

As for the Rip look-alike...

My eyes fall to him the most.

I can't help it. I keep trying to pick his appearance apart, as if I can spot all the differences. Yet apart from the empty space where his aura should be pulsing, there's nothing I can see that gives me any hint as to who he really is.

"King Midas, I don't think I complimented you on the throne room yet. It was positively stunning," Queen Kaila gushes.

"A gift to Prince Niven," Midas says smoothly, as if he did it for anyone other than himself.

"It was very generous," the boy murmurs in monotone.

Queen Kaila's lips pull up in a smile. "You know, I have always been captivated by your power, King Midas."

"It's nothing," he replies with an easy smile.

I bristle. My ribbons sharpen like bared fangs.

It's nothing.

Nothing.

My fingers clamp tightly around my spoon. So many

times I've drained myself for this man, just for him to pretend that it's *his* power and it's *nothing*.

That angry creature prods my ribs, rapping to get out. Coils of ribbons slither down my legs like serpents searching to pierce a vein and tear into sinewy muscle, but I hold them back.

"Oh, I'm so glad to hear that your power comes so easily to you," Kaila replies. "Magic can be a fickle thing."

"It can," he readily agrees. "But I mastered it long ago."

Mastered it.

It feels like my stomach turns to ash, burnt down by the flare of fire erupting from the throat of my cloying fury.

Mastered *me*, he means, this complete and utter piece of shit—

"So magnificent," Queen Kaila says. "Could you show us?"

The hand on his goblet goes still, his eyes locking onto her. "Show you?"

The queen nods with excitement, her eyes glittering. "You wouldn't mind, would you? I've heard so many stories of how awe-inspiring it is, and I would *love* a demonstration. I assumed since you've mastered it so completely, it isn't such a terrible imposition? My brother and I would adore seeing it."

Midas may look at her with that courtly smile still plastered on his face, but I see the tightness in his jaw. Feel the six taps of his heel on the floor.

In just a few short sentences, Kaila has trapped him. If he were to deny her, it would make him appear either weak or disagreeable. Neither of those things are what Midas is trying to prove.

After a silence that stretches on a few beats too long, he tips his head. "Of course, Queen Kaila. I would be happy to."

She beams at him, looking so young and pretty, and yet there's a thread of cunning that gleams in her gaze, as if this is a test.

"Auren, pass me your goblet, would you?" Midas turns to me, eyes flickering with pointed demand. We've played this game so many times. We've fooled so many people.

But right now, the fuming anger is in control, and the only person I want the fool to be is *him*.

With a saccharine smile on my face, I pick up the goblet and hold it out to him. In the past, I'd make sure to do a quick sleight of hand to make my skin touch the object at just the right moment as I passed it over, so that by the time my gold was spreading, it was firmly in his grasp.

But I do nothing.

Midas's carob-pod eyes darken and deaden, falling

off a branch to land down at my gloved hand. When he lifts that gaze again, we stay in limbo, both of us holding the cup, staring at each other in equal challenge.

His gaze is an order.

Mine is a threat.

In these loaded, heavy seconds, a tense silence stretches across the table, bound by the unwavering looks knotted between the Golden King and his gilded pet.

A tic appears in Midas's jaw, and while his smile is still plastered on his handsome face, there's a fury there buried in the depths, ready to dig me out and crush my defiance with a fist. I manage to keep the smile on my face with innocent levity, but my golden irises spark with the light of a fire.

He's always towered over me to cast me in his shadow, and a shadow doesn't like it when you burn it straight through. My chest leaps at the power I'm manipulating by *not* using my power at all. At everyone staring, waiting for him to perform.

And he can't.

"Are you going to let go?" he asks lightly, as though it's a joke, though it's belied by the hardness in his jaw.

Are you going to do as you're told? he's really saying.

What would you do if I didn't? my gaze says.

Seconds drag by of this public power play.

Several chairs down, I swear I can feel a rumbling

laugh, though it's silent inside a black-clad chest. My own seems to puff up a little bit more.

Midas yanks the goblet away from me and looks down the table with an amused look. "Apologies, I'm often distracted by my favored," he says to excuse away our exchange, making a few people laugh politely.

His eyes move to the windows behind us, and I see the infuriated panic in the tightening of his lips as he realizes that night is about to descend. He has minutes, maybe even seconds. My power is about to go dormant, and his temper is burgeoning.

"Understandable. She is a beauty," Keon says, shooting me a wink, but everyone is wondering. Doubting. Not quite understanding. For the first time, the pet has turned on her master, and the master doesn't like seeing fangs bared that he thought he'd muzzled.

Midas leans in, not near enough to touch my skin, of course. He's far too meticulous for that. "Careful, Precious," he whispers, voice dropped down to a breath.

My rebellion falters beneath his smile pitched in threat. Midas looks at me to imbue his warning, though he pulls away like a king who just whispered intimate secrets to his favored saddle.

Digby. I have to think of Digby.

Crunching up my pride like torn paper in a fist, I discreetly tug off my glove in my lap. Lifting back up, I pretend to reach for a serving spoon, thankful for the icicle centerpiece that juts up in front of me. With intent attention, I time it precisely so that as soon as Midas sets his goblet down, I drag my bare palm against the glass tabletop right beside it and let my power unleash.

Gold erupts like a gushing wound bleeding across the table.

Several gasps ring out as the liquid spreads from beneath Midas's goblet and spills into the entire length of the table like reaching floodwaters. It swallows the glass in its shiny pall, dripping down the sides and curling down the edges to spread beneath. Within moments, the entire table is gilded, the centerpiece of jagged icicles now reaching up like clawed fingers of golden greed.

Midas's shoulders noticeably relax, and across from him, Queen Kaila claps. "How exquisite, King Midas," she says with a grin, her tanned fingers running over the polished metal.

Keon laughs jovially. "Indeed. Why go for the goblet when you can gild the whole table?"

Midas gives a bared-teeth smile. "Exactly what I was thinking." His malignant attention settles on my face, scraping it raw. "Did you enjoy that, Precious?"

"I did."

I really, really did.

He turns back to his food, and I pull my glove back on, my gold-slicked palm sticking to the inside of the fabric. Taking care to stay composed, I keep my expression shuttered while my insides riot.

Stupid. That was a stupid, foolish risk I shouldn't have taken. My pride is not worth Digby's life.

But damn, it felt good to make him squirm.

A few minutes later, the sun dips away, and the dying day gives in. With the descent of night, I feel my power empty out of me. The claggy gold remnants on my hand soak back into my skin, and I let out a ragged, tired breath. Too much power too fast has left me lightheaded, and I'm clearly still recovering from my drain.

Everyone is talking around me, Queen Kaila fawning over the golden table while the others continue to eat and make small talk. Somehow, I manage to eat my tacky, cold porridge and wash it away from the roof of my mouth with a gulp of water.

All I want to do is run back to my room and escape to the balcony, to breathe in the crisp air, far away from prying eyes and courtly conversation. Midas's presence beside me is the bow of a ship, looming ever closer, no matter how fast I try to swim.

When I bite into some syrupy fruits, I have the sudden urge to cry. But that wouldn't do. It's odd enough that I'm sitting here like a spectacle at a royal dinner. If I start weeping into my dinner bowl, I'll be the talk of the court. But I hate this. Hate *him*. Gritting my teeth, I tell myself to pull it together, to not let him get to me.

Why is it that a man can make you feel like nothing, when you have given him *everything*?

Suddenly, like a whisper in my ear, I feel the faintest breeze of magic brush against my cheek. So subtle, like dipping a single fingertip into still water. Rather than the nauseating power he usually gives off, this is the balm of a cool caress that I've grown accustomed to when he's in his spiked form.

At the stroke of his essence, I'm able to let out a normal breath. My throat bobs, swallowing down the regret and worry, and I grasp that composure I need. Just like that, Slade has calmed me, grounded me on stable earth.

Since I can't look at him, I let my eyes lift to Fake Rip again instead, his slitted helmet pointing straight ahead, hands clasped in front of him. Who would I find if I pulled off that dark metal that hides his face? What other secrets does King Slade Ravinger have?

"Did you hear me?"

My head snaps to the left at Midas's voice. "What?"

Brown eyes darken as his gaze skips from me to the commander I was just caught staring at. My stomach drops, and I know I've made another grave mistake tonight. All of the calming reassurance I received from Slade is instantly gone, crushed beneath the threat of Midas's stare.

Midas jerks his chin up, eyes dragging to the harp by the windows. "Go play some music."

Not a request.

Not even really appropriate, considering the setting and that I haven't finished eating. He caught me looking at Rip, and he doesn't like it. Not one bit.

"Your Majesty, don't feel like you have to add entertainment on our account," Manu cuts in across the table. "Besides, that harp looks awfully complicated, doesn't it, Keon?"

The man looks up from the leg meat in front of his mouth. When he doesn't reply right away, Manu elbows him. "Oh, right. Yes, awfully complicated."

"My Auren is self-taught," Midas boasts with another fake smile. "Well?" he prompts.

"Now?" I ask thickly, stalling.

Displeasure bleeds through his features. "Yes, *now*."

I'm on thin ice, I know that. I honestly don't know what's come over me tonight. Or maybe I do.

It's nothing.

I've mastered it.

He's already insulted me, embarrassed me, sat me here to be his trophy, and bolstered his own image by pretending that he gilt the table. The last thing I want is to go over there and perform like a puppet.

Still, I'm surprised when I hear myself saying, "No, thank you."

Someone's fork screeches against their plate like a startled musician squeaking their violin string. The chattering along the table dims. From my peripheral, I think I see Slade smirk.

I learned long ago to read Midas's subtleties, and right now, he's so sharp with anger that I'm in danger of being pierced straight through. His voice drops low, like the threat of rain on a drowned-out sea. "*No?*"

I attempt to smooth his ruffled feathers by giving him a placating smile. "It's been so long since I've played in front of anyone. I'm out of practice…"

He smiles, but it doesn't reach his eyes. No, there's a sort of furious yet gleeful anomaly there that sets me on edge. "Oh, Precious, you play so beautifully. You'll get the hang of it again and be just as you were before."

His double meaning is clear.

"I had no idea your gold-touched was so talented," Queen Kaila says, drawing his attention.

"Yes, she has learned some very good skills to *entertain* me with over the years," he says, looking back at me. "Isn't that right, Precious?"

The innuendo has me burning from my cheeks to my ears.

He's doing this on purpose. Humiliating me. Putting me in my place. Reminding me and everyone else here that I'm his possession.

"She's always happy to entertain others as well," Midas goes on, and for that split second he looks away from me, I allow my gaze to dart to Slade.

He's sitting back in his chair, one elbow leaning on his armrest, and a goblet balanced in his other hand. He looks relaxed. Bored, even.

Except for the whites of his knuckles where he's gripping his goblet so fiercely I worry he might shatter it.

Maybe shatter *me* in the process.

There's a cough from the back of the room, and my eyes shoot to Fake Rip, whose hands drop back down in front of him.

This time when Midas's hand comes up, his fingers pinch *right* on the sensitive underside of my arm. Even through the sleeve, it hurts. I stiffen and suck in a breath, tears springing up from the sharp notch of pain as he digs in.

With the way his hand is wrapped around my bicep, I'm sure to the rest of the table that it simply looks as if he's bestowing me with an affectionate touch instead of this move of punishing dominance.

Some of them keep up polite conversation, but they're really paying attention to us. After all, it's not every day one gets to observe the Golden King with his elusive gold-touched favored.

As if that scrutiny weren't bad enough, I can feel Slade's eyes burning into the side of my face. I don't know how I know he's watching, or how I can feel his attention stitched to the place Midas is touching me, but I do.

"Don't be shy now, Precious."

One of my ribbons lifts, a beveled end perking up

like a snake scenting the air. Every second that passes makes the pinched spot even more painful, feeling like a pin bolted straight through my skin.

Midas smiles at the look in my eye before blessedly releasing me. Though he finally lets go, it doesn't remove the hurt, and isn't that fitting? Every part he's touched has bloomed with a blatant spot I'm left to ache with. Every touch radiates out with a mark from the spot he savaged.

"My leg and arm are a little sore," I reply quietly, dropping a pointed look to my thigh that's no doubt already forming a bruise as well.

"I forget how delicate you are," Midas says, the pleasantness in his voice nothing but a farce to the edge in his eye. "Since your leg is so sore, perhaps the commander can carry you to the harp. He seems to have some practice at that."

Shit. My heart stammers, a clumsy, knocking pulse to rap against my ribs. *How much does he know?*

Damn the guards for reporting my every move. Now that I think about it, the only reason I didn't get Midas storming into my bedroom was probably because Queen Kaila arrived last night.

He was preoccupied.

He isn't preoccupied anymore.

Now, I'm going to pay for letting someone else touch me. No matter that it was his own damn fault I couldn't walk up the stairs in the first place.

He lets his kingly voice boast out, "Commander, come help Auren to the harp."

I have to hand it to him. The asshole really has some nerve, ordering Rip around like that, considering the commander's reputation and the fact that Midas isn't even his king.

All of Midas's attention is pinned to Fake Rip, but the man is still standing stoic against the wall, powerful thighs shoulder-length apart. He cocks his head, not in Midas's direction, but in Slade's, and my embarrassment comes to a head.

"That's not necessary," I quickly state.

"Oh, but it is. I *insist*." Midas's tone is sharp enough to cut.

My teeth grit and grind. Desperate now, I look around the table, but everyone's pointedly pretending not to be paying attention to this exchange. Even Manu and Keon are in deep discussion with their queen.

"I don't need to inconvenience the commander." I scoot my chair back too fast, the legs wailing out a shrill screech against the stone.

Before I can stand fully, Midas's hand is on my wrist, halting me. "If it wasn't an inconvenience last night, then it certainly shouldn't be now." The cold challenge is a blatant flex of control shoveled out from his words before he levels a look at Slade. "You don't mind, do you, Ravinger? Your commander took such good care of my Auren last night, so I know he can do so again."

My Auren.

Half of me is surprised at how blatant his play of control and possession is tonight. Yet it makes sense to me too, since I know he learned about last night. If there's one thing he hates, it's anyone touching me.

Slade regards him, head cocked, expression apathetic. Even when his eyes drop to skim over the spot where Midas is holding me, there's nothing. Not a flicker of any kind of emotion.

I think that's what bothers me most of all.

At least until Slade says, "By all means, Midas. Whatever you need."

Something in me deflates at that, my ribbon settling down to lick invisible wounds. Was I imagining the bite of anger I saw earlier with his grip on his goblet?

Slade's every action is always unexpected. But it isn't until I feel this pebble of disappointment dig in that I realize I thought he was going to intervene on my behalf.

But he doesn't.

Fake Rip is already stalking toward me, the black sheen of the spikes looking scarier on him than they do on Slade. All too soon, he's right in front of me, taking my arm into the crook of his stiff elbow.

I turn and start the humiliating walk over to the harp,

wishing I'd never opened my big mouth. I should've known that Midas would find it necessary to immediately put me in my place.

We've only taken a few steps when Midas calls out, "My favored can't possibly walk on her own, Commander."

Heels stuck to the stone, this stranger and I stay frozen for a moment. Then, nearly too quietly to hear, a sigh sounds within the hollow spaces of his helmet.

My shoulders tighten. "Don't you da—"

Before I've finished my sentence, I'm picked up in Fake Rip's arms.

Not bridal style. Not even flung over his shoulder like a brute.

No, he carries me like a sack of potatoes, hauling me up by my waist with one arm, balancing me against his side.

I'm too stunned to offer an objection as he stomps the rest of the way to the harp, every step jostling me like I'm an errant toddler on a mother's hip.

I get dropped unceremoniously onto the stool in front of the instrument, and I hiss in protest, shooting a glare up at the man, while my ribbons practically turn to poke silken tongues out at him. I'm not positive, but I think I might see him wink at me through the slits in his helmet before he turns and strides back to his spot.

What the hell?

The dining room is achingly quiet for a second until Manu demands, "Why don't you carry me around like that?"

"Because you weigh about a hundred pounds more than me," Keon drawls.

"That's a terrible excuse."

Thankful that Manu and his husband have filled the awkward gap of quiet, I straighten my back and lift my chin before I let my fingers pluck against the strings.

I don't play any particular song. There's no need. Midas doesn't actually want me to entertain anyone with a tune, that's never what this has been about in all my years of playing. It's a performance, but not one that has anything to do with music.

For the next hour, while the rest of them eat and drink and talk, my gilded fingers strum over the strings. It's an indolent, vagabond melody with no focus that plunks through the flicks of my fingertips.

Not once does Midas say anything to me again. Not once does Slade, or any of his Wrath, glance my way. Manu eyes me every once in a while, but I don't know him well enough to judge the expression on his face.

Behave tonight

Sit pretty

Play your silly music

Leave the men to speak

Those old words sing along in soundless lyrics. Same shit, different castle.

CHAPTER 20

AUREN

My fingertips feel raw.

It's been months since I played the harp, and it shows. After hours of sitting at that stool, plucking discordant strings with bare hands while my gloves stayed in my lap, my fingers are now tender and offended, puffed up with indignation.

The thing is, I *like* music. I like that I can control the thrum of every note, steer every melody. Perhaps I like it in the way a bird likes to sing. But being *ordered* to play, like a pet performing for background noise, makes me resent the act altogether. I want to sit at the harp because *I* want to. Not because I've been *mastered*.

In a way, it's good, what happened tonight. Midas's asshole tendencies rearing its ugly head, the public embarrassment, even Slade's reaction. It's good, because it reminds me to stay on track. Reminds me why I need to find Digby and get the hell out of here and to not put my faith in males.

Prove it, I told him.

He didn't.

Midas walks me back to my room as soon as dinner ends. His temper burns like a double-ended candle, flaring hot with anger on one side and arrogance at the other. I'd be trembling in my slippers right about now if I were still the same girl in Highbell, and that's what he wants. The giant always expects the ones at his feet to scramble for his bidding, if only not to get trampled on.

As soon as we reach the hall, the guards in the corridor whip open my bedroom door so that we don't even break stride as we enter. I go straight to the balcony doors and toss them open, not caring that the piled up snow blows into the room, scattering like salt over a sloppy dinner plate.

I need the fresh air. I need the *openness* these doors represent. Because after tonight, after that display of dominance, my spirit needs the reminder.

I'm not trapped.

I'm not weak.

I'm not *his*.

The door shuts with a snap, the sound dancing with the crackle of the fireplace as the flames gnaw and bite at the burning wood.

I turn around, hands clasped in front of me, and Midas grips me with his gaze like he wants to shake me from the inside out.

"You acted abominably this evening."

I want to snort at the hypocrisy, but I keep my lips sealed like wax on a letter.

The right side of his face glows orange, making his tanned skin speckle with the flames. "Do you have any idea what Queen Kaila must think of you?"

As if I care. But *he* certainly does. Midas obsesses about appearances and how to use them to his advantage.

"I've allowed you a lot of freedoms, Auren. But I will *not* abide disrespect, and after our discussion, you should know better."

My chin rises, right along with that feathery companion that seems to have nested in my anger. "Digby did nothing but be a loyal guard for years. You have no right to threaten him."

He laughs.

It's a cruel, cold laugh that contradicts the firelight he's bathed in. Midas eats up the space between us until he's blazing at my front while the reminder of an escape chills my back.

"Being a king gives me every right in the world. I *own* the rights, the rules, the laws. You've pleased me with your work this past week, but that stunt you pulled tonight won't be tolerated."

My winged anger sits up, a dark trill in the back of her throat that sounds like a promise.

"Explain to me what the hell you were thinking letting that disgusting man touch you last night?" His words lash, one after another. "If he was *any* other soldier, his severed head would already be draining in your bathtub for you to gild."

Tepid bile crawls up the back of my throat, my stomach churning with the visual of that. Of Rip's— *Slade's*—head cut right through his neck, pale skin glossed over with the paint of red blood. It wouldn't be the first time Midas has carried out something that gruesome and ordered me to gold-touch it as an example to others.

Midas leans down, and I blink the vision away, breath stuttering in my chest as his fury soaks up the oxygen in the room. "If you let anyone ever touch you again, you won't like what happens. To you, to the other person, *or* to Digby."

"I nearly collapsed on the stairs, and your guards wouldn't help."

"And they shouldn't!" he bursts out. "No one is allowed to touch you except for me. That's twice now this commander has disrespected me."

A line digs between my brows. "Twice?"

"He lifted you off the horse when he brought you back," he seethes. "I should have ordered an arrow to shoot him down right where he stood."

And had the might of Fourth's army attack him back? Not likely.

"Did you fuck him?"

The question lands like a crack renting the earth.

I blink in surprise. "*What*?"

"You heard me." His tone is the low rumbling of a shaken ground, possessive fury coiling through every word. "Did. You. Fuck. Him."

A churning, bitter hate coats my eyes, glossing it with a golden haze, and my angry beast roars in my ears. "No."

Back and forth, his eyes flick between mine, fatal jealousy boring through them and snapping past his teeth. "Do you want him, Auren?" he croons with loathing. "Do you want that grotesque, ugly, spiked-up, magic-tainted monstrosity to bend you over and fuck you like a whore?"

The air decompresses, collapsing in on me like it's broken up into shards that slice my lungs. I can't think past the clamor in my skull, not with my outrage blaring so loudly.

How dare he.

How fucking *dare* he.

"You were watching him. I saw you."

"Yeah?" I bite out. "Well, I saw *you* fucking your royal saddles all the time in front of me, so I think you can handle a glance."

"*Watch it*," he warns.

My tone drips with snarky disdain when I answer, "*I did.*"

It happens so fast.

One second, I'm standing there mouthing off, and the next, Midas's hand connects with my face hard enough to rattle my brain.

I stagger back, head snapped to the right, my cheek flaming from the punishing blow. Tears drip unbidden down the aching flesh, like my eyes want to caress the spot he just smacked.

Time seems to stop.

A line forms between us, a fissure of cracked earth broken through from the force of a single hit.

He's never struck me before. *Never.*

The pinching he did earlier was a shock in itself, but even so, that was a controlled punishment. A pointed reminder to stay in line, like a master yanking on a leashed collar, and very in-line with his usual temper.

But this is different. This was Midas losing control in a wave of anger, and he prides himself on his control.

Stunned silence stains the room in a void of dark shadows as I take in what just happened. The roaring creature inside of me takes it all in too, her beak bared to flash a row of razor-sharp teeth.

There seems to be a crashing sea of fury rising up, and my anger relishes in it, ready to swim beneath its depths. My entire body trembles with the force to hold her back. I can feel those waters closing in on me, a whirlpool ready to pull me under.

That love-stained girl inside of me is gone. The one whose heart was broken with the pieces used to pin her up like a bug to a board. She was burned down with the force of his palm. Her ashes are now nothing but soil to sprout the stems of the wickedness that seems to suddenly bloom brighter.

I take a fortifying inhale and turn back to look at Midas. At the man whose greed has so ruined him that he doesn't even realize it. He's swam out so far in a gilded sea and doesn't even see it's drowning him.

I hate him. I hate him so much that I know the truth gleams from my eyes.

A pregnant pause billows between us like a roiling cloud.

Midas's eyes are wide, face pale as he looks at me in shock. Abruptly, his breath shatters the air. "*Shit...*"

Hands come up to my face, and his palm cups my jaw, thumbs stroking down my throbbing cheek. "Precious...I...I didn't mean that. I was angry. I didn't... *Shit!*"

Anguish bleeds through his tone, and my stomach tightens at the thundering noise. I try to jerk out of his hold, but his grip tightens, like he's afraid to let me go. Afraid I'll disappear into thin air.

That's *exactly* what I intend to do.

He tips my head up, forcing me to look at him. "You make me so crazy, Auren." I nearly scoff. Those are words to lay fault at my feet. "I'm not used to you behaving this way, but that was wrong of me. I lost my temper, but you know how much I love you. How much I need you."

His touch gentles on my face, thumb wiping away the tear tracks like he wants to erase my every emotion, control everything I do, everything I feel. He wants to wipe me clean like a slate.

I almost feel sorry for him. I feel sorry for me too, that this is how we've ended up. However, once I'm gone, I can start over. I can have a life. But him…

By losing me, he loses *everything*.

"This is getting out of hand," he says, tone quiet, the last of his vitriol expended and soaked up by my face. "Let's go to bed. Let me take care of you. Let me show you how much I love you."

I blink, incredulous horror spiking my pulse as I realize what he's implying. Does he actually believe I'm going to have *sex* with him right now?

He either doesn't see the look on my face, or he's sure he can turn this around by physically distracting me, because the next thing I know, his mouth is descending, ready to capture mine for a kiss.

My abated anger rushes back like a held-back tide.

As fast as it takes to blink, my ribbons are up, curving around my front like a cocoon of ribs. With a powerful push, they shove him back, and Midas goes stumbling, nearly landing on his ass.

He stares at me with wide-eyed shock, eyes glancing warily at the ribbons poised at my sides, held up in the air with cocked ends. All that's missing from their stance are fangs dripping with venom and a rattle in their tails.

"*Don't touch me.*" My voice singes, landing against his ear and making him twitch with the burn.

Midas recovers by straightening himself, shifting on his feet warily. "You're worked up," he says placatingly, and although he's trying to sound calm, to seem sure of himself, there's a tremor in his hands as he tugs down his golden tunic, fingers running over the buttons. "It's understandable."

I say nothing. I'm too busy breathing shallowly through my nose while my ribbons strain at my back, tugging against my muscles like they want to rip from my skin and tackle the bastard.

"You know I love you, Auren," he says quietly, shoulders slumping down in a rare show of remorse. "You're the most precious thing to me in the world, but I let my temper get the better of me. You embarrassed me at the table in front of the queen, and we *need* her alliance," he says, as if I care. "And I don't like the way the commander thinks he's entitled to touch you without my permission. Make sure it doesn't happen again, and just...*behave*, alright? I don't want this constant tension between us." It's nearly a plea, as if I'm causing him strife.

My eyes stay hard as stone. "I want to see Digby."

"Soon," he promises, eyes darting to the throbbing spot of my cheek. "Get some sleep, and we'll talk later, alright?"

The moment he leaves, the very second my door is shut with a click of a turning key, I stumble out onto the balcony and slam the door behind me. Then I pick up the snow-sodden pillow left out on the chair, and I scream into it with a pent-up bellow of rage.

It doesn't seem to come from my own mouth, but from the throat of the beast.

I scream and scream and scream, and the sky thunders back with an answering roar that makes the mountains shudder.

Yet the creature born from a withered heart and suppressed fury isn't satisfied. My ribbons writhe around me with spitting savagery, so I throw the pillow down and then wrap their lengths around the banister.

I haul myself off the balcony in three simple swings, executed solely by my pent-up rage. Then I'm stalking through the snow, running toward the decrepit stairs that will lead me to that forgotten antechamber with its locked doors and frigid air.

Because I can't stay still. I can't stay in that room where he laid his hands on me.

I have to move, or I'm afraid whatever this *thing* is inside of me will claw out of my skin and devastate everything in its path.

I have to find Digby.

I have to escape before I finally snap and become the monster I'm trying not to be. And the only way I can drown out that demand for violence and bloodthirst is to focus on my plan.

It's the only thing keeping me from plunging into the flames that burn pure gold.

CHAPTER 21

QUEEN MALINA

Tensed fingers gripped around my arms make my eyes fly open, body jolting upright.

For a moment, I'm disoriented, mind scrapping between sleep and wakefulness, caught in that groggy, heart-pounding in-between.

With a spewed exhale, my vision adjusts to the darkness of night, and I stare up at Jeo. "*What* do you think you're doing?" I bleat, the jarring way he woke me up setting my mood to plummet.

As soon as Jeo sees that I'm coherent, he turns on his heel. "We have to go. Where are your shoes?" He walks away without waiting for a reply and disappears into my dressing room.

What in the world?

"Jeo?" I call. No answer. I run a hand down my face,

trying to wipe away the lingering slumber as I attempt to get my bearings in the dark room.

Jeo comes out of my dressing room a second later, and with only the low-burning fire to light the room, I squint at the bundle in his arms.

"What are you doing with my clothes?"

I push the covers aside and get up, still dressed, the cut of my white fabric now horribly wrinkled.

He stops at the bed, tossing down random bits of clothes before he starts shoving them into a knapsack—the same kind of bag that Pruinn carries for his bric-a-bracs.

"Jeo," I snap, watching him frantically shove everything inside, his own clothing in disarray, blood-red hair sticking up in places like he just rolled from bed himself. "Tell me what's going on right this instant."

He looks over at me, blue eyes washed out from the light of the fire. "They breached the castle walls."

"Who?" The stupid question falls from my mouth, unbidden. Of course I know who. I just don't know *how*. I told the guards to have them all killed if they dared to come up the mountain.

"The rioters. They'll be inside the castle within moments. You must get to the safe house."

I feel my head shaking, feel the blood drain from my face. "That's not possible. The guards—"

Fingers grip my arms again, shaking me, just as he

did to wake me up. "The guards abandoned their posts. They *opened* the damn gates."

"*What*?"

A nightmare. That's all this is. I'm still sleeping, and this is a nightmare.

My temples begin to throb again.

I lift my fingers, pressing against the pulse, trying to flatten the pain out. "Send for some food. I can't think with this incessant headache."

"*Food*? That's what you're thinking about right now?" he asks incredulously. "No food will be sent up on silver platters. Your servants are gone, already fled."

The remnants of sleep bob in the water, my headache yanking at the anchor.

"Fools!" I curse. "Then the servants have betrayed me as well as the guards."

"Malina, you ordered your soldiers to slaughter the people. *Their* people," Jeo hisses, his fingers digging into my arms, forcing me to be present, to fasten me to the here and now. "That's their families down there in that city. Their friends. Neighbors. And you commanded they all be killed."

The accusation in his voice has my shoulders stiffening, lips pursing. "The people are *rioting*, Jeo! They needed to be punished, and I needed to put them in their place. It's my duty as queen, and it's the soldiers' duty to obey me," I snap. "The wall guard let them in? Well, I'll see that they're all punished too."

With a disgusted scoff, he uses his grip to push me down and sit me on the bed. He kneels and shoves my feet into a pair of ill-laced boots. "You don't get it, do you?" Deft fingers begin lacing me up, so tightly my ankles twinge. "You just lost the last of whatever power you thought you had here. They've turned on you. *Everyone*. You need to flee before they get inside."

My head is shaking again, a mantra of disbelief in control of my neck. "Get my advisors. Call in the palace guards. No one will get into Highbell without meeting a bloody end."

He finishes lacing me up, standing to jerk me back to my feet, and slings the bag of clothes over his shoulder. He pulls me to the door, while I try to extract my hand from his, but he doesn't relent.

When I pound a fist against his back, he spins around to face me, eyes blazing. "Your advisors are gone. Most of your guards are gone too, and probably raised up arms to join the mob. It's over, Malina!"

My throat clogs, fear and denial like clumps of gravel to scrape me up. "No."

"Yes," he persists, and that's when I see past his anger, past his rush, and notice something else.

Fear.

That's unmistakable, raw, frenetic fear there, his freckles made starker by the cold terror that's paled his face.

I swallow hard, those jagged pieces of rock cutting down, cleaving my reality.

"What do I do?" It doesn't even sound like my voice. No haughty confidence, no poised decorum. The tone is ragged. Vulnerable.

Jeo's eyes soften for a heartbeat, and my own chest compresses at this saddle, at this man I've called my own for these past several weeks.

"You didn't abandon me."

He shakes his head slowly. "No, my queen."

"Why not?" I'm not a kind woman. I'm not an easy personality. I'm certainly not warm. And I can't even boast that I'm good in bed, because he's my first other than Tyndall. So why he's shown me so much loyalty is beyond me.

If the roles were reversed, I would've been gone. No guilt. No hesitation.

Yet here he is, shaking me awake and packing me a bag, ready to sneak me into safety.

Jeo doesn't answer, either because he doesn't want to, or he doesn't know why himself.

"We must hurry," he says instead, a dagger I've never seen before held in his fingers. "Stay with me, and if you hear any violence, I want you to duck your head, alright?"

My heart pounds against my ribcage, threatening to cave it in, but I manage a nod.

"As soon as I open this door, your Queen's guards will

surround us and take us to your safe house. You need to keep moving, no matter what happens. Don't stop. Okay?"

Dogged eyes look between mine for confirmation, and the moment I nod, he opens the door and pulls me through it. I gird myself, expecting the worst, head spinning like it's still trying to argue that this couldn't possibly be real, that I'll wake up any moment.

But this is no nightmare. At least, not the kind you sleep through.

Just as Jeo said, my guards surround me the moment I'm in the corridor. I keep my head down, shoulders bunched as I'm rushed down the halls. My guards know how to get to the safe house, but it's not common knowledge. Though if any of them told, if they're leading me into a trap...

"What if the safe house is no longer secret?" I whisper to Jeo as we hurry side by side, his arm slung around my back protectively.

His grim face lets me know he's considered this too. "It's the best option we have left."

My thoughts spin, trying to plot a way out of this. "The timberwings—"

"All gone. All taken with Midas."

I curse beneath my breath, nearly stumbling when my too-tight boot catches against one of the new rugs placed on the floor, the glaring white fur an idiotic attempt at covering more gold.

Though when we get to the main floor, I hear it.

A cacophony of rage.

Voices, hundreds of them, bleating outside the castle walls. They're all shouting something different, words or jeers or wordless hollers, joined in a clamor of unmitigated outcry.

When we race through the main hall, that's when I hear the hacking. The destroying.

"What are they doing?" I cry out, the slashing and sawing noises growing so intense I can *feel* it vibrating through the castle walls.

"Getting their due," Jeo answers grimly, his hold around me going tighter. "They're splitting Highbell apart brick by brick, stealing the gold that they've been forced to see every day while they starve and freeze."

Sour acid bubbles up my throat and coats the back of my tongue.

I hate the gold that Midas tainted Highbell with, but this...this desecration of my castle, of my *home*, makes my hands shake. I didn't want this. I didn't want any of this.

How did this happen?

How did I lose control so *fast*?

A horrible booming noise shakes the walls, making the chandeliers sway as if dozens of people are out there heaving a beam to force entry.

"Will the doors hold?" I ask. They're gilded, not

solid, but even so, it should mean that they'll be harder to break.

"The last of the guards who didn't abandon their posts are on the other side," the man covering my left tells me. "They'll hold it as long as they can."

Jeo makes me go faster until we're full on running. We head for the doorway that leads to the bell tower, except instead of going through it, we take a sharp right into a corridor that appears to dead end. My guards shove aside a hanging tapestry to reveal a hidden doorway latched into the wall, obscured by wainscoting.

As soon as they muscle-open the secret door, I look down into the yawning darkness of a forgotten passageway. One that hasn't had to be used by any royal for generations. Now, I'm forced to flee down it.

The way is so dark that all I can see are the first few steps of a narrow set of stairs before the darkness surrounds them. No gold down there. It's nothing but raw cut stone, drab and gray, soiled with stale air.

"Torches. We need torches!" one of the guards demands, making another sprint out of the room to go get something to light our way.

I watch the doorway he just left through, mind churning with the horrible question of whether or not he'll actually come back. I nearly jump out of my skin when a tear-stained servant walks past, hair in disarray, panic in her wild eyes.

"Go!" Jeo shouts at her, making her flinch. "You need to run. Hide. Don't be caught serving in here when they break in."

The girl doesn't have to be told twice. She turns and flees, steps drowned out by the ongoing attack outside, wrathful voices echoing through the mountains.

"This can't be happening..."

No one hears my whisper, but to me, it's as loud as a shriek.

The seconds feel like hours while we wait, the entire castle shuddering with hammers and scraping with blades as the people pillage whatever gold they can pry away.

All his fault. This is all Tyndall's fault.

Running footsteps pound down the floor, and my heart leaps into my throat before bursting with relief when the guard returns. He's carrying three sconces he must've ripped right off the walls, and one crudely made torch with torn curtains wrapped around the top of what looks to be a broken broomstick handle.

He immediately passes the sconces to the others, but the end of his makeshift one refuses to light. The gilded curtain is resistant to the puckering flames, no matter how long they hold the lit sconces to it. "It won't fucking light!" he spits, shaking the useless torch in his hand.

"Just leave it. Three is enough," another argues.

"Do you know how far down those take us? It's pitch-black down there! We need all the light we can get or this will be meaningless because we'll all fall and break our damn necks."

"Fancy another light-holder?"

Everyone whirls around at the voice, but instead of a servant, it's Pruinn who walks in, carrying a candelabra, three candles already lit.

"What are *you* doing here?" Jeo snaps, his arm tightening around me.

Pruinn comes up to us and shrugs. "By the time I made it to the gate, the guards had already abandoned their post. I didn't fancy being slain in the angry horde, so I came back."

"Yeah? Well, shove off. You can't come with us," Jeo snipes.

Pruinn grins handsomely, but it doesn't reach his eyes. No, those silver pools are hard and austere, a serrated blade ready to cut.

Jeo doesn't like him, hasn't since my first encounter and every impromptu visit thereafter, but now isn't the time for male dominance plays.

"We don't have time for this. You want to come? Then you can go first, Sir Pruinn," I declare.

Jeo tenses and lets me go, but my words are a challenge all their own, and Pruinn knows it. He gazes down into the shadowed depths with an unenthused expression. He covers it up a second later when he gives me a reverent nod. "It would be my honor to lead you, Your Majesty."

Jeo makes a rude noise beside me that the merchant ignores completely.

My guards move out of the way, but just as Pruinn takes the first step down, a deafening crash comes from the direction of the kitchens.

"They've broken in!" one of the guards shouts, setting off all four of the armored men to lift their swords from their scabbards in a swish of metallic scrape.

"Go, Your Majesty! Go!"

There's no time for me to hesitate or to dread the trek, because the horrible frenzied shouting has multiplied, rending through the air. The screams and chants out there are like a pack of rabid wolves with the scent of blood in their snouts.

Cries like yips echo while glass smashes and footsteps pound in time with my galloping heart. All hesitation on Pruinn's part is erased in a moment as he rushes down the steps. I barely have time to register the great boom of noise that shakes the ground before I'm shoved forward after Pruinn, my body plunging into the passage.

"You two go with the queen!" one guard shouts. "We'll close you in!"

My boots skid against the steps, slipping until Jeo's fingers curl around my arm. "I have you," he says behind me. "Keep going."

We shuffle downward, every stair narrow, making my toes hang off the edge. My palm skims against the filthy stone wall at my right, and I stay glued onto Pruinn's heels, while Jeo stays on mine.

The shouting is closer now, more breaking, more horrible hacking.

Just when I don't think it can possibly get any worse than this, the two guards who stayed behind suddenly slam the secret doorway shut.

Darkness devours me.

CHAPTER 22

KING MIDAS

There's a gloom over the morning light as I watch the sculptors chisel into the ice.

Two of them are working on a block taller than me, their bodies poised on stepladders as they chip into the frozen slab in the courtyard. I'm told they're working on a sculpture of Niven. A gift for the prince's upcoming birthday. Apparently, they'll be making a total of thirteen sculptures in his likeness.

I have to suppress a sneer.

The boy is nothing but an overindulged brat who seems to think he can play at being a ruler. Fulke did his son a disservice by giving him the entitlement of the crown, without any of the actual aptitude to be effective. His youth doesn't excuse anything. When I was his age, I was already running my household, making and stealing wages to ensure I had food on the table. Nothing was handed to me, I had to *take* it.

The only thing Niven takes is liberties with my patience. He's been a splinter in my thumb since I arrived, a prickling annoyance that I can't pluck out.

Not yet.

Timing is everything. I need to have this kingdom eating out of my hand. It's begun to happen already, especially now that Ranhold is growing richer room by room, touch by touch. Gold always sways favor.

I look around, the gentle tap of the chisels thrumming in my ears as I make a mental note to have this gazebo gold-touched next. I'll be able to see it from my rooms, and with any luck, it will far overshadow any of the prince's sculptures. All damn thirteen of them.

A presence jars me from my thoughts, and I lift my head as Queen Kaila steps into the gazebo, her form-fitting blue skirts flaring out at the knees.

"Queen Kaila." I rise to my feet at the smiling woman as she tips her head.

"Good morning, King Midas," she says, cinnamon eyes filled with amusement. "This is the second time I've caught you out here. This must be a favorite haunt of yours."

"It is. Would you like to sit?" I ask, gesturing beside me.

She shakes her head, the fur-lined hood of her cloak

glittering with leftover frost. "That's alright, I was just taking a walk."

My smile tightens. I imagine that during these so-called walks, she's using her magic to try and suss out secrets. It's what I would do if I were her. I'll need to have another discussion with the guards to make sure they're all keeping talk to a minimum. Men in uniform seem to gossip more than schoolgirls.

"It is a pleasant morning for it."

"Very quiet and calm," she replies, though I have a feeling she isn't talking about the weather, and I have to suppress a smirk.

The queen's power intrigues me, even as it sets me on edge. It's an impressive magic to be able to gather the words of others. It would certainly have its uses. It's why I invited her here.

Queen Kaila wants to solidify an alliance because her kingdom needs income. I want to further my reach. What better way to do that than by aligning myself with someone who's easily bought with gold and who can steal the whispers of others? It's better to keep her close so that she shares those secrets rather than steal them from me.

"I hope you haven't had too much of a shock adjusting to Fifth Kingdom."

Kaila glances around, her smooth black hair hanging loose around her shoulders. "I have to admit, the snow has its charms," she replies, the husky timbre of her voice dipping into seduction.

I tilt my head, a grin sloping up. "It does. Though the private islands of Third Kingdom are said to be the most beautiful in Orea."

"I'd have to agree with that assessment," she says coyly, playing at the wrap of shells hanging around her dainty wrist. "Though I'm decidedly biased about the subject."

I let out a pleasant chuckle. "Every monarch should think their land is the best, should they not?"

"They should." She nods. "But in this case, perhaps I could invite you to one of those islands someday soon so that you may get a look at it for yourself and decide if it warrants the claim."

My grin widens.

I let my eyes run over her pleasing figure. Perhaps Malina's defiance will work out in my favor after all. Why settle for a cold shrew and a saddle's bastard when there may be other...options to explore?

"Would you like to dine with me tonight in my personal chambers?" I ask. "I'm sure I could request for the kitchens to make a popular dish from your kingdom."

A pleased look comes over her expression. She really is a beauty. I wonder if the rumors are true about her *much* older, and now deceased, first husband. It's been said that she heard a secret she didn't like, and he died soon after.

"That would be lovely. Will your gold-touched favored be joining us?"

If I weren't versed in these sorts of conversational leads, her question might have caught me off guard.

"Not tonight," I reply smoothly. "Though I'm sure you will grow quite fond of her."

Kaila smiles. "I'm sure I will."

The dreary morning around us begins to let out a glaze of wet snow, fat flakes melting over the ground like sugared icing.

The queen shivers. "Well, I'd better get inside. As charming as the snow can be, I am not overly fond of how cold it is." She casts me a smile. "I look forward to our dinner, King Midas."

"Tyndall, please. And as do I."

With a pretty tip of her head, she turns and walks out of the gazebo, hips swaying as she catches up to her guards and brother, Manu, who are waiting for her by the castle wall.

Manu casts me a gaze, one that's careful not to show anything but polite pleasantness, though his shoulders are just a tad too stiff. For all of his outward affability, I have a feeling he's a sharp judge of character. Since he's so deeply in his sister's ear, I'll have to be careful to gain good footing with him.

When Kaila disappears inside, I turn back to the sculptors now being dusted with the wintry spritz, their hoods pulled up and gloves shucked on. My eyes follow their movements, but my mind goes over the conversation with the queen, the possibilities splaying out like threads for me to wield.

She has an interest in Auren, but I knew she would. *Everyone* is interested in my Auren.

Including that thorn-backed bastard, Commander Rip.

A tic pulses in my jaw, anger coming up to brew in my chest like a temperamental boil. I'm still fuming that he touched her. He even had the nerve to carry her right in front of the guards. What I don't yet know is if he did it because she was weak or because he's taunting me.

Either way, the situation sets my teeth on edge. If it weren't for the fact that he's under the protection of Ravinger, I would've locked him up already and plucked the spikes from his spine. My hands coil into fists, and the sudden urge to do just that—to *punish*—makes my arms go stiff.

He will need to be dealt with.

Auren will need to be dealt with too.

I don't like the way she's been looking at me, or the guardedness she now shutters over her expression. Her time away from me has changed her. After years of careful grooming, of teaching her to behave properly, I thought my influence over her was firm. Yet just a few weeks away from me, and her behavior slid like footsteps on ice. She'll need to be reminded of who takes care of her, of who her master is.

I've never struck her before, but she pushed me to it with her antics at the dinner table. I glance down at my hand, as if I can still feel the sharp hit to her cheek. The look on her face after I did it…

Something ugly twists in my gut. I shouldn't have let my anger get the better of me. So much is riding on every minute I spend here. I need her to fall into place, need to stop her backwards slide.

So I'll give her this time to sulk. To lick her wounds in peace, away from curious eyes. I'll separate myself so she can process things at her own pace. She'll come around, though—she always does.

In the meantime, I don't particularly care to see the reminder of my lapse in control on her bruised face. I'll let her be for now. Let her settle. Enough gold has been bestowed on Ranhold to staunch talk, and I've plenty of other things to see to before the ball.

First and foremost, Commander Rip will need to be dealt with. Rankling aggravation stews in my gut every time I even *think* about him touching her, about what might have occurred between them while they traveled together, out of my reach.

My guards and staff know better than to touch her, so I'll simply have to make sure the army commander *and* Ravinger know better as well.

My finger taps against my thigh in vexation.

I need to have a better grip on these strings that are trying to loosen. Auren, the commander, Malina, Niven. Two entire damn kingdoms that need constant attention.

I knew moving forward to push my influence into Fifth would be a challenge. Yet it's a challenge I relish in overcoming, and I *will* overcome it. I'll accept nothing less.

But this constant pressure is growing. Every time another thread is strewn in my lap, it takes incredible planning to keep it from tangling everything else. If only these threads wouldn't be so difficult to weave.

My fists loosen and tighten, flex and relax, again and again.

A groaning creak of the sculptor's ladder draws my eye, and my gaze lands on the man as he steps down to pick up the hammer he'd dropped. His face is angled toward me, giving me the perfect view of him.

Deep-seated hate brims at the sight of him. It happens every time, and yet, I still come out here.

I cock my head, fists tingling. I've spent weeks watching him, this man with my dead father's face. A father I abhor to this day, even though he's nothing but ashes now, body left to burn in a scorched desert.

At first, I watched the sculptor because I enjoyed feeling like my father was here, simpering around me, laboring beneath my eye. But perhaps I've been missing the real purpose. Perhaps the gods left him here for me to ease my lack of control when I feel it fraying. To remind me that I overcame *him*, and I can overcome anything and anyone else.

Perhaps the gods gave him my father's face so I can make use of it.

My fists relax as he reaches up to dust off the iced slab. His hood falls back, revealing his bald head lined with prominent wrinkles, the deep ridges shaped like frowns. His white beard is yellowed against the snowy background, his eyes slightly more tilted. His are clear and brown, while my father's eyes were always bloodshot with the veins of alcohol brewing beneath hooded lids.

The sculptor seems to feel my attention on him, because he turns his head, meeting my gaze for a moment before he defers, head bowing. The only time my father ever bowed was when he was kneeling over me to beat me with his belt or a jug of ale he drained dry.

Sometimes, I regret leaving him to burn in our hovel. It was too quick a death for him. But maybe I can amend that now. It seems I've been given a chance to wreak authority over another without it messing up any of my plans. I've been given the perfect person to indulge in for punishment.

Dark delight fits into the recesses of my chest as I lift a hand, signaling to my head guard. Always attentive, he immediately sees the gesture and hurries over, stopping just outside the gazebo. "Sire?"

"That man there," I say, tipping my head. "Bring him to the dungeon."

I can see I've caught him off guard, but he's well trained, so he recovers quickly. "Yes, Your Majesty. It will be done."

Turning, he signals to one of the other guards, and together, the two of them stalk straight toward the aged sculptor.

At first, the old man frowns at their approach, confusion pleating his brow. Saying nothing, my guards each grab one of his arms, and his body lurches in surprise before he drops his chisel and hammer to the ground. The other sculptors all freeze in shock, watching with wide eyes as my guards start to drag him away.

His hoarse shouts clap in the air with peaked desperation, bald head whipping left and right. "What are you doing? Where are you taking me? I-I haven't done anything!" he cries, his twig-like legs and scrabbling feet making drag marks through the snow.

Uneasiness passes through the courtyard, but no one questions me. No one tries to stop it.

Head craning, the man's wild eyes lock onto me. "Please, Your Majesty! There's been a mistake! Please, help me!"

My chest puffs in gratification as I imagine that

it's my father being dragged away, that it's *his* voice begging.

A garroted cry rises up his throat. "I'm guilty of nothing!"

You look like him, I say in silent reply. *Your guilt lies right there in your face.*

His bent, arthritic hands grapple at the guards' uniforms, but he's far too frail to really put up much of a fight. With one last shout torn into the air, they drag him around the side of the castle where they'll take him to a discreet entrance into the dungeons.

After his voice is drowned out, the courtyard is left to lull in its silence.

I stand there, arms crossed in front of my chest, staring out boldly at everyone who's left. Scattered Ranhold guards, sculptors, a stable hand, they're all frozen in place. I wait to see if any will dare to speak out, but none of them do.

When they notice my attention has turned to them, they quickly get back to work, averting their gazes. So quickly people will turn a blind eye to the misfortunes of others. It's the dark voice in their ear, whispering, *just leave it be. Don't get involved, lest it happen to you too.*

I let my arms drop and then stride out of the gazebo, wet spackles of snow landing on my forehead as I go through the main entry of Ranhold.

Excitement buzzes in my palms as I head for the

main entrance to the dungeons. For every difficult thread, for all of the anger I can't dole out on those responsible, I'll mete it out on *him*.

Because the gods left me a gift, and I intend to *take* it.

CHAPTER 23

AUREN

There's still a bruise on my cheek.

Bright side? Midas hasn't bothered me for three blessed days since he struck me. He hasn't summoned me to gild anything, hasn't made me attend any more royal feasts.

But this reprieve is a gift of guilt. Midas doesn't want to see the proof of his loss of control darkening my face. Out of sight, out of fault.

Still, I enjoy the break, because it's given me time to myself.

All three days, from the moment I wake up in the morning until the sun goes down, I've stayed in my room and trained. Simple exercises like lunges and curls, and I also turned a pair of shoes solid gold so I could lift them and build up my arm muscles. I also run through the few things I remember that the Wrath managed to show me when I was with them. When my body is shaking with exertion, which, granted, doesn't take long, I switch off to work my ribbons.

I focus on learning how to move them one at a time and then together too. It's a bit like rubbing your stomach and patting your head at the same time, or trying to write two separate words with either hand simultaneously. It takes concentration and a lot of time. When I'm sick of doing that, I practice lifting things with them and moving them around. Back and forth I go, from practicing with my ribbons to working out my body.

I'm pathetically weak, but I've decided to fix that by doing what I can on my own.

As soon as the sun goes down, servants come in to feed my fire, draw my bath, and bring me food. By then I'm a sweating, shaking, cranky mess. Even my ribbons are getting snappish from all the hard work. But...I also feel *good*. Like I'm doing something productive. It satisfies the creature pecking at my chest.

For now.

True to his word, Midas has allowed me to wander the castle at night with a guard. So after a bath where I soak my tired muscles, I leave my rooms like I have for the past few nights. I've been visiting Rissa, sneaking her one gilded item at a time.

I also have the guards take me up to the forgotten

entrance of the library that no one seems to use or really care about. I lie and say that the scribes gave me special permission to enter that way since it's more private. They didn't question it. Scofield and Lowe wait there in the cold antechamber while I pretend to be reading up on Fifth Kingdom's history to kill the time.

I already broke into the other locked doors in the antechamber the night after Midas hit me. I'd hoped one of them would bring me to the dungeons or a secret passage, but they didn't. They led to the cellar, the kitchens, an exit near the stables, a couple of random corridors, and what I think must've been King Fulke's rooms. All fruitless.

So tonight after I visit Rissa, I'll go back to the library and try to search again for blueprints of the castle. I'm hoping I can figure out where Digby might be kept, or find secret passages that might help us get out of Ranhold undetected.

It's going to be another long night, no doubt.

Every night that I don't find anything, I grow more worried. Rissa is becoming antsy. With every visit, her eyes seem to darken like the shade of a sundial counting down the time.

So it's almost funny that my conflicted thoughts of her impatience have me so engrossed that I bowl right into her in the corridor on my way to the saddle wing.

"Shit." I stagger back, shoulder hitting the corner I just rounded, while Rissa barely manages to catch herself on the wall.

"My lady?" Scofield blurts, eyes wide, though he doesn't move closer to me or try to help. He knows better.

"Watch where you're going!" Rissa snaps, hands going to smooth her blonde hair.

I straighten up, cringing. "Sorry."

Thank the Divine it's nighttime.

She puffs out a breath, her tone and expression losing their hard edges as she looks me over. "It's fine. I didn't know it was you."

Her hands fiddle with the low-cut bodice of her dress, and I notice the guard behind her. He doesn't look at all concerned that the two of us nearly butted heads coming around the corner. In fact, he doesn't do much other than let his eyes stray to Rissa's cleavage. At least Scofield and Lowe don't ogle me that way. Granted, I do break my corsets every time I put one on, so my boobs don't look nearly as perky and full as hers, but still.

Rissa's cool assessment crawls over my face. "You're looking better."

I brush a palm over my cheek that's still slightly bruised and swollen. "Yeah," I say simply. She never asked what happened, and I didn't offer up the information. But she knows. Women always do.

"Come to visit again?" she asks as she continues to walk in the direction away from the saddles' rooms.

The presence of the guards makes my words careful. "Yes, I was hoping we could chat."

"Well, I'm not in the saddle wing as you can see, but you're welcome to join me."

I shoot a look over at the guard before facing forward again, the sound of Rissa's heels clicking against the marble. "Oh, are you...umm. You're not going to an *appointment*, are you?"

She snorts and shoots me a derisive look. "No, I haven't been called to go fuck someone, Auren," she replies dryly.

"Well, I thought it prudent to check..."

I can practically hear Rissa's blue eyes roll in their sockets. "Do you think I would really invite you to watch me get ridden?"

"Wouldn't be my first offer."

A reluctant laugh trundles out of her. "True. I used to hate when he made you watch."

This surprises me. "Really?"

"Of course," she says as we turn another corner, heading to a part of the castle I haven't been to yet. "Do you think any of us enjoyed it?"

"Polly did," I answer without hesitation. "She liked that I was stuck behind bars while the king...well. Just believe me when I say it amused her."

"Maybe, but not me. Having the king's gold-touched favored watching, judging, seeing everything..." She shakes her head. "I hated it. Hated you."

She says it without venom, just stating facts.

"And now?"

Rissa looks over at me. "Now what?"

"You don't hate me now."

There's a narrowing of her eyes. "I tolerate you."

"You're so warm and fuzzy."

I catch the slightest quirk of her lips as she smiles. Just a flash, and then it's gone, but it makes my distracted, weary soul feel lighter.

"We're here." She stops in front of a door where a second guard is stationed just outside, sitting on a stool with a toothpick balanced on his bottom lip.

"Where's here?" I ask, looking at the unfamiliar door. "What are you doing?"

Rissa arches a blonde brow and smirks at me. "I'm here to visit Mist."

Mist.

As in, the saddle who has tried to claw my eyes out on more than one occasion. The woman who publicly cuts me down with verbal hate. The woman who's pregnant with Midas's illegitimate child.

I actually back up a step, eyes gone wide as saucers. "*What*? You know I can't go in there!" I hiss.

"That's too bad. If you don't come in there with me, we won't be able to *chat*, and believe me, I have some very juicy gossip," she says pointedly.

I look around the corridor like I'm hoping a trap door will appear, but the gossip bit is her telling me that she has news. I also need to get rid of this gold leaf that's currently burning a hole in my pocket.

A sigh ripples from my chest. "Are you sure you don't hate me anymore? Because it seems like you do."

Rissa's grin widens, like my reaction is thoroughly amusing her. "You're going to want to hear my gossip, Auren."

Dammit, she has me. She has me, and she knows it. "You know, I have the sudden urge to throw a book."

Melodic laughter lifts from her, and she finally seems to lose her weighed-down shoulders, her eyes sparkling for a second. "Don't be so dramatic. I've just come for a quick visit. One of us saddles comes each day, and today is my turn."

I debate for another second but then give in. "Fine. But I feel like I need a safe word."

With a sly grin, she knocks on the door, and at the call to enter, we both go inside while the guards stay in the hall, the door closing securely behind us. I look around at the periwinkle room, noting the feminine bedding, the matching sitting area near the fire complete with a dainty table already set up for tea time.

That's where Mist is now, the profile of her round face visible beneath a neat coif of black hair. Rissa rounds the chaise and plops down on the single chair, her body sinking into the plush purple cushions.

"Oh. It's you," Mist says, glancing up at her.

Well, shit, if that's the sort of welcome *Rissa* gets, mine is going to be positively peachy.

"Nice to see you too, Mist," Rissa replies with a smile as she plucks up a teacup from the table and helps herself.

I assumed the two of them were friends, so this exchange surprises me. Then again, I usually only saw the saddles when they were...visiting Midas. They always seemed *very* friendly then, but that was an act—their job.

I hang back awkwardly. "Nice room."

Mist's head whips around so fast I'm surprised she doesn't crack her neck. "What are *you* doing here?"

"No idea, to be honest," I mutter as I lean against the door. I don't want to come any closer. Mist has claws, and I don't trust that feathery creature that's taken up residence beneath my ribcage.

Her dark eyes flash over to Rissa. "You brought her here?"

Rissa takes a dainty sip of her tea, as if she's not at all affected by the tension. "You're the one who requested to have company every day. Now you have two people at once."

Mist jabs her finger in my direction. "She doesn't count as a person."

I blink at the insult, and my ire flares, but Rissa cuts in before I can reply. "Your pregnancy hormones certainly haven't improved your manners, Mist."

"Why should I have manners in front of her? She gets doted on enough."

Rissa levels cold blue eyes on her. "Yes, and now here you are, getting doted on too. Your own suite, servants at your beck and call, a nine-month break from working on your back. Should the rest of the saddles act like bitches toward *you*?"

Mist's cheeks darken, and for a second, I think she's about to tell us both to get out, but instead, she pins me with a glare and says, "Well? Don't just lean there like a stick," she snaps. "Sit down."

So pleasant.

I give her a wide berth, taking a seat on the chair beside Rissa's. I don't help myself to the tea or tray of cookies, though. I can tell Mist's tolerance only reaches as far as the cushion beneath me.

We regard each other across the table, while a cheery fire flickers beside us, like it's trying to burn through the incivility. The three of us sit there in stiff silence, years of watching each other from opposite sides of my cage somehow compiling into this moment.

Mist lays a hand on her slightly protruding belly, and my eyes fall to the touch. When I first found out about her pregnancy, it gutted me. But now...

What do I feel now?

I was expecting some echoes of jealousy to knock against the hollow spaces inside of me. But it doesn't.

She's showing now. Just a small bump, but it's enough behind her form-fitting dress. Funny how the proof of Midas is in her burgeoning belly, while for me, it's on my darkened cheek.

And just like that, my mood shifts.

Mist is jealous of what she thinks my status is in Midas's life. I know that now, and I knew that before, but seeing her belly puts things in perspective. Because...how would I feel if I were in her shoes?

This isn't a normal pregnancy. Mist is going to be giving birth to the child of a king. A king, who, other than keeping her as his royal saddle, doesn't hold any real care for her.

She's probably afraid. Of pregnancy in general, of giving birth, of what will happen to her afterward. She will have no control, and I, more than anyone else in the world, understand that.

Mist is going to have Midas's baby. The man who just struck me, hurt me, left bruises over my body. Sympathy, like a heavy, wet raincloud, drizzles over my mood, saturating it in sorrow for the woman sitting across from me.

It could've been me. I could've been the one carrying his child, and then what would I have done?

I'd never have been able to get away from him.

Mist's life has been irrevocably changed forever. She's now shackled with the master manipulator and reigning narcissist, a man who just showed me he's not above hurting someone physically.

She thinks Midas's attention is a good thing. It's *not*. It's more toxic than the jealousy she's stewing in.

I don't mean to be staring at her belly all this time while these thoughts flood through me, but I'm so in my head that I don't notice her glare until Mist slams her teacup down. I drop my gaze to my lap.

"When is Polly coming to visit me next?" Mist asks, clearly unimpressed with her current company.

"You're lucky she was here a couple of days ago. She can't be bothered to get out of bed most days."

I look over at the sudden quiet and notice something passing between the two of them, the irritation from earlier seeming to lessen just a bit. "She needs to stop taking dew."

"Why don't you try telling her that?" Rissa lobs back.

Mist grits her teeth before her hand moves to grab a lump of yarn I hadn't noticed. She puts it on her lap and starts to fiddle with it while shaking her head. "I know dew is a delicacy here in Fifth, but I don't like it. It makes her..."

Rissa fills in the gap. "Sloppy. Uncaring. Addicted to fucking and nothing else, while emptied of every single thought from her head."

Mist's lips pinch, fingers digging harder into the yarn. "Yes."

I'm certainly not a big fan of Polly, but I don't like the thought of her or any of the other saddles being addicted to that stuff.

"It's disgusting how they treat saddles here," Rissa says, pink growing in her cheeks as though anger is blooming there. "And that drug is just making everyone worse."

Weighty silence descends between them, only disturbed when Mist begins to knit. The *click click click* of the needles tapping against each other is the only noise in the room for a few minutes until Rissa sets down her teacup and says, "Polly did mention you were still getting sick in the mornings."

Mist shrugs. "The servants bring me ginger tea. I'm managing." She curses under her breath, yanking out the loops she made, a line of frustration drawn between her black brows.

She struggles for a minute before I say, "I could help you knit that."

Her dark brown eyes surge up, fingers pausing. "Excuse me?"

I tip my head at the yarn she's currently tangling. "Knitting. I could help if you'd like."

Disdain drips from her expression. "I don't want you touching any of my baby's things."

The offer drops like a lead weight, and I swallow uncomfortably. "Alright."

She keeps at it, practically stabbing with the needles, getting more and more frustrated with every sloppy loop. "How do you even know how to knit?" she demands.

"You learn a lot of things to occupy yourself when you're forced to be sequestered every day of your life." I speak with more sadness than I mean to, but I can't help it.

Knitting, sewing, embroidering, harping, reading, napping, drinking. Mindless, pointless things to take up my time. So many days spent without purpose, without joy or heart or *life*. I may as well have been a statue, should've turned myself solid gold and saved Midas the trouble.

"What happened to your face?"

I get yanked off my troubled trail of thoughts, gaze springing back up to see Mist studying my fading bruise. It's just getting all sorts of unwanted attention tonight. I consider lying for a moment or brushing her off, but...a part of me wants to warn her. To get through to her.

Because I'm not her enemy, despite the hurt that's telling her I am. I'm not competition. I'm simply the woman who was on the other side of the bars.

My fingers press gently against my cheek. "This is what happens when King Midas loses his temper."

Something skims across her almond-shaped eyes, but it's gone in a flash, and then she sniffs and lifts her chin. "You shouldn't displease him. He gives you so much."

A laugh ruptures out of the clefts of my cynicism.

"What's funny?" she snaps.

The bitter amusement slips off my face, and I feel my head shake, as if trying to displace the sadness that wants to settle in. "Nothing," I tell her. "He has given me a lot, it's true."

But he's taken so much more.

"Of course he has." The bristling of her shoulders has raised them a notch, but she smooths them out as she plasters on a fake smile. "Now me, I'm grateful for everything he's done. The moment he found out I was carrying his child, he removed me from the saddle wing and put me in here." She looks around the room like it's the best thing she's ever seen—as if she can't see the invisible bars.

I hesitate. "Has he spoken with you about what will happen after the baby is born?"

It's the wrong thing to ask, because Mist's face goes from syrupy to fuming. "That's none of your damn business."

My lips press together, wishing I could snip those words off and shove them back in my mouth.

"This room is very nice," Rissa intervenes after taking another dainty sip of tea. "You must be very comfortable here."

Mist glares at me for a moment longer before turning her attention on the blonde. She runs a hand down the armrest like she's alleviating her own inner ruffling. "Yes, it's beautiful, isn't it? The king is very thoughtful. It's nice being so well cared for."

Watching her is like watching an old version of myself. She's dazzled by him, by all the pretty things, by all the security that his promises come with. How could she not be? When that man turns his smiles and nice words onto you, it's hard not to fall under his spell. Mist and I are more alike than she'd ever want to believe.

"I'm giving him something that no one else has." Honest pride shines through her expression as her hand settles over her bump once more. "He makes sure I have everything I request. Food, clothes, mender visits... He's already so devoted to me, surrounds me with every comfort."

Instead of her and this pretty purple room, I'm seeing my bedroom at the highest level of Highbell, and all the pretty things he gave to me. I'm seeing my walls slowly closing in with gilded bars, an invisible chain clamped around my ankles.

I clear my throat, trying to sort through the pity that's risen inside of it, but the lump won't go down.

"It bothers you, doesn't it?" Mist asks, taking in my expression.

"Yes," I answer honestly. "But not for the reasons you think."

Her grip on the needles tightens, and the mood in the room tightens with it. "What's that supposed to mean?"

"I'm not a threat to you," I say, but I can see she doesn't believe me, and honestly, why would she?

"Of course you're not," she retorts with prim derision. "I'm carrying his *baby*, Auren. One day, my child will wear a crown."

I blink at her in surprise. "I...I thought...well, considering you're not his wife..."

"The king told me himself," she bites out, face flushing with anger. "My child will be claimed as legitimate and be given everything, while I'll be taken care of for the rest of my life."

I'm so shocked by this that all I can do is stare at her.

A pointed finger jabs toward my face. "See? You're jealous. *You* wanted to be the one to carry his child, but it's *me*, and you hate it." The venom from her words makes her heave with breath. "Nothing was ever good enough for you, I saw it. We all did, Rissa included."

The saddle in question arches a brow but says nothing to argue that fact.

Mist is on a roll she won't seem to stop, wanting to flatten me, a boulder of weight to ostracize me. My ribbons tighten like a fist around my hips as she gets to her feet, the sorry scraps of her baby's knit cap falling forgotten at her feet. "It's me the king adores right now, it's me whose baby will one day sit on the throne, and you hate it. *Admit it*."

I get to my feet stiffly, because my spine is itching, like my golden lengths are anticipating her to lunge at us.

"I'm giving him an heir," she hurls at me, the anger of her words like nails she wants to rake down my face. "What did *you* ever give him other than a gilded cunt?"

My ribbons squeeze so hard around me that they nearly cut off my air.

What did I give him?

A queen. A kingdom. A crown.

Immeasurable wealth.

Myself.

But this irate woman standing in front of me, she wouldn't listen to any of that even if I confessed every sordid piece of it. I can see the truth of that in the sheen in her narrowed eyes, emotions clinging and threatening to spill. Her hate for me is all sharp corners and staggering weight, but beneath it, there's a bleak fear that I know all too well.

"I'll see myself out."

Mist's face twists. "Yeah, get out!" she snarls, attention flicking to Rissa, who rises to her feet. "I don't want her in here ever again."

Rissa murmurs something placating, but I'm halfway across the room already. Whatever it is that she said didn't settle well, because Mist's tone goes shrill. "I don't care. I'm carrying the king's baby and she's jealous. She's jealous that I'm his new favorite!"

I tug open the door and stride out, passing the guards without a word. I just walk. Walk and walk and walk, as if the distance I put between Mist and me will dispel the hostility she spewed.

Before I can reach the end of the corridor, Rissa catches up to me, dress swishing against the floor. She says nothing for a moment, but I find myself falling into step with her as she heads back to the saddle wing, the guards trailing after us.

"Mist is... She's not in the best place right now," she finally says.

"You don't have to apologize for her. I'm not angry."

Rissa glances at me out of the corner of her eye as if she's not quite sure she believes me. But it's true.

Mist doesn't hate *me*. Not really. She hates the threat I represent. She's acting like a cornered animal because she thinks that I can take away her comfort, her safety, her *relevancy* in Midas's life. How can I be angry when she thinks I'm going to ruin her life?

With a sigh, I try to shrug off everything from that room, glancing at Rissa as she practically glides down the hall. "How can you stand to wear those Fifth Kingdom corsets?" I ask, changing the subject.

She smirks over at me. "I take small breaths."

I chuckle a little, grateful that she's helping me leave behind what just happened with Mist. "It makes your boobs look great, though," I say, and one of the guards behind us coughs.

Rissa nods. "It really does."

When we reach the door to the saddle wing, we step inside and leave the guards behind in the hall. My anticipation notches up, curiosity burning to know what she has to tell me. We tuck ourselves into the corner of the empty sitting room, checking first to make sure no one is around.

"I didn't find any blueprints or maps again last night," I say immediately.

"And your guard?" she asks, because I've already filled her in on that—on my need to bring him along.

I shake my head. "I've tried sneaking out to look for him, but the lower levels where I suspect he's being held are always guarded."

Her lips turn down with disappointment. "So, basically, this is the same news as yesterday. And the day before that."

A frustrated sigh escapes me. "I'm trying."

She holds out a hand. "You do have gold for me at least, don't you?"

Digging into my pocket, I pull out a gilded leaf and pass it over. She inspects it before tucking it away in her cleavage, and then without preamble, she says, "Well, you'll be pleased to know that your failure to find the maps or secret passages isn't a problem any longer. I have a different plan."

I blink at her. "What do you mean?"

"We don't need a hidden path away from the guards'

eyes. We're going to walk right out the front doors of the castle."

My brows dig in close together. "And exactly how do you expect we're going to do that?"

Determination solidifies in the pull of her shoulders. "We leave the night of the celebration ball."

"The *ball*?" My head is already shaking. "You want to try to leave the night this place will be filled with hundreds of eyes as opposed to dozens? We can't slip out then, Rissa. We're expected to attend. The king will notice our absence immediately."

"He'll be distracted," she argues. "It's the only time. There will be hundreds of carriages, workers, deliveries, enough bustle to create distractions. No one will be paying attention to people coming and going in their finery."

I bite my lip, mind spinning.

"You haven't found a path for us to sneak out of, Auren. This is the only other way. And I'm sorry, I know you want to bring this guard with you, but you might not find him by then, and..." Her words trail off, but I know what she isn't saying. He might not even be here. He might be dead. He might be too hurt to travel.

My stomach twists in knots.

"The ball is too risky. He'll notice our absence much quicker."

"It's *all* a risk," Rissa points out. "And I won't wait any longer for you. I can't miss my chance."

The warning is as clear as her blue eyes—there's no talking her out of this, because she's already decided.

"I arranged transportation for that night. It will be tight with the four of us, not at all comfortable, but we'll be hidden, and we'll get away without anyone the wiser. All we have to do is get past the gated walls."

"I—wait. Did you say *four*?"

Rissa's eyes shutter, but she tips up her chin. "You added this guard you want to bring along. I added someone too."

"*Who*?"

"Polly."

"Rissa!" I hiss, head shaking. "Polly can't be trusted. I know she's your friend, but she *hates* me, and she—"

"This is non-negotiable," Rissa replies, tone hardened. "If you get to bring your guard, I get to bring her."

My panic reels. "You didn't tell her about this plan, did you?"

"Of course not," she snaps.

I run a hand down my face, my mind blaring with all the reasons this is a bad idea. "Rissa…"

Her bottom lip is trapped between her teeth before she drops her voice and says, "Look, I know how you two feel about each other. But Polly and I have been through a lot together, and she deserves better than being stuck here with her thighs spread and her mind jumbled. She's addicted to dew, and it's *killing* her. I can't just leave her here."

I stare at her a moment before letting out a sigh. "Ugh. Fine."

Her body relaxes a fraction, the corners of her eyes not looking quite so strained.

I can't fault her for trying to save Polly, especially not when I'm doing the same thing with Digby. And she's right about the night of the ball. Things around the castle will be hectic, crawling with a crowd that perhaps even a gold-skinned female can blend into.

But...the ball is only four days away.

Four days.

And suddenly, that number of days seems very, very small.

"So the ball? You'll find your guard by then and be ready to leave?" she prompts, heeled foot tapping against the polished floor. "I need an answer, Auren."

I swallow down a lump that's formed in my throat and wipe my slick palms against my dress, nervousness flooding my skin. "Yes."

Somehow, I have to find Digby, and then we'll be making an escape right under Midas's watchful brown eyes. This is what I've been working toward. This is what I decided is best.

Yet as I leave Rissa to head for the library, my eyes

aren't filled with the excited determination. No, they're filled with tears.

Because in order to escape one king...I have to leave behind two.

CHAPTER 24

AUREN

fter talking to Rissa, I head for the antechamber, leaving Scofield and Lowe to stay perched on the benches while I go into the library. I creep around inside, trying not to get caught by the robed scribes, who are way too protective of the mildewed books and unreadable scrolls.

If I wasn't in constant worry of being caught, I'd be able to look for the castle's blueprints unhindered and uninterrupted, but I don't have that luxury. So I search the forgotten stacks, rifling through neglected shelves as I squint in the terrible lighting. On hands and knees or stretched up on tiptoes, I scour the place, only to have to skitter away whenever someone walks by.

But what have I found during all my time searching? Nothing.

Which tells me I'm not looking in the right spots. I have a bad feeling that they might be kept at the front of the room, but that's the one place I can't go, because there's always that one scribe there who caught me before, body bowed over the table and scratching away with his quill.

I'm probably going to leave empty-handed again tonight, and that terrifies me. Because with Rissa's new plan, time is breathing down my neck now more than ever. I might have to abandon this idea of finding a map and start searching on foot instead. I have no idea how I'm going to avoid all of the guards in this place though.

I don't want to fail—myself *or* Digby. And I don't want to *be* failed, either.

At that awful dinner, with the way Midas treated me, there was a moment when I wanted Slade to intervene. To show me that his previous words were true.

I let myself *hope.*

Since we kissed on my balcony, this thing between us has grown. Expanded. Just like he was accused of encroaching on Fulke's territory, Slade has encroached on *me.* On my emotions.

I tried to fold it up. Creased it with denial, tucking it beneath the furthest recesses of my thoughts. But like a finger slipping beneath the flap of a letter, I couldn't resist the temptation to open it, to see what was inside.

Now, all I have are empty words and paper cut pains

radiating from my chest, because he didn't prove it to me like he said he would.

My stupid heart hasn't learned its lesson, it seems. So I have to get out of here before it ruins me completely.

Suppressing a sneeze from the dusty air, I get to my feet, sore knees popping from all the time I've spent kneeling on the hard floor rummaging through scrolls. I didn't find anything in this stack but old birth records of Fifth's monarchs.

Real exciting stuff.

With a huff, I drag myself away, delving deeper into the cavernous room and wishing for the hundredth time that there was more light in this place.

I wander over to a bookshelf that's cut right into the wall. A single sconce hangs on the left, a good foot away from the nearest shelf and casting off a pitiful amount of light. Honestly, there's enough dust on these books that they'd probably smother any flame that dared try to burn anything.

Squinting, I let my fingers drag across the book spines just enough to read the titles. When nothing helpful leaps out at me, I stand up on my tiptoes to look at the scrolls at the top, but just as my fingers close around some, footsteps clop my way.

With a silent grumble, I abandon the shelf and hurry in the opposite direction, cursing whichever scribe is interrupting me. I'm never going to find these stupid maps at this rate.

As I head for the first bookcase to duck behind, *another* pair of footsteps sounds from that direction. The two scribes begin to talk quietly as they near each other, their voices echoing off the walls and making it sound like they're much closer than I first thought.

I whirl on my heel and rush back the way I came and then dart between two shelves, not even paying attention to where I'm going, so long as it's far away from them.

The voices converge somewhere to my left, and then their steps fall into unison as they walk together. Toward me. *Again.* I shoot a look at the ceiling as if I can see straight through to the night sky and curse the goddesses hiding in the stars.

I cut a sharp right to the next aisle of stacks, and then another one, and another. The library swallows me in its dark belly, but it's worth it, because soon, I put enough distance between us that I don't hear the scribes speaking anymore. I stop to catch my breath, ears straining, and finally relax after several seconds when no other sounds greet me.

Unfortunately, the deep breaths I keep pulling in means I inhale a whole lot of dust, and my nose tingles violently. All I manage to do is slap a hand over my mouth before the sneeze ruptures out of me.

It echoes.

Loudly.

I freeze in horror, heart taking off like a wild horse, not daring to even *breathe* as I listen for the scribes to come running my way.

"Bless you."

A shriek clutches my tongue and crumples beneath my throat. Hand on heart, I spin around and find none other than Slade leaning against the stone bookshelf. With dark clothes, piercing green eyes, and power curling over his sharp jaw, he practically basks in the shadows.

"Don't do that!" I snap, though my voice is barely louder than an exhale. I've made enough noise as it is.

With his arms crossed in front of him and a smirk on his pale face, the bastard looks perfectly at ease and amused as hell.

"Do what?" he asks with a cock of his head. "Say bless you?"

I look over my shoulder as if I'm ready for the scribes to storm the row and grab me with their frail, age-spotted hands.

"Be quiet!" I hiss.

This time, he does nothing to hide his amusement, because his teeth gleam in the dark as a smile spreads over his face. "Only you would dare tell *King Rot* to be quiet."

"Maybe more people should..." I mumble.

A low rumbling chuckle rolls around in his chest like loosening stones before the rockslide.

He doesn't get a chance to reply to my rudeness, because just then, a scribe suddenly appears at the end of the aisle, making my stomach drop like a boulder.

Face aglow with the lantern in his bony hands, the orangish cast-off makes the man look scary, long white hair like a drape of fire. Dressed in heavy purple robes that sweep against the floor, his eyes immediately land on me with an indignant glare. "What are you doing in here?"

My mouth goes dry, mind fumbling with an excuse. "Umm..."

He comes closer, and I back up a step, my hopes and plans crashing down around me. All of this because of a stupid sneeze.

"You don't have permission to be in here."

I don't know if the lantern light is throwing off his vision or if the shadows surrounding Slade are too heavy, but the scribe doesn't seem to notice the king behind me until Slade moves.

Like the wind, he picks up and brushes past until he's standing at my side like a cool caress. "*I* gave her permission to be in here."

The scribe's eyes widen, mouth gaping for a moment. "King Ravinger. I didn't see you there," he says, bending his hunched spine into a bow.

Slade says nothing, but all previous signs of his amusement are gone. There isn't a single lingering touch of his easygoing energy left, but I'm honestly grateful. It makes it easier to keep an emotional distance from him when his *kingly* mask is on.

"Apologies, Your Majesty, but this is the *royal* library. Those outside of royal lineage are not allowed inside," the nervous scribe says.

A pulse of power seeps into the air. Not Slade's magic in full force by any means, but just a *push*. An undertone that ripples from him and spreads out, making a chill trickle over my skin, my ribbons quivering.

Despite the lighting, I can see the blood drain from the scribe's face as he's suddenly reminded exactly who he's talking to.

"I...of course. If she's with you, then that rule is negated."

Slade looks at him with an expression cut from stone. "Good. You can go."

The scribe nods, not daring to glance my way before he turns and leaves without another word. As soon as he's gone, an exhale of relief expels out of me. "Thanks," I say, and then I start to walk away too, because being alone with Slade is bad for my plans.

Much to my irritation, he follows me, sticking like a thorn in my side. I shoot him a look. "Do you mind?"

Hands tucked into pockets, the bastard *strolls*. Leisurely. Like he has nothing better to do. "Not at all. I enjoy long walks in a dreary library."

"*Royal* library," I snip. "And great. Go enjoy that walk somewhere else."

His brow furrows with a frown. "Are you...mad at me?"

The fact that he even has to ask...

A bitter laugh pops from my mouth. "Mad? No, of course not. Why would I be mad?" I reply breezily. "Now, I'd like you to stop following me and go do...whatever it is you were doing here before I sneezed and leave me alone."

His footsteps falter. "Auren."

I ignore him, but that's never stopped him before.

"Auren," he says again, tone insistent, an edge of impatience cutting through.

I stop in my tracks but don't turn to face him. "What?"

Slade comes up to my side so that every word he speaks paints my lips with his air. "Tell me what's wrong."

The breath that comes in my chest is shaken, because my heart can't take this constant disappointment, this circle of hope and distrust.

My eyes flick left to the bookcase, and I stare at the bindings, like I need to fasten my gaze onto something solid. Onto something other than him.

"Midas was always different in private," I hear myself say, my lips feeling cold in this forbidding place. "In public, he was the king, and he acted like it. It was necessary, he said. It was necessary for him to marry Malina. Necessary to start calling me his favored gold-touched saddle. Necessary for appearances to use me like a shiny trophy to dangle in front of others. No matter that I was in love with him when he dragged me across the kingdoms and brought me to that horrible icy place."

I shiver and cross my arms around me, and my ribbons cross right along with them, as if they're trying to ward off the chill. Too bad this one is *inside* of me.

Slade is quiet. Listening. Like he's hearing every word but looking at them in a hundred different directions.

"I put up with all of it because he was different in private," I admit. "He said *just* enough of the right things. When we were alone, when there were no other eyes around, he whispered pretty words and swore grand promises."

One of my ribbons slinks down to wrap around my palm, twining around my fingers like it's giving my hand a squeeze of comfort.

"I don't understand." He sounds almost...at a loss. Which is impossible. Slade Ravinger is always sure of himself.

"I told you to prove it to me, and yet you sat there at that table and you were a *king*."

He sucks in a breath. Like he's trying to pull in my truth. Trying to taste it, understand it.

I turn to look at him, ribbons dropping to my feet,

chin lifted, my expression unyielding. "Pretty promises in private, and the uncaring king in public." I shake my head, letting him see the disappointed look on my face. "I've been down that road before, Slade. I won't do it again. I asked you to prove it, and you didn't."

He expels a breath and turns away, shoving a hand through his thick black hair. "*Fuck.*"

I turn to leave, but faster than I can track, he somehow steps in front of me and blocks my way before I can take a second step. I try to turn back the other way instead, but that's a mistake, because he stops my turn by jutting out an arm to cut me off.

Now I'm stuck, back against the bookshelf, his hands braced on the shelves on either side of me. He takes another step forward into me, even though there's no space for it. His body crowds mine, making a gasp balk from my mouth.

"Move," I tell him.

"No," he quickly says with a shake of his head. "Let me explain."

I scoff and roll my eyes, because how many times have I heard *that*? I don't want to be that person anymore, that rug for everyone to walk all over.

"Things with Midas and I are precarious at best," Slade tells me, his fixed eyes like emeralds, glinting unnaturally in the dark.

"You hate him. You've made that perfectly clear,

so why not just kill him?" I ask, because I'm honestly curious. I don't think his level of loathing has been a farce.

Slade's eyes go shuttered. "Believe it or not, I don't go around killing without thought. He's a king. If I were to end him, especially using my magic, there would be implications to that, which would set off a chain of events. He rules people, and right now, he's making plays to rule even more. But sometimes, if you cut off the head of a monster, two more crop up."

Realization dawns. "You're worried that if Midas weren't king, someone even worse would take his place?"

He gives me a terse nod. "Better to play the game and be ten moves ahead of him, to learn his weaknesses and to cut him where it hurts. If I simply lashed out and killed him, I'd have more than just his kingdom to worry about. I'd have the other royals banding against me. They're nervous enough about my reign and my magic as it is. I have the wellbeing of my own people to consider. No one likes a rotten king, but it's my people who would suffer, as well as the innocents in the other kingdoms if any of the monarchs strike out against me and force war."

I can see the shifting marks of his power move beneath his skin, each one as thin as a hair strand. They move up his neck and disappear beneath his stubble like fishing line dipping beneath water.

I've offended him, that much is clear. And for a split second, I see the male beneath the crown. I see the way the world perceives him and the damage that can do to a person. If anyone knows about being made notorious, about being made into a *thing*, it's me.

My chest hurts all of a sudden, my resolve jabbed-through with little pinpricks of pain.

His voice lowers, eyes bright and sharp, poking even more holes through me. "You think I *wanted* to sit there and do nothing while that asshole spoke to you that way?" he bites out. "You think I enjoyed his childish power play by ordering you to be carried to that harp? I wanted to leap over the table and crush his throat with my bare hands."

As if to demonstrate his words, he lifts his arm, and his palm wraps around my neck. Except he doesn't squeeze, doesn't hurt. His dark words coil around my thumping heartbeat, while his touch encompasses my throat. His thumb brushes against my drumming pulse, not in a threat, but as a caress.

It takes a lot of willpower not to let my eyes flutter closed at the intimate touch, not to lean into his chest, though I feel the warmth of it like a blanket around my body. Aside from Midas, he's the only person who touches me.

Every grip and stroke seems to fill an empty well inside of me. Despite the fact that he knows what touching my bare skin can do, he never hesitates. It's like he can't help himself, like he *needs* to feel me.

Midas never touches me like *that*. His touches are

always placating—a pat on my head, a tap on my jaw. Either that, or it's possessive. But with Slade, it's neither of those things. He touches me like he can't resist, like he can't go one more second without feeling me.

Resisting him is difficult. But somehow, I don't let myself surrender to that heat he spreads, don't give in to that aching feeling that thrums to life between my legs. Instead, I slap his hand off me.

He lets go, hand dropping down to his side, and I take a mental fist around my ribbons, stopping them from reaching out. This close to him, it's too hard to curb my feelings. So I turn my cheek, because I don't want to get caught in the trap of his eyes or taste the lure of his words.

But as soon as I turn my head, he goes utterly still.

It's an *unnatural* stillness. The kind that makes my breath shrivel up while confusion and fear slithers through me.

Fury pumps into the air around us, and then, with a voice as dark as the pits of hell, Slade says something that makes my eyes go wide. "Why the *fuck* is there a bruise on your cheek?"

CHAPTER 25

AUREN

I have to hand it to him, the fact that Slade is even able to see the faded bruise in such terrible lighting is a credit to his fae eyesight.

My hand automatically goes up to the spot he's staring at, fingers pressing against my cheek, but just like I did to him, Slade knocks my hand away so he can see it better.

Turning my face, featherlight fingertips graze over the spot of burnished gold, like he doesn't want to put any pressure on it in case it hurts me.

It wouldn't, not now. It's a hell of a lot better than it was. A few hours after Midas first struck me, it swelled up pretty badly. I went to sleep that night with a cold compress resting on it, made from snow I collected off my balcony and stuffed into a rag. It reminded me of Hojat.

The bruise is barely showing anymore. My gold skin always marks up darker, bruising in shades of bronze and rust before it fades back to my usual gleam. But at least nearly all of the swelling is gone. The darkened mark can be mistaken for a shadow if you're not really paying attention.

Clearly, Slade *is* paying attention.

His touch makes my nerve endings come alive, and it feels like my chest is swelling far more than my cheek did.

"It's nothing," I say with a hard swallow before jerking my head away from his scrutiny.

"That is *not* nothing. Did someone put their hands on you?"

I just look at him warily, which I guess is answer enough.

"Who?"

"Slade—"

"*Who*, Auren?" he demands, his dark, seductive voice so contradictory to the violence held in his tone.

Because he knows the answer. I can see it in his face.

"*Midas*," he snarls, like a predator with its eyes trained on a trespassing hunter in the woods. He waits, looking at me to confirm, yet I don't reply, don't even nod my head.

But I don't deny it either.

At my silent confirmation, Slade *loses it*.

All of a sudden, his eyes flare, going from startling

green to a bleed of pure black. Spikes rip from his arms and pierce through the sleeves of his shirt, making a gasp fly out of my mouth.

I watch as he struggles, shifting back and forth between his forms with the click of his jaw, fury bunching his muscles. The lined power that marks his flesh writhes beneath his stubble, reaching, *growing*.

A cold sweat breaks out over me as I feel his power dominate the air. It thickens like syrup, and a wave of nauseating *death* ekes from his body.

"Slade..." The nervous plea falls from my lips as I move to back up, only to remember I can't. I'm still pinned against the bookshelf, his presence blocking my front.

It's a shock to see him like this, the way his body seems to be warring back and forth. But as his forms flicker, his essence does too—part corrupt magic, part comforting aura. Both of them beating like drums with a singular reaction.

Anger.

And just as quickly as the fear washed over me, it dissipates, like a burnt-up mist. Because his anger, it feels *familiar*.

The feathered creature in me, the one ruffling for a reckoning, she sits up and cocks her head. She pays attention.

Slade's clash of manifestations stems from

something dark and writhing. Something that's cleaved the two halves of him, making him battle within himself. But that thing...it's letting out a silent call, creating a palpable rhythm in the air. A strained song of discord that my bloomed anger can hear.

Breath buckling in an accordion bellow, I stare at him, not in fear, but in recognition as the beast in me rises up and answers to the beast inside *him*.

All twenty-four of my ribbons lurch to attention. They become charged with energy, as if they've felt the erratic spike of his magic and are answering in kind.

Yet instead of them lashing out at him like they did with Midas, they form a cocoon, like they're creating another layer upon his aura that's already surrounding us. These parts of ourselves feel so alive. So *decadent*.

"Look at me." My voice is stoic, unafraid, even as his body struggles to hold its form.

His green and black flashing eyes latch onto me, hypnotic in their frenetic oscillation. I don't know what would happen if he were to rupture, but power flows from him and pounds in the air. This time, it doesn't make me want to vomit. Instead, it's like a singing siren, and I want nothing but to be lured in.

"Can you feel that?" I whisper as my hand rises to his chest, my open palm connecting with the chiseled muscles over his racing heart.

The moment my touch settles against him, Slade's

eyes bleed back to a forest of green, like the needles of a pine appearing out of the dark. My breath catches, his heart beating beneath my palm in a rhythm that seems to match the push in my veins.

His touches I've savored have coalesced into the one I now press against him. And as innocent as it may seem, it's somehow intimate.

"Your heartbeat…"

"What about it?" His tone is hoarse, breath gone ragged.

"It sounds like mine."

Twin beats pulse, just as two tears rip down my cheeks in perforated anguish. Because I can *hear* it, this perfect harmony, like a hum of sun and soil, of depth and rise. But the moment is tainted, cheapened, because I had my head pressed to another's chest, hearing a song that wasn't singing for me. So how can I trust what I hear?

"Auren."

My shining eyes rise up, and I fleetingly note the spikes sinking back beneath his skin and the scales disappearing from his cheeks. I start to pull my hand away, because I suddenly feel so undeserving of the touch. Yet before I can, his hand comes up to trap mine, and he holds it there as he watches me with an intensity that I can't fathom.

"You're warm," he murmurs.

I nod, feeling the heat circling from my palm, dipping into the soft fabric of his shirt, sinking into the hard chest beneath. The drag of his calloused thumb against the back of my hand shouldn't feel sensual, but it does.

Heat drips down from my navel, settling between my thighs and making my muscles go tight. His fingernail scrapes against my knuckle, an abraded edge of nearness that carries the hint of a need to dig in deep. Right then, I want to let him. To peel my layers open so he can get to what lies beneath.

"He hit you." Slade grinds out the words, each one spoken from sharp back teeth.

Midas has done far more than that, but emotional assault doesn't leave any marks on the skin.

Lines of power snap against Slade's jaw like miniature vipers, and my gaze follows their insipid movements. "How long has he been doing this?"

"That was the first time."

He looks wholly unconvinced. "And at the dinner table?"

"What about it?" I hedge.

"There was a moment when your expression changed. Was he hurting you then?"

"Just a pinch." I don't dare hint that the *just a pinch* was more than one, or that they left such dark bruises on my skin that they're still sore to the touch. The only good thing about Midas's physical assault is that he's left me alone since then.

"He won't ever touch me again," I declare, because I already made that promise to myself.

Something boils inside of Slade, burning so hot that my hand sears beneath his. "You asked me why I don't just kill him," he says, his hard, pitiless eyes hooked on my face. "But why don't *you*?"

I blink in surprise as he throws my question back in my face, and my ribbons wilt, falling onto the floor like plucked petals.

His finger comes up to skim against my cheek, and even though he doesn't lose control again, he's no less angry.

"Since the moment I arrived in Fifth Kingdom, I've thought about little else other than ripping him to shreds with my bare hands. But do you know what stops me?" he asks, his thumb still caressing, our beats still in rhythm. "More than politics and potential world wars."

I don't want to ask, but I do anyway. "What?"

"*You*."

My mind recoils at the way he spits the word, at the bitterness that stains his exhale, and I yank my hand away from his chest, like I've been scalded by it. "Me?"

"Yes. You would hate me for it, because for whatever reason, you still care for him."

"I *don't*," I argue, saying it again when he scoffs at me.

"Oh, really?" he challenges. "Then ask me."

My mind stumbles, like I'm riding too fast downhill and the speed is getting away from me. "Ask you...?"

"Ask me to kill him for you."

I blanch, feeling the blood drain from my face. That was the very last thing I expected him to say.

Everything about Slade right now is fierce, unfettered, and completely fae, despite those parts of him hidden from view. "You say the word, and it's done. You hear me?" His hand lifts, and he snaps his fingers so loud that I flinch. "That quick, Auren. I'd end him in a breath, in a room full of people who'd run screaming, with monarchs who'd band together against me. But if you wanted me to do it, I would. *So say it.*"

"It's not just about me," I try to explain, but he doesn't even seem to hear me.

Slade looks at me with that crude, horrible challenge in his expression. "Say it!" he shouts, making me flinch.

"I-I can't."

A flash of utter disappointment crystallizes in his eyes. And that gesture as sharp as glass cuts me to the bone. It's a wound much worse than the one I sustained on my cheek.

"*Exactly.*" He turns and moves away a few steps, and I feel the space between us like a chasm that I have no hope of crossing. "Which is why I refuse to ruin my chances over that *worthless fucker*," he hurls out the insult between bitten teeth. "If I killed him—and make no mistake, Auren, I would *gladly* kill him for you, damn the consequences. But if I did, the truth is right there on your face. You'd resent me for it. Even if you don't want to admit it. And isn't that just a fucking cruel twist of it all?"

Tears build up in my eyes with every pent-up word that peels off him, but I don't let them drop this time. Not even as they burn and puddle on my lids.

He tilts his head in my direction, particles of dust clinging to the air between us like it's waiting for us to settle. But we don't settle, that's the problem. We never do. Every time I think we're on even footing ready to stand still, one of us takes another step.

"I'm..." My mouth closes. I'm what? *Sorry?* Am I apologizing that I can't ask the male in front of me to kill the one I've put *behind* me?

"Is that what you think I should do? Is that what you want?" I ask instead, the question genuine.

He tips his head up and sends a bitter smile to the cobwebbed ceiling. "What I want..." His laughter is soaked in somber asperity, eyes casting for wisdom from a sky that can't see us. After a pushed breath through his tense chest, he looks at me again. "There's only one thing that I find I want anymore."

There's a churning in my stomach, his declaration twisting me all up so much that I don't know if I'll ever be able to disentangle myself. Based on the woven look in his grass-bladed eyes, he feels the same.

"I'll be returning to Fourth Kingdom the day after the ball," he says suddenly, and something painful tears through my chest. "I've been away too long as it is, and I'm needed there."

You're needed here too.

He looks at me, and there's a wait there, an opportunity for me to ask him to stay, and it terrifies me.

Like a confession of pilfered spoils, I hear myself say, "I'm trying to leave him."

Slade's attention sharpens, my eyes dropping from the piercing gaze that lands against my face. "I'm trying to just...*leave*." My words tear off, like shorn parchment right in the middle of an apology letter. "To disappear."

That stillness in him has returned, the unmoving mountain standing solid against fits of wind.

I don't know why I told him, and yet, he feels like the only one I *should* tell.

Because despite my determination to get away, Slade's right. It would be so easy to end Midas, to turn him into the gold he covets so much. To bring an end to that tyranny. It would be even easier for Slade to rot him inside out.

But...I can't.

And great Divine, doesn't *that* just leave me

conflicted. I hate myself, I'm proud of myself, I'm right, I'm wrong, this is best, this is worst.

Around and around and around I go.

"Judge me for it—for not being able to end him," I say softly, almost like I *want* him to. And maybe I do. Maybe it would be a good punishment, fit for the girl who fell in love with her captor and let herself flounder. "I know how pathetic I must seem to you."

Whatever he sees on my face makes his eyes soften, the angry frustration smoothing from his heavy brow. He walks over to me again, not nearly as close this time, but at least he's sealed the gap, making the air between us not so cold and jagged when I inhale.

Slowly, Slade lifts a hand to sweep a knuckle across my bruise. I melt into the touch like the brim of wax on a candlestick, and all I can think is, *what would it be like to just catch and burn in his heat?*

One simple skim is all I get though, and then his touch drops away, leaving the track to tingle. He stuffs both hands into his pockets, as if he needs to keep them there so he doesn't reach for me again. I keep trying to convince myself that separation from him is what I need, and yet every time I get just that, it feels like someone is fisting my paper heart, crumpling it whole. A pang resonates through me as he stands there, suddenly seeming untouchable.

It doesn't matter that his shirt is torn on the sleeves

from where his spikes ripped through. It doesn't matter that he's here in a begrimed library full of rotting books. It doesn't even matter that I saw him lose a sliver of control. Somehow, he still manages to look kingly. Intimidating. *Gorgeous*.

"You're not pathetic," he murmurs quietly, a somber sort of song. "You just haven't found it yet."

My golden brows pull together as I search his expression for meaning. "Found what?"

"We all have our edge, Auren. One day, you're going to find where yours is." The darkness of his essence brushes against my skin like a whisper's caress. "You're going to find out just how far you can be pushed until you're tipped over. And when that happens, when you find your edge, just promise me one thing."

My voice comes out like a croak, a single tear dashing down. "What?"

"Don't fall." Time stands still as he leans in and places a kiss on my temple, lips turning to whisper into my ear. "*Fly*."

I don't even realize my eyes fluttered closed until I blink my damp lids open again. But by then, Slade's already gone, swallowed up by the shadows without a sound.

CHAPTER 26

SLADE

The library door doesn't slam shut behind me. It would've been more satisfying if it had. Not for the scribes, who'd surely curse me in their heads, but it would've pleased me immensely given my current mood.

Instead, all I get is the quiet snick of wood. Yet somehow, Osrik hears it and appears around the corner, his black leathers peeling him from the shadows as he waits for me.

For a big bastard, he's quiet when he wants to be. All my Wrath are. They've had to learn skills like that over the years. Some of those skills are as harmless as learning to move silently, while other skills are...not so harmless.

Osrik takes one look at my expression and cocks a

bushy brow. Stroking a hand down his brown beard, he studies me as I stalk down the hall toward him. He steps up to my side and matches my pace, and even though I'm not a short male by any means, Osrik's height dwarfs mine, his bulky body swaying with every booted step.

"So, nice visit with Auren then?" he asks wryly, a smirk playing on his mouth.

I pin him with a glare. "Why don't you take that piercing in your bottom lip and stick it through your top one too?"

Osrik lets out a chuckle, tongue flicking over the tiny piercing of Fourth's twisted tree branch sigil. It's one of his only tells. He flicks at it when he's thinking, or pissed, or amused. So actually, I guess it's a pretty shit tell.

"She's done a number on you, huh?"

My irritation twitches with the vein in my temple. Beneath my skin, I can feel my power writhing like infected veins, rooting around for a source to latch onto. My fury feels the same, but I know *exactly* who I want to take it out on.

"He fucking hit her."

Osrik stops in his tracks. I turn to face him, and his brown eyes blink at me, his round face going ruddy beneath his scruff. "What the fuck did you say?"

Only because we're in a deserted hallway does he know he can talk to me like this. When we're around others, we have to keep up the act of formality. But I don't consider my Wrath my subjects or servants. They're the only people in this whole damn world I trust. So when we're not forced to play court, we can speak freely.

I'm glad for the anger I see on his face. Misery may love company, but anger *thrives* on it.

"Midas struck her. After the welcome dinner. She has a fucking bruise on her cheek."

Osrik curses under his breath, but just saying it aloud makes me fist my hands at my sides. I hadn't noticed the mark at first—I'd thought the dim lighting and the shadows were the reason behind the slight darkening along her cheek. Just the thought that the slimy shithead put his hands on her makes my blood boil.

"What do you wanna do?" Osrik asks evenly. "Kill the fucker?"

I have to smirk at the way he so effortlessly proposes we kill a king.

The thing is, if I asked them to, any of my Wrath would do it in a heartbeat. No hesitation, no questions asked. They'd slit Midas's throat and be happy for the bloodstain on their blade.

Yet like I told Auren, there's a reason why I've held back. Not just because of the political problems that would arise—and they *would* arise. Especially if it became known that I killed him or had any hand in it. I don't even want to think about the repercussions my kingdom would face, and my people don't deserve that.

The other kingdoms would form an alliance to get rid of me, no doubt. Then my people would be forced to live through more war, and if the others succeeded, my kingdom would have to live beneath a new king or queen.

Fuck that.

However, aside from those reasons, I'd still kill him if Auren asked me to. But she won't. Just like she didn't ask me not to leave Ranhold.

I let out a frustrated sigh. "As much as I want to...no."

Auren's eyes are opened now, she sees the bars for what they are, but killing the captor she loved is another matter entirely. So for now, I can do nothing, and that alone makes me rage, makes my irascible power grow moody and demanding. Or perhaps it's the thought of her leaving, disappearing. As if she needs to run away from not just Midas, but me as well.

At my reply, Osrik lifts his lip in a disappointed sneer. "What if I just maim him a bit?"

A chuckle comes out of me, helping to dispose of the black cloud that's looming over my thoughts. The two of us start walking the halls again while I think. Ranhold is a maze of corridors and staircases, and it can be easy to get lost within its stone and glass walls, though I've made a point to familiarize myself with most of it.

"I'll let you know on the maiming," I reply. "I wouldn't mind castrating him."

Osrik gives me a grunt in return.

"No moves on the prince?" I ask, switching subjects.

He shakes his head, the fasten around his long hair pulled at his nape. "No. Lu's just left her watch for the night. If Midas is planning on killing the little twat, he's not doing anything yet."

I hum thoughtfully. "Where are the others?"

"Already back at camp. We received the hawks for updates back at Fourth."

"All is well?" I ask.

"Yep."

I roll my eyes in amusement. "Always so loquacious, Os."

"Low what?"

My lips twitch. "Nothing."

By the time we make it down to the ground floor, I'm feeling more in control, though my moody power is still brimming and volatile. I thought I was going to have to expel some magic right there in the library. I let my anger surge so much that my forms shifted back and forth, which hasn't happened in years. It took everything to hold it back, but even then, I thought I was going to lose it. Until Auren touched me.

One touch, and she brought my magic to heel. I could practically taste her sunlit aura as it swept against mine. It's a good thing no one else can see it but me, because people would've figured her out a long time ago. But distance and my own damn anger has my power stretching and slinking, like it wants to crawl out from beneath my skin and rot this whole damn castle.

I let out a controlled breath to get a handle on it, just as Osrik says, "You need to get rid of some of that."

He and the others know better than anybody what can happen when I don't use my power and I let it build up too much. "Later."

The two of us stride across the great hall, ignoring the guards propped up like posts along the walls. I'll feel better once I'm outside, away from this damn castle and Midas's guards who watch us entirely too closely. Yet just as we round a corner, we come across the last person in the world who I want to see right now.

Midas.

Beside me, Osrik makes the barest of grunts, loud enough only for me to hear. I've had a long time to decipher his wordless noises, and this one is basically the equivalent of calling Midas a fuckhead.

I more than agree with his assessment.

Upon spotting us, the *Golden King* stops on his way into the ballroom, and I barely hold in a glower. The prick looks as pompous as always, with pure golden threads on his tunic, little extra embellishments along the hem and cuffs of his sleeves that he probably stared at in the mirror while he had his hair combed.

But what really bothers me about him are his shoes.

You can tell a lot about a man based on the shoes he

wears. Midas always wears a new pair. Something shiny and gaudy, with soles that make a metallic click against the tiles like he enjoys boasting that he literally walks on gold.

"Ah, Ravinger. I'm glad at this chance meeting," he says as Osrik and I approach. His king's guard is six men strong, but every single one of them seems unnerved by Osrik as they cast him quick glances.

Midas is strict about my Wrath's presence. If they're in Ranhold, they have to be accompanying me, which is why Lu's had to sneak around to keep her eye on the prince.

"Are you?" I reply smoothly, coming to a stop in front of him. My magic tightens like a fist, wanting to punch through my skin and rot him where he stands.

Midas nods. "I'd actually like to speak with you."

I'd actually rather chew iron nails and shit them back out, but the life of a king isn't easy.

"Fine."

Together, Osrik and I follow Midas inside the ballroom, and my eyes immediately narrow at the sight of the space that's been partially gilded. Golden tapestries bracket windows nearly forty feet high. Huge pillars along the far wall with darkened veins that were once marble now gleam in metallic luster. The banquet tables are covered in gold tablecloths, and the candelabras set atop them probably weigh more than I do. A corner dais has been erected for musicians, each and every instrument and stool gilt by magic.

The rest of the room still looks like it did before, with polished white floors and stone walls encased in glass, and a plain mezzanine balcony above. But the amount of power Auren would've had to use in order to gold-touch everything else must've been exhausting. The pillars alone are an incredible feat, and it pisses me off. That Midas has her use her power like this, nearly draining herself, all to boast his own image. Because this gold does nothing. It's not for the people to use, it's not counted in the royal coffers. It's just a useless, wordless brag.

There are servants all over the place, cleaning windows, polishing floors, making repairs, or bringing in countless flower arrangements. Ladders have been erected in here too, and palace workers are installing candlesticks and dusting off grand chandeliers that look like sharp icicles ready to plummet.

Midas runs a critical gaze all around, and the workers seem to stiffen under his presence, each and every one of them making a point to stay busy. He stops walking to better assess the room or maybe just to make himself feel important. "They're readying the space for the celebratory ball," he explains.

Osrik stands to my right as I lean against the wall. "I can see that."

From where we just entered, a line of women file

inside, and I immediately recognize some of them as Midas's royal saddles we took from the Red Raids and brought here.

Dressed in scantily clad gowns that hug every curve, the women all curtsy to Midas, some of them clumsily, their movements too languid, as they follow an old man who's chattering away at them with obvious orders.

"My royal saddles," Midas says with a smile. "Beautiful, aren't they?" When I say nothing in return, his eyes move over to me. "If you'd like to make use of them, you need only ask. I'd be more than happy to gift some of them to you for the night."

I have to work to keep the disgust off my face. How easily he uses people, like they're nothing but possessions, toys to be traded. "No, thanks."

Midas shrugs. "They'll be tending to the room during the ball," he says, once again watching them. "Odo is explaining their duties so they can prepare accordingly. Some of them will be performing, while others will be serving drinks, or whatever else I require of them."

He'll flaunt them as much as he flaunts his supposed wealth.

"Did you really bring me in here to talk about your ball preparations?" I ask in an impatient tone. The sooner I'm out of his presence, the better.

A peeved look crosses his face, but he quickly

staunches it behind his fake facade. "Always ready to cut to the chase, Ravinger."

"It makes for a more honest conversation, don't you think?"

Midas gives a sly grin that makes me want to punch it right off his mouth. "Indeed, but one does not stay a king with *honest conversations*, as you well know."

He's right. When you're a king, you have to play the game of conversation, and you have to do it better than everybody else. Normally, I'd be able to word twist with the best of them, but I have no patience for that right now. Not with the vision of Auren's bruised cheek so fresh in my mind. Not with my power itching beneath my skin, begging to be let out. Not with *him*.

"What do you want, Midas?"

He loses his grin and turns to face me, but I don't like the look in his eye. "I simply wanted to thank you for your continued alliance with Fifth and Sixth Kingdoms. Now that there is no worry of a boundary war, our people can rest a little easier. And after all, that's what this ball is all about—celebrating alliances and a strong Orea."

My mind tries to read between the lines so I can hook onto the words he's not saying. Midas always has an angle. For years, I let him do what he wanted, so long as he didn't try any shit with my kingdom.

"Like the stronger alliance you're forming with Third," I put in.

"Precisely." Midas pretends to appraise the room again before he goes on to say, "I was so pleased we could come to an agreement to avoid battle. That plot of land you bargained for seemed to be such a small sacrifice in the name of peace."

My shoulders go tense.

His brown eyes flit over to me, and I can see the bastard trying to read my expression, though he won't be able to. I learned a long time ago how to shutter every feeling and thought away from my face.

"Deadwell," he says, running a hand along his shaved chin. "A fitting name for the place you encroached on with your deadly rotting power. Such a curious piece of land, is it not? I'd thought it was nothing but a frozen wasteland at the border of Fifth, but that's not entirely true, is it?"

My teeth grind. Out of all the times he could've approached me, it *had* to be right now, when I'm pissed beyond belief and my power is scraping beneath my skin.

When I don't reply, Midas turns toward me fully, smug arrogance bleeding through his expression. "Drollard Village, ever heard of it?"

My insides turn to ice. The chunk of sharp freeze appears right there in the center of my chest, ready to stab straight through.

Because of my encounter with Auren, because frustration is clawing relentlessly at my back, I let my expressionless mask crack. Just for a split second.

But Midas sees.

"Yes, I thought you had," he goes on, and I don't fucking like the gleam in his eye. Not one bit. "Drollard Village, an unsanctioned town, right there at the edge of Deadwell."

Beside me, Osrik has gone as still as I have.

"Not very pleasant names are they?" Midas muses, toying with me. "But then, it's not a very pleasant place."

Fuck.

"Strange how it's technically been a part of Fifth Kingdom all this time, yet there's no record of it. Not part of any historical data or population information. The people there have never paid any taxes. In fact, Drollard Village isn't even on any Fifth Kingdom maps. And now, it's part of *your* territory," he says, and the shrewd edge of his gaze tries to scrape over my expression, attempting to glean anything from my reaction.

I force a bored look over my face. "Yes, it is mine now. As you said, my power encroached on it, so I've simply made it officially part of *my* domain. As such, it's not Fifth Kingdom's interest anymore, seeing as how you gave up the rights to it. Unless you're going back on your trade?" My question is a threat and we both know it.

"Not at all," the slimy bastard replies. "I am a man of my word."

I nearly roll my eyes at that.

"Of course, I had a few of my advisors escorted there

in an official capacity to mark the new boundary lines. A king must keep up on his precise record-keeping, but I'm sure you agree, don't you, Ravinger?"

My eyes drop down to where I know for a fact he has his little journal of scribbles hidden away in an inside pocket. "Yes, the notes a king keeps are *very* interesting."

Midas finally loses the smarmy look on his face at what I'm implying. Good. Let him worry about whether or not I would've ever had a chance to get my eyes on his notebook.

It takes him a few seconds, but he springs back. "You know what's also interesting about that tiny village? The people there were very forthcoming. It seems you visit quite often."

There's a roaring in my ears, and my power coils and snaps at my skin. Yet I hold it all back. I learned control a long time ago—I had to.

"What can I say? They make good jerky out there. I'm a repeat customer," I drawl.

Midas's lips tighten ever so slightly that I'm not rising to the bait. It's obvious now that he has assumptions and inklings, but he's fishing for more information.

"Since Deadwell is no longer Fifth's concern, I'm confused as to why you seem so interested in it. As you said, it's not a very pleasant place," I add.

"No, certainly not," he agrees with a tip of his head. "And my people will be out of Drollard Village the moment they finish drawing the new boundary lines, of course. It belongs to you now, and I think it's important that we respect what belongs to others."

And there it is—the knot he's trying to weave. Always so many steps to get the perfect loops he likes to tie.

If I didn't already have a tight leash on my reactions, I might have wavered again and given away too much. I need to get my shit together. I know better than to let my guard down while in his presence.

Temptation ferments on my tongue. The forbidden knowledge of his greatest secret is baiting me like a worm on a hook. The king in me wants to do it, to meet Midas on his playing board and tell him that I know *his* secret too, and his is a hell of a lot more damaging than mine. I'd enjoy kicking his arrogant feet right out from under him and putting panic in his eyes. But I hold back, because as gratifying as that would be, it would negatively affect Auren, and that isn't something I'll allow.

"What do you want, Midas?" I say with a sigh. "I have affairs to see to."

"Then I'll speak plainly." Midas has lost the fake pleasant look on his face. "Deadwell is yours? Well, Auren is *mine*. I want your army commander to stay away from her."

I knew something was going to come of his little power play at the dinner.

My gaze goes impassive. "*You* were the one who had him carry her to the harp. He has no interest in her."

But I fucking do.

Midas's lips press together in a hard line. "My people will leave Drollard Village when your commander leaves Ranhold."

Last loop, pulled tight.

"Deadwell isn't yours anymore, so you can pretend that you sent your *advisors* there in an official capacity, but I want them out of *my* village," I remind him.

"It's within my rights to re-mark boundary lines after a land exchange."

Leaning in close, I let the fucker see the magic lines crawling up my neck. He can never look at it without flinching.

I need him out of Drollard. Every second he has eyes there is time for him to find out more shit I don't want him knowing. No one has ever uncovered the secret I've kept buried there, and I sure as hell am not going to let him of all people gain entry to one of my only vulnerabilities.

Since he's shorter than me, I lean my head down, albeit exaggeratedly, so that he can feel smaller than me as I look him in the eye. "I don't like when people try to coerce me, Midas. It would serve you well to remember that I still have my army on your doorstep. Do you really want to get on my bad side?"

"Not at all," he says easily, that annoying amiable

tone back in his voice. "It's about respect, is it not? As allies, we respect what belongs to others."

The fact that he thinks he *owns* Auren makes me see red.

Just then, the old man leading around the gaggle of saddles interrupts with a bow. "Your Majesty, I have a few questions we need to address for the ball."

"Of course, Odo," Midas replies to the robed man before turning back to me. "I must see to some affairs," he says, regurgitating my own damn excuse. "I'll let my people know they can leave Deadwell at your earliest convenience. Although, I think they're rather enjoying getting to know everyone there." He sends me a smirk that makes me want to knock his teeth out. "Enjoy your night."

Midas turns and walks off with his man, the saddles trailing after him in a sweep of perfume and swaying hips.

I can feel Osrik shoot me a look, but I shake my head imperceptibly, and then we stride out of the room, both of us knowing better than to speak until we get outside. Even when we pass through the main castle doors and are greeted by the stark night air with nothing but fog and frost, we wait.

Seething silently, the two of us pass through the front gates of the wall, where Ranhold's soldiers spring to attention and open it for us in haste as soon as they see us coming. I don't know who scares them more, Osrik or myself.

When we're well enough away from the castle's

walls and heading for my army's camp just over the crest of the snow-clad hill, Osrik finally lets out a curse. "That fucker," he growls. "How the hell did he find Drollard?"

"Scouts, obviously. I should've anticipated that he'd send people when I traded for Deadwell," I say, pissed at myself for not preparing for that. I was preoccupied, distracted. I've had tunnel vision with Auren and let some of my responsibilities slip through the cracks.

"We didn't expect for him to put in the effort. Not for a land known for being empty."

"I still should've planned for it just in case," I reply, the frustration in my voice coming out in a cloud of cold.

The two of us walk in silence for a moment, the only sound coming from the trek of our boots as we cut through the snow. The glow of campfires hangs at the top of the hill where most of my soldiers are gathered. The rest are probably still in Ranhold City finding whatever entertainments they have enough coin for.

"What are you going to do?" Osrik asks.

"I need Midas out of there," I reply with frustration. "Maybe I should send all of you. Make sure the situation is handled."

Osrik cuts me a look as we get to the top of the hill, just as countless leather tents fill my view.

"Fuck that. We're not leaving you here with that golden prick."

I cast him a look. "Worried about me, Os?"

He stops walking, turning his huge bulk to block my path. "If you really want us to go, you know we will. We're your Wrath, and we will carry out whatever action you want, you just say the word. But Lu is gonna be pissed if you have no one to watch your back."

"You're a bunch of mother hens," I mutter with a shake of my head.

Osrik just smirks. "Yep."

With a sigh, I scrub a hand down my face. This was the last thing I needed right now. My responsibilities are piling up, and now I have to deal with Midas sticking his nose where I can't have him or anyone else sniffing around. I didn't go through all of this trouble to finally lay claim to Deadwell, just for Midas to figure out why I want it.

"Make Midas back off by doing what he wants and send your *army commander* to Deadwell," Osrik suggests with a wry twist of his lips. "I'm sick of the fucker anyway."

I chuckle low, watching some of my soldiers walking around in the distance, dark shadows moving from tent to tent. "We need to get back to Fourth. Maybe we should all move out."

Osrik's bushy brows rise up. "Leave? Without...?"

My teeth grind at the thought.

It goes against every instinct, but if I don't respect her wishes, I'm no better than Midas.

I sweep my gaze along the castle as if I can see straight through the walls within. "We'll leave in two days. Fuck the ball and the priggish prince. I should let them all plot and scheme to their graves. Stay in Fourth and forget all about these fucking monarchs."

Osrik hesitates, probably at the frustration sharpening my tone. "You sure about that?"

My nod feels heavy, the roots of my power pinching at my skin. I'm surging with restless energy. "I'll get Midas's spies out of Deadwell myself. They'll have nothing to report if they're rotting corpses."

"If that's what you want to do, then we'll make it happen."

Simple as that. And yet, leaving is anything *but* simple.

"But are you *sure* you want to leave so soon?" he presses.

My magic snaps at the thought, and I'm forced to fist my hands at my sides. Instead of answering him, I turn on my heel, heading away from camp, my boots clomping through the deep snow as I cut toward the copse of trees in the distance.

"Where are you going?" Osrik calls behind me.

"Need to go rot something," I reply over my shoulder. I hear him grumble something under his breath, but he leaves me to it.

It's time to face facts. Like I told Auren, I've been

away from my kingdom for too long. She's made her choice, and I have to accept that, no matter how strongly my instincts try to convince me otherwise. No matter how much my magic rebels.

I abhor the politics that Midas plays, so perhaps it's time to cut ties and just let it all play out. I'll return to Fourth, shore up my borders, and go back to not caring about the other kingdoms, so long as they don't try to fuck with mine. Since Midas is big on appearances, it'll piss him off immensely if I leave early and skip his celebration, so that's one bit of silver lining I have.

I'd really only been staying here for one reason anyway, and it certainly wasn't for a fucking ball.

CHAPTER 27

AUREN

I toss and turn in bed, twisted up in both my blankets and my thoughts. Only after the sun comes up do I finally fall into an exhausted sleep, but even that doesn't bring much rest.

Every single word Slade spoke to me replays over and over. Not just what he said earlier in the library, or when he carried me upstairs and sat on my balcony, but even further back too. When we were together in a coal-lit tent, or fighting in a snowy circle, or walking along the edge of his army's camp.

Small, stolen moments.

Dangerous, forbidden moments.

Tell me.

I can't.

I'm a once-clear pond gone all murky, like Slade

dove in and splashed around in my depths. Without me realizing it, he slipped into my veins and now swims through my every thought, steeped into every drop.

When I drag my eyes open again, it's late in the day, although I feel as if I haven't gotten any rest at all. How could I, when even in sleep, Slade seems to have soaked into every inch of me?

You've chosen to sit back and wither.

Sometimes, things need first to be ruined in order to then be remade.

Listen to your instincts and stop holding back.

The silence of the room only makes his voice louder in my skull. Ripping back the blankets, I get up with a restlessness that prickles my skin. Liquid gold bleeds from the soles of my feet as I begin to pace, covering the parts of the stone floor that my power hadn't yet reached. But even that use of magic doesn't help moor me. I'm drifting in a sea of my own tangled thoughts, caught up in the swell.

Hitching my body against the wall, I let my forehead rest on the gilded wallpaper and squeeze my eyes closed. Taking steadying breaths, I lean there for a moment, palms pressed to the doorframe and a war crowding my chest.

Three more days until the ball. Three days until I'm supposed to leave. Somehow, the sum of those days seems to equate to the missing pieces inside of me.

Right or wrong, trust or doubt, mind or heart.

I'm at a fork in the road, and I can't linger at its point anymore. I have to choose a path.

With the sudden clarity of a cloudless sky, my eyes spring open and my body lurches upright. I cross into the dressing room and pull on a long-sleeved gown, the silk molding with gold the minute I tug it over my body. For once, I leave the corset be and don't cut or break it, but I don't bother to do up the back either.

My ribbons plait my hair as I tug on undergarments, stockings, gloves, boots, and a coat, and then I tear out of the room and through the balcony doors. The dogs are already back from their daily hunt, most of them out in the pen and sniffing around in the snow.

The sky is as broody as I am, with simmering gray clouds dropping lazy flakes of snow to float in the air. I do a quick check to make sure no one is near before I climb up onto the railing. I loop my ribbons around the banister before letting them drop like ropes that I then use to climb down. My arm and leg muscles are sore from my exercise sessions, but I hold on tight as I lower myself.

I keep a steady grip and manage to curl the ends of my ribbons like a hook to solidify them enough to hold my weight. Looking down, I judge the distance of the balcony a floor below to my left. I know I have to time this just right and jump with enough distance so that I don't break a damn ankle. But I did it before, and I can do it again.

So without giving myself time to overthink, I swing my body forward, once, twice, three times, and then I release my ribbons and *jump*.

I land hard onto the balcony floor, and a jolt of impact shoots up both of my legs, but I smile in victory that I made it. Below, the dogs whip themselves into a frenzy and start to yip and howl at me. The last thing I want is for someone to come investigate why they're making such a racket and find me up here. I wave my hands at the dogs below, but they just start barking louder.

"Okay, doggies, *shh*!"

They don't shh.

I glance around nervously, but no one has come to check out the noise yet—though they will. I hurry to the door, thanking the Divines when the knob opens and I'm able to rush inside. I yank my ribbons in with me and shut the door, blocking out the howls and hoping that they'll settle down now that I'm out of view.

My ribbons coil around my waist like loosely hung belts, and I inhale a steadying breath as I take in the room. It's blessedly abandoned and freezing cold in here, clearly closed up from disuse. White sheets cover the bedroom furniture like cumbersome ghosts, and a fireplace lies empty and stained with soot.

"Alright. I made it this far," I whisper to myself, equal parts determined and impressed. I check that my gloves are secure and pull up my hood before I cross over to the door. I cock my head to listen, making sure there aren't any sounds before I open it just enough to peek out.

The hallway is empty.

I'm not about to waste my chance, so I quickly exit, closing the door softly behind me, and then I walk as fast as I dare in these boots without making my tread too loud.

"Opposite side, snowflake door. Opposite side, snowflake door..." My whisper carries me forward, down the hall of icy blue. The stony glass walls reflect my body as I go, and I pass white pillars cut like rough icicles dripping from ceiling to floor.

I'm approaching a corner when I hear noise coming from the staircase just behind me, and my heart kicks up a notch. I can't be seen by the guards. It's not an option.

Picking up my pace, I round the corner, and then I nearly gasp out in relief. Right there, at the end of this short corridor, is the snowflake door.

My hurried steps bring me right to it, and I stop, hesitating. A quick look over my shoulder shows that I'm alone, aside from a lone pillar standing sentry.

I bite my lip as I look at the door.

Do I just...knock?

Nervousness writhes in my stomach all of a sudden, but there's no turning back now. I rushed over here without letting myself overthink it, but now that my mind has had a chance to catch up, I hesitate.

"Come on, Auren. Just do it," I mumble to myself in a pep talk.

With a determined breath, I lift my fist to knock, but the door suddenly swings open. I blink in surprise, barely stopping my knuckles from rapping on the metal chest plate now in front of me.

"Rip?"

The black helmet tilts down. "Ah. The little golden girl."

A wisp of breath leaves me as I realize the voice is all wrong. "You're not Rip." I should've known the moment he opened the door, but I'm too wound up.

He glances at the spikes along his forearms. "No? Who am I then, my lady?"

I narrow my eyes at his mocking tone. His voice is deep, but it's not Slade's, and there is no aura hovering around him. Yet his build and height is the same, and from this close, even the gleam of his spikes looks identical to the real thing.

"No idea. Why don't you enlighten me?" I reply.

He watches me for a moment and then says, "No, I think not."

Of course he's not going to tell me.

I let a little disappointment roll in my eyes. "Right. Can you get Slade for me?"

"*Oh*, on a first name basis, are we? That's very informal," he replies, amusement dancing on the edge of his gravelly tone.

I drop into an exaggerated curtsy and plaster on a smile. "Apologies. May I speak to King Ravinger, Ruler of Fourth Kingdom and Rotter of...Things?"

A jagged chuckle comes from him, but he still doesn't move out of the way. "You sure you wouldn't rather pass along your message to me than to talk to the Rotter of Things?"

Irritation huffs out of me, but for a second, I'm worried that Slade doesn't want to see me. Maybe after our talk in the library, he's decided to wash his hands of me and told Fake Rip and the others to send me away. "Look, you spiky stand-in, may I speak to him or not?"

"Impatient, aren't we?"

I grind my teeth. I'm all too aware of those footsteps I heard on the stairs, and I don't want to get caught right at Slade's doorstep. "Never mind," I grumble, feeling deflated.

I start to turn around, but Fake Rip stops me when he says, "I was just messing with you, golden girl." I eye him as he steps aside, leaving the doorway open. "Go on ahead. He'll be back shortly."

My foot pauses in the threshold. "Wait, he's not even here?"

"No."

433

"And...you want me to wait in there? In his private rooms? Without him present?"

Fake Rip shrugs.

Flabbergasted, I shake my head. "You're a terrible guard."

"Not a guard," he counters. "And even if I were, King Ravinger, Ruler of Fourth Kingdom and Rotter of Things, wouldn't need one."

Can't argue that.

He jerks his chin up. "Go on. Unless you want the guards who are about to round the corner to see you."

My eyes go wide, and I practically leap inside the room before Fake Rip latches the door behind me with a low chuckle. Now alone, I look around the space that's decorated in deep purples and blues. The ceiling has been painted to look like a snowfall sky, with puffy clouds and snowflakes.

I'm in a small sitting room that has a blue painted desk in the corner. There isn't a single piece of parchment, book, or quill on top of it, and the chair seems to have been relocated. Several mismatched chairs are bunched together in front of a low burning fire, as if Slade and his guests slid them over to talk together.

Were all the members of his Wrath here? Lu, Osrik, and Judd? I suppose Fake Rip would be considered a member of that as well. But who the hell *is* he? It has to be someone Slade trusts implicitly to carry this facade. It's a massive secret pretending to be two different people, and I wonder why he does it. There's so much about Slade I don't know.

I remove my coat and let it drape over the back of a chair before I take a seat near the fire. I let my mind spin, but I'm too bunched with nerves to sit still for long, so I get right back up again nearly as fast. I stoke the fire with the iron poker, watching the sparks blink lazily to life, and my gaze wanders over to the inched-open door to my right.

Don't do it.

I turn away as I put the fire poker back, but I cast another look over my shoulder. Surely it's no harm if I just take a quick peek?

I'm going to do it.

Just a teeny tiny little look. That's not weird, right? It's just a guest room, after all. It's not as if it's his *actual* bedroom.

Before I can talk sense into myself, I walk over to the door, whipping a guilty look behind me first to ensure I'm still alone. The moment I slip inside the bedroom, I'm immediately shrouded in shadow. The windows are covered beneath thick floor-to-ceiling curtains, though I think I see a peek of a balcony door between the two panels.

My shoes skim across the plush carpet, my gaze taking in the black shirt left haphazardly on the ottoman by the fireplace. The bed is swathed in royal blue, with most of the pillows tossed onto the floor, as if they were far too fluffy for Slade's liking. For someone who sprouts spikes from his skin and who sleeps in an army tent a lot of the time, I guess he's more accustomed to firm rather than soft.

I head across the room and wander into another open door, because why not? I've already come this far.

Inside, I find a dressing room, but instead of each rack being stuffed with clothing and the floor lined with shoes like my own dressing room, this one is pretty empty. There are only a few shirts and pants hanging up, all of them black or dark brown. Some armor is set in a pile in the corner, and there's also a single pair of boots. But my gaze falls to an alarming number of weapons that are leaning up against the wall.

"That seems aggressive," I murmur.

What does it say about a male who owns more daggers than shirts? It's probably not the best idea to sneak into said male's personal chambers, but here I am.

Just as I turn away, something catches my eye, stuffed at the front corner where I hadn't noticed before. My gaze latches onto the peek of brown as I slip forward and then shove aside one of Slade's shirts to have a better look.

As soon as I do, my breath is yanked from my chest

like a fist grappled it out of me. I stare at the familiar coat, my fingers running over the dappled feathers and gilded lining. Memory flashes of Slade transforming in front of my eyes for the first time, of me throwing this coat in his face when he called me Goldfinch.

He kept it.

I don't know when, but he snuck back into those rooms, took this coat, and kept it. My eyes burn and my chest tightens, and for a moment, all I can do is stare at it. Stare and wonder.

With a shaky breath, I turn away and reenter the bedroom, trying to regain my composure. I need to get back into the sitting room, but the sight of that coat has left me reeling.

My dazed eyes drag across the bed, remembering the way he looked when he slept in the army tent, back when we had smoldering coals and a mountain of distrust between us. Closing the distance, I let my fingers trail along his pillow, noting the obvious dip in the feathers and silk where his head must've rested. Without thinking, I find myself leaning down to smell it.

Eyes closed, I breathe in Slade's scent. I hadn't really considered what he smelled like before, but there's something very earthen and distinct about it. It reminds me of damp wood chips and churned soil, but something heavier and darker too, like the bitterness of chocolate.

Something in me settles, makes me remember the

feel of his hips when I trapped them between my knees on the railing. I breathe in again and my pulse calms, like last night's troubled tossing and turning is draining out of me.

As if my ribbons are taking a cue from my relaxed state, I feel them loosen and then slip down onto the bed. They start to twirl like dogs rolling around in a scent they like. I can't even blame them though, because Slade smells *delicious*.

I take in one more indulgent sniff, but I lean just a little bit too close, and a trickle from the tip of my nose has my eyes snapping open.

Oh, shit.

I flinch backwards, watching in horror as a single golden droplet spreads from where I accidentally brushed up against the pillow. My gloved hands come down in a frenzy as if I can wipe the stuff off, which, of course I can't.

"No, no, no..."

Since I'm not still touching it with my bare skin, I can't even control it enough to stop it from turning solid, either. So instead of just infusing the fabric with gilded threads, my magic spreads until the pillow goes completely stiff, the metallic surface reflecting my panicked face.

Within seconds, the silk and feather is now completely gold, solidifying Slade's head indentation forever, encased in my own idiotic carelessness.

I stare at it for a moment, grimacing at the way it's now weighing down the bed so much that the mattress has flattened out beneath it, and the bed frame wails an angry creak like it's threatening to crack.

"Maybe he won't notice?" I muse, swiping at my nose before I make a fist and lightly knock on the pillow. The bed creaks in protest again.

Alright, yeah. He's probably going to notice.

At a tug along my back, my attention is pulled away from the pillow statue to see that my ribbons are diving beneath Slade's blankets like hyper kittens.

"Oh, great Divine," I mutter as I try to shove them away. They never used to act this way before. It's like ever since they burst out to attack Slade in the fighting circle, they've just taken on a life of their own.

"Get out of his bed!" I hiss, but the damn things are strong. I try to get them off, but they pull right out of my grasp again and continue doing barrel rolls. With an exasperated sigh, I lean over and shove my hands beneath the blankets, grabbing hold of the ribbons like a twenty-four stranded rope.

I start pulling on them when a deep, sensual voice stops me cold. "If I knew you had interest in tangling yourself up in my bed, I would've at least had the forethought to be in it already."

Slade.

Bright side? None. Absolutely none. Because I just

turned his pillow solid gold from *sniffing* it like a lunatic, while he watched my ribbons dive into his sheets like fish in a Slade stream.

Fantastic.

CHAPTER 28

AUREN

S *lade is leaning up against* the bedroom wall with one foot kicked up behind him, casual as can be. With his arms crossed in front of his chest and his sleeves rolled up to show off his strong forearms, he looks ridiculously sexy with his ruffled black hair and perfectly molded clothes.

Even with the shadowed light, I can see the amusement in his expression, and I'd be able to appreciate how sizzlingly gorgeous he is if it weren't for the fact that my face is now flamed with embarrassment.

I just *had* to sniff the damn pillow.

"Well, I doubt *that* will be very comfortable to sleep on," Slade muses.

Snapping out of the shock of being caught, my body jerks upright, and I try to act properly, like I wasn't just clawing through his bedsheets, though mortification bleeds through my voice. "It was an accident."

"And the rest of you was rooting around in my bed because…?"

"I was trying to get my ribbons out of your blankets," I explain, as if that somehow makes this any better.

His eyes fall to my hands where I have the golden lengths bunched in my fists, but the ribbons immediately go limp like I made the whole thing up and they weren't doing anything at all.

Traitors.

I shove them behind me and cross my arms, trying to gain some semblance of calm, though my heart is pounding hard enough to rattle my ribs.

Creases of light fold in from the gaps between the curtains, casting shards of glowing lines between us. We regard each other in silence for a moment, while my nervous embarrassment grows.

"I'm sorry," I rush out. "Fake Rip let me in, but I should've stayed in the sitting room. It was incredibly rude of me to come in here."

He tilts his head. "So why did you?"

My mouth opens and closes, but no words come out, because what am I going to say? *Well, I just wanted to snoop?* That doesn't seem like a good answer.

When I don't reply, he says, "You just decided to come in here and rumple up my blankets because you were bored?" His tone isn't impatient or angry, even though I've clearly overstepped. If anything, he's just amused, though there's an underlying wariness too. His green eyes seem darker than usual, his shoulders tight with a tension that won't let go.

The blush on my cheeks burns hotter at his teasing tone. "Are you angry?"

"Very," he replies steadily, and my heart drops until he adds, "but not with you."

I swallow hard, unsure how to respond to that.

"What are you doing here, Auren?"

"Here, as in...Ranhold or...?"

I'm stalling. I know it, he knows it, but I can't seem to help it. Not now that he's here in front of me.

Mirth flashes across his face. "Here, as in my personal chambers."

Our conversation from the library replays in my head again. "I...well, I came here to see you."

He may look relaxed to others, but I've paid enough attention to Slade to know that's not the case. He's watching me in that intense way of his, like he's studying every inch, noting every gesture.

"Why?"

I twist my hands into my skirts in a nervous gesture because this is so much harder than I thought. Or maybe I just didn't really let myself think it through because I didn't want to chicken out.

"Auren?" he prompts.

He's always doing that, isn't he? Prompting me, pushing me, and it's exactly what I need. But I'm not only hearing him now, I'm hearing him *then*. When he gave me words and fight and a choice.

Listen to your instincts and stop holding back.

I can't wait to see the rest of you.

You're so much more than what you let yourself be.

Do you want to stay?

My throat thickens like I've gulped mud, but I manage to look him in the eye. "I'm here because I wanted to say something to you."

The only indication that I've surprised him is in the way he slides his propped-up foot onto the floor, as if he's bracing himself for what I have to say. "...Alright."

Before I can lose my nerve, I take a deep breath. "When I was five years old, war came to Bryol, where I lived in Annwyn. It arrived with fire and smoke and death. My parents tried to sneak me out with the rest of the children on the street, but our escorts didn't last the hour. We were stolen long before we ever reached safety."

Slade's attention intensifies, like this was the last thing he expected. Even a part of me is surprised that this is how I've chosen to open up. Then again, maybe this is exactly what I needed to say.

"Even though I didn't have my magic yet, hadn't even sprouted ribbons from my back, I was too recognizable to be bought by any fae. So, I was smuggled into Orea—I still to this day don't know how. All I know is, one night I was in Annwyn, and the next, I was here in this world where I didn't belong, where the sky didn't sing and the sun wasn't right. I was bought by a man in Derfort Harbor who smelled like alcohol and pipe smoke. A man who taught me how to steal and to beg. That same man who later made me into a street rat saddle, who made sure I opened my legs for any paying customer who wanted a night with the *painted girl*."

Slade goes entirely still.

His eyes are trained on me as fierce as a hawk, and that intrusive power of his seems to tremble the air while it cloys forward to press against my skin. Like a feline's rough tongue come to lick against invisible wounds.

"I didn't run away until I was fifteen, and then..." My eyes drop down to my gloved hands. "Well. It doesn't matter. Things didn't go well for me."

The first teardrop falls from my eye, the brined water of old hurts turning gilded the moment it slides down my cheek, though I dash it quickly away.

"I'm telling you this so that you can understand. When Midas came along, I was broken. I'd never known a kind touch by a man. I'd never known what love was or even real friendship. I didn't even know *myself* yet. I may not have been innocent, but I was naive—unsure of who I was, who I could be."

Vulnerability pierces me right in my chest, but I know I can't stop now. Even though I've run out of breath, I have to keep on exhaling, keep on purging, or else I'm going to suffocate in my own poison.

I lift a shoulder. "I thought I loved him. I thought he loved *me*. For a long time, I convinced myself that was what love and friendship was, because I didn't know any better."

From across the room, I see Slade's pale throat bob with a hard swallow, the roots of his power twisting around his neck. "And now?" he rumbles.

"Now, I know that I was a girl clinging to my own stagnancy, because I was terrified of being thrown back into the world that had abused me. I couldn't face the truth that Midas was abusing me too, just in a different way." My admission is a heavy burden lifting from my tongue, every word weighed down. "If Midas ever loved me at all, he buried it beneath his love for gold and the love for himself. Buried it so deep that he doesn't even remember what he covered."

Slade's hands hang at his sides, and something ripples in his eyes. Something I can't read. "What are you saying, Auren?"

Everything.

I'm saying everything.

Because there's no time. Because I'm supposed to leave. Because he's leaving too.

I take a deep, shaky breath. "All my life, I have been coveted or bought or possessed because of the gold that drips from my fingers and lusters my skin. I have been used and kept, and I learned to accept that life. I learned to accept that the best I deserved was Midas and that I shouldn't ever hope for more because I knew just how much worse it could be."

An angry look slashes across the shadows of Slade's face, his mouth pressing together above his stubbled chin.

My wet lashes drag against my cheek with every blink. "But then you came along. And never, not once, has anyone looked at me the way you do."

He goes tense, breath bated to hear what I have to say. There's a long pause held between us, like hands cupping water, desperate not to let a single drop leak out. "And what way is that?"

"Like I'm a person instead of a trophy. Like you don't just look at me and see gold," I answer honestly. "That's never happened before," I admit with a sad smile. "You challenged me to be more than what I've been made into. You showed me how to see the world without my blindfold."

He shifts on his feet, allowing a slash of light shining from the balcony doors to land across his black-clad chest. "Good."

"But when you did that, you didn't just open my eyes. You shifted my vision entirely, and now, all I keep seeing is *you*."

My voice cracks with the truth, but I let it spread, let it split, just as I've been torn down the middle for weeks. It's so hard, standing here in this raw honesty, bleeding out words. But for better or for worse, I've chosen a path in that forked road.

"I was going to just run away. To continue denying and doubting this...*thing* between us. I kept telling myself that you lied to me, that you'll fool me like Midas did, that you can't be trusted. But you're under my skin and stuck in my head, and I'm furious with you for that."

Slade rears back and his eyes flash. "*Why?*"

A shaky sigh slips from my lips. "I'm furious because every waking hour, every sleepless night, I'm trying to convince myself that running away is the best option, but I'm *failing* at it. I have these things inside of me now, this anger and this fear and this *want*, and I should walk away—I *should*. But it's not enough to just get away from Midas anymore, to run and hide. Because you dug around and unraveled me, and now, I want *more*."

Tears gleam across my cheeks as they fall. I don't think Slade is breathing. There's this look on his face that's somehow a perfect mix of determination and devastation. His power crackles, and although I brace myself for a wave of sickness, it doesn't come.

"Auren," he rasps, just a slip of my name that somehow sounds like a promise rent from his soul.

"I keep blaming you for things so that I can push you

away. But you've done nothing wrong. Not really. You've challenged me and pissed me off and lied, but it's nothing I didn't do right back. You're not the villain in my story."

"I am," he says without remorse, his sharp jaw tight with tension. "But I'll be the villain *for* you. Not to you."

"I believe you," I say immediately, because it's true. I *do* believe him, not just in this, but in everything. I can only hope that doesn't make me the fool.

The moment I say that, Slade takes a step forward. Just one, yet I feel the air between us condense and thicken. As if all these words I'm saying are filling up the divots we've created by digging in our heels.

I watch him and he watches me, and in my head, I hear him saying, *you are my own good.* In the tingle of my lips, I'm feeling the heat of his mouth when he kissed me.

"All my life, men have had me, but I have never had a man."

The barest of breaths sucks in through his teeth. A stillness passing between us like a fragile pane of glass.

"I am no man."

"No. You're more," I agree. "Because no matter what I do, you cling to my skin and burrow into my conscience, and as angry as I am at you for that, I don't want to lie to myself anymore. I am *sick to death* of repression. Of denial. Of holding back. After twenty damn years, I don't want to tell myself no."

"So *don't*," he says, practically cursing the word.

"What do you want, Auren? Admit to me what you *really* want."

There's an internal compass inside of me that laid still for so long, stuck behind its arc of glass, listless and without hope. But it's been spinning since the moment I left Highbell, begging me to follow my instincts. To move toward something better.

It's time I start following that compass. I just didn't expect for it to point to him.

My pulse pounds and my hands tremble, because when denial drains out of you, it leaves you shaken and scared. What are we without our white lies and protective walls? I'm laid bare, heart raw and vulnerabilities wrenched open, thoroughly ruined while somehow feeling inexplicably *right*.

Which is why I let that last wall tumble down when I look Slade in the eye and say, "You, Slade. I want you."

CHAPTER 29

AUREN

Time crawls. *With bent knees* and flat palms, it skulks forward with a painful, pitiful drag, scraping at my nerves as it goes.

Slade stares at me, and an unbearable silence fills the spaces where seconds should be ticking by. It's unfair how beautiful he looks just by standing there. Midas called him ugly, because he can't fathom the perfection of Slade's anomalies. The strange marks of power that root beneath his skin are striking. As are the thorns that sprout from his spine and the scales that dust his cheek when he's in his other form. Every sharp plane of his face, every strand of tousled hair, every muscle sculpting his body is perfect.

Why did he have to be so *consuming*?

My life would be easier if he weren't. But I've stepped

too close to him and gotten caught in his quicksand. No matter which direction I go, I just end up sinking deeper.

My heart beats so hard that my temples throb, palms slicking up with nervousness as he continues to stand there, watching me.

I just told him I want him, told him bits of my life I don't share with people, and yet...he's saying nothing.

Finally, I can't take it anymore. The silence, the scrutiny, the confessions lying at my feet like plucked fruit left to rot. "Are you going to say anything? I just admitted that I want you, and you're just standing there."

Slade blinks. "I was processing."

"You process really slowly."

His mouth hitches up. "What do you mean, exactly, when you say you want me?"

I thought I couldn't be more embarrassed, but I was wrong. I wasn't expecting this reaction, and it makes me feel...rejected. Snubbed. It hurts more than I can put into words. "You know what? Forget it."

The second I move toward the door, Slade easily sidesteps in front of me, stopping me in my tracks. "You think you can say all of that to me and then just walk out?"

I shoot him an incredulous look. "Yes, because *you're not saying anything*. If things have changed, if you don't want me back, then…"

A frown tucks in, creasing in place between Slade's brows. "*Don't want you*? Is that what you think? You think I've been hanging around Fifth Kingdom because I'm excited to attend a ball?"

"I don't know what to think!" I cry out, hands flinging up in exasperation. "I just said all of those things, and—"

"I've wanted you since the moment I laid eyes on you, Goldfinch. I was just waiting for you to catch up."

My breath hitches to the steady gait of his voice, my gaze reined in to his piercing eyes. It's everything I didn't know I needed to hear. His words instantly calm the turmoiled waters that were splashing around inside my chest, and just like that, my fear of rejection washes away.

When he takes a prowling step forward, my pulse jumps, like I've suddenly found myself playing the prey in a hunt. "Tell me, do you remember how it is between fae?"

"Umm, no." I give a slow shake of my head, confused by what exactly he means.

"Fae are not like Oreans," Slade explains as he walks over to the fireplace and crouches down in front of it.

My eyes drop to his powerful thighs, and I watch as he meticulously layers the grate with kindling from the neat woodpile before he lights it with a piece of flint. Sparks come to life, and he leans in closer, blowing softly until flames lick up the wood. I don't know why I find that sexy, but I do.

"Fae are wilder in our instinctual drives. We can be demanding and ardent, dominant and jealous." He stands up and faces me again, and even though he's no closer than he was before, it feels like something between us has compressed. Like the world is shrinking into this moment. "Especially with...someone we want."

I'm hot all over, my ribbons unable to hold still any longer as they twine against my back.

"I didn't answer you right away because I need you to understand something first," he tells me, that dark, brooding voice of his caressing my ears.

I force myself to let go of my skirts and smooth out the wrinkled parts I'd clutched onto. "Okay..."

Newborn firelight flickers at his back, but his gaze gleams brighter. "I was going to make myself walk away. I was going to leave early—tomorrow actually. I had every intention of respecting your decision. Whether it was to stay with *him* or to run, I was going to force myself to accept it and leave you be."

I don't like hearing him talk about leaving. Just the thought of it makes me squirm.

"But make no mistake. I would've still wanted you."

My eyes prickle with his declaration.

Right now, with the intensity of his attention on me, I can *feel* that wild edge he just mentioned. "It's all or nothing, Auren."

"What do you mean?"

"I want *all* of you," he tells me, a newfound hunger in the depths of his green eyes that stirs heat beneath my skin.

"Every piece, every memory, every minute, every inch. This isn't going to be some casual dalliance. This isn't going to be temporary. I want you soul, mind, and body. I want your trust and your thoughts. I want your past, your present, your future. So make *very* certain that you want me for the right reasons. Be certain that you're choosing this, because once you do, there's no turning back."

An overwhelming rush of emotions drenches me. I've been caught in the rain of Slade's storm, not a single part of me left out of the torrent. But surprisingly, my doubts don't sprout up. Worries don't flood me. Instead, I feel an inner resolution, like bobbing ice that's finally settled and gone still.

"I want it," I tell him with a resolute nod.

A slow, wicked grin curls his lips, and my toes curl with it. When he looks at me like that, my skin seems to shimmer, though it has nothing to do with being gold.

"But I get all of you too. I won't ever again give myself to someone who doesn't give himself back to me. So make very certain that *you're* choosing this, King Ravinger," I parrot back to him. "Because once you do, there's no turning back."

He chuckles, the sound like a gravelly baritone that's music to my ears and makes my own lips lift.

"Oh, I'm certain," he replies. "I chose you the moment you called me a prick, and your ribbons tried to knock me on my ass."

A surprised laugh escapes me. "*That's* when you decided?"

"Yep. No need to admit when you chose me. I know it was when you were admiring my ass outside."

My mouth pops open, cheeks going hot. "For the last time, I was *not* looking at your ass!"

"Mm-hmm," he replies, sounding unconvinced as he walks over to the curtain and drags it open, filling the room with the silvered light of the sun stuck behind a veil of snowdrift clouds.

When he opens the balcony door and looks up at the sky, I frown. "What are you doing?" I ask as he comes back in and shuts the door.

"Gauging the time. We have about half an hour, I'd say."

"You have somewhere to be?"

He gives me a sardonic look. "Do you honestly think I'd leave after you just told me you're in love with me?"

I blink in shock and rear back. "I didn't...I'm not in love with you," I quickly say. "That's *not* what I said."

He rubs at the black scruff on his chin, regarding me. "Not exactly that phrase, no. But with you, I have to hear what you're not saying in order to read the whole page of your words." His voice pitches lower, right along with my stomach. "I assure you, I've heard you loud and clear."

I shake my head, dashing away his claim with a slash

of my hand. "That's not...no. Don't be ridiculous. I said I wanted you. I don't love you."

He cocks his head, looking infuriatingly calm as he leans against the wall and crosses his arms again. "Are you sure about that?"

My expression is incredulous. "Yes, I'm sure!" I exclaim, cheeks gone feverish. "I admit I feel something for you, but not *that*, you arrogant ass. Love doesn't happen this way."

His brows hitch up. "Love happens in all kinds of ways. Fast. Slow. In bits and pieces, or immediate. Filled with lust, one-sided longing, a snap realization never noticed before. Deeply. Thoroughly. Love is a whisper we didn't hear or a sound that drums in our ears and drowns out everything else." Slade edges toward me, though I barely notice because I'm so hooked on his words that I've forgotten to blink. "You're incredibly private. Closed-off. Conditioned to shut out your true feelings and deny yourself what you want. So you wouldn't have said all of those things unless you were in love with me, Auren."

Do I love him?

No. He's delusional and pretty damn self-assured. There's a pull between us, sure, an undeniable spark of *something*, but it's not love...

Right?

My teeth grind as I take a step back. "You're wrong,

and you're also a presumptuous jerk, and I no longer want you, so I'm leaving now."

His grin widens. "And you're a gorgeous little liar, but that's okay," he says with a shrug. "I've made you face your other truths, and I have no doubt I can make you face this one too."

My stomach jumps with a thrill I don't want to admit. *He thinks I'm gorgeous.*

Okay, yeah, he thinks I'm a liar too, but the takeaway here is the gorgeous part.

I cross my arms and tip my chin up as if he didn't just tilt my world on its axis. As if I'm not feeling exposed and terrified. "Don't say love."

"Why not?"

"Because," I huff out, feeling overwhelmed. "That's... I don't have the best history with that particular word, so I'd appreciate it if you wouldn't say it."

The bastard grins. "We'll work on that."

My eyes narrow, though my damn heart is pitter-pattering like a flock of feet. "Okay, goodbye."

His lips twitch and he shakes his head. "As I said before, you're not leaving, so you should know better than that."

"I know that my ribbons are going to push you out of the way if you don't stop teasing me."

His eyes flick down, and I follow his gaze to see that my ribbons have once more started to slither up to his bed and wriggle around. "Great Divine," I mutter.

Slade tries and fails to suppress his grin. "I'll take my chances with them. So…since you're staying, will you undress for me?"

My heart stops, eyes going wide. "Excuse me?"

"Soul, mind, *and body*, remember?" he says, a devilish spark in his eye. "I want all of you, and I'll have you."

A full-body flush streams down my skin and pulses low in my stomach. "*Now*?" I squeak.

He lifts a shoulder. "We can play this push and pull game for a little bit longer if you prefer. I enjoy our verbal sparring. The challenge makes the reward that much sweeter. But we both know it's just a matter of time before I have you under me, spread out and gloriously naked with your sunlit skin pressed against mine as I take you hard and slow."

"Good goddess," I breathe, pressing a hand to my hot cheek. "You're a crass one, aren't you?"

Carnal amusement crosses his expression. "Oh, Goldfinch, if you think that was crass, then you don't want to know the things I'm thinking, because they're positively *filthy*."

The intensity that's always between us flares from the pit of my stomach and pulses between my thighs. This heated temptation has been building with every interaction, and I can't help but feel like all the moments between us have led us to this. That it was just a matter of time before we were going to collide.

"Now, are you going to strip, or are you going to lie to yourself and pretend that this wasn't what you wanted when you came here to see me?"

The cocky prick.

I arch a brow. "You can't have me yet."

His eyes flare with challenge. "Is that so?"

My hand waves toward the balcony. "It's still daylight. Which means you can't touch me." I let a smug smile cross my face.

But Slade doesn't look deterred. In fact, he starts prowling over to me, and the sly look he wears makes my own grin falter. "Why do you think I asked you to undress yourself?" he purrs as he comes closer. "If I could touch you right now, I'd already be doing it. Like I said, we have about half an hour, but just because I'm forced to wait until I slide my hands over your luscious body doesn't mean we can't have plenty of enjoyment in the meantime."

"I don't know if that's a good idea…" My heart slams against my chest, and I retreat as he keeps coming forward until my back hits the wall.

"I wholeheartedly disagree."

He doesn't stop until he's right in front of me, his hands coming up to brace on either side of my head. His power presses against my skin, making chills scatter down the side of my neck. In one inhale, I breathe in his scent like it's my very own aphrodisiac.

This dangerous closeness is heightening *everything*. Desire coils between us so thick that I can taste it. The temptation of him is just a breath away, and yet, we can't touch.

Not yet.

Holding back from him is its very own sweet agony of craving ache.

When Slade inches his face closer to my ear, I don't dare move or blink or even breathe.

His voice is a seductive grit of palpable hunger that has my ribbons twisting on the floor and my own want surging. My eyes flutter closed as his words stroke my ear and slip inside to settle beneath my ribs like they carry their own beat.

"It's fucking *torture* to have you stand there and tell me you want me, and not be able to do anything about it. But I'm a patient male, and as soon as I'm able, I'm going to touch and taste every inch of you. I'm going to have you writhing and begging, and I'll give you every bit of pleasure I can wring from your delectable body," he murmurs in a wicked promise. "The moment that sun dips, Goldfinch, you're *mine*."

CHAPTER 30

AUREN

I have never wanted someone as much as I want this male. I have never felt as wanted as Slade makes me feel.

My chest heaves, my heart pelting out a percussion against my ribs that somehow matches the timbre of Slade's carnal promise.

"Tell me, Auren."

I didn't even realize I'd let my eyes flutter closed until I spring them open again, my head braced against the wall behind me, Slade hooking me against it with forbidden closeness. "Tell you what?"

"Tell me again that you want this. That I can have all of you. I want to hear it."

Parched heat forces me to lick my lips, and Slade's eyes flare as he watches my tongue drag across before I can answer him. "I won't ever be an object for someone to possess ever again, but I don't think that's quite what you mean."

"It's not," he replies, the flames behind him bedecking his silhouette in its gleam. "I don't want to be your master, Auren. I'm not asking to keep you like property. I'm asking you to give me your all and not hold back, because I'm far too deep with you to settle for anything less. It's what our fae nature demands. It is what *I* will demand. Once I have you, I'm not going to give you up."

"I don't want you to," I whisper, and the vulnerability I let slip softens his eyes. The green of them is so deep it reminds me of the darkest grass at the very cusp of summer. Of sunburnt moss stained against shoreline rocks. It's the green of secret forests so thick no one ever attempts to traverse them. But me, I'd let myself get lost in it just to remind myself of this moment.

"Undress for me, Goldfinch," he murmurs. "I want to see you."

I bite my lip with hesitation, though my body pulses. "Promise you won't touch me yet."

"Until the sun sets." He makes it sound like a sensuous warning, and I find myself shivering when he pulls away. I miss his presence immediately, even if our proximity was entirely too dangerous. The fact that he even *would* be that close to me during daylight is a big deal. He trusts me enough to be a mere breath away. He wants me enough to risk it.

Slade walks out onto the balcony and drags in a chair, the iron feet scraping against the floor as it comes to a stop in front of the fire. He shuts out the wintry air with a click before striding back over, and then sits down with a cocked brow. "I'll stay right here in this spot."

The breath I let out is shaky, but not in fear. Instead, I'm full of anticipation.

For the first time in my life, *I'm* choosing the person I take to bed. I get to see what all of this sexual tension and spiking chemistry between us is going to surmount to. It just took a restless night and a dwindling hourglass to face my truth.

I want him.

I'm sick of pushing him away, of trying to confine myself to denials and doubts. I understand the importance of him doing his kingly duties, of not playing into Midas's hands. But I also want to know what it feels like for Slade to be truly mine, and that's what I had to face when I woke up. Because if I were to leave without telling him, without giving myself this, then I would have regretted it forever. I would've always wondered.

I'm sick of wondering.

There comes a point in your life when you have to choose between having regrets and the possibility of making mistakes. I'd rather make those mistakes than live without ever taking a chance, because I've missed out on too much already. Taking chances can be like walking through a mudslide, where every inch of you gets stained, but regrets are the stagnant pools of deprivation, and I've been wading in them for far too long.

It's time to get a little dirty.

Slade's attention is solely on me as I peel myself away from the wall. The fire blazes behind him like the mouth of a demon, but the wickedest thing in this room is *him*. The way he watches me leaves no doubt in my mind that his thoughts are as filthy and debauched as he claimed.

"You know, this hardly seems fair that I should be undressing while you aren't," I point out.

Slade grins from his seat. "If you wanted me to strip, Auren, all you had to do was ask." When I narrow my eyes on him, he clicks his tongue. "Shy?"

Of course I'm a little shy. I'm about to bare myself to him, to let him see every inch of me, and it's nerve-wracking.

As if he's caught the tremor of hesitation that moves through me, Slade says, "Do you remember when I accidentally walked in on you in my tent when you were changing?" At my slow nod, he goes on. "I wanted to touch you so damn badly it took every ounce of self-restraint to walk away. I'll admit, I thought about that moment many, *many* times."

"That's not very gentlemanly," I tease.

His lips tip up. "I'm no gentleman."

Why does something as simple as that send a trill of excitement reverberating down my spine?

Before I lose my nerve, I look down at the ribbons that are still somewhat wrapped around me to hold up my dress. One by one, I let them slowly unravel all the way until the loose back of my bodice parts like paper unfolding.

When all of my ribbons are lying on the floor behind me, they shake out and stretch. I lift my fingers to the top of my gown, more to keep it up than to peel it off.

One look at Slade, and my face heats, but I don't want my nerves to get the better of me. I want to be confident, sexy, in control. *Empowered.*

Keeping that frame of mind, I turn around until my back is facing him, and the heat of the crackling fire trickles up my spine. With my fingers digging beneath the collar, I drag my dress off my left shoulder, feeling like I'm exposing far more than just my skin. Two of my ribbons come up to help tug the sleeve the rest of the way down, and with my pulse ricocheting in my veins, I do the same to the other side, until the bodice sinks around my waist.

"Not a fan of the corsets here, love?"

That damn word.

"No," I tell him with a shake of my head. "And you wouldn't be either if *you* were expected to wear them."

A low chuckle. "I suppose I wouldn't."

I start to pull the dress down, but Slade says, "Slower."

Just that single word spikes desire low in my belly. "Bossy."

"King," he reminds me.

My lips tilt up, and then with a careful drag, I start to take my gown off. I give a slightly exaggerated shimmy of my hips, and behind me, I hear Slade groan. A thrill shoots through me, and my confidence grows enough that I haul it down the rest of the way and let the dress pool at my feet.

I look over my shoulder, careful to keep my body still as I turn my head.

He's leaning forward, bent elbows propped against his thighs, hands clasped in front of his chin. There's nothing bored or stony about him right now. No, he's pure heat and restrained hunger, and I *love* that I'm the person who's put that look in his eyes.

"Let down that gorgeous hair of yours."

My ribbons come up instantly, two of them unthreading the braids they created. A gentle comb through, and then my scalp is relaxed, my golden tresses hanging down my back in gentle waves.

"I can't wait to thread my fingers through every strand," he tells me. "To twist it around my fist and tip your head back so I can look you in the eye as I take you from behind."

A stuttering breath slips past my lips at his wicked words, and I watch as his eyes dip lower. *Lower.*

Slade hums. "I'm inclined to agree with you about the corsets, but I have to say, Fifth's undergarments are a different matter entirely."

A nervous laugh comes out of me as his gaze settles on my ass that's currently encased in gold lace. Glittering stockings hug my legs, the tops stopping at my thighs. His hands move to the armrests, his fingers curling over the ends to give it a white-knuckled grip, as if he has to hold himself back, or else he'll pounce on me.

"Turn around for me, Auren." His voice simmers and strokes.

I don't know how he can affect me so much, but every gravelly instruction he speaks adds weight to the lust that's already piled inside of me. I step out of the dress and turn in a slow circle until I'm facing him fully, in nothing but my gloves, stockings, underwear, and boots.

His lips quirk up when he sees my long hair hanging perfectly down in the front to cover my breasts. "Tease."

"I'm only following directions," I say with an impish grin.

Movement on the floor has both of us looking down at the same time where we see my ribbons trying to slither closer to Slade.

"Now these, on the other hand, seem to be quite brazen," he says, sounding entirely too pleased about that.

I give them a tug. "They're just trying to get closer to the fire."

"Liar." With a smirk, he tips his head. "Come here."

My eyes narrow. "*Slade*."

"I won't touch your skin, I promise. Put your foot right here," he says, widening his legs and tapping the spot between.

A hard swallow travels down my throat when my gaze drops down to the very visible bulge in his pants. Walking forward, I carefully lift my foot and brace it on the edge of his chair, right between his muscled thighs.

There's a slow drag of his gaze that goes up the entire length of my leg. Slade hums, and the noise seems to settle right in my core, making it pulse. "You are the most stunning female I have ever seen."

His compliment sends butterflies fluttering past the crevices of my chest. I don't look away from his face when he lazily trails my every curve as if he's taking his time to see every part of me. I have the sudden urge to reach down and thread my hands through his hair, so I hold them behind me instead, my fingers tangling into the base of my ribbons.

With my foot propped up like this, Slade has the perfect view of, well, *everything*. I suck in a breath at just how intimate this is, and he looks up at me with a glint in his eye.

We're so incredibly close, and even though my lace

panties cover me, and my hair hangs over my breasts, I still feel so *exposed*. In the firelight, my skin gleams, the tight weave of my stockings glistening.

"Don't move," he tells me, and then his hands come down to the laces of my boots.

Transfixed, I watch his deft fingers untie the knot and then begin to meticulously loosen the ties. When he's slackened them all, he gives my boot a tap, and I carefully switch legs until my right foot is propped up. He does the same thing to that foot, and then he looks up at me again.

"There," he says quietly.

Setting my foot down on the floor, I back up and slip out of my boots, and then I back up a few more steps, putting some safe space between us before one of us pounces on the other.

"Go sit on my bed."

I shake my head. "I'll gild it."

"I don't care," he says roughly.

"I do. The servants will see."

"They're not allowed in here."

Looking around at the messy space, I smirk. "Maybe they should be."

His lips twitch. "The bed, Auren."

Great Divine, the way he says that. The command sparking through his tone is ravenous, impatient, *dominant*. Like he's been waiting for me all this time, and he's ready for the clash. The lascivious need inside of me craves it, wants to see just how hungry I can make him.

"Hmm, I think I'll stay right here," I tease. My tone is flippant, though I have to work not to let a smile out.

I'm careful to stay next to the wall, letting only the back of my head rest against it, my hair covering my skin enough not to gild anything. Then, with a boldness I didn't know I possessed, I let my fingers play against my collarbone, then a slow stroke down between my breasts.

A low, rumbling growl escapes him.

He brings one hand up to run a thumb over his plush bottom lip, and my gaze follows the movement, wondering what it would feel like if it were *my* lip he was touching like that.

"Lower."

His gruff command makes me press my legs together, trying to feed into the sudden need for friction.

With my eyes locked on his, I let my fingers trail down slowly between my breasts in a leisurely scrawl. I drop beneath to the curves of them, my hair moving in the slightest ripple of tantalizing tease without revealing anything beneath.

"Lower," he says again, and my nipples pebble.

I let my touch drag down to my stomach, circle over my belly button, and then pause just above my panty line. Slade leans back and tips his hips up slightly to adjust himself in his seat, and I don't know what it is about the move, but it sends a rush of heat between my legs.

"You have no idea what you're doing to me."

I steal a look at the length that seems to have grown between his legs. "I think I have *some* idea."

Another drag of his thumb against that bottom lip. "You look good against that wall, but you're going to look even better pinned up against it while I fuck you."

"Great goddess," I murmur, flooded with a newfound throb.

"It's nearly dusk."

My eyes flit over to the balcony door, its glass frosted with little veins of freeze hanging from every corner. Outside, the light's gone murky, the gray giving way to obscurity.

"So it is."

As if he can't hold back anymore, Slade unfurls from the chair and straightens. His power coils around him, reaching out in invisible fingers to stroke against my skin. My breath catches, and once again, there's no nausea or sense of wrongness. Instead, his magic seems to blow around me in an unmoving breeze.

Like a caged predator, Slade goes to the glass doors of the balcony and then grins. "You're very nearly mine now."

My teeth trap my bottom lip in anticipation, everything in me nearly trembling beneath the wait. When he reaches for the top button on his black shirt, my eyes go wide, and even my ribbons go still.

At seeing my expression, he pauses. "I can leave it on, if you prefer."

For a moment, my brows lower in a frown of confusion, but then it dawns on me. My gaze traces over the shifting stems along his skin, the reaching ends peeking above his collar.

"Don't you dare," I tell him. If he thinks I don't want to see him, he's wrong. I'm not put off by those strange roots beneath his pale skin. If anything, they make me want to run my fingers over each and every one.

My reply earns me a roguish grin, but I don't miss the flash of relief in his expression. He undresses slowly, and with each button that comes undone, my heart seems to beat harder.

I saw him shirtless in the fight circle, but that was when he was in his Rip form, and great Divine, was he *ripped.* But when Slade shrugs out of his shirt and tosses it to the floor, my breath catches, because...

"You're beautiful."

A surprised laugh escapes him, but I'm not kidding. Every inch of him is sculpted to perfection. My attention is latched onto his body, and I'm unable to look away.

Those intrinsic threads of his power seem to sprout from his chest, right at the chiseled line below his pecs. They're thick at the bottom and a perfect mirror image on both sides of his chest and neck as they root upward, like they're searching for a sun. They're thinnest right where they end at the edge of his jaw, barely bigger than a needle, yet as thick as my finger at the base.

If it weren't for the fact that they move ever so slightly, like a field of wheat in a breeze, I'd think they were tattooed onto his pale skin. I find myself aching to let my lips drag over them, to taste them as they bend.

Slade stands there, letting me drink him in, while his power pools around him. My gaze slips down to see his perfectly cut abs, the V that disappears below his pelvis. His arms hang at his sides, muscles bulging, the strong veins down his forearms enough to make my mouth water.

When I'm finally able to lift my eyes back up to his face, I realize I've taken two steps closer to him, as if drawn to him, needing to close the space between us.

"I'd touch you if it wouldn't turn you solid," I admit.

"One part of me is plenty solid already," he says with a devilish smirk.

My face heats, and Slade begins to pace in front of me like a wild animal waiting for the bars of time to drop away. He kicks off his shoes, and the impatient energy he's now giving off is mixing with the rampancy of his frenetic power, causing my nerves to jump with edginess.

His hands drop to the button of his pants, and my eyes are glued to the movement. But instead of popping it open and showing me the rest of him, he pauses, and I actually *whimper*. Out loud.

Slade chuckles at me, now being just as much the tease as I was before. "Impatient, Goldfinch?" he asks, enjoying himself way too much.

I open my mouth to reply, but the words die on my tongue because right then, I *feel* it.

The telltale prickle that travels along my exposed skin, making chills scatter like tossed dice. I look toward the glass of the door, the dying gray light breathing out with the last exhale of day.

Finally, I tug off my gloves, letting them drop like a weight on the ground, more indicative than any bell toll. The moment my hands are bare, I reach back and touch the wall, and Slade freezes when he sees my bare skin collide with it...and no gold comes.

"Thank *fuck*." In five long strides, he demolishes the space between us. He's suddenly there, gripping me by the waist, hard lips fused to mine, and *finally*, we combust.

CHAPTER 31

SLADE

uren latches onto me as desperately as I do her.
There is no holding back. Not anymore. The rest of my will snapped with the sunken sun, the tie of daylight severed, and not a moment too soon.

I walk her backwards until her back hits the wall, and then I completely devour her mouth, tasting her the way I've wanted to since I found her in my room. Tipping her head with a firm hold along her jaw, I make her open for me, my tongue licking up her intoxicating taste.

This isn't a kiss. It's a *demand*, and she meets my terms beautifully. I've been waiting for this moment. Waiting for *her*, so I hope she was sure when she pledged herself, because I'm just enough of a bastard to hold her to it.

It was all I could do to keep my ass planted in the chair and not reach out and drag her into my lap. It took all my willpower not to touch her while she leaned against the wall, tantalizing me with peeks of her nudity like a temptress come to test my resolve.

Fucking gold-touch.

Auren pulls from my lips to take in a gasp, but I chase her mouth, not done with her. Nowhere close to being done. And to think, I was going to leave tomorrow.

"I need to catch my breath," she says, pulling away again to pant against my neck.

"*I* get your breaths right now." My tongue darts out to lick at the burnished edge of her neck, making her shiver deliciously.

Stroking along the edge of her cheek, I dive my fingers into the long strands of hair hanging down her back. Angling her just where I want her, I nip at her lips until she opens her mouth even more. When I reach down to grip her thigh and lift it over my hip to get closer, she melts against me. She is supple eagerness wrapped in seductive grace.

I pin my hips against her, and the little nymph grinds her pelvis into me, tearing a groan from my throat when her heat seeks out my hard length. I reach down and grasp her waist, holding it against the wall with a firm push. "Naughty thing. I'm in control right now."

Her eyes flare with impatience, but the hooded look

of them diminishes any anger she might've been trying to display. Her ribbons wrap loosely around my torso, as if she's going to use them to drag me closer.

"I've waited long enough," she tells me, her voice gone husky, while that golden aura of hers flares around her like she's my own personal sun.

"I waited longer," I counter.

Not only did I wait, I was going to *let her go*. I almost can't believe that she's here, warm and willing, choosing *me*.

Without warning, I lift her up, because I can't wait anymore. Auren made her decision, and that was the affirmation I needed.

She squeaks in surprise as I carry her, but both of her legs automatically come up to squeeze my waist. She feels so damn perfect that I consider just taking her like this, with her hoisted in my arms.

Next time.

For now, I want to worship her body on the soft mattress like she deserves. I want to wring out every drop of pleasure I can. I set her down on the bed so I can—

CRACK!

With another feminine squeal, Auren goes pitching to the left toward the headboard and probably would've ended up in the splintered bed frame if I hadn't quickly pinned her in place with my own body.

The two of us look over at the head of the bed that's now collapsed down, the whole thing tilted. There's also a gaping hole where my pillow used to be. It broke straight through the mattress and the frame, landing with a resounding metal clang while feathers from the mattress flutter down around us.

"Think the gold pillow is going to break through the stone floor too?" I ask curiously.

Her brows pull into an adorable frown. "I'm sure it's fine," she quickly says, though she doesn't sound convinced of that at all.

With a smirk, I cup her face and pull it back to me again, wanting her full attention. "You know, that wasn't the way I envisioned we'd break my bed."

A beautiful blush bronzes her cheeks, and she lets out a little laugh, but my attention dips lower. With her beneath me like this, my cock is so hard I'm surprised it's not ripping through the seam of my pants.

She licks her lips as I lift up on my knees braced on either side of her. I brush her hair away from her breasts, finally seeing what I only had teasing peeks at before. The sight of her makes something surge in me, an almost animalistic drive to claim her.

Hair fanning around her head, eyes filled with lust, lush lips parted, and breasts moving up and down in time with her fast breaths. I look down at this gorgeous creature, and all I can do is stare. Stare and pray to the gods that I can memorize every inch of her. I want this vision burned into my mind for all eternity.

I lift her leg, my hands trailing over her calf and up to her thigh. I drag her stocking down slowly, wanting to appreciate each exposed part of her soft skin. I do the same to the other leg, relishing in the way she shivers as I pull them the rest of the way off.

To my surprise, she directs two of her ribbons to come down and start pulling her panties off. "Impatient again?" I tease.

"Yes," she says seriously before the ribbons toss them away, and words flee from my mind as I stare down at her.

She's completely nude, everything revealed to me, body glistening in the light of the low burning fire.

"You're fucking *perfection*," I growl, unable to keep the roughness out of my voice. Not when her breasts look like they're aching to be touched, her dusky nipples hard and wanting. Not with her spread out in front of me like a feast, looking better than every fantasy I've ever had of her.

I reach down to pluck up one of the loose feathers from the broken mattress and drag it between her breasts, making another shiver travel down her skin. "If I were an artist, I'd paint you just like this."

She laughs, the sound like music to my ears, and I can't help but swoop down to swallow it up. She moans into my mouth as my tongue dips in, at the same time that I slip my other hand between her thighs to find what's waiting for me.

Heat.

Delicious, sinful, *wet* heat. Another groan escapes me, and I grow impossibly harder in my pants. Auren is going to bring me to my knees. But who would complain with a view like this?

"You're already wet for me," I say against her lips before I kiss my way down her throat. I want to take her. Hard, slow, fast, lying down, against a wall, I don't fucking care. I just want to make her mine.

She lets out a noise low in her throat. "Slade, please."

"Please, what?"

Her eyes flutter. "Are you going to make me say it?"

A grin takes over my face. "Yep."

"Don't be an ass."

I shrug. "I want you writhing. I want your blissful moans in my ear. But I also want that pretty mouth to whisper the wicked words I want to hear."

"You're *very* demanding."

"I warned you."

She hums in consideration and then shocks the hell out of me by suddenly bringing one of her ribbons up to my pants. But she doesn't just have it undo the button. No, she makes the damn thing as sharp as a razor and cuts the button clear off. Then my pants are being tugged off without hesitation, and my hard cock springs out.

I guess I'm not the only demanding one.

Auren's breath seems to stick to her throat as she takes me in. She sits up to get a better look, and with a nibble to her lip, she reaches forward. Looking up at me through her lashes with adorable apprehension, she then closes her fingers around me.

"Fuck." I drop my head back and let out a groan. Her touch is like being caught in the sweetest snare.

Her grip is light and experimental at first, but then she seems to gather her courage and starts to work my length, fist tightening.

"You're so thick that my fingers almost can't close all the way around you," she says breathily, eyes locked on my dick. Any other time, I'd let her touch to her heart's content, but not now. I'm too impatient, too hungry for her.

Without warning, I clamp around her wrist and then push her back on the slanted bed. An *oomph* escapes her as I pin her hands above her head.

Golden eyes look up at me in surprise. "Hey! I wasn't done touching you."

My lips lift at her sass. "You're done." I lean in and drag my mouth against her neck, wishing I was in my other form so my fangs could scrape against her sensitive skin. "Come on, Auren. I want to hear you tell me that you want my cock buried inside of you."

Her aura flares with heat. It's a challenge and we both know it. One last chance to back out. "Great Divine, that *mouth* of yours," she chastises.

My lips spread into a wolfish grin. "You'll like this mouth plenty when I lick your clit until you scream."

Her eyes dilate, breath quickening. "I want to feel you."

"Want to feel me *what*?" I coax, pressing my cock between her legs, making a shudder travel down her body as her own wetness coats my length. She tries to move her hand out of my hold, but I keep her still as I drag against her once more, her face the perfect picture of sexual frustration. "I'll give you what you want as soon as you say it. Be specific."

"Fine," she huffs on a rasp, looking pissed, but she can't fool me. Her aura gives her away, just like the blush on her cheeks and the quick pulse of her neck. She *likes* being teased. And she likes my dirty talk even more. "I want to feel you inside of me. I want you to fuck me hard, I want you to bury your cock in my—"

Before she can finish her sentence, my hips punch up, and I surge into her with one hard thrust.

"Oh, goddess…" She cries out, spine arching, head thrown back, while I get damn tunnel vision because being inside her is fucking *sublime*.

A ground-out noise drags up my throat, and it's all I can do to not spill inside her right here and now. Her cunt squeezes my cock like she was made for me, so tight that

I have to grind my teeth to keep from fucking into her like a madman. I probably should've gone slower, but I just couldn't wait another second to be sheathed in her heat.

I force myself to stay still, to let her body get used to me so I don't hurt her. But she clearly has other ideas, because she starts to gyrate her hips. "Stop that, I'm letting you adjust," I reprimand playfully, leaning down to run my mouth over her breasts, tongue flicking out to lap at her peaked nipple.

"I'm adjusted," she pants out, making me chuckle. "I want more. I need you to move."

I need to move too. Having her pinned like this, her body hugging my cock, is enough to make me lose my mind. But I want her to lose hers too. "Look at you, you've had my cock for two seconds, and you're already begging for more."

Her scowl is damned adorable.

I grab her thigh and hook it around my waist, right where I like it.

"*Move*," she urges, lifting her hips up again.

"I'm enjoying the view."

Smirking at the impatient frown on her face, I take my time to stroke behind her leg and then travel up the curve of her ass, loving the way it feels in my palm as I squeeze it. I use my hold to tip her hips up slightly, and then I drag my length out of her before slowly pushing back in, her frown morphing from one of frustration to pleasure.

"*Yes...*" she whimpers.

I do it again, but this time, I drive in so hard I make her body slide up the bed. Her ribbons shoot up to curl around the bedposts, and they go firm to hold her in place.

I can feel my eyes practically light up. "Oh, the things I'm going to do with those ribbons..."

Her tongue darts out to lick her lips like the idea excites her, and I lean down to nip at it, punching my hips forward with another deep thrust that makes her gasp. "You like the sound of that?" I love the way her cheeks flush, the way her eyes dilate. I'm going to make it my personal mission to bring that blush of heat over her as many times as I possibly can.

"Y-yes."

"Good."

Another hard thrust, but her body doesn't move away this time, not with the way her ribbons hold her in place. Both of my hands grip her hips, tilting her up to the perfect angle.

The second she's where I want her, I drag my cock out and start fucking her harder, relishing in the way her breasts bounce with every drive of my hips, at the look on her face as I drive into her. She begins to writhe beneath me, her back arching up in a bended beg, and I'm all too happy to oblige her.

My head dips down to lick a line over the slope of her breasts, and a little mewl escapes past her plush lips. "I'm going to fuck these too. Spill my seed on you, mark you as mine everywhere."

"Oh, gods, I *need*..."

"What do you need, Auren?" I say against her breast before giving the other one just as much attention. Her nipples are darker, almost bronze, the tight tips practically begging for my touch. I flick my tongue over it, promising myself I'm going to taste every inch of her. Take her as many times as I can before the sun dawns.

"Faster," she begs. "Harder. Make me feel good."

"You want to come, baby?"

Her eyes flare at the endearment. "Yes."

"You want me to fuck you hard and fast while my fingers play with your clit?"

"Yes!" she cries out with wanton restlessness.

I reach down and pick her up, her ribbons instantly giving me the slack I require as I reposition us on the broken bed. She's on my lap before she can blink, and I lift her by her waist, dragging her up my cock and then slamming her back down.

"*Fuck!*" The curse flies from her mouth, and her hands perch on my shoulders, little nails digging into my skin. I hope she leaves a mark, makes little crescents of claim all over my back.

I grip her hair and pull her face back to look at me, her hooded eyes dragging open with effort. "When you called me by my name for the first time, all I could think was that I wanted to hear you say it while I was buried deep inside of you."

Her exhale stutters out, body quivering.

"That's right," I nod as I lift and lower her body over me again and again until both of us are panting, the cusp of pleasure dragging us upward. "I want to hear you scream my name while this perfect pussy squeezes my cock and milks me dry."

Her eyes fall closed. "Oh goddess... Please, please, *please*!"

My resolve snaps.

Whatever control I'd had left unleashes with her chanted plea. As quick as a blink, I have her pinned to the bed again, and I start to power into her like a male possessed, and then I well and truly start to *fuck* her.

I slip my hand between us to play with her clit, and she jerks so hard she nearly comes up off the bed.

"Oh my…" She starts to moan unintelligibly, head whipping left and right, ribbons tangling in the sheets.

"Take the pleasure I give you, Auren."

The sounds our bodies make together is the dirtiest song I've ever heard. Moans, skin against skin, a bed creaking in protest. All while her delectable body gives me everything I ever wanted and more.

My fingers pluck and circle and stroke as I watch her, note every movement that makes her pussy flutter. I want to learn her, I want to know every trick, every spot, every move that will make her body sing for me.

And sing she does.

"Yes, yes. *Don't stop*," she begs, and I lean down to take her mouth as I drive into her, because I want *all* of her, every fucking part.

When she whimpers against my lips, I drag my mouth down her neck to the sensitive flesh beneath her ear. "Do you feel how tight you are around me? Do you feel how hard I'm fucking you?" I say, lips skimming over her flushed skin. "I'm going to have you again and again and *again*. I will learn every inch of your body, drive you to pleasure, and then do it all over again."

"*Oh...*"

My hand doesn't relent as I pinch and play with her nub, and I feel her wetness coating me. I drive my cock into her faster and harder, my circling strokes on her clit an unrelenting demand to see her fall apart.

I feel her pussy tighten, feel her whole damn body go tense, and I know she's *right there*. I use my other hand to tip her hips up even more, earning a mewl. "That's right, baby. Come for me. I want you to finally unravel."

She curses, eyes clamped shut, breasts bouncing, looking beautifully wanton, and then her aura surges with light. That's all the warning I get before she screams out my name, pussy squeezing me as tight as a vise. "*Slade!*"

My name on her lips in the throes of her orgasm is

enough to tip me right over the edge with her. My cock pulses, and then I'm exploding inside of her. I come so hard I damn well almost black out. "*Fuck.*"

The collision of our shared pleasure encompasses all the pent-up attraction, all the push and pull we've had since we met. She is so damn perfect that even while I'm buried inside of her, I still want more. I want *everything*, just like I told her.

The pleasure stretches on, my thrusts gone ragged, each drag slower than the last, because I don't want this to end. I want her right here against me, want to feel her perfect pussy clamp on my cock as she wraps her arms around my neck.

Her body shudders, lips letting out a small, blissful noise, and my chest goes tight. For a second, we just look at each other, breaths panting, skin slick.

A grip of brooding disquiet seeps in as I think about how we almost missed this. If she'd run away, or if I'd left early like I planned, I would've missed her giving herself to me—and not just her body, but *her*.

I know how difficult it was for her to place her emotions at my feet, especially considering how many people have trampled and manipulated them in the past. I know what it took for her to trust me, and I also know that I'll destroy myself before I ever let her down.

Auren blinks at me with kiss-puffed lips. There's a sated, beautiful look on her flushed face, and she looks so damn sexy I already want her again. She settles my magic, calms my anger, calls to my fae nature. She's a burst of light in my dark, erupting life in the rotting depths of my soul.

She is everything I don't deserve.

But I'm going to keep her anyway.

Gripping her close, I turn us so that I can fall on my back and have Auren draped over me, her body fitting perfectly against me. We pant together as we come down from our high, our hearts slamming in tandem as we catch our breaths. She molds to my body, jellied and satiated, her ribbons lying limp on the bed like they're just as pleased as she is.

I press a kiss against her head, my arm coming around to hold her in place against me. After a moment, she looks up, her chin resting on my chest, fingers drawing over the lines that stretch up and curve toward my neck. Her touch is familiar. Intimate. And it makes me pleased as hell.

When I stroke a finger down her cheek, her head leans into my touch ever so slightly. I'm not sure if she even realizes she does it, but even *that* is gratifying. I want her every reaction to sway toward me like branches in the wind, caught up by the force of our synchronicity.

"What are you thinking about?" she asks, her voice still rasping.

I smooth my hand down her spine, loving the way she shivers when my fingers caress over the base of where her ribbons grow from her back. "You," I say simply, gaze roving over her like I want to drink her in. Her gleaming eyes, her pillowy mouth, and the arch of her brows—every feature is perfect because it's *her.*

She shows me her gorgeous smile, and the shy charm in her eyes makes me want to kiss her all over again so I can taste her happy.

When she tries to shift away from me, I hold her in place, and amusement flashes in her face. "Are you going to let me up?"

"Not likely."

She laughs. "You're still inside of me."

"Yep."

Her smile turns impish, and I know I'm going to have my hands full when my temptress says, "Well, if you're going to stay there, then can we do that again?"

I grip her chin, male satisfaction bleeding through my expression as I look at her, my cock already hardening again. "Oh Goldfinch, we're just getting started."

CHAPTER 32

AUREN

My ear is pressed against Slade's chest as I look out at the glass doors of the balcony. The dying night is the stroke of an artist painting over the sky, lessening the black into shades of muted gray.

Beneath me, Slade sleeps, the tempo of his even breaths like the pull of a breeze. Yet I haven't slept, not for a single minute.

I've soaked up every moment, relished in each touch, reveled in all of him. Right now, in the quiet of a coming dawn, my spirit is content in a way I've never experienced before.

It reminds me of the feeling I used to get when I read those beautiful books of poetry back in Highbell. That sense like I'm suddenly hearing life as a song, an entity with more depth than I could ever possibly fathom.

Everything I've experienced or thought suddenly joins, makes sense, has bigger meaning.

That's what it feels like as I lie here, draped over Slade's body, our skin pressed together in shared warmth. As if the veil of life has peeled back, showing me the greater deepness, the vibrancy of a moment and my place in it all.

I want to stay here forever.

But of course, I can't.

My fingertip traces over his rooting ropes of power, watching the thin lines as they sway beneath his pale skin. They're slower now, sluggish, as if they too are sated and drowsing sleepily.

I give myself another moment of pure indulgence, enjoying the way our legs are tangled together and our bodies slanted, the feel of his arm wrapped around my back. It's so achingly perfect that I've become melancholic, dropped in a dread of knowing that life won't stay this way.

But I wish it would.

When the sky has well and truly blurred with the drab of impending daybreak, I finally force myself to get up. I need to do it slowly so I don't wake him. Using my ribbons, I lift his arm enough to slip out from under him. I freeze when he makes a noise, but instead of waking, he shifts his legs. I use the opportunity to extricate myself the rest of the way.

With careful movements, I rise up from his broken bed and get to my feet, making my ribbons slip out just as gently. The fireplace is just a collection of smoldering coals by now, and the chill of the room raises bumps along my arms.

I start to pick up my discarded clothing around the room like birds to scattered breadcrumbs. My body is sore—deliciously so—and I'd really like to get back to my room and soak in a bath before the sun comes up.

I quickly pull on my gloves, dress, and stockings and then pluck up my boots, stuffing them beneath my arm. On tiptoes, I head for the door, hand grasping the handle and hoping that the hinges don't squeak.

When I open it an inch and it doesn't make a sound, I let out a little breath of relief, only for that breath to turn into a squeal as a hand slams the door shut again.

I whirl around finding a very naked, very *awake* Slade standing over me. "Going somewhere?"

"You scared me!" I admonish, pressing my hand against my racing heart.

He crosses his arms and leans against the door, effectively keeping me in. "Why are you sneaking out?"

"I'm not *sneaking*," I reply. "I just didn't want to wake you. You've barely been sleeping an hour."

A devilish smirk tips up his lips. "Whose fault is that?"

My cheeks immediately heat, despite the cold air. "Yours!" I insist.

He pretends to cock his head in thought. "Mmm, I'd have to disagree. You were quite insatiable. Asked for us to *go again* on multiple occasions as I recall."

I groan in embarrassment, which just makes him grin. "Come back to bed."

"I can't," I tell him with a shake of my head. "The sun is going to be up soon."

His green eyes flit over to the glass doors, to the horizon we can see over the castle walls. "We can fit one more time in."

"I've fit enough in for one night," I quip.

Slade laughs, and the delicious sound makes my toes curl. "Alright, let me get dressed, and I'll walk you back to your rooms."

My eyes nearly bug out. "What are you talking about? You know you can't do that."

He strides across the room, and I become momentarily distracted with his strong back and firm ass until both disappear from view when he enters his dressing room.

Shaking my head, I take the opportunity to open the door and walk out. I expect for the sitting room to be empty, so I startle when I find Fake Rip sitting on one of the chairs, a map rolled out on his lap and a platter of breakfast laid out on the table in front of him.

"Do you *always* wear that helmet and armor? It's only four in the morning."

He doesn't even turn his head in my direction. "Trust

me, it's not my favorite look," he murmurs. "It makes it a pain in the ass to eat...and take a piss."

I scrunch up my nose. "I didn't need to know that."

Spotting my coat hanging on the back of the chair he's sitting on, I walk over and tug, but it doesn't budge beneath his weight. "Can you get off?"

"I suppose I don't have to ask the two of *you* that question," he jokes.

My mouth drops open in mortification, but before I can form a response, Slade strides into the room half dressed, pants hanging low on his hips, black shirt unbuttoned. He walks straight over to Fake Rip and smacks him on the back of his head, helmet be damned. "Don't make me rot your tongue this early in the morning."

Fake Rip chuckles with a shrug, barely glancing up from the map. "Just wanted to see what color her skin turns when she blushes."

"Don't be an ass," Slade says as he starts to button up his shirt, hiding all those sexy muscles I love looking at. "Apologize to her."

Fake Rip reaches behind him and grabs my coat, holding it out to me. "Sorry, little golden girl."

I snatch the coat and pull it on before I sit down and shove my feet into my boots and do up the laces. From my peripheral, I notice Fake Rip looking at Slade. "So I take it we're not leaving now."

Stealing a look up at Slade, I notice his face has gone stony.

"That's what I thought," Fake Rip says, though his tone has taken on a slightly bitter edge. "Then are you going to send me?"

"I don't know yet."

A curse grits out from behind Fake Rip's black helmet. "Dammit, you know we can't fuck around with this. We need to go and see—"

"*I know*," Slade bites out. "We'll talk about it later."

Fake Rip shakes his head, grumbling something too low for me to hear. I quickly tie up the rest of my boots, feeling both awkward and curious about overhearing this conversation.

"Ready?" Slade asks, coming up to stand beside me as soon as I'm finished.

"You can't come with me."

He frowns. "I don't like the idea of you creeping out of here alone like a dirty secret. I'll be discreet."

"*Right*. Because no one will notice King Rot walking the gold-touched favored down the halls at four in the morning," I say with a snort. "We both know I need to go alone so that no one sees."

His eyes narrow, and for a moment, we're stuck in some sort of standoff. Then, without looking away, he says, "Give us a minute."

Fake Rip makes a noise of irritation, but he gets

to his feet and stomps out of the room, heading for the balcony.

When we're relatively alone, Slade runs a hand through his mussed, coal-black hair. I can say from experience that it's just as soft as it appears. But instead of saying anything, he hesitates, looking torn.

"I appreciate the sentiment of you wanting to walk me, but we both know it's not a good idea. I really do need to go." Something flickers in his eyes, making me frown. "What's wrong?"

"Nothing. Everything," he replies in frustration. "I don't like having you slink out of here on your own. What if Midas is there?"

"He won't be," I reassure him. "He hardly ever comes to see me during the day unless he needs me to use my power. And he's been avoiding me since..." I trail off, biting my lip, but Slade hears what I don't say, his deep green eyes flicking to my cheek.

"He better not touch you again."

"He won't."

Still, Slade doesn't seem to be placated. "Tell me you aren't pulling back."

My brows crease. "Pulling back?"

"You're not having regrets, are you?" he asks me, gaze intent on my face.

So *that's* what this is about. My eyes soften, voice

gentling. "Last night was a lot of things, but a regret isn't one of them."

Relief seems to evaporate the tension from his shoulders as he lets out a breath. "Good. It would've been really time-consuming to tie you down on the bed all day."

My lips part in surprise. "You wouldn't dare."

He leans down so our faces are level, that wicked mischievousness I love so much coming back into his eyes. "All of you, every part, and I'm not giving you up, remember? I would *definitely* tie you to the bed if you tried to back out on this. Your ribbons would probably even help me do it."

My stomach flutters at the teasing implications. I can't even deny the part about my ribbons, because they're currently trying to slither up his damn legs. "Well...pretty soon, you can't touch me," I remind him.

His warm breath skates across my cheek. "Have a little faith in me. I could have you begging again, even without touching your skin."

Great Divine.

I swallow, trying to get rid of the lump of lust that's risen up. "I need to go now, or I won't have time to take a bath before the sun comes up."

Seemingly satisfied by my blush, he straightens up. "Have some breakfast first."

I look over to the table, and my stomach chooses that moment to growl, which makes Slade smile in victory.

"One croissant," I relent.

"And some eggs," he adds. "Also fruit. Maybe some ham too."

Rolling my eyes, I turn and sit down on the chaise, where Slade immediately takes a seat next to me. He grabs a plate and starts piling it up while I look around at the spread of croissants. Before I can pick one, he pushes the plate into my hands, and I blink down at it in surprise. "I can't eat all of this."

"Of course you can. Besides, you need to replenish your body. We expelled *a lot* of energy last night," he says with a grin.

How many times can I blush before dawn?

I choose to stuff my face instead of reply, while Slade eats from his own plate, albeit much more slowly.

I clear my throat and jerk my head in the direction of the balcony. "Are you going to let him come back inside? It looks cold out there."

"He's fine," Slade says dismissively.

"No, I'm not!" Fake Rip calls in through the glass, though he doesn't turn around from where he's leaning on the railing. "It's fucking snowing again!"

Slade just snorts out a laugh and continues to eat.

We sit in comfortable silence for a bit, but I find myself getting distracted several times as he bites into his bread, his lips dusted with sugar that I really want to lick up.

"You keep looking at me like that, and I won't be letting you leave."

My eyes shoot up to his teasing gaze that has an entirely different sort of hunger in it that has nothing to do with the food. Finishing my bite, I set the plate down and get to my feet. "Okay, I'm going to head back to my room. Thank you for breakfast."

Slade's eyes trail up my form, and my body reacts to it, my stomach dipping while my nipples pebble. "You should eat more first," he says after a quick glance to the windows, which are growing lighter every second. "I don't think you've had enough."

"No, really, I'm…" I trail off, my eyes narrowing in suspicion. "Wait a minute. Are you…are you trying to purposely stall me?"

He gives a single blink before reaching down and pouring himself something from the pitcher and taking a swig. "I don't know what you mean. I simply enjoy your company, and I think you should stay until well after dawn."

"You *are*. You're stalling me. Why?"

Slade is trying to look *entirely* too innocent. "No reason. So…if you try to bathe during the day, do you turn your bath water liquid gold or solid?"

"I *could* make it solid, but that would take a lot of power. The water would go liquid gold as soon as I touched it, and that's no way to bathe. Which is why I need to get going. Washing with gold water just isn't very cleanly."

"That's unfortunate," he says, though he doesn't sound like he thinks it's unfortunate at all.

My eyes widen in realization. "Oh my goddess, Slade! You're trying to make me late so I can't wash?"

Instead of denying it, the perverse bastard has the nerve to smirk. "I told you fae are a bit wild. I like having my scent all over you. I want to keep it there."

I should be grossed out, but the fact that he wants me to keep his *scent* on me makes my stomach do a little flip. "You're crass."

"We've already established that."

With a little snort, I turn and head for the door. "Okay, I'm going to go bathe like a normal person. You should do the same."

He lets out a put-upon sigh and follows me to the door. "Fine, but come and see me tonight at the camp. I'll get Lu to sneak you out."

I give him a hesitant look. "I don't know if that's a good idea."

"No one will see. Trust me. I'll have her wait for you outside your balcony." A glint of amusement shines in his eyes. "I heard she knows where it is."

I wince. "She told you about that?"

A grin spreads over his lips. "Yep. She said it was one of the funniest things she's ever seen, the way you dangled off the balcony like that." I smack his arm, but that only makes him chuckle.

Slade opens the door for me, popping his head out for a moment before he faces me again. "It's clear," he confirms.

"Thank you."

I slip past him, though I can feel his eyes on my body as I start to walk down the dark corridor.

"Tonight, Auren," he says quietly, and the ends of my ribbons twist at the decadent promise edging his voice.

Stopping at the end of the hall, I look back at him over my shoulder, a secret smile lifting my lips as forbidden excitement fills me. "Tonight."

CHAPTER 33

QUEEN MALINA

*J eo's fingers are red lik*e his windblown hair, as if the cold slipped its unforgiving grip between his palms and squeezed tight.

I watch him from my spot in front of the window while he jerks on the crude fishing pole, its line buried within the depths of the hole in the frozen lake. Every few minutes, he has to hack away at the ice that tries to reform, as if nature itself is working against him.

With another tug, a gray fish the size of his hand comes flailing out, and he tosses it behind him onto the small pile he's already caught, their sides having long since ceased their rise and fall.

He then sets the pole aside and bends down, gathering all the fish in a tin bucket that was used to remove ash from the chimney before he redesigned it for the task of holding our food.

A few seconds later, his boots tap against the doorframe, and an icy chill blasts in the moment he walks inside. He quickly shuts the door behind him to keep out the wintry air, but I don't turn away from the window. Not even as I hear him set down the bucket in the tiny kitchen or when he pulls off his heavy boots to dry in front of the fire.

I just keep staring out this dirty window layered with grime and dust that's frozen to the pane. Keep staring past the snowy mountain blocking my view of Highbell Castle right on the other side of it.

Four days we've been in this safe house. Four days since I fled my castle to descend a stone stairwell that seemed to never end. I walked until it felt like my legs would give out, swallowed by that tunnel of darkness while my eyes strained on the candlelight that Sir Loth Pruinn carried as he led the way.

The five of us made it here that night without anyone coming after us or discovering the secret passage. The safe house's location wasn't discovered by the rebels. Yet the cost of that confidentiality was paid by my other two guards, who stayed behind to ensure we weren't followed. They never met up with us and are probably even now lying slain somewhere in that gilded room.

"Did you get some sleep?" Jeo asks from behind me.

I look over at him as he pulls out some fish from the bucket and slaps them on the small counter surface. The scent of it immediately clogs my nose, and I wrinkle it in distaste.

"Must you do that?"

"Unless you want to starve, yes." My back stiffens at his tone, at his lack of respect, but if he notices my irritation, he does nothing to appease it. He grabs a knife from the drawer and begins to cut the fish in uneven strokes, half the meat getting ripped off in the process of him skinning it. "Sleep?" he asks again.

"I can't rest in that awful bedroom." My eyes shift to the wooden stairwell tucked in the corner of the house as if I can see all the way to the space in question. I detest it. The lumpy mattress, the fireplace that throws off more smoke than heat, the linens that smell of mold and dust. "It's horribly drafty."

A frown appears between his brows, and his mouth pinches tight. "This house is old, but we're lucky we have it."

Bitterness rises up in the shape of a jagged laugh. "Lucky? You think it's *lucky* that I've lost my castle, lost control of Highbell in the course of a week?"

"That's not what I—"

"I'm the rightful ruler of Sixth Kingdom," I interrupt, my eyes feeling as icy as their color. "This is Tyndall's poison that's spread through the city, so much so that I've been forced out of my *home*. Forced to hide in this corner of squalor."

"Right." The knife slams down as he starts to chop— to butcher the fish like he's envisioning hacking off something else entirely. "Well, I'm sorry that this place isn't lavish enough for you, Your Majesty."

A cold burn comes up to sear through my eyes. "*Excuse me*?" How dare he talk to me in such a way.

"Look around," he says, flinging that knife about like it's an extension of his hand. "Rioters took over your palace. Most of your own soldiers turned on you. You've only been ruling here alone for several weeks, and look what's happened."

My jawbone is solid ice. One more clench of my teeth and it'll shatter. "This was all *Tyndall's*—"

"Yes, it's all *his* fault," Jeo cuts in, turning to look at me fully. For the first time, I notice how chapped his lips are, how the smooth skin of his face has been made rough with lines of pink, like slaps landed there from winter's windy hands during his many hours of fishing outside.

And in those lines, that peeling skin, those circles beneath his eyes, I see it. The way I have *diminished* in his mind. If I were in Highbell, wearing my fine gowns and opal crown on my head, he wouldn't dare speak to me in such a way.

But I'm here. Run out of my own castle, wearing decades old clothing found in a trunk and half-eaten by moths. I have no servants, no cooks, no advisors, no crown, no *castle*.

"A queen's saddle doesn't speak to her in such a way," I reply coolly, a warning for him to staunch his tongue.

Redness crawls up his neck, caught low from the stretched out collar of his tunic and coat that's been worn for too many days. But it's not embarrassment coloring his freckled skin, it's anger. "This *saddle* has been working day and night to keep you fed and warm and comfortable, while all you've done is sit around and complain and stare out this dirty window instead of *doing* something!" he spits.

Shock pools before my lips like a puff of cold air as I stare at him.

After a moment, his anger falters, blue eyes softening an inch. I hate him all the more for it. "You can't keep waiting for everything to be handed to you and then get angry when it isn't," he says quietly.

"If I have a question on how to spread my legs and fuck for a living, I'll consult you, Jeo," I say coldly. "But when it comes to being a monarch, you're vastly underqualified to be giving me any advice."

He laughs without lifting his lips, the sound without any joy whatsoever. "Of course. How silly of me."

Jeo slams the knife down and stalks toward the door, making to leave.

"Where are you going?" I demand.

He stops to chuck on his snow-crusted coat and boots. "I'd rather stand out there and try to catch the cold-blooded fish. They're better company."

I ignore his little tantrum and motion to the kitchen where the fish he's already started to maul are still lying on the countertop, mouths agape and bones shucked from their bodies. "What about supper?"

Jeo shrugs as he buttons up. "I'm not a cook, just a saddle, right?" He looks over at Sir Pruinn, who's just sitting there beside the fire, watching our exchange unabashedly. "Maybe the merchant could get off his arse for a change?"

Without another word, he lets himself out into the snow, slamming the door behind him like a child. A noise crawls up my throat as I watch him walk away, down to the edge of the lake and out of view.

My stomach tightens.

Footsteps click over, and then a pair of hands are on my shoulders, turning me around. My glare drops to the pair of pale hands. "Unhand me, Sir Pruinn."

The silver-eyed merchant smiles jovially despite my warning. Instead of letting go, he drops his touch to my arm and pulls me away from the tiny kitchen and into the sitting area in front of the fire. "Your royal saddle will be back. He simply needs to work off some steam. You should come and rest your feet."

"I don't appreciate being manhandled," I say, though I do sit down on the stiff cushions of the chair nearest the flames. It doesn't matter that we feed the fireplace day and night from the logs in the woodpile. No amount of fuel can make me feel those orange flickers. I haven't lost the chill that's gathered on my skin since the moment I walked out of Highbell.

Sir Pruinn settles himself on the chair opposite me where he's been reading some book from the inane collection on the dusty shelf. For a moment, he simply watches me, one ankle resting on his knee, elbow tucked on the armrest so his hand can prop up his head. His idle attention irks me. "What?"

His nickel eyes seem to twinkle. "You don't deserve any of this. Not at all."

The defensive knots I have tied in my gut loosen ever so slightly.

He waves his free hand around the room. "You should be in a castle, ruling over subjects who adore and respect you."

"Of course I should," I reply, sitting up straighter. "I would be, if it weren't for my husband."

"He wanted you to claim an heir that wasn't your own."

My nostrils flare, shock coursing through me. "Where did you hear that." Not a question—a demand for an answer.

He doesn't cower under my command. Instead, the pale-haired merchant smiles. "I hear many things. That's why you continue to meet with me, remember?"

I sit back in my seat, hating the way the cushion beneath me feels as if it's been stuffed with straw. I don't care how long ago this safe house was built, the prior monarchs should have kept it furnished with things worthy of the royals who may have needed to flee here. The moment I get out of this horrible place, I'll be having it fully renovated.

"You didn't hear enough," I accuse. "You should've been able to tell me what was happening sooner, how Tyndall used his messenger to spread such violent discord."

"A couple of days earlier wouldn't have mattered. The result would have been the same."

"You don't know that," I snap. "I could have turned the tide. Highbell is mine. It's all I want, and I will have it."

He leans forward. "You know, there's another way to get the thing you want most."

Our gazes clash again, ice boring through magnets. "I will not speak of your so-called destiny reading. I've said it before and I'll say it again, there is nothing left of Seventh Kingdom."

Pruinn lifts a shoulder, his clothes somehow still looking impeccable. "Magic doesn't lie."

"Magic lies plenty, Sir Pruinn, and so do people who wield it. If you haven't learned that yet, you're a fool."

He's quiet as he regards me, but I don't look away from his assessment. I meet it head-on, let him see the steel frozen in my spine. "A queen does what she must to secure her queendom," he finally says, his hand waving in the direction of the door. "Your saddle might not understand that, but I do."

"You are a traveling merchant who dabbles in fortune-telling. You know nothing."

A smile cracks his handsome face, a hard grin split into an indecipherable expression. "As you say, Your Majesty."

The posturing in his tone annoys me, as if he's deferring not out of respect, but from disappointment. He picks up his book and starts to read again like he hasn't a care in the world. As if the putrid scent of fish still sitting in that bucket doesn't bother him, or the fact that we're holed up here isn't any inconvenience at all.

I chew on my irritation. It's become a tangible thing, a wedge between my back teeth. No matter how many times I gnaw and grind, it's still there, making my jaw ache with it.

Several minutes of silence pass, and I have nothing to do except sit on a hard cushion and chew.

Noises break up the monotony spinning through my head, and I look up just as my two guards come stomping in the house. Snow falls off of them like splatters of mud, wet clumps to seep into the floor.

Their faces are brittle with frost clinging to their eyebrows, reddened cheeks behind scarves they've wrapped around their mouths and nose. Jeo walks in behind them and shuts the door, and I get to my feet expectantly.

"Well?" I ask as they begin to remove their iced capes to hang near the fire.

The blond haired one named Tobyn bows first, while Nile, the older one with a peppering of gray, leans down to take off his boots.

"We weren't spotted, my queen," Tobyn tells me, still slightly out of breath.

"But what did you learn in the city?" I press. "Are they still rioting? What sort of force has taken over the castle?"

"They aren't," Nile says, heavy shoes landing with a thump.

I blink at him, noting the look that he and Tobyn share. I don't care that they've walked miles in the snow both ways from the city to our little hidden hub behind the mountain. I've been waiting for over twelve hours to hear what they found. "Explain."

"Here." Jeo comes up, pressing tin cups of steaming tea into the men's hands. Both of the guards murmur their thanks at him. "Have a seat, you're probably ready to keel over." I suppress a sigh of impatience as they take their time drinking half the cups and sit down beside the fire.

My look of displeasure lands on the side of Jeo's face, but he doesn't turn to acknowledge it, even though I know he can feel it clinging to his profile like a frost.

"I want to know what you found." My tone grinds against the irritation like a worn cog. "I need to send word to my allies and order for the noble houses to bring their soldiers to me. I will need every last sword, but once they've all gathered, I can take back Highbell."

Tension pulls between the guards like a sharpened string.

"Your Majesty," Tobyn starts, looking like he's swallowed a bug. "King Midas sent forces..."

My body goes still. "What do you mean he sent forces?" I exclaim. "The rest of his army is in Fifth Kingdom with him. They couldn't possibly have gotten here that quickly."

"If I may?" Sir Pruinn cuts in. With a sharp glance from me, he says, "I informed you that King Midas had sent his messenger man to deliver his...deal with you, knowing more than likely you wouldn't agree to it, and he was ready for such a response. He had his messenger and possibly others help speed discord throughout the city. It wouldn't be a great leap to believe that, since he had the foresight to spread the rebellion, he'd have a way to snuff it out too."

My sharp nails dig into the wood of the armrest. My tone is so even, so quiet, that every man in the room goes tense from the taut line of it. "Are you telling me that this rebellion that Tyndall *engineered to happen* was just as easily squashed by the very person who machinated the entire thing?"

"I don't know anything about all of that..." Tobyn says, scratching the back of his head nervously. "But we can confirm that the riots have been controlled. It seems King Midas's force re-took the castle, arresting most of them, and the revolters backed down. The king then offered payment to anyone who ceased their part in the destruction of the city, and is allowing some to relocate to Fifth Kingdom."

I leap to my feet and pace toward the window, my fists bunched at my sides so hard that it feels as if my bones might shatter.

"Your Majesty?"

I stare out the dirty panes, across the frozen water, into the back of the mountain. Gaze boring through the ice and snow and rock to find my castle behind it.

He took it from me. *Again.*

My throne, my crown, my castle, my home.

He's not even *here*, and still, he managed to take it right out from under me.

"Send word to my allies," I say, turning around. "The ones who swore loyalty to the Coliers. Tyndall couldn't have sent many forces, not if he's kept some with him in Fifth. With their men, I can take it back, I can—"

Tobyn cuts me off with a shake of his head. "My queen, the nobles have fled to Fifth already, and..."

"And *what*?" I demand past a snap of teeth.

Tobyn shares another glance with Nile, and my attention bites into the older guard. He straightens up, as if he's anticipating a blow to land after he says, "There was a public announcement yesterday. That you were... well, assassinated in the rebel attacks. King Midas's sigil was branded on the statement."

Assassinated? "He's claiming that I'm dead?" I say, voice gone shrill.

"Yes, Your Majesty."

Some say rage burns hot.

Not mine.

Mine turns solid ice. It goes crystalline, reaching fingers of frost covering every inch of my insides, chilling my nerves, frigidity coating my expression.

"We were able to bring a cart and a couple horses back," Tobyn blurts. "It's no royal carriage, but that would only draw attention, anyway. The city is crawling with guards we don't recognize. We don't know who we can trust. If the king made that announcement...we have to assume that he's set on making sure you *stay* dead, if you catch my meaning. We could get you away from here. Get you somewhere safe."

"No." My head shakes in time with the windstorm that begins to rattle outside. "I will not be run out!"

"Malina," Jeo says gently. "It's over."

My eyes flash to him and his cowardly words, and my mask cracks, revealing the fury beneath. "It is *not* over."

He walks to me, frustrated concern bleeding into the blue of his irises, and I hate that look of pity, hate it when his hands come up to cradle my arms. "It's over, Malina," he repeats quietly. "He's taken back the city, the soldiers, your allies. He's just declared that you were killed. You need to leave before he actually does that too."

"For the last time, you are a *saddle*," I spit. "You are beneath me, bought to be ridden. A whore will not dictate what a queen does!"

His hands fall, the weight of the drop slamming at our feet, its reverberation traveling up my legs.

Perhaps later I'll be able to care about the hurt I see in his expression, but right now, I feel nothing as I stare back at him.

"You sure are one cold bitch, Malina."

My teeth clench. "That's *Queen* to you."

He gives me a humorless laugh. "Is it?"

Taken aback, I glare at him. Before I can chop out a scathing response, a shadow passes in front of the window, making me turn. "What was that?"

The mood in the room immediately shifts, everyone going tight with tension.

Jeo moves to look out, swiping his sleeve against the glass to see better. Behind me, the guards are up, already moving. Nile goes to the door, Tobyn to the back window.

"Do you see anything?" I ask.

"No, nothing," Tobyn answers. "I'll go out and do a perimeter check."

He opens the door, wind and snow battering the threshold before he manages to shove it closed.

I walk over to the window to look out, but Jeo stops me. "Wait."

I start to push aside his arm, but before I can, the sound of Tobyn screaming outside makes me freeze in place. My heart stops, a paper-thin exhale rustling past thinned lips. Yet what's even worse than the blood-curdling scream that seems to echo through the mountains is what follows it.

Deathly quiet.

"Great Divine..." Jeo breathes, all the blood drained from his face.

Horrible fear consumes me, locking my limbs, my feet like blocks of ice frozen in place. Tobyn's cut-off scream echoes in my ears.

Jeo slams the shutters closed while Nile races over to the door and throws the bolt down. "We need to get her Majesty to the cart!"

Pruinn is beside me in an instant, his ever-present bag slung over his shoulder.

"There's no other door out," Jeo says, dagger in hand and anxiousness stiffening his fingers. "We have no idea how many men might be out there."

"How far away is the cart?" Pruinn asks.

Nile shakes his head. "Not far. Twenty feet at most. We tried to leave the horses beneath the overhang of the roof where the wood is kept."

Jeo licks his lips, turning in place as he thinks until his eyes land on the shuttered window behind us. "Okay, one of us goes out the door, the others help the queen out the window. It's the closest to the cart, and they won't be expecting it. We'll cover her from all angles," he says, nodding his head as if his body is convincing his mind.

Nile nods grimly. "I'll go through the door, you two get Her Majesty to the cart."

The men pass a look between them, while something heavy and horrible sinks onto my shoulders. "He sent men to kill me," I breathe. "I can't believe that arrogant bastard, who only became a king through a marriage to *me,* would dare try to have me killed!"

"Malina!" Jeo snaps. "We don't have time for your indignation. We have *one* fucking shot at this, alright? Or we're all dead like Tobyn."

He turns back to Pruinn and Nile while they peer out windows, whispering their hurried plans back together.

"Ready?"

I blink at Jeo numbly, because no, I am *not* ready. "We should stay in here."

"We stay, we're dead, Your Majesty. There aren't enough of us here to defend you. Fleeing is our only chance," Nile says.

They don't wait for me to give the approval. Jeo grasps my hand and squeezes. "Keep your head down and keep running, just like before. Alright?"

My nod is heavy, my vision tunneling with adrenaline my body doesn't know what to do with.

Nile takes up position at the door, while Pruinn and Jeo work together to carefully open the shutters, checking outside as far as they can. "Nothing," Pruinn confirms. "And the cart is just there."

Jeo looks over at the guard. "On your move."

This is all happening entirely too fast.

Nile throws open the latch, making as much noise as he can at the same time that Jeo and Pruinn break through the window. Then Nile is racing through the open door with his sword held high and a threat from his mouth while Jeo jumps out the window.

The moment Jeo's on the other side, I'm shoved and pulled simultaneously by the men. I topple out, my saddle's hands gripping my waist as he yanks me the rest of the way. But the skirts of my dress get snagged on the serrated edges of the window as I'm pulled forcefully out, and the glass cuts right through, making blood rise from the tears in my skin. Right when I let out a hiss of pain and land on my feet outside, a scream rents the air.

Nile.

Just like before, the shout echoes and stretches, until it suddenly cuts off in a way that you know life was cut with it.

With horror and terror pounding in my veins, Jeo takes my hand just as Pruinn jumps out of the window behind me. Then we all race toward the cart, feet slogging through snow that's up to our knees. The horses are stomping, heads shaking, blowing out frenzied breaths of fearful whinnies. Pruinn sprints past us and jumps into the driver's seat, grabbing hold of the reins before the animals bolt.

"Hurry, Malina," Jeo prompts, nearly dragging me through the snow to the back of the cart. Right as my hands brace against the rough wood and his hands come to help lift me up, something dark moves in my peripheral. I turn my head just in time to see a shadow move against the side of the house, and terror stabs down my spine.

"Jeo…"

He whirls around with his dagger in hand, but nothing is there. My eyes dart around, because I know I saw something, but the shadow is gone, and—

There.

My eyes fly over to the left as wisps of strange black smoke seem to peel away from the house's shadows. I watch, frozen in fear, as it dissipates slowly, coalescing into a man with a hood over his face. The man seems to be shrouded in a dark veil, like shade is clinging to him. Even the sword in his hand is obscured, fresh blood dripping from its edges to land like a menacing threat.

Jeo whips around and shoves me hard. "GO!"

My body topples forward, hip bumping into the edge of the cart, head smacking into the frozen wood. I clamber the rest of the way in just as the reins crack like a whip from Pruinn's hand. The cart lurches forward, and I scrabble to find a handhold as Pruinn's hoarse "Ya!" calls out.

Jeo sprints after us, just a foot away from the cart, and he manages to grab the back ledge. Yet the man is right on his heels, racing forward. His shadows conform and melt over his body so that he turns almost invisible against his surroundings, perfectly blended in as he distorts both dark and light.

Jeo nearly trips in the thick snow, and I know within seconds, the speed of the horses will make him lose his chance, and he knows it too. With a determined grunt, he pushes himself forward and manages to grip the edge.

Yet just as he starts to pull himself up, a sword appears in the air, held aloft by this invisible demon who wields it. I open my mouth to call his name in warning, but it's already too late.

The sound it makes as it stabs straight into Jeo's back and through his chest is like the gasp before a scream.

My saddle's wide blue eyes lock onto me. With shock, with fear. With *death*.

Jeo's hands slip away from the back of the cart as blood blotches his coat, and he staggers in place. The cart keeps racing on without him, but his gaze stays stuck to mine, horror etched in both of our expressions.

Just a second later, the hooded shadow man wrenches his sword from my saddle's back, making a scream tear from Jeo's mouth.

Blood drips, stains, leaches from the hole ripped through his body, the color perfectly matching his hair.

Jeo's scream breaks off as his knees land in the snow. I get one more second of his eyes on me, and then he falls face-first in the snow and doesn't get back up.

The horses have gained their momentum now, going so fast it nearly sends me skidding off the back, but I hold on, eyes frosting over as I stare and stare at where Jeo lies.

I know it's shock, but I have no breath to scream, none to whisper. My tongue is frozen to the roof of my mouth, unable to form his name. All I can do is watch as shadow and light swirl together beside Jeo's discarded body, hiding the man responsible. Magic clings and splits in deathly calm wisps that not even the punishing wind seems to touch.

Tobyn and Nile lie unmoving in front of the safe house like a macabre garden planted by Death. Planted there where their blood has taken root, where the ground has soaked in their life and sprouted their end.

Pruinn yells again at the horses to hurry, and the assassin's power dissolves in the air. I suck in a breath as he stands there like Menace made flesh. Not a force of soldiers sent to kill me, not a band of cutthroats. Just a single deadly man with evil power curling around him.

The man pulls back his hood slowly, and then I see his dark eyes watching me from a patchwork face of two-toned skin. As if that too is playing with light and shadow.

Our eyes lock, and I'm unable to tear my gaze away, unable to do anything except stare as bile battles with my throat. He looks at me with a dangerous promise, but I look at him right back.

You, we both seem to say.

You.

Then, the cart cuts a sharp corner against a rocky hill of snow, and my view of him is gone, the sound of the horses' pounding hooves somehow sounding like Jeo's knees as they slammed into the ground.

Far off, I hear the toll of the castle's bell echo through the mountains, a warning for the storm that's beginning its furor. It will rage with ice and wind, and come morning, Jeo's body will be nothing but a lump of snow, hidden by the sky and stolen by the ground. Come morning, Highbell will be out of my grasp again and under the control of the man who used me to get it in the first place, while I'm forced to flee from the shadow he sent to eradicate me.

Fury like I've never known before hardens like jagged waves of a sea gone glacial, stuck in a freeze that it has no way of thawing. When the blizzard hits, I don't even notice it. I'm far too cold on the inside to feel it.

CHAPTER 34

AUREN

I sleep like the dead, so deep that it's like clawing out from six feet underground to pull myself into consciousness. But I do it, because my subconscious is warning me that something is...off.

Peeling my blurred eyes open, I jerk upright, trying to bat away the last dregs of slumber, my senses prickling.

When I catch movement in my dim bedroom, I experience a moment of panic before my eyes land on the intruder.

"*Lu?*" My voice is croaky and cracked, but I stare at the Wrath incredulously. She's sitting in front of the fire with her feet propped up, a book in one hand and a wine glass in the other.

She casts me a look. "Took you long enough. The sun went down an hour ago. You were snoring."

Embarrassment makes me grumble indignantly, "I was not."

I probably was.

Gaze flicking over to the balcony and windows, I see that Lu was right, I slept right through the entire day. Not only did I get a bath in before dawn, but I passed out just as the sun was cresting, and I've been sleeping ever since. Slade's attentions wore me out in the best way.

Rubbing my face, I shove the covers back and stand up, stretching my arms over my head, feeling little twinges of soreness all over. Although, I think those have more to do with my nighttime activities than my exercises, and I have to keep a blush from my face as the swarm of memories crop up.

"How did you get in here?" I ask as I wander over to Lu, noting that not only is she drinking my wine, but she's also helped herself to my tray of food that the servants sent. She must've built up my fire though, because it's blazing warm and bright.

I flop into the chair across from her and look over the remnants of food on the tray. Looks like Lu helped herself to the cuts of meat and whatever used to be in the bowl. All that's left is one chocolate scone, some gritty fruit, and half of a sandwich with a cinnamon crust that has a bite taken out of it.

I raise my brow at her. "Enjoy my food?"

She shrugs. "I've had worse. But why this kingdom

thinks it's a good idea to slop sugar on everything, I'll never know. In the city, I ordered the beef stew, and it was smothered in syrup."

My nose wrinkles as I take a bite of scone and help myself to some water. "How did you get in here?"

"Easily. Came right in through the balcony."

A frown pulls my brows together. "That door was locked."

"Was it?" she hums. "Well, then you need better guards. No one even patrols below the grounds over here, and the ones in the hall never hear a thing."

When she says *better guards*, Digby's face suddenly flashes in my mind. Just like that, the sugary breakfast goes sour in my mouth. I manage to swallow the bite down, but it feels like guilt settles in my stomach instead.

"What's that look for?"

"Nothing. Just...I had a good guard," I say, fidgeting with one of my ribbons in my lap as I think of Digby and Sail both. "*Two* great ones, actually."

"Had?"

"It's my fault," I answer, unable to go into any more detail. It's my fault Sail was stabbed by the captain of the Red Raids. My fault that Digby is being held by Midas and dangled over my head.

I feel suddenly awkward, because I didn't expect this unrestrained sadness to cut my knees right out from under me like this, for me to suddenly stumble on grief. Especially not in front of Lu.

I need to talk to Slade about Digby as soon as possible—about Rissa too. I should've done it last night, but...I was preoccupied. I just wanted a moment for myself. I didn't want to let reality flood in and taint our time together.

Yet that was selfish of me, to indulge and shut away all my problems. Guilt claws down my back now, because Digby might be wasting away in a dungeon somewhere for all I know, while I'm up here indulging in Slade's company and complaining about how sweet the food is. What kind of horrible person does that?

Cutting through the thick silence, Lu says, "I know how it feels when bad shit happens and it's your fault," she says matter-of-factly. I appreciate her no-nonsense tone. I'm grateful that she doesn't try to tell me it wasn't my fault, to absolve me from my guilt. "When Rip put me in charge of the right flank, I was cocky as hell about it. But then we had our first battle, and I lost a lot of good men and women."

I glance up at her, watching her eyes cast into the flames of the fire, her dark skin aglow with its warmth.

"Every life lost...it was on me, you know? I was responsible for commanding them, and every direction caused some to live and others to die."

She lifts a hand to scrub over the shapes of daggers

cut into her hair, and I suddenly wonder if there's a significance for those symbolic blades.

"When you feel responsible for death...that stays with you. It sticks to the soles of your feet every time you take a step."

I nod slowly in understanding, and Lu lets out a breath, face stoic as she sits up straighter. "But that's the curse of the survivors. We have to live with our dead."

When I think about all the people who have died because of me, my shoulders weigh down. "Living with the dead is harder than living with the living."

Her gaze jumps to mine, turning mischievous. "Unless that living happens to be the golden king prick."

I snort and shake my head. "You have no idea."

With a laugh, she sets down the wine glass and points at it. "Our wine barrel is better than this stuff."

"I agree." Abandoning the scone, I set it down and get to my feet. "So, you're really going to be able to sneak me out of here?"

Lu gives me a look. "Don't insult me, Gildy."

I hold up my hands placatingly. "Alright, alright. Let me just get dressed."

It just takes me a few minutes, and when I come out of my dressing room, I'm in a new gown and my hair is no longer a rat's nest. I also may have taken a little bit of extra time on my appearance for a certain king, so I chose my dress with care and only snapped *two* of the boning inlays in the corset. The things you do for the males you sleep with.

"Okay, I'm ready," I say, coming back out as I pull on my coat.

Lu springs up fluidly from the chair. "Finally." She walks over, holding out the book she had this whole time.

When I look down and see what it is, my eyes go wide. "How did you get that?"

"It was just sitting out."

I pin her with a look. "It was stuffed into one of the gowns in my dressing room."

Lu shrugs and slips into her thick black coat. "You need better hiding spots."

Shaking my head, I take the fae book and put it into the inside pocket of my coat. Lu leads the way out of the balcony, and before I even close the door behind us, she's leaping up onto the railing.

"Lu—"

Without hesitation, she bends her knees and then goes *flipping* right off of it.

I gasp and rush over, but Lu's perfectly maneuvered herself and somehow managed to grab onto the railing of the next balcony over. In some crazy acrobatic feats, and making it look much easier than it actually is, she kicks off and spins her body and then lands in a perfect crouch onto the snowy ground below.

I just gape down at her in the dark. "How the hell did you do that?" I hiss.

She smirks. "Easily."

With a huff, I wrap all of my ribbons around the railing before climbing up onto it. Gripping half of them, I have my ribbons slowly lower me down as far as they'll go. The other half stretches to the next balcony, and I swing myself over, and then I repeat the process again.

When I finally land on the ground, my arms are shaking and I'm breathing hard.

"Took you long enough," Lu admonishes. "But I'll admit, that was a bit better than the first effort I witnessed."

I glower at her. "We can't all be flip masters who just go careening off three-story-high balconies."

With a grin, she starts to walk, and I follow behind her, noting that the dogs are put away in the kennel house for the night, the pen empty and quiet. "Your arm strength is atrocious. You need to come back and get training with us again."

The very few training sessions I had with the Wrath were the most challenging and rigorous thing I'd ever done, but it also made me feel good mentally—a way to rid myself of my own vulnerabilities and weaknesses.

"I'd like that," I admit.

Lu seems pleased, and she sends me an enigmatic look. "I'm glad you came to your senses, Gildy."

I don't think she's talking about the training.

I smile. "Me too."

"You seem to be controlling your ribbons with greater skill," she notes, and I can't help but puff up a little at her compliment.

"I've been trying to practice with them when I can."

"Good," she says with a sharp nod of her head. "Now I need you to shut up, okay?"

Taken aback, I mutter, "Rude."

I follow her past the row of greenhouses until we reach the corner of the castle walls. The sky is growing darker with every passing minute, gated shadows enclosing the land into night. She stops and looks around it, holding her hand up for me to wait, and then after a moment, waves me forward again.

I look around nervously as we creep past the stables, and then once again, Lu stops me just at the corner of it, but this time we stay there for a few minutes, and I notice Lu checking a brass pocket watch clipped to her belt.

"You worked out the guards' rotations?" I whisper, keeping my back pressed against the rough wall of the stable.

"Yes. Now shh," she snips.

Pretending to button my lip, I let my eyes scan the castle grounds, noting the ice sculptures in the distance. They're pretty during the day, but at night, they look like creepy spectators, their silhouettes menacing and eerie. I keep darting a look at them, and my heart nearly jumps into my throat when I notice movement. Realizing it's two guards heading toward us, I stiffen, but Lu just shoots me a look to stay still and quiet.

I'm barely breathing when they come nearer and nearer toward the front of the stable. Yet before they cross right in front of us, one of them mutters something too low for me to hear, and then they both start looking around behind them, momentarily distracted. I have no idea what caught their attention, but it couldn't have come at a better time.

Lu gives a sharp jerk of her head, and I follow her hurriedly as we dart in the opposite direction. I steal looks behind us, but the guards never glance our way.

She stops us again when we reach the garden gazebo, her eyes intent on the face of the pocket watch like she's memorized every guard route and is counting down the seconds.

"That was close," I whisper, my heart still beating fast from the residual adrenaline rush. "Good thing they got distracted." I rub my hands together, the cold air seeping right through my gloves. "So what's the plan? How are we going to sneak out?"

"The guards open the castle gates in three minutes for the outer perimeter watch change. We'll slip out then."

An incredulous look drops over my features. "What

are you talking about? We can't just...*slip out* through the front gates of the castle."

She doesn't even look up from her watch. "Yes, we can."

I feel like I'm suddenly talking to a crazy person. "The front gate has to be swarming with guards."

"Usually has about thirty," she replies with a shrug.

My mouth drops open. "And yet, you expect us to just walk right out? Are you out of your mind?"

"Gildy Locks, your voice is going a little high-pitched, there. I'm going to need you to loosen your ribbons and take a breath."

Okay, I might be panicking a bit, but she doesn't have to sound so damn amused.

"We'll get caught if we try to go out that way," I insist. "I thought you had found some secret way out or had bribed a guard or something."

"I don't need to," she tells me. "Ready to go?"

"No!" I hiss.

She rolls her eyes, looking entirely too calm about this. "Just don't talk, and we'll be fine. Now come on, or we'll miss our chance."

Grumbling a curse, I follow her as she pushes off the gazebo and heads down the swept stone walkway. We pass the last of the ice sculptures, then go past the bailey, and then all too soon, we're nearing the castle gate.

Torches are braced high along the wall, like iron

fingers jutting out from the stone with sharp fingernails of flames. I can see armored soldiers on the top parapet, their purple cloaks wagging in the cold wind.

There are some unhitched wagons and empty carriages on the ground off to the left, and a stone statue of whatever past king sits smack dab in the middle so that the first thing you see when you enter the gates is some long dead monarch with a saber held in his hand.

Lu stops us in the shadow of an alcove stacked with sandbags, probably to pour over the ground when they need to pack the snowfall down. Even in our current hiding spot, we're way too out in the open for my liking.

"Lu..." I breathe. I don't care how stealthy she is. There is *no* way we are sneaking out of those gates when they open.

She shoots me a sharp look, effectively silencing me. Slade trusted her implicitly to sneak me out, had absolutely zero doubt she could get me to the camp, and that, plus my own trust in her, makes me stay right where I am.

When two guards walk over to the gate and begin to lift the heavy beam stretched across it, Lu whispers, "Get ready, Gildy."

Despite the cold temperature, I'm sweating with nervousness. The gate opens, and a line of guards come filing in, looking tired with slumped shoulders and dragged steps. Several of them head straight across the grounds, while some begin to talk with the other soldiers, not in any rush to put the beam back in place.

When Lu starts walking toward the gate, I grit my teeth and hurry forward. I stick to her like a noon shadow, my eyes darting every which way as I note the dozens of guards around, just waiting for one of them to spot us and raise the alarm.

My pulse pounds in my ears, but Lu continues to stride confidently forward, not a single step faltering. Her birdlike steps are silent, like she's able to flit from one place to another, her body lithe and graceful in every movement, making me feel lumbering and noisy beside her. Even when we finally lose the last of the wall's shadows and can only head straight down the middle toward the gate, she doesn't slow.

The moment we're out in the open, two guards on the wall turn their heads in our direction, and I brace myself. But as quickly as they looked down at us, they look away again.

What in the world?

I'm not sure how they didn't see us, but I don't have time to fully appreciate the close call, because we reach the gate just then. The group of guards several feet away begin to turn toward us too, and I tense up, ready to sprint through the gate.

But once again, they get distracted, their attention

jerking away a second before their eyes land on us. The men all grumble and start kicking at the snow with their boots, pointing at something I can't see. A nudge from Lu has me whipping my head back around, and then we're slipping out the gate together.

I take a breath the moment we're outside the castle walls, disbelief furrowing my brow.

We got out.

I can't believe we actually just walked right out the front gate, right next to all those castle guards. I know Lu was critical of Ranhold's security, and now, I can see why. And yet, something is off. No way we got that lucky.

As we walk quickly away, I feel like there's a giant target on my gold-clad back, but...nothing happens.

Nothing at all.

I steal a look behind us, squinting through the dark at the guard towers that I know must be manned, but not a single shout rings out. When Lu and I reach the crest of a hill and are far enough away from the castle walls, new perimeter guards come filing out, and then the gate doors are closed again.

Lu nods in satisfaction. "We're fine now," she says briskly. "Good job not talking. That would've made things more difficult for me."

"How the *hell* did we just pull that off?" I pant, trying to keep up with her as we hurry through the snow.

"*We* didn't. *I* did," Lu replies, brown eyes sweeping the landscape.

I send one of my ribbons to grip her by the arm and pull her to a stop. "Tell me what just happened. What was that?"

Lu frowns down at my ribbon and bats it away. "I have a little magic."

My brows shoot up. "You have magic? What kind?"

"Nothing too extreme, I can't rot people alive or turn a castle gold, but I can divert attention."

Surprise has me shaking my head. "How does it work?"

She shrugs. "I can sense when people are paying attention to me, and then I just...make them pay attention elsewhere."

Well, that's a handy trick.

"And you can do it for the people with you?"

"To an extent," she replies. "One person with me is easy. But more than that, and it gets a bit more difficult."

"This would've been nice information *before* you snuck me out."

Lu grins, her white teeth flashing in the night. "But this was more fun. You should've seen your face back there. I thought you were going to pee yourself."

"Thanks a lot," I say drily.

"Come on, it's colder than a pecker in the Barrens. I'll take you to see the others."

A smile pulls my cheeks as I follow her, noting the orange glow of the campfires up ahead. When giddiness rises in my chest, I realize just how excited I am to see Slade again, as well as the other members of the Wrath. Even big brutish Osrik, who still scares me a little.

It's funny, but walking past the tents of Fourth's army feels so much more comfortable than the luxuries of the castle behind me. In fact, it feels a little bit like coming home.

CHAPTER 35

AUREN

The camp atmosphere is exactly how I remember it. Soldiers are gathered around the motley fires, leather tents dusted with snow while the scent of smoke and cooked meat chars the air.

The deeper into camp we go, the more soldiers notice me as we pass by, and I quickly become self-conscious at the way their eyes follow me. It's not quite as contentious as it was before when I was a prisoner in their eyes, but there's something definitively wary in their expressions.

Not that I can blame them—I can only imagine what they think of me, have no idea what they've been told or if there's camp gossip. One group we pass goes completely silent, voices cutting off mid-sentence when they notice me. I try to send them a quick smile, but they look away.

"Do they hate me?" I ask, unable to staunch the question from leaking out.

"For the most part, they don't trust you," Lu answers as we walk side-by-side. "They never will, so long as they see you as Midas's pet."

Nodding, I repress the urge to pull up my hood and cover my face. I don't want to look like I'm concealing anything or that I have anything to be ashamed of. It wouldn't do me any good with this crowd.

Instead, I keep my chin up, my shoulders back, let my ribbons trail after me in the snow, their golden ends playing and jumping over the glittering ground. If I'm going to try and fit in here, to earn the trust or at least tolerance of these soldiers, I can't do it by hiding.

Beside me, Lu gives a nod, like I've made the right move, which fuels my determination. As we continue picking our way past tightly packed-in tents, a woman comes up who I recognize. Inga, the soldier who ran into Judd and me when we stole the wine barrel back from Lu's right flank. I still can't get over the embarrassment I felt when Judd told her I had *women's troubles*. The prick.

Just like then, Inga has a flop of brown spirals on her head and a wooden pipe stuck behind her ear. She comes up on Lu's other side, falling into step with us.

"How did the training go?" Lu asks her by way of greeting.

"It went well. Got some of the new routines down before I let them go off into the city for the night."

"Good," Lu replies. "Why don't you go into the city yourself? You've earned it."

"Thanks, but I'd rather stay here. Ranhold doesn't appeal to me. Too bloody cold. And have you seen the corsets the women wear here?" Inga asks, lip curling up in distaste.

"Right?" I exclaim, leaning around Lu to see her. "They're terrible. I'm not sure how anyone breathes in this kingdom."

"The clothing in Fourth is much better," Inga tells me.

Lu casts her a droll look. "You don't wear civilian clothing. In fact, I don't think I've *ever* seen you out of your uniform."

The woman looks down at her black leathers, fingers patting the brown straps that crisscross at the front. "They're comfortable. Got them broken in just the way I like."

Lu snorts.

Inga plucks up the pipe from her ear. "Need anything else, Lu?"

"No, go relax. Thanks, Inga."

She nods and then looks at me. "See you around, Gildy." With a wave, she walks off, joining a rowdy group of soldiers playing cards.

"Your nickname for me really caught on," I grumble. Lu's grin widens.

Soon, she and I get past all of the close-knit clusters of tents. The privacy is instantly more prominent, the breathing room of empty space given to a larger tent that I recognize immediately. There's a fire burning several feet in front of it, and a familiar group is gathered around. They're sitting on stumps of wood and talking quietly, and a smile instantly appears on my lips.

The moment I step forward, a pair of black eyes dart up to meet mine, and just that look steals the breath from my chest. He's in his Rip form, and my stomach does a little flip at the sight. His pale face glows orange from the flickering flames in front of him, but the charge between us burns hotter.

Lu notices my steps falter, and she looks over at me with a frown. "Feet broken?"

"What? No."

She glances from me to Slade and back again and then rolls her eyes and mutters something that I don't catch. I can't, because I'm still staring at Slade. I can't help it. Not when he's looking at me like that.

The slow drag of his attention is like the stroke of his fingertip against my bare skin. Which, after last night, I know very, *very* well. The look in his eye somehow reflects every single erotic thing we did together, making a blush rise to my cheeks. Slade quirks up one side of his mouth.

That smirk.

Oh Divine, *that smirk*.

"Gildy! Get the hell over here!"

My attention wrenches away to Judd, who's waving me over. With a little embarrassment, I realize Lu has already walked off without me even noticing. Tucking some loose hair behind my ear, I head over to their fire, avoiding the puddles of melted snow on the ground.

"Thought I was going to have to drag you over," Judd says with a grin as he leans over a barrel and pours out some wine. "Here."

I take the tin cup gratefully and give it an indulgent sniff before I breathe out in a smile. "You're good to me, Mustard."

Judd grimaces and rubs at his mustard-seed hair. "It's not *that* yellow."

I cock a brow. "Listen, I'm *gold*, okay? Don't whine to me."

He laughs, and his tan complexion makes his teeth stand out white and bright. "Fair enough."

When he starts filling up more cups of wine, I turn around, all too aware of Slade's attention on me. Instead of letting myself get caught up in his gaze again, I watch Osrik yank off the roasted meat that's cooking over the fire and start to peel chunks off of it.

The big brute is wearing a leather vest, with straps

wound around his massive biceps, and his brown hair is hanging down loose around his shoulders. His scowl is as fierce as ever, but at least he gives me a nod in greeting instead of threatening my life. It's a big improvement since the time we first met.

Judd passes my line of sight and gives wine to the others, and my gaze zeroes in on Slade again. He's still watching me, his aura smoky, reaching toward me with tendril fingers of a dark want. In answer, my ribbons begin to inch closer, slithering on the ground, tugging me forward until I stand right in front of him.

"Hi," I blurt out.

Hi? *That's* what I say?

This male bent my body in all sorts of ways last night, brought me more pleasure than I've ever experienced, and I just stand here awkwardly and say *hi*?

His lips twitch in amusement. "Hello, Goldfinch."

He doesn't say it. He practically *purrs* it. So instead of hearing a simple greeting, I'm hearing him whisper filthy things into my ear. I'm feeling his hot breath against my neck, seeing the lines of his abs hidden beneath his leathers.

I'm staring again. I know I am, and yet, I just can't stop, because there's this energy rippling from him that's filled with lust and affection, and I wouldn't be able to break away from it even if I wanted to.

He was in his kingly form last night...but what would

548

it be like to be with him while he's in this Rip form? What would it be like to feel the tips of his spikes above his brow, or press my lips to the murky streak of gray scales along the tops of his cheeks? Would he tease me with that hint of fang by dragging it along my—

"Leg or breast?"

My head snaps in the direction of Osrik's voice, and my cheeks flame. "What?"

His brown eyes blink impatiently beneath bushy brows. "Leg or breast?" he grunts, pointing to the meat he's tearing apart.

"Oh. Uh...leg?"

He nods before ripping off the biggest damn leg from some poor animal he probably hunted down himself with his bare hands.

I stuff my gloves in my pocket and then grab the hunk he passes over. I have to grip the end of the leg bone in both hands just to hold it up. I'm no food snob, but this is a little ridiculous.

Taking pity on me, Slade relieves me of the giant leg and tears a strip of meat off, before he hands over the much more manageable slice. "Thanks." I sit down on the empty stump of wood just beside him and then bite into the meat, which practically melts in my mouth.

"Os, stop tearing into it like that. You're massacring it," Lu gripes. The three of them sit a few feet away from us, the firelight making their uniforms brighten.

He glowers. "What's wrong with it?"

"Looks a bit like something a pack of rabid wolves have been at," Judd says helpfully. Before Osrik can so much as shoot a glare his way, the mustard-haired Wrath smoothly shoves a cup of wine in his direction.

Osrik swipes up the cup before shoving a hunk of meat in Judd's direction in return, making fat go dripping all over the ground. "You're lucky I'm thirsty."

Judd grins and sits next to Lu, making her shove over on her stump. "Did I say you could sit here?" she asks with an arched brow.

"Well, if I try to share a stump with Os, he'll probably tear my legs off and roast them over the spit."

Lu tilts her head contemplatively. "True."

Osrik grunts, teeth gnashing onto a bite of smoked skin that crackles as he chews. But he doesn't disagree.

I watch in amusement as I finish my food and drink my fill, all while relishing their easy interactions. It makes me relax bit by bit until I find that I'm just... enjoying myself. I'm not on edge. Not having to watch what I do or say. I don't have to play a part. I can simply be myself and not look over my shoulder. We might be on Ranhold's front doorstep, but in this moment, I feel an ocean away.

"I take it you and Lu had no trouble coming out here?" Slade asks me.

Using the snow at my feet, I wipe my hands the best

I can before I hold them up to the fire to thaw them out. "No. Nice trick she has, by the way."

"It is," he replies simply before taking a drink from his cup and stretching out his legs in front of him.

"Do all of your Wrath have *tricks*?"

He gives me a mischievous look. "Guess you'll have to find out."

One glance at Osrik still mauling his food and I'm not sure I want to know.

Lowering my voice, I ask, "Do they...know?"

Amusement dances in his eyes. "Do they know what exactly? That we..."

"No," I hiss, darting a look at the others. Luckily, they're occupied with making fun of Judd about something.

Slade grins, and I know the ass did it on purpose. The fact that Fake Rip might or might not have heard some things is embarrassing enough as it is. "Not *that*. Do they know that you change *coats*?" I ask pointedly.

He snorts. "Yes, they know I change forms. They're the only ones, apart from you."

Emotion swells in my chest like water soaked up into a sponge, until I'm saturated with a flattered sense of humbling pride that he let me into his small circle of people who he trusts with his secret.

"Poor guy, huh?" Judd cuts in, proving that they are, in fact, eavesdropping. "Has to choose between spikes coming out of his ass, or magic lines down his... unmentionables."

My brows pull together in a frown. "He doesn't have magic lines on his—" I cut myself off, but it's too late. Lu chokes on her wine.

Judd barks out a laugh. "Ha! Told you!" he exclaims, slapping his knee with delight. "Pay up, Os."

Mortified, I bury my face into my hands. "Oh goddess."

"Don't feel too bad, Gildy," Judd tells me. "We always know everything about everything. I even know how many times Os takes a shit every day." Osrik shoots him a glare. "*Four*, in case you were wondering."

Gross.

"I wasn't," I mumble against my hands, still keeping my face buried in them. It seems safer, considering the direction of the conversation.

"Hey, Judd?" Slade calls, and I peek out from between my fingers.

He perks up, looking pleased with himself. "Yeah, Commander?"

"Shut up."

A quick nod precedes Judd's cheerful reply. "Yep, will do."

I laugh against my palms until Slade's firm fingers wrap around mine and tug them away from my face. "Don't mind Judd. He can't help but be an unendurable prick."

"It's true," Lu chirps. "He thrives on it."

"Yeah, but I keep you lot entertained," Judd defends.

Shaking my head, I turn back to Slade and look him over cautiously. "So...just to be clear, you *don't* have a spike that comes out of your ass, right?"

Lu, Judd, and Osrik all howl in laughter.

Slade just sighs. "No ass spikes to speak of."

Bright side.

"So, are you still glad you came out to camp?" Lu asks with a smirk on her face.

"Apart from all the ass and shit talk? Definitely," I reply, and the others grin at me, as if that was the right thing to say.

The easygoing camaraderie between them all is visceral, filling me with a sense of comfortable friendship that I've never experienced before in my life. There's no underlying bitterness or competitiveness in the way they joke with one another. There's no sense of jealousy or resentment. Instead, there's an intense certainty about them. As if they're family, that they know each other inside and out, and even when they're mocking or joking, I can *feel* the loyalty they have for one another.

"So, you're Rip tonight," I note, looking over the spikes jutting up from Slade's uniform.

"I am." He glances down as two of my ribbons start toying with the laces of his boot, and his lips quirk. "Little flirts."

I shrug, because I give up on trying to hold back the cheeky things. "Do you change forms a lot?" I ask curiously.

"Sometimes it's necessary. But other times, I do it when I don't feel like being the king and dealing with everything that comes with it."

"It's like an escape for you."

He nods. "It's not always easy being King Rot," he replies sardonically, but I can see the edge of bitter truth to that, and my heart aches for him. I can't imagine what he carries on his back as not only a monarch, but a feared one. Sometimes even a despised one.

"I can understand that. I actually envy it," I admit quietly, watching my ribbons continue to twirl around his shoes and ankles playfully. "If I could stop being the gold girl even just for a night, I'd jump at the chance to not be me."

Slade's finger and thumb suddenly come up to grip my chin, and he pulls my face to look at him, his intense eyes boring into me. "Never say that," he rumbles, the timbre of his voice pitched in firm demand. "The world would be a dreary place without your light."

My chest constricts, something warm scattering over me with the brush of his thumb.

"Shit," Judd says in a groan. "Rip is being fucking cute, and it's making me want to vomit."

Another sigh passes through Slade's lips as he drops his hold from my chin. "Hey, Lu?"

"Yeah, Commander?"

"Smack Judd for me."

Quicker than Judd can dodge, she smacks him on the back of the head, making him grunt. "Ow! Why are you so violent?"

Lu flashes him a grin that's all teeth. "Because it makes me happy."

I can't stifle the laugh that bubbles out of me.

"Come on, Mustard," Osrik grunts as he gets to his feet, yanking up Judd by his sleeve. "Let's go find some more wine for Lu. She's always much nicer after she has a few pints."

"That's true," she agrees.

The three of them wander off, and then it's just Spikey Slade and me alone in the company of a wisping fire with fingers that taper up toward the icy sky.

"So...Goldfinch." His voice has gone gravelly and decadent, his dark aura coiling around me. The look he gives me is both indulgent and sensual, and it makes my stomach spark with embers of heat. "Now that we're alone, what should we do?"

The words may be a question, but his voice already has the answer, and it matches mine.

A coy smile appears on my face. "I have a few ideas."

CHAPTER 36

AUREN

I don't know who kisses who first, but our lips come together in a clash of craving. It's both cold from the winter air and hot from the heat of the campfire, the temperatures warring as much as our drive to fulfill the lust pumping in our veins.

Slade cradles the back of my head, fingers digging into the strands of my hair like he wants to dig deeper into me, keeping me against his mouth so that he can have his way with mine.

And he does.

His dominant hold tilts my head right where he wants me so his tongue can sweep in further, as if he's drinking me in.

When I pull away to take in a breath, he growls, like a predator being taken from his catch. "Don't turn away from me," he rumbles.

Laughing, I say, "You have to let a girl breathe."

"*I* want to breathe you in," he counters. "Your every exhale, your aura, your very essence. I don't want to miss a single part of you."

My stomach leaps right up to my chest, his words elevating me like the climb of a mountain and taking me right to the peak. My ribbons lift up and wrap around him as much as he's curling his arms around me, and once again, the rest of the world just fades away until it's just us. Just here.

Bringing up a hand, I let my fingertips graze against the ashen scales along his cheekbones, marveling at the smooth texture of them. They reflect the firelight, making the fae in him stand out.

"Did your parents have scales?" I ask curiously.

"My father."

I try to decipher the tone of his answer, but I get distracted by the light puffs of snowfall that land in his black hair. Slade looks up and glowers at the sky. "This place is always snowing."

"It's Fifth Kingdom, what did you expect?" I tease. "At least here it isn't constantly blizzarding. The snowstorms have been pretty mild."

"I can't wait to be back in my own kingdom where I'm able to see the sun."

Nostalgia floats over me like a warm summer breeze. "Goddess, I can't even remember when I spent a day in the sun. It's always overcast and cold in this part of Orea. In Highbell, it was always snowing, and even if the sun *did* come out, which was *very* rare, I wasn't outside to see it."

Agitation snaps in his gaze like impatient fingers. "You will see the sun again, Auren. You will see everything and anything you want."

My heart swells at the determination in his voice, at the way his fingers tighten on my waist. "I will," I agree.

He nods, as if we just made the same vow. "Let's get you inside where it's warm." I expect him to step away and just grab my hand, but instead, he sweeps me up in his arms, making me let out a noise of surprise.

Striding through the snow, he carries me toward the tent, and when we're closer, I send some of my ribbons out to hold up the tent flaps to make it easier for us to duck in.

As soon as we're inside, I'm wrapped in warmth from the coals simmering in the center. Slade sets me down on the furs, and I look around, noting that everything is exactly the same, except...

"Got rid of my pallet?" I wander over as I note the metal armor stacked in the corner where I used to sleep.

"Not exactly," he replies, nodding toward where his own pallet is. "I just shoved yours against mine since our sleeping arrangements are a bit different now."

I send him a sly smile. "Awful presumptuous to think I'll be sleeping with you, Commander Rip."

"Call it presumptuous all you like," he replies smoothly. "We both know I'm going to be buried inside of you soon."

"Is that so?" I peel off my coat, but the fae book that I'd forgotten about drops from its pocket and lands on the ground.

"What's that?"

I lift it up, checking to make sure the pages are still intact. "A book I found in the library," I explain, and I see Slade's eyes light with interest. "But...we'll talk about that later." I place the book and coat carefully on top of his armor before I sit down on his—*our*—pallet. I cross my legs, lips lifting up in a seductive smile. "For now, I'd like to do something else."

He stalks forward and then braces his hands on either side of me, leaning down until our faces are right in front of each other. "All I could think about today is what you felt like last night," he murmurs before he leans in to run his nose against my neck, skimming over the sensitive parts ever so slightly with his hot breath. "All I could smell was your skin, and all I could hear was the noises you made while I was deep inside of you."

I shiver, my head tipping back and my eyes fluttering closed as he begins to press his wicked mouth against my skin. He crouches down in front of me, dragging the sleeve of my dress with him to bare my shoulder. "You've bewitched my senses, taken over my thoughts. Every time I blink, all I see is you, like you've seared yourself into my eyes and I'll never close them again without envisioning you. And you know what?"

My voice is as breathless as my thoughts. "What?"

He leans away to look me in the eye again. "I wouldn't have it any other way."

This time, it's definitely me who presses forward to claim him for a kiss. To claim him for so much *more*.

He is everything I never thought I could have. Every sip I never thought I'd taste.

As if I'm worried he'll be ripped away from me, I hold him a little bit tighter, let my ribbons wrap around him just a little bit more.

When I get too overenthusiastic with my kiss, I bite down on his lip hard enough to draw blood. But he doesn't pull back. If anything, it just seems to spur him on even more, and I swallow up an appreciative growl right from his tongue.

"Hungry?" he teases against my lips.

"I've been starving for a long time," I whisper. As soon as I say that out loud, I realize how true it is, how undernourished my soul has been. I thought it was only freedom that I craved, but it was this too.

My life was a flat, barren plain. My horizon was stale and endless, with the constraints of others' control.

There was nothing but a bland, lackluster existence with no growth, no change. Just an arid land that held no rise.

The world taught me that things could always be worse. I learned to always look up, to take what I could get, to settle.

I became too blinded by my bright sides to see the truth.

Sometimes, you look at the silver lining so much that you drift into denial about the clouds.

Slade's black brows pull together, and he sweeps his finger beneath my eye, making me feel the wetness there. "What's this?" he asks, rough voice carrying his worry like rainfall in buckets.

I shake my head through the bouts of breath I pull in, taking in his scent with it. Freshly turned soil, wood chips wet by the rain, bittersweet chocolate left on my tongue. "I'm just...happy."

His face softens, and then he pushes me gently until my back hits the furs, and he props himself over me. He has snowfall in his cold hair and adoration in his warm touch, and if I could, I'd melt into him forever.

Slade looks at me like he cherishes me, the sweep of his thumb against my cheek like a kiss of touch.

"I'm happy too, Goldfinch."

"There's so much we have to talk about," I say, letting my hands run over the supple leather on his shoulders.

"But for now, I want you to be the commander and me to be the goldfinch, and not have anything to do with cages or crowns."

Understanding dips into his expression. "I'll stay in whatever form you like. I'll give you whatever you need."

"You," I answer honestly. "I just need you."

Slade stands up, eyes never leaving me, while he systematically begins to undress. His coat, shirt, boots, pants, everything comes off, until he's standing naked in front of me, pale skin and dark spikes on full display.

Along his shoulders is another brush of scales I hadn't noticed before, the gray of them swept from the blades, nearly up to the sides of his neck.

My eyes trace over every part of him, counting the six spikes up his spine, following the slight arc of them, as if they're talons from a predator's feet. The four spikes along his forearms jut out proudly too, but not as much as his thick cock.

Impatient to feel his body against mine, I sit up and lift my arms, and Slade grasps my dress and pulls it off. Just like the night before, he carefully removes my boots, dragging my stockings down right after. "Like unwrapping a present," he murmurs.

His gaze rolls over me like thread on a spindle, taut against my body. I can practically feel him weaving scandalous thoughts to twine around my skin until I'm wrapped in attentive want, and it makes my whole body flush.

He kneels down on the ground in front of me, his rough fingers skimming up my thigh. "I couldn't take it slow last night, but right now, I intend to lick your clit until you come all over my tongue."

My eyes flare, but I click my knees together, trapping his hand. "I, umm, I've never…I mean...I don't know if I'd like it..."

Slade goes still, but his aura seems to stretch out around him, a shadow converging. "Are you trying to tell me you've never had someone pleasure you with their mouth?"

I shake my head, my cheeks heating in uncomfortable vulnerability.

Slade reaches up and grasps both of my cheeks, drawing me into his gaze. "Then I'm the luckiest bastard in the realm, because I get to be the first one to taste you."

Before I can try to talk him out of it or voice my worries, he leans in and hooks the lace of my undergarments with his teeth and then slowly begins to tug them down. The sight is erotic, his movements smooth and confident.

Once they're to my knees, he pulls them the rest of the way off and then tosses them away. "Have I told you how sexy you are?" he asks, black eyes moving up to my face.

He leans in and blows lightly on the inside of my thighs, making me jolt from the barest of sensations. "I don't remember," I answer distractedly.

"Hmm," he hums. "Then I'll have to make sure you remember it now. Trust me, alright?"

The second I nod, he swoops in, and his tongue licks over my clit. My hips buck upward in surprise and sensation, but Slade pushes me back down, his strong hand grounding me in place against the furs. His dark aura writhes in the air around him, easing in closer like it wants a taste of me too.

I'm wound tight, my body stiff with tension, and he looks up at me from between my legs. "Relax. Trust me to give you what you want."

What I *don't* want is to ruin this because I'm feeling so exposed. So with a hard swallow, I nod my head and let my fidgety hands fist in the furs beneath me as I lie back down. "I trust you."

He lifts my leg, his spikes curved from his forearms like the glint of predatory fangs. When he sees me watching them warily, he gives me a wink. "They won't hurt you, but for now..." In the next blink, his spikes sink back into his skin until his arms and his back are just smooth skin again. All that's left are the tiny ones above his eyebrows, stubs of black that somehow make him look even sexier.

Slade drapes my right leg over his shoulder, securing me while also ensuring I'm spread before him. The scruff of his jaw scrapes lightly against my inner thighs as he kisses his way up again before a slow drag of his tongue licks up my slit.

"Oh!" My hands claw into the furs, and my knees try to snap together again, but since one is draped over Slade's shoulder, they can't. His tongue drags up again, tasting my wetness, and I can't help but feel overwhelmed. This is wicked and intimate, and I don't know if—

"*Relax*," he commands again, voice vibrating against my center.

I'm honestly not sure if I can, but then, his mouth descends on my clit again, and I buckle. He goes at it like he knows exactly what I need to make all my thoughts disperse. With his tongue lapping, flicking, and swirling, I forget to think, forget to be unsure, and I just start to *feel*. And when he presses a finger into my opening and thrusts it inside of me, I let go of the insecurities and the unknown, and I finally just melt into the sensations.

"Good girl," he growls against me, masculine pride jutting through his voice. "Your taste is my new favorite flavor. I want you on my tongue every night."

His dirty words are followed immediately by his mouth fastening onto my clit again. And then...he *ravages* me.

Slade licks and sucks, and my body comes alive with bliss. Squeezing my eyes shut, I let go beneath his devouring devotion. It's like he's worshipping my body, kneeling in supplication with earnest faith in the skill of his divinely decadent tongue. His hand stays braced on my hip to keep me in place, while the other pushes his finger in and out, dragging with my slick. Everything else blacks out as he works me up a high peak, even as his hand pins me down, demanding my pleasure.

Two of my ribbons delve into his hair, twisting and tugging, keeping him *right there*, while my hands fist more and more of the furs, my spine arcing up.

"Don't stop, don't stop." I squirm against his mouth, my scattered thoughts of need bursting through my mind one after another.

When he thrusts his finger in, he curls it this time, hitting a spot against me that makes me see stars. "Slade!"

"Come, baby," he purrs with dark decadence. "I want you to come with my tongue lapping at your clit and my finger in your sweet cunt."

"Oh goddess..." I groan, feeling like a bubble about to pop.

His digit thrusts into me like a prelude of what's to come, and when he drags the flat of his tongue against my clit one more time, I fall into bliss.

I cry out, without any idea of what I say or what noises I make. I'm too lost in the gust that sweeps over me, tossing and turning, pushing me deeper into a spiral of pleasure.

I'm still riding the waves of its invisible tempest when I feel Slade rise up, knees bracing, and then his cock pushes inside of me an inch.

My eyes pop open, and I look down, biting my lip.

"More," I pant, needing it, needing to feel that connection with him. Needing to make *him* feel as good as I just did.

His lips twitch, but his black eyes flare. "Don't be greedy, Goldfinch. Just take what I give you."

Heat coils in my belly, even as I raise an indignant brow. "Then *give me more*," I retort.

With a widening smirk, he leans down and nips at my lips. "Always so impatient."

Hooking my legs around his ass, I try to pull him deeper, but he just chuckles and shakes his head and then moves *out* of me before dipping back in with the same shallow thrust. "I should make you writhe and beg for *hours*."

I blink, horrified. "No, you absolutely should *not*."

The sexy-as-sin smile he flashes me behind his dark stubble would make me melt if I weren't growing increasingly impatient. He eases out and pushes in again, only going another inch deeper.

"*Slade*."

"Yes, Auren?" he croons teasingly.

That's it.

I bring up my ribbons from my left side and wrap them around his body, and before he can so much as tense, I use their strength to flip us over so that I'm on top. The second I'm in control and straddling his body, I sink down on him all the way, making him hiss out a breath.

My head tosses back with a gasp. "*Yes...*"

He reaches up to grip my waist, fingers digging into my skin. "Look at my wanton female riding my cock," he says, tone trimmed with pleased arrogance. "It's sexy to see you take what you want."

I barely hear his words, too caught up in lifting myself over him. One of his hands comes up to stroke over my breast, thumb dragging over my nipple, making it go hard and stiff against his touch.

"Harder, baby. Fuck yourself on me harder," he demands. He uses his other hand to help bring me up and down over his cock, making my body start climbing that pinnacle again.

I let my palms graze against his muscled abs before I brace my hands against his bare chest, using it for better leverage. I do exactly what he said, fucking myself on him hard and fast, while he continues to help lift my body over his thick length.

"Give me your eyes, Auren," he commands.

When I don't listen, he sits us both up, dragging me impossibly deeper as I sit in his lap, my legs shifting to wrap around his waist. His hips jut up into me, stealing a groan from my chest.

"That's right. Look at me with those gorgeous golden eyes of yours. I want them on me when your perfect pussy wrings out every drop of my cum."

A needy noise leaves my throat, his filthy words their

very own aphrodisiac that heightens my desire.

Hands trace down my spine, his touch feathering over the base of each ribbon, right where they grow from my back. His fingers pluck them lightly like a harp, making my body sing, but only he can hear its song. Chills scatter down my skin, ribbons shuddering with ecstasy.

Bracing my arms on his shoulders, I bend my elbows so my hands can dig into his soft hair. I'm so overwhelmed with needy fervor and the intensity of our connection that my eyes burn with it.

Both of his hands come back to my waist, biceps bulging. This time when he thrusts his hips up, he goes so deep that it's like he's rooted inside of me, causing my pleasure to sprout up higher.

And I want more, I want *this*.

Using my thighs, I start bucking on top of him as fast as I can, spine undulating, hips grinding, my swollen clit being pressed against him every time I slam down.

"Fuck…" Slade grits out, and the curse from his lips just spurs me on to go faster, and then I'm nearly there, so close…

"Slade!"

"Come again, just like this," he growls. "I want your pussy to choke my cock, Auren."

My whimper slips out from the filth of his words, and I feel myself become impossibly wetter, my core going tight. My body purrs for him, back arching, hips in his grip, pussy clamping down around him. Our gazes fasten, gold and black anchored together like ships to the sea.

"That's it, Goldfinch," he purrs.

Utter rapture overtakes me.

My orgasm washes over me like crashing waves until I become submerged entirely. I cry out, nails scraping down his skin as my entire body seems to clamp down around him.

"*Fucking yes...*" He roars in my ear, burying himself deep, stretching me around him. He groans out my name like a rugged prayer as he comes, while the last of my rippling orgasm laps over me in lingering licks.

I'm floating in the depths he brought me, basking in the weightlessness of it all, in awe of the force of our joining. As I shudder and pant against him, I let my forehead rest against his. We sink against each other, breaths shallow, feelings deep, wading in waters that are completely uncharted.

So this is how it can be with the right person.

All my life, I thought sex was just...sex. A commodity to be sold, a job to perform. With Midas, sex was the only time he'd give me the touch I so desperately craved, a way for me to make him love me. But I *never* felt anything like this before. No one ever gave me such pleasure or made me feel so treasured, so sexy, so *wanted*.

I watch him with a sweep of sated awe, his aura languid, flowing from his shoulders to drip across mine like a cool stream. We breathe together, chests rising and falling in tandem. My ribbons lazily stroke up his back, playing with the spikes that are once more protruding from his spine, and I hum in pure happiness.

Once again, this is a moment I never want to end.

But I know it has to.

As if he can see it in my face, Slade lifts his forehead from mine, eyes searching my expression.

"We should talk," I tell him, my voice filled with regret, even as it still carries a husky note to it. Those three words break the spell we're in, and then it's not simple anymore. It's not just him and me.

All too soon, we're breaking apart, bodies separating, my ribbons drooping like they're mourning the loss of him. I don't blame them. All I want to do is curl up beside him and fall asleep in his arms, but we don't have that luxury. I don't know if we ever will, and that thought hurts my heart.

Maybe these stolen moments of a forbidden romance are all we'll ever get. Moments where we forget about the outside, but the outside doesn't forget about us. The world has a way of blowing past your bubble, poking and prodding until evaded reality pops its way in.

So, as much as I want to keep on ignoring, keep on melting into him, I don't. If I want him, if I want *me*, it's time to face those harsh realities, because there is no future with Slade if I don't fight for it.

Which is why I clean up and get dressed in heavy silence, letting every concern and thought and worry rush back in as violently as churned rapids from the falls.

Slade watches me from his pallet, pants on, shirt off, spikes out, an army commander waiting for a problem he can attack.

"Tell me."

Not a command. He says it in a way that lets me know without a shadow of a doubt that he's here as my ally. That he's not just my lover, but someone I can depend on, can trust, and *that's* what gives me the strength to finally unburden myself and let my tongue unravel from the secret knots that have tied up my throat.

"Midas has him," I say, and the weight is like a boulder dropped from my hunched shoulders. "He has Digby."

CHAPTER 37

AUREN

I tell Slade everything.

About Digby, about how he went missing before the attack of the Red Raids and how I'd thought he was dead. Dead just like Sail.

I tell him about Rissa too, our plans to escape that keep changing, from trying to find a secret passage to deciding to leave during the ball and take Digby with us.

After I go over everything with him, he finishes getting dressed and brings me to the meeting tent where his Wrath are already waiting, and he has me relay everything to them too.

When I'm done, Judd exchanges a look with Osrik, running a hand over his yellow hair thoughtfully before he says, "It's possible Midas doesn't actually have Digby."

"It's definitely possible that he's lying," I agree. "But...I can't take that chance. I need to find him."

"How much of the castle have you searched so far?" Osrik asks from across the table. We're in the same positioning that we were back when I thought I was a prisoner in their army, only this time, Slade is sitting next to me.

"Not much," I admit. "The few times I've been able to look around, I've had to stick to the places that weren't guarded. There's an antechamber that connects a bunch of passages, one of which goes to the library, but when I searched the rest, they didn't lead me any closer to finding Digby."

Everyone looks at Lu, and she shakes her head. "I've checked them. She's right."

Osrik crosses his thick arms in front of him, tongue flicking his lip piercing as he looks at Slade. "He's gotta be in the dungeons."

"That was my thought as well," he replies.

Judd tilts his head at Lu. "You been down there yet?"

"No," she says. "I've been keeping to the top passages of the castle, mostly familiarizing myself so that I can get a handle on everything in case Midas tries to off Prince Niven. My time has been busy with making sure he doesn't end up dead."

I blink in surprise. "You've been guarding the prince?"

She shrugs, her leathers crinkling along her shoulder. "The last thing we want is for the little twit to be killed off and Midas have an official hold on Fifth Kingdom."

That makes sense, considering I wouldn't put it past Midas for a second. "What about Queen Kaila? Do you think she's in danger?"

The Wrath look contemplative, but it's Slade who answers. "We aren't sure. Midas always has plans, but I don't think he intends to assassinate her. Even if he tried to make it look like an accident, there would be whispers. She is much loved in her kingdom. I doubt it could happen without repercussions."

I wish I could help and say that I knew what Midas's plans for Queen Kaila are, but I have no clue.

My gaze goes back to Lu. "Do you think you can find him? Digby, I mean?"

"If he's in the castle, I can find him," she replies with certainty, her brown eyes full of promise before flicking over. "Rip?"

Slade nods. "Yeah, go ahead and pause your watch on Prince Niven and focus on finding the dungeons to search for Digby there."

"What about the prince?" she asks.

He tilts his head in thought. "So far, no move has been made against him, but I still want him watched. Judd, can you take over?"

The man nods. "I got it. I'm no Lu, but once I'm in, I can keep an eye on him."

I should probably feel guilty that I'm messing up their plans and taking Lu away from watching over the prince, but I can't bring myself to. Just the sliver of a chance that she could actually find Digby and get him out makes my chest go tight with hope, a band around my ribs that binds every breath.

"Alright, I'll start searching for Digby later tonight. Tired guards are easier to work my magic on," she explains.

"You can get started after you get Auren safely back into her rooms," Slade tells her, and she nods in reply.

Osrik scratches his shaggy brown beard. "How about this saddle, Rissa?" he says. "Is she trustworthy?"

I hesitate before answering. "She's not *un*trustworthy," I say carefully. "But..."

"But if you didn't follow through on your end of the deal, she'd sell you out," Slade finishes for me.

"Yes, but she warned me she would."

Osrik snorts. "Well, at least she's honest."

"I don't begrudge her for it," I tell him. "The life of a woman saddle isn't easy. She has to do what's best for her."

Judd blinks at me. "Gildy. Come on. You can't afford to be naive here. She might be silent for now, but what happens if she does make it out of here and then runs out of money? She's going to squawk your secret to whoever will buy it. Or maybe she won't even get that far. Perhaps she'll get caught before she can leave Ranhold, and she'll spill it then," he points out. "She's a liability."

"She's a *person*," I reply, a sense of protectiveness rising up. "And she gave me her word."

Slade looks at me, his spiked brow furrowed. "Auren, Judd has a point."

My spine stiffens. "Don't," I say with a shake of my head. "Don't even suggest—"

"We should kill her," Osrik butts in gruffly, as if he's not at all bothered by the suggestion to kill an innocent woman.

"Don't touch her," I snap, on my feet before I even realize I've stood up. "She's done nothing wrong."

"Yet," Osrik drawls.

Both of my lips press together in a hard line. I look to Lu, hoping for another female advocate on my side, but even she looks dubious.

"Look, I get that this isn't the best situation, but Rissa doesn't know the whole truth," I tell them. "I let her come to her own conclusions when she saw me turn the Red Raids captain solid gold. She thinks that Midas's power fed into me when he gold-touched me."

"Yes, but that's dangerous enough," Judd puts in.

I shake my head, growing more and more nervous that they'll take this out of my hands and do something unforgivable. "If we kill her for knowing, we're no better than Midas. It's what he would do if he found out Rissa knew," I argue, my conviction bleeding through my throat to coat my words. "She's done *nothing* wrong. The only thing she's guilty of is being in the same room when I gold-touched Captain Fane. She doesn't deserve to be killed because of that."

Osrik opens his mouth to argue again, but a shake of Slade's head has him snapping it shut, a glower lowering his heavy brow.

I turn to look at Slade. "You won't hurt her. Promise me."

His hesitancy has my tension rising and my ribbons ruffling out behind me, but he tips his head. "I give you my word. In fact, I'll even extend an offer to her and to the other saddle she wants to escape with."

"What do you mean?"

"When we leave, both women can come with us. It'll be grueling travel, but they'll be safe. It's not completely selfless, of course," he explains. "It would also mean that I could keep an eye on her and ensure she didn't speak your secret."

My lips part in surprise at the offer, and I lower myself back down on my seat. "You'd let Rissa and Polly go with you?"

"Go with *us*," he corrects, black eyes boring into mine. "If you think I'm leaving without you, you're out of your damned mind."

A soft smile tilts my lips, and I have to stop myself from reaching up to smooth away the frown puckering his brow. His shoulders have gone stiff, as if he's anticipating me telling him I'm not leaving.

"I'm ready to leave as soon as we find Digby."

Relief washes over his expression. Beneath the table, his hand comes down to rest against my thigh, warmth spreading from his comforting touch. "Good."

"It has to be secret," I warn him. "Midas can't know."

"Midas can go fuck himself," he retorts hotly.

This male.

"I'm serious, Slade. I don't want you two waging war. Not over me. No one deserves to die."

"That fucker does," Osrik cuts in. "I can't wait for Midas's smug head to get chopped off from his neck."

"I'd like his limbs to get cut off one by one and for him to bleed out slowly," Judd puts in cheerfully.

"Or Rip could just rot him from the inside out," Lu offers with a contemplative tap against the piercing of twisted wood above her upper lip, its ruby end glittering like a slitted pupil.

The Wrath nod in satisfactory contemplation while I gape, seriously questioning their sanity. "You three have issues."

They don't disagree.

With a chuckle, Slade shakes his head before looking

back at me. "It's late. If you're going back to the castle tonight, you should leave soon."

I can hear the other option hanging in the air—*if* I go back. "As much as I want to, I can't stay. I can't risk Digby's life. Whatever I do is a direct consequence to him, if he really is in Ranhold."

Please be in Ranhold.

Slade nods, though I don't miss the disappointment that flashes through his eyes before he looks at Lu. "Can you take her back?"

"You got it, Commander," she says, hopping to her feet. "Ready, Gildy?"

I don't want to leave. Going back to the castle feels a bit like walking into a trap, the clamps of iron teeth ready to shackle my feet in place with its piercing hold. But I don't say that, because I know as well as Slade that I really *do* have to return. I have to keep up the facade until Lu can find Digby.

Slade gets up, his hand taking mine as he follows beside me out of the tent.

"I'll walk you to the camp boundary. Then I'll let Lu take you so that she doesn't strain her magic. I want to make sure you have no problems getting back inside," he tells me while we begin to make our way through the snow. A fog has settled around us, socked in with milky condensation, giving the camp an eerie glow that hugs the campfires.

With Slade on one side and Lu on the other, I feel protected, reinforced just by their presence. "Thank you," I tell them, watching my boots sink into every slogged step.

Slade tosses me a look. "For what?"

"Everything." That one simple word encompasses a vastness I can't quite express. I can tell they're waiting for me to elaborate, so I say, "You're all just so willing to help me. Even though I'm nothing to you."

Slade stops in his steps like he just ran into a wall, his aura suddenly gone pitch-black, like a moonless night. His scales shimmer as his head turns toward me, eyes narrowed. Lu whistles low and steps a few feet ahead.

He raises his finger and says, "I'm going to let that slide *once*." His tone is the steady rumble of a brewing storm that makes the hairs on the back of my neck stand upright. Not in fear—I'm not afraid of him—but in response to the utter impact that lands with each word. It's a force as great as the quaking of the ground, threatening to topple me if I don't dig in my heels. "But hear me now, Auren. You are *not* nothing." Fierce eyes take me in, holding me hostage. "Understand?"

I nod slowly, the weight of his declaration settling in my bones, not as a burden but a bolster. "Understand."

He searches my face like he wants to make sure I'm telling the truth, and then he nods sharply. "Good."

I breathe out, embarrassed to admit that I'm a little turned on right now. But *damn*, that was intensely sexy.

When we start walking again and catch up to Lu, she smirks at me. "You got in trouble," she singsongs.

"Shut it," I grumble. "I didn't mean it like that, anyway."

"Good, because this is how it is, Gildy. You're one of us now. We always have each other's backs. It's us against the world."

I've never had real friends before, people I could trust and depend on. "It's going to take some getting used to," I admit.

Slade grunts next to me, and I smile at the stubborn look on his face. "Now who's the impatient one?" I say, nudging him with my elbow.

An entirely different sort of look hoods his eyes. "If you intend to go back to Ranhold, then it would be prudent not to tease me."

"Prudent, hmm?" Lu puts in. "Awfully fancy talk for our bloodthirsty commander."

He rolls his eyes.

"How did you all start working together?"

"I scouted them," Slade replies. "They all became soldiers under my command, and they proved to be smart and skilled. But the loyalty...that came with time. Osrik was originally from First Kingdom. We actually battled one another—he belonged to a team of mercenaries."

My brows lift. "Really?"

He and Lu share a smirk. "Yep. The big bastard nearly knocked me off my horse, so he impressed me. After the scuffle was over, Judd and I persuaded Os to join us and train as my soldier instead. He took the deal," Slade explains.

"Course he did. He had my sword to his balls," Lu chirps, sounding happy about it.

I wince a little. "That recruitment method seems a little violent."

Lu snorts. "It's better than when the commander tossed Judd's ass in jail."

My eyes go wide. "You did?"

Slade nods. "He was a wanderer with sticky fingers, kept stealing from noble houses. But once we finally caught him, the prick made a game of it. He'd break out of his cell nearly every day and then wait like the cocky bastard he is, *outside* of the bars, amused as can be. I had to offer him a deal just so he'd stop making a mockery of our jailhouse."

I laugh, shaking my head as I imagine it all. "That sounds like something Judd would do. What about you?" I ask Lu. "How'd you come to join Fourth's army?"

All the easygoing openness shutters in her eyes with a single blink, and her expression goes stoic. "A story for another day."

My curiosity burns, but I have enough in my past

that I don't like to think about, let alone talk about, so I know better than to press. Instead, I say, "The way you guys are with each other...so much trust there."

"We've been together for a long time," Lu replies, casting Slade a smile. It's not flirtatious in any way, but familial and affectionate.

A sudden shout cuts through the air. "Ho there!"

My head whips around at the call, and I squint through the fog to see a large campfire where a group of soldiers are gathered. Right there in the center of it all, stirring something over an iron pot and grinning from ear to ear, is a familiar face.

"Hey, Keg." I wave as I walk over with a smile.

Without taking his eyes off me, Keg slops a spoonful of stew into the bowl of the soldier in front of him. A bunch of it splashes out, and the soldier grumbles before walking off. Good ol' Keg.

"Gildy, I thought that was you," Keg says, shoving back his long, twisted black hair, making the dangling bits of woven-in wood jangle together like chimes. "What are you doing out here slumming it? Shouldn't you be up in that fancy ass castle?"

Not knowing how to answer, I look over my shoulder to Slade, and Keg follows my gaze. "Ho there, Commander. Didn't see you there. Sad to tell you, Gildy Locks outshines you."

Slade shakes his head, the corner of his lips twitching. "I don't disagree."

"Oy, can you serve me?" a soldier in line asks, eyeing the spoon in Keg's hand like he's hungry enough to try to snatch it from his grasp.

The army's cook pins the man with a look, wiping his free hand over his uniform, the leather as dark as his smooth black skin. "I *can.* I can also kick my foot right up your arse."

"I missed you, Keg," I say with a laugh. "I'll catch up later, okay? I better get back to my fancy ass castle now."

He serves the stew for the poor waiting soldier before he points the dripping spoon right at me. "Alright, fine. But next time I see you, I'm feeding you. Double helpings."

"I'm not going to fight you on it. If anyone can make army slop taste good, it's you."

Keg's brown eyes shine with satisfaction. "That's right, girl. Don't you forget it. The other cooks in this army try to sabotage me constantly. But *someone* won't do a thing about it," he says, looking perfectly serious as he glares at Lu.

She rolls her eyes and comes up to grab my arm. "Yeah, yeah. Cry your tears in the pot, Keg," she tells him as we begin to walk away.

"I will!" he shouts. "How do you think I get it so salty?"

The soldiers in his line groan.

Laughing, we head toward the edge of camp, but right before we get there, a hawk dive-bombs us, and I don't even notice it until it's careening through the fog, coming right toward us.

I yelp in surprise, but Slade lifts his arm and the bird lands on it, talons perfectly placed between his spikes.

I blink in surprise and watch him stroke the hawk's head and let it nip his fingers before he reaches down to the metal vial attached to its leg. When he does, my gaze zeroes in on it. "Wait, is that..." The question trails off as I recognize the golden bell insignia. "That's a Highbell vial." My eyes go wide. "This is a *Highbell messenger hawk?*"

He pops off the top to get the missive inside, his black eyes scanning over it while the large bird lifts a wing, burying its beak beneath like it's scratching an itch.

"He didn't tell you?" Lu asks, sidling up to me. "The commander has trained his hawks to intercept others. They're smart and skilled enough to snap the vials right off the other birds' legs. Then they bring the vials to the commander, he straps them on one of *his* hawks, making it look like it belongs to whatever kingdom he wants. In this case, Highbell. But instead of delivering messages, his spy birds know to bring every letter to the commander first."

"Wow, that's...pretty diabolical," I say, though I

can't help but be impressed. "Wait, is that how you knew I'd sent a message to Midas?"

"Yep." He finishes reading, passing it over to Lu, a grim look settling on his face.

"What's wrong?" I ask. Lu scans the letter before she hands it to me, and I frown at the words.

"The cold weather has gone from Highbell. Clear skies ahead."

"Clear skies?" I ask in confusion. "Highbell *never* has clear skies. And the cold weather certainly never leaves. What does it mean?"

Slade takes it back from me, not at all seeming worried that he broke the wax seal. "I'm not sure yet. It's in code. I'll talk to the others about it." Settling his dark gaze on me, I can tell that his mind is working. "I've got to get this hawk back to the cart so I can reseal the letter and send her on her way. You'll be okay with Lu?"

"Yep."

"Good. I'll be returning to the castle as the king tomorrow afternoon. Meet me in the library at dusk? I'll update you if Lu finds anything."

"I'll be there," I promise.

Reaching up, he gently strokes a knuckle down my cheek. "Good. I'll see you soon."

I have to suppress the urge to lean in and kiss him. He probably showed too much affection as it is, even though the fog shrouds us beneath the dark night sky.

"Lu, be careful."

"Always, Commander."

With one last look at me, he turns and strides away, and I follow Lu, trying to fight the urge to turn around. Every step closer to Ranhold's walls feels wrong, my ribbons coiling as tightly as my dread.

Just like before, Lu manages to use her magic to distract the soldiers, perfecting our timing so that we slip inside the walls during another guard shift.

"Think you can get back up to your rooms through the balcony?" she whispers, her quick steps leading me past the side of the castle. The gray stones are covered in frost, its higher stories impossible to see as the heavy fog thickens with the drop in temperature.

"Yeah, no problem," I say quietly, the air clotted with swollen silence. "Thanks for sneaking me in and out. It was nice to spend time with...Rip."

She smirks. "I'm sure. Better company than the golden prick, huh?"

"Much better," I agree, my lips curling up.

Yet that smile drips right off my face when we round the corner to the back of the castle and find four people standing there in the murky air. We skid to a stop, and I can tell by the way Lu's body goes stiff that she hadn't even realized we had company.

For a second, my heart drops at the shadowed figures, and I fully expect Midas to step out from the fog.

Instead, it's someone else who steps forward—the last person I expected to see wandering the grounds at night.

Queen Kaila.

CHAPTER 38

AUREN

T here's a suffocation of noise and a pause in the air when Queen Kaila stops before us. Lu bends her waist into a stiff bow, and I drop into a hurried curtsy, my pulse racing. "Queen Kaila, forgive us. We didn't know you were outside. I hope we didn't interrupt anything."

"Oh, you didn't," she replies, her umber gaze skipping across us like stones.

Anxiety churns in my gut as we stand there awkwardly. Every breath I take clings to my lungs, the frigid humidity coating my mouth and pressing dingy exhales across my skin like I'm clogged in a cloud.

The thick fog suddenly feels like an enemy, rather than a boon that kept Lu and me better hidden on the trek back to my room. It's the air closing in on us, an opaque mist shoved down from the sky as if the gods want to trap us.

The gray-blue of Queen Kaila's gown shimmers beneath her thick cloak, the hood drawn up over her straight black hair. There are three guards escorting her, the one to her right holding a torch in his hand. Their armor is worn down silver with the sigil of Third Kingdom molded to their chests, a proud insignia denoting their coasts with the rising fin of a predatory shark stalking beneath a line of ocean water.

Kaila pushes back her hood, and though no crown sits on her head today, she looks no less queenly than before. "What luck, that the two of us should run into each other like this."

I only smile politely in response, but despite my calm exterior, my heartbeat is sprinting. The only *luck* this is, is the bad kind. Uneasiness has quickly drenched my spirits, my mind racing with what the implications might be of her seeing me. I don't know Kaila's character, barely know the main facts about her.

I tried to put all things Third Kingdom out of my mind a long time ago, but I wish I hadn't. I wish I'd studied up on this woman, because right now, every instinct is telling me that Kaila is dangerous. I overlooked her at the dinner, her entertaining brother taking up more of my attention, plus Midas's demanding presence and a certain brooding king.

Kaila is here on Midas's invitation, but I have no idea why he specifically invited her. But maybe the more important question is, why did she agree to come?

"Interesting that you should be out at this hour," Kaila muses. "I would think that King Midas prefers you safe inside the castle."

Quickly scrambling, I say, "I couldn't sleep, so I decided to take a walk outside. Ranhold's night air is dense tonight."

"Indeed. I too wanted to take a walk. I find it mentally stimulating. You can hear so many interesting things at night."

My shoulders go stiff, and I feel Lu's attention sharpen on the queen. Kaila must feel it too, because her gaze flicks over for a second before she once again settles her attention on me. "Walk with me?"

I blink in surprise, my hands fisting into my skirts. The last thing I want to do is walk with her, but there's absolutely no way I can deny her, because we both know it wasn't really a request to begin with.

"Of course, Your Majesty."

When we both step aside for Kaila to lead the way, she cuts Lu a saccharine look. "You're dismissed."

Lu opens her mouth like she's going to argue, but I subtly shake my head. I don't want her to get herself in trouble or hurt. Queen Kaila is making my nerves strum with a steady chord of alarm, and I don't want Lu anywhere near her. She may be a warrior and the perfect spy, but I've dealt with my fair share of royals over the years.

With a loaded look at me, Lu nods tersely before she turns on her heel and strides away. Her steps are silent, dark silhouette disappearing into the fog like a forgotten ghost fading into the ether.

Now alone with Kaila and her guards, the queen begins to walk, and I dutifully match her steps, my palms sweating nervously beneath my gloves.

"Strange," Queen Kaila hums.

Goddess, I don't want to rise to her loaded bait, but I can't *not*. Verbal trapping is a royal's favorite pastime. Instead of learning to wage war on a battlefield, they've learned to do it in court.

"What's strange, Your Majesty?" I ask, trying to keep my tone light, despite the way my throat tightens.

"That you should be accompanied by a soldier from Fourth Kingdom, instead of your king's guards."

My ears ring with the dangerous pitch of her words, temples pulsing with the underlying threat I can sense in their inflection.

Yep, I should've paid more attention to her.

Along my spine, my ribbons stiffen, the satiny lengths bracing against my skin like an animal backed into a corner, hackles raised and poised for the strike.

"My other guards are waiting for me," I lie.

"Actually, I should probably get back to them before they come searching..."

Kaila gives me a look that lets me know she sees right through my pathetic attempt at leaving. "Come now, Auren. I can keep a secret. I keep lots of them, in fact."

Well, that makes me feel not at all better.

I worry my lip as we continue to walk past the castle, the heavy blue skirts of her dress swishing against the ground, collecting little bits of snowfall like white pebbles sewn to the hem.

Her guards hang a few feet behind us, but their presence is an oppressive wall at my back, like at any moment, they could come down on me and pin me in place.

How the hell did Lu not hear them and distract them from our presence?

I try to keep my anxiousness squelched, while the air does its best to blanket us in its dour mood, but Kaila seems oblivious to both. Or perhaps she likes the weighted presence that clings to us.

"Secrets are important, wouldn't you agree?"

It takes every ounce of willpower for me not to allow my expression to crack. I don't want her to see the flash of fearful trepidation drumming beneath my skull.

"I suppose so, Queen Kaila."

"You suppose?" she repeats, her throaty laugh adding husk to the syrupy atmosphere. "Whispers are my greatest resource. You do remember my power?"

I swallow hard, trying to keep the nervous tremble from my hands. "Your magic controls voices."

"That's right," she says, nodding with a smile. "I can send whispers across the room. I can make people hear voices that aren't there. I can steal someone's ability to talk for as long as I like, leaving them mute. But one of my favorite things to do is pull words toward me—murmurs of forbidden knowledge not for outside ears. Those are my greatest wealth."

My stomach tilts, a tremble radiating up my spine.

She heard. She heard Lu and me talking. I desperately try to recall exactly what I'd said, but there's no need.

Kaila stops and turns toward me with the stone of the castle at her back, her tawny skin glowing from the socked-in torchlight. I watch as she purses her full lips and then blows out a stream of smoky vapor.

The prickling presence of magic blows out with it, and then I hear something that lifts every hair on the back of my neck.

"Thanks for sneaking me in and out. It was nice to spend time with Rip."

"I'm sure. Better company than the golden prick, huh?"

"Much better."

My voice along with Lu's echoes slightly as it replays. The disembodied words play along the fog in an invisible wisp of an unnatural breeze that imbeds itself upon my rising fear.

The whispers replay over and over, making my teeth lock, a cringe trying to overtake my expression. All the while, Queen Kaila watches me, a pleased look painted on her face. I have to suppress the urge to shove my hands over my ears, but luckily, she raises a hand in the air, and the voices disintegrate, fading into silence.

"You snuck out of the castle to spend time with Fourth's army commander."

I feel all the blood drain from my face. "I—"

She cuts me off. "Don't try to deny it."

Regret shoots up in stems from my gut, threatening to branch out and hang me.

Presumably happy with my silence, Kaila turns and starts to walk again. "This way."

I follow her numbly, feet leaden with bricks of dismay.

"So, Auren, do you have a family name? A family?"

The change of subject has me flicking her a wary gaze. "No, Your Majesty. I'm an orphan."

She makes a humming noise, taking us around the corner of the castle and past the courtyard filled with ice sculptures. The moon might be only half lit and hidden behind clouds, but it's still reflecting off the moisture in the air, casting everything in an eerie haze.

"A shame. Family is important."

"It is. You and your brother seem to be quite close," I reply, trying to steer the conversation toward her instead.

The queen's lips bend into a wistful smile. "Manu is my closest advisor and friend. He's quite fond of you."

Well, that's good. Right?

"Of course, Manu likes most people," she goes on, cutting across my hope and the castle grounds. We head to a part I haven't been to before, passing by a short wall made of stacked rocks. "He's a sweet soul who wouldn't dream of using information against others. But then, that's why the goddesses didn't bestow a power on him, isn't it? I'm a better fit to rule Third Kingdom, because I will do whatever it takes to ensure I keep my throne." She nods at her own affirmation, as if she's had this conversation with herself many times before.

The sick feeling in my stomach only grows as she veers off the stone path and begins to walk through the thick snow. The guard carrying the torch hurries in front to cut an easier path across the grounds for his queen, the burning eye of his fire glaring at me through the haze.

My dread builds and builds until it teeters over into distress, and the silence frays the ends of my nerves until I finally ask, "Where are we going, Your Majesty?"

"Just a bit farther."

I keep darting a look over my shoulder, but it's not like I can make a run for it. Based on the way her guards are eyeing me, I wouldn't get far unless I used my ribbons, and I don't want the queen to know about them if I can help it. She doesn't need any more of my secrets.

Finally, we approach a huge stone building that looks five stories tall if not more, its true height gripped by the fog. At the front, there's a stone archway salted with frost, wide enough for twenty men to walk through it shoulder-to-shoulder.

Four Ranhold soldiers outside bow to the queen as we pass through the archway, and her three personal guards stay with them. As soon as I'm inside the building, I look around in surprise. The distinct smell of animal fills my nose in layers of hay, dusty musk, and something almost woodsy. "This is..."

"The timberwings perch," Kaila finishes for me, stopping in the middle of the huge open room. Beams crisscross the tall ceiling of the cylindrical space like toothpicks caught in the teeth of the stone walls.

There are dozens of the animals inside, feathers and talons as far up as I can see. Some are huddled together in their tree branch nests built on the beams, some are scratching at the hay on the ground, others are nosing at the trough where raw meat has been dumped.

Kaila walks over to one of them on our left, the feathered beast dozing with its head nestled beneath a tucked in wing.

"Riawk," she murmurs.

The timberwing immediately responds to her voice,

muddy brown eyes snapping open as its head whips up. It opens its mouth, and I flinch at its sharp, brutal teeth, but the creature only lets out a loping tongue to lick against the queen's hand in greeting.

Kaila looks over her shoulder at me. "Have you ever been close to a timberwing?"

Hell no. These things freak me out.

"No," I reply simply with a shake of my head.

Kaila strokes his feathers of brindled bark, and the animal lets out a purr. "Riawk won't bite."

Riawk looks like he wants to maul my whole face off, but sure.

I jump in alarm as a timberwing behind me suddenly flaps its huge wings, kicking up hay and dirt and other things I probably don't want to think about, before it runs through the open archway and takes off into the night.

While I attempt to dust off my dress and coat, Kaila continues to scratch Riawk unscathed. "Auren, let's talk woman-to-woman, shall we?"

Hesitantly, I say, "Alright."

She looks me steadily in the eye. "I came here because Fifth Kingdom has untapped resources—resources I want. But the late King Fulke was a shortsighted swine, and his son is a snot-nosed prig."

I have no clue why she's telling me this, but I feel it building up. With each word, she's shoving me up a craggy mountain of her own making.

"King Midas's presence in Fifth Kingdom and his extended invitation turned out quite fortuitous for me."

"Oh?" I ask cautiously, being dragged up another foot.

"Yes. After all, aligning with the Golden King has its very own advantages, doesn't it?" she asks, dragging her eyes over my gilded form. "Luckily, King Midas and I came to a mutual agreement," she says matter-of-factly, though her eyes bore through mine, her timberwing staring at me just as intently. "Marriage."

For a moment, I think I've heard her wrong, and my brows pull together in a confused frown. "Umm...but he's already married."

She tilts her head. "Oh, he hasn't told you? Queen Malina was killed."

I'm pushed right off the peak.

Utter disbelief has me shaking my head. My mind spins in circles with this news, but I can't even fathom it.

Malina...*dead*?

How can that be possible? The woman hated me from the start, but she's a queen I knew how to deal with. Became a fixture in the background of my static life. To hear she's suddenly dead...

"How? When?" I ask, bewilderment sticking to the roof of my mouth, my tongue a rasp of sandpaper scraping off the words.

A pleased gleam enters Kaila's eyes. She enjoys

catching me off guard. I wonder if this is something she used her magic to learn or if Midas actually told her.

"There were riots in Sixth Kingdom because she was trying to commit treason against King Midas. The people rebelled against her, of course. She wasn't able to subdue them, and they stormed the castle and killed her. The king sent forces, but it was too late."

I rear back in shock. I can no sooner imagine riots happening in Highbell than I can Malina being murdered by them. How the hell did this happen?

Suddenly, I remember the coded letter that Slade intercepted.

The cold weather has gone from Highbell. Clear skies ahead.

Comprehension is a landing of wreckage overhead, trapping me beneath convoluted rubble.

The *Cold* Queen. That's what the letter was talking about. It was a confirmation that Malina is gone.

"I can see this is quite a shock to you," Kaila remarks, though her pitying tone doesn't fool me.

My eyes blur with erratic thoughts as I plunge down and down.

I stare at the timberwings, but I'm not really seeing them. Instead, I'm seeing Malina, always looking down her nose at me. Formidable. Cold. Utterly unflappable.

And then there's Highbell itself. I may have been a self-inflicted prisoner there, but it was the place I called home for a long, long time. I literally poured myself into that castle to make it what it was. I gave so much of me without ever considering the effect it would have on the people who had to look at it every day.

Kaila is still speaking, and I have to forcibly jerk my thoughts from my inner spiral to focus on what she's saying. "He's gotten it well in hand. The late queen obviously did not know how to quell such things, but King Midas is a competent monarch who knows how to rule a kingdom. Which is good, because my first husband was a fool."

Completely at a loss and too unsteady to care, I ask, "Why are you telling me all of this?"

Her finger traces over the shell necklace that droops below her cloak. "This is the woman-to-woman part of the talk, Auren. I need to know, are you going to be a problem?"

So far, this conversation has been the equivalent of a kick to the gut, the shove off the cliffside, and now, I'm just falling.

"A problem?" My eyes skip over to the timberwing as it starts to nuzzle her arm.

Kaila's thick black brows arch up ever so slightly. "I'm not a fool, and I've been married before. I know the ways of kings and their saddles, but you're so much more than that, aren't you? The gold-touched favored one." She drags her gaze from my head to my toes. "I'm not sure if he loves you or if he simply fucks you every once in a while and keeps you as his garnished prize."

My lips part in shock, and I shoot a look over my shoulder to see if the guards are listening in, but Kaila says, "Don't worry. I've been controlling our voices since we walked in this perch. No one can hear us."

"Not even if I scream?"

A slow—and quite frankly, scary—smile spreads her lips. "Not even then. I can tug every whisper to my ears, push any voice from its box. I can grab conversations and pitch them across the room. I'm a master at voices, Auren, but it's yours I want to hear. Are you going to be a problem?"

How is someone so young so damn terrifying?

"No."

She regards me like she's taken my voice and is studying it behind the lenses of her magic. "That's very good to hear. And the other saddles, are any of them going to be a problem?"

I swallow. "No."

"It isn't a good idea to lie to me, Auren," she chastises, her dark eyes gone barbed. "But it's alright. I already know about the pregnant one. *Mist.* I can't have my betrothed having bastards, so she won't be an issue for much longer."

Chills flee down the length of my spine, and my heart drops down into my stomach.

Won't be an issue. What a generic way to talk about having someone killed. Adrenaline rushes me, like my body is begging me to turn and run, to find Mist and warn her, but my knees are locked in place.

"This is a business proposition and nothing more," she goes on. "Still, I need the public to accept me. I won't make the same mistakes as Malina did. I won't be shoved aside for the *favored* or give the people a reason to rebel against me at the first chance they have."

My ribbons tense like fisted fingers.

"I will have the people celebrate this union, Auren. It's the only way they're going to accept us joining our kingdoms. I want you gone. Which is why I'm so glad I overheard you tonight. In fact, that's the only reason we're talking, rather than me taking care of the issue of *you* as well," she says pointedly.

Killed. She was going to have me killed.

Goddess, who *is* this woman?

She considers me for a moment, her onyx hair pulled back tight, enhancing her cheekbones. "Oh, don't look so shocked. I can't have anything threatening my reign. Certainly not an orphan girl—I don't care if your hair *is* made of strands of pure gold. So I'm going to make you a deal, and I don't do this often, so I'd take it if I were you."

I have to suppress a wince at the underlying threat that prods up through her voice. Maybe it's her magic, or maybe it's just her, but either way, I feel the menace that nudges past her charming lips.

"I want you gone, but I don't want to dirty my hands when it comes to you. So, I want you to run away with your army commander," she says, and I gape at her in shock. "If you leave of your own volition, I won't tell Midas that I saw you tonight."

I have a feeling she wants me to leave so that if Midas *does* find out about her schemes, she won't be responsible for killing me.

Kaila's eyes are sharp, grating against my face. "If you *don't* leave, I'll tell him all about your little liaison with the spiked soldier, and I don't think he'd take that very well, do you?"

My plummet ends in a violent crash against an unsteady ground, body left to sprawl amongst the threat. Kaila smiles at me, the beauty of her young face indisputable. I have to admit, blackmail becomes her.

The fact that I already planned to run away with Slade works in my favor, especially if she's telling the truth about not alerting Midas about tonight. But I'm terrified that she holds this information that she can use on a whim. And what will she do once she sees that Midas won't give me up?

I'm not sure what Kaila sees on my face, but whatever it is makes her grin. "I see you understand. I'm glad we had this little chat, aren't you?"

My stomach twists with my placating lips. "I am, Your Majesty."

"Good," she nods before turning to scratch her timberwing's chin. "The king and I will be making our announcement at the celebration ball. With the rebellions in Sixth and things tentative here with a prince not yet old enough to hold a throne, it's imperative that we bring stability to Orea."

The only thing this union will bring to Orea is two very power-hungry monarchs having access to even *more* power.

"Would you like to pet Riawk?" Kaila asks suddenly.

This woman must really enjoy catching me off guard.

"Oh, no, thank you."

"Give him a pet," she insists. "He's very sweet."

About as sweet as she is, would be my guess.

With a pinched smile, I turn to the animal and lift a hand. As soon as I do, it whips its head with narrowed eyes and snaps at me. I jerk my hand back with a yelp, barely missing the bite of its teeth.

Queen Kaila tips her head back and laughs before tapping the timberwing on its nose. "Naughty, Riawk," she croons, though she's still smiling. "Males are always biting at the hand that strokes them."

I know that all too well.

"I'm glad I could talk to you, Auren. We women understand things between each other, don't we?"

"I understand perfectly."

"Good," she replies with a nod. "You may go."

Adequately dismissed, I waste no time turning and fleeing the building, the growled chirps of the animals following in my wake. When I exit through the stone archway, my ears pop, like I just passed through her magical sound bubble.

As I rush back to the castle, my head is in chaos, panic gripping me at Queen Kaila's conversation—at her terrifying power.

Midas just might have met his match with her.

I need to tell Slade and the others what happened, but I don't dare try to sneak out without Lu, and I don't know where the messenger hawks are being kept. I really wish we'd come up with a way to communicate with each other for instances like this, but for now, I'll have to wait until I see Slade tomorrow night in the library.

For right now though, I have to try and save someone who loathes me. I'm not sure if *that* discussion is going to be any better than the one I just had.

Mist might hate me, but I hope that hate will dim in the light of my warning. Because if it doesn't...her life, and the life of her unborn babe, are in danger of being snuffed out.

CHAPTER 39

AUREN

The problem with my mind being so frantic is that I forget just how late it is. I make it to the saddles' wing, only to be barred from entry. There are two guards sitting there, both of whom I recognize as the usual ones watching over the saddles' door. The gray-haired grumpy one and the younger blond with the patchy beard, who I've just permanently decided to call Grump and Patch in my head.

Grump shakes his head as I approach. "Can't let you in, my lady."

"I know it's late, I just need to speak with—"

"None of the saddles are here anyway, Miss," Patch tells me.

All my bluster blows out of me in a puff of disappointment. "Where are they?"

Patch scratches his jaw absently, his golden armor gleaming despite the darkness of the corridor. "In town. King's orders. They were sent to...entertain some of Third Kingdom's visiting dignitaries."

My shoulders crumple in misfortune. "Okay. Sorry to disturb," I murmur before turning away.

Behind me, the guards have an exchange, and when I hear shuffled footsteps, I look over my shoulder to find that Grump is following me. When I frown at him, he says, "You shouldn't be walking at this time of night alone. I'm surprised the king doesn't have a whole legion with you at all times."

My smile is tight. "He's happy to give me a bit more freedom these days," I say before I turn back around, hoping like hell he won't report this to Midas and find out just how badly I'm lying. However, I'm not *actually* breaking the rule. It's still dark out, which means I'm allowed out of my rooms so long as I have a guard...which I now do. Sneaking out part notwithstanding.

"Shall I bring you back to your rooms?"

I shake my head. "I need to speak with someone."

"At this hour?" he asks.

"The king asked me to tell her something."

That shuts him up, which is good, because my nerves are frazzled enough as it is. I was hoping I could've spoken with Rissa about this, but since she's not here, I have no choice but to go directly to Mist.

Keeping my steps quiet, I try to tamp down my driving need to run. I don't like this castle at night. It makes the glassed-in walls cast off a dark reflection of my silhouette, like a specter to mirror my movements in sinister intent. No matter how much I try to brush it off, I swear I can still hear the disembodied voices of Lu and me replaying in my head.

Remembering the way to Mist's rooms is a little bit difficult, but I somehow manage it without getting lost. It's just my luck too, considering I'm dreading the confrontation.

There's one guard walking his rounds on her corridor, but he doesn't try to intercept us once he notices me. Stopping in front of her door, I take a deep breath and try to steel my spine. I'm not sure it works.

Not wanting to prolong this, I raise my hand and rap on the wooden door. Once. Twice. By the third time, the guards are looking at me like I'm crazy, but I don't stop. I just keep knocking persistently, louder and louder, my mind racing.

When I'm practically pounding on it with my fist and Mist still doesn't answer the door, I start to really panic.

Did Queen Kaila already do something to her? Is she lying in there right now, body already growing cold?

The door suddenly wrenches open. "Mist," I breathe out, relief like a crashing wave that surges past me.

"What the hell are you doing?" she snarls, hastily

closing her robe as she ties a knot at the front, clearly disheveled.

"I need to speak with you."

Her eyes have dark circles beneath them, and I've obviously pulled her right out of her bed, a fact which has not softened her toward me at all. "Get away from my door! It's the middle of the damn night, and even if it wasn't, you're the last person I'd ever want to see."

Grump clears his throat at the awkward exchange, but I can't let her deter me.

"Look, I know you don't like me, but I have to talk to you, it's important."

She looks over my shoulder to the men. "Get her away from me. These are my personal chambers that the king gave me, and I don't want her here."

Her guard steps forward, not close enough to touch me, but he gives me a beseeching look. "My lady..."

Nope. I didn't get this far just to get scolded away. Gritting my teeth, I grip Mist's arm and push myself inside, dragging her with me before anyone can react. I slam the door shut on the guards, throw the lock in place, and then lean against the wood with my arms crossed.

"Who do you think you are?" Mist shouts in my face with outrage.

She tries to get past me to unlock the door, but I shift over to block it. "Just listen for two minutes and I'll leave."

"Fuck you, cunt!" she yells furiously, her hands balled into fists at her sides.

Panic spikes in my gut, and I look around, as if Queen Kaila is lurking somewhere, ready to steal more words. "Keep your voice down!"

Mist must hear the frenzy jumping in my tone, because she actually shuts up with her screaming. "Why should I?"

"Because these walls have ears, and trust me when I say, you don't want the queen to hear you."

A frown hooks her lips downward, the shadows of the dark room broken up only by the low-burning fire. Taking advantage of the way I've caught her off guard, I decide to just blurt out what I have to say, though I keep my voice quiet. I don't want the guards to hear, and I have no idea how far the queen's powers can reach. "Your life is in danger, Mist. Queen Kaila is going to have you killed."

She blinks and backs up a step, confusion warring with the anger that mottles her face. "*What*?"

"It's true," I say, taking a step away from the door. "Malina is dead, and Midas is planning on remarrying the queen of Third Kingdom so that he can have control over yet another kingdom. Queen Kaila doesn't like competition, and she *definitely* doesn't like the idea of you bearing his child."

Mist places her hand on her slightly rounded belly,

though her dark eyes narrow in suspicion, their almond shape tightening. "You woke me up to spew lies?"

"I'm not lying," I insist, begging her to see the truth of my words right there on my open expression. "The queen spoke to me tonight, threatened me, and told me in not so many words that she's going to make sure you aren't an issue."

Mist scoffs before her hand comes up to fiddle with the tie of her robe. "Sure she did."

"It's the truth. You need to leave."

A look of pure contempt crosses her face. "So that's your play? Trying to scare me into leaving?" She shakes her head, the fury returning in twin patches of red on her cheeks. "Well, it's not going to work. You're so caught up in your jealousy, hating that I have special treatment, that I have the king's *heir*, that you're willing to try and trick a pregnant woman?" She sneers, looking me up and down with hatred. "You're pathetic."

"I'm trying to save your life," I hiss.

She laughs, but the sound isn't humorous or even pleasant. It grates against the cold air of her sitting room, dark claws of catty dislike to leave me in stung shreds.

"Get out."

"Mist—"

"I said, *get out*!" she screams, the violent lash making me jolt backward, and the guards start to knock heavily on the door behind me. Great Divine, I *really* hope Queen Kaila and her power is nowhere nearby.

"Fine, I'll go," I say placatingly, hands raised.

Mist is shaking all over, the color on her cheeks now moved down to her neck and chest. I don't want to cause her distress, and I'm obviously not getting through to her.

But I don't care how much she loathes me, I don't want her or her baby to be killed. If it were anyone else telling her this, she might listen, but she's too blinded by her hatred of me.

With a defeated sigh, I turn around and grip the lock, but before I turn it, I speak quietly, hoping for one more chance at getting through to her. "I know you hate me, and that's okay. But I swear to you, Mist, I'm telling the truth. I don't want you or your baby to be hurt. Talk to Rissa. She'll tell you that you can trust me. I can get you out where you'll be safe, but I'll need your answer at the ball."

I glance over my shoulder at her, and I catch the tail-end of doubt flashing through her expression.

"A new queen isn't going to tolerate a bastard born from another woman, Mist," I say gently. "Just...please. Talk to Rissa. Consider it for your baby's sake."

"Even if it were true, which I don't believe it is, Midas would never—"

"You can't trust Midas," I snap vehemently. "He's always going to choose the best option for himself to get ahead, and with a new wife, you're no longer it."

She knots her arms in front of her defensively, but despite the aggravated posture, I can see the anxiety in the tightness of her eyes, in the way her toes dig into the flooring. "Why would you even tell me this?"

My shoulder lifts in a shrug. "We saddles should stick together, right?" I say it lightly, but inside, it's a deep-seated, melancholic thought. If only we could stop competing, stop the petty jealousies, stop letting men pit us against one another. Imagine what women could do if we started being loyal to each other?

Mist's lips press into a thin line, and an indiscernible look crosses her face before she jerks her chin up. "Leave."

Giving her a stiff nod, I turn around and flip the lock. I have no idea if she's actually going to talk to Rissa, but if I managed to put even a sliver of doubt in her mind, then it was worth it. At the very least, I hope that she looks over her shoulder.

With the click of the lock, the door is swung open, and I walk out past the guards, ignoring their disapproving looks.

On the way back to my rooms, emotional and mental exhaustion crushes me from the inside out, until my spinning mind and curdling heart have made my temples throb and my eyes burn. The jarring impact of this night is like being stuck under the brutish steps of a burden, heels driven down to squash me under its weight.

When we get to my corridor, Scofield and Lowe are

the ones stationed outside my door, and their eyes widen at the sight of me.

"My lady! How... You were in your rooms all day and night," Scofield says with clear distress, pulling at his light brown hair in a nervous gesture.

I can't answer him. I don't have the mental capacity right now to try to come up with a plausible lie, nor the emotional availability to care to.

Instead, I move past him without a word and close the door, locking it behind me, and then I fall into the bed, the forbidding disquiet in my chest taking up too much space.

I need sleep, and then first thing in the morning, I need to speak to Rissa. Then I can meet Slade at the library and tell him everything. Together, we can get a handle on the situation with Mist, on Queen Kaila, and hopefully, Lu will also have found Digby.

Despite those rational thoughts though, anxiety flutters through my system like provoked wasps stinging up my insides, because I'm not sure if I've done enough.

I fall into a troubled sleep, praying to the goddesses, but it's a silent voice to a starless sky, and when have they ever listened to me, anyway?

CHAPTER 40

AUREN

I wake with a determination steeped into my bones.

Midas, Digby, Mist, Rissa, Kaila. These obstacles piled up on top of me last night, but sleep and restless thought did one good thing for me. It stoked my anger and my resolution enough to drive away the anxiousness.

I'm too close to getting what I want to mess it up now.

Getting up from bed, I tromp over to the curtains and pull them open. I'm greeted by a milky morning, six inches of snow already piled up on the floor.

I dress hurriedly, with the backdrop of the baying dogs coming from outside. Wearing a simple silk gown, corset snapped impatiently, boots and gloves and cloak secured, I rush outside to the balcony, determined to sneak out so I can try to talk to Rissa again. It can't wait until nightfall.

Yet when my hands come down to grip the railing, my body jolts to a stop. There's a guard standing just below, gold plated armor subdued beneath flakes of snow. He's walking along the front of the dogs' pen, stance relaxed as he strolls along, but my stomach drops.

Backing away slowly, my steps take me to the balcony door, and I rush inside, heart suddenly racing with apprehension.

Midas knows I've snuck out. There's no other explanation. I'm not sure what the implications of this are, but the grounds below my balcony have never been guarded before, so I know it's to ensure I stay inside. Honestly, I've been careless. Last night, I was so concerned with getting to Rissa and Mist that I didn't think about myself.

Not good. This is not good at all.

With my lips pressed into a thin line, my eyes flick to my nightstand, and an idea sparks to life. If I can't go to Rissa, I'll just have to get Rissa to come to me.

The fire hasn't yet been lit, but I ignore the chill as I walk over and yank open the nightstand drawer. There are a few sheets of parchment inside, and I grab them along with a quill and ink, and hastily scrawl a note for her.

I don't dare say too much. Everything I write will undoubtedly be relayed to Midas, so I simply invite her to come up to my rooms for tea. A seemingly innocent request, but Rissa will know something is amiss.

I'll tell her about the offer to leave with me in Fourth's army, and I'll get her to convince Mist to come with us. I have a feeling I'm going to need to give her a hell of a lot of gold.

Meanwhile, Lu will find Digby, and then we'll get out of here.

I'll finally be free.

Heading over to my bedroom door, I open it, startling Scofield and Lowe, who are sitting just outside. I just can't shake these two.

"My lady, did you need something?" Scofield asks.

With the message folded between my fingers, I pass him the paper. "Can you have this delivered to the royal saddle wing? It's for Rissa."

His light brown eyes flick down to my outstretched hand for a second before I hear, "I'll take that."

My head turns at Midas's voice, and the guards practically jump out of the way. He grabs the letter before I can react, reading it with a skim of his gaze.

"No need," he says, folding it back up and slipping it into the pocket of his golden trousers. "You won't be here for tea today, Precious."

My stomach bottoms out, but he comes inside before I can reply, and I instinctually move out of the way, not wanting to be anywhere near him. The golden buttons on his tunic are shaped like bells, filigree thread reaching up toward his collar and down each cuff. He's immaculate as always, smooth jaw and pressed pants, shoes so shiny that they reflect the room.

The base of my ribbons lift like hackles, and when he motions to someone behind him, I watch as a maid comes inside and heads right for the fireplace, setting it alight with fresh wood and kindling.

I stay right where I am, back facing the wall next to the door, my eyes not leaving him as he saunters around, probably noting whatever else I've gilded in this room since he was last here.

The corporeal anger borne beneath my ribs makes her presence known once again, the creature bloomed from soured soil tilled in the resentment of my soul. I'd had a reprieve for a while—distracted from my fury by Slade's presence, but now she's back in full force.

I haven't seen Midas since he struck me.

My cheek may be healed, but the mark he left on me doesn't show on my skin. It's soaked in, saturated far below, twined to the crevices of my contained fury.

I look at him and think, *do you know? Do you know that Queen Kaila intends to kill the woman carrying your child? Do you even care? Did you give Kaila your blessing?*

The sad truth of it is, he probably did. Why settle for a bastard child from a saddle when you can have a legitimate heir from a young queen?

When the maid leaves and I'm alone with him, Midas

finally looks at me, smoothing a hand over his honeyed locks. His brown gaze flicks to my cheek, relief there for one second before it's gone again.

I was right about him avoiding me. He didn't want to see the guilt of his actions tarnished on my face.

"How are you, Precious?"

I'd be really fucking good if he never called me that again.

"Fine." Everything about my posture is stiff, unable to fake any sort of pleasantness.

There's a hesitancy in his demeanor, but it's not him trying to tread carefully. It's something else. Something I can't quite pinpoint.

He gives a sharp nod. "I apologize for not being more attentive. I've been very busy, gone most every day to meet with Queen Kaila or make appearances in the city or deal with my advisors and the prince. Fifth and Sixth Kingdoms have needed my attention as well as a firm hand."

I swipe a finger along my cheekbone. "Well, I think it's safe to say you definitely have the firm hand perfected."

He sucks in a breath, jaw tightening, but just as quickly, he exhales out the anger, shaking his head before he shoves his hands into his pockets. "I'm sorry. You know I am. I've been riddled with guilt since that night."

"Guilt doesn't assuage the guilty."

The narrowing of his eyes precedes his brows pulling in, a line divided to separate the charm on his face from the true nature beneath. He opens his mouth like he's going to spout back something combative to douse me with, but instead, he closes it again and seems to reconsider.

I keep waiting for him to tell me about the betrothal to Queen Kaila, for him to inform me of Malina's death.

But he does neither.

I used to think he confided in me, that our murmured conversations late at night in the privacy of my cage were something special. Yet I see now that he only told me things when it served a purpose, a manipulation. A way to steer the reins he trussed around his *gold-touched saddle*.

"The ball is tomorrow night," Midas reminds me as he strolls leisurely over to the fireplace and lets his hand rest on the mantle. "I would like you to come with me today and add some finishing touches around the castle."

Of course that's why he's here. It's not really to apologize. He just needs my power. I probably should be grateful for the reprieve I had from him for so many days, earned by the repercussions of his strike, but I wish it'd been even longer.

I tilt my head in thought, because...this could actually work in my favor. "On one condition. I want to see Digby."

A hush cascades between us like silent falls, placid water to hold us in the plunge.

"Okay."

I jerk back in surprise. Even my ribbons twitch around my waist. "You mean it?"

"I'll take you to see him tonight. You'll have earned it."

It's on the tip of my tongue to demand that I see Digby first, but I know Midas. If I push him, he's more likely to scrap the whole thing. Which is why I nod and say, "Alright."

One more day of letting him use me for my power. One more, and then I'll know where Digby is—finally confirm that Midas has him. Then I can save my guard and leave this place forever.

Midas smiles, pure charm dripping from his features. I wonder if he charms himself too. "Excellent. Let's get to work, and when you finish, you can see your guard."

Midas's "finishing touches" turn out to be more like relentless gropes. With bare feet and slicked hands, I turn whatever he asks me to, blocking out everything else, my mind's eye tunneled into one goal: get this done so that I can see Digby.

I become so focused that the hours of the day are no longer made up of minutes. They're made up of drips of gold. Precious metal replaces the grains of sand in an hourglass, each drop I create another second to spend.

So I spend.

And I spend.

And I spend.

Clothing and plates, walls and coins. Tapestries and bannisters, ice sculptures and sconces.

It's not the morning that passes, but me as I move through each room, touch every item. It's not the afternoon that lengthens, it's the stretch of my magic through Ranhold, creating more wealth in Midas's name.

He keeps me busy through it all, one thing after another, my power pervading every item until it gleams. But I do it all gladly, tirelessly, not once complaining even as the day drags on and my gold-touch clogs up.

Because I'm not going to do a single thing to risk seeing Digby tonight. I will let Midas steer my reins one last time, and then I will take a page out of Slade's book and rot them to proverbial dust.

One thing. He has one last thing dangling over my head, and I'm about to take it back from him.

I'm in the ballroom when the familiar tingle across my skin occurs. With heavy-lidded eyes, I glance over at the window, though I don't need to see the sky to know that the sun has set.

Finally.

I set down the empty pitcher I'm holding, as the

628

last of my power dries up. The weakened magic swirls around the pewter base, only making it halfway before it solidifies and stops mid-gild. I let go of it, turning my palms up to look at the damage. They're coated in sticky gold, clumps like curdled milk drying on my skin.

"You've done so well, Precious," Midas praises.

He stuck to my side the entire day, which is different from his usual "watch from afar" habit. Maybe he was being more careful in the ballroom in particular, since a random servant tried to come in once. Or perhaps he simply wanted to be more involved. For whatever reason, I was able to keep my head down and just go through the motions, so I didn't let him get to me.

Despite the long day, Midas's clothes still look impeccable. His neat hair is nearly as gilded as the floor, handsome face lacking any stubble, still looking as fresh as this morning.

On the other hand, I probably look a wreck, because I feel like one. My weakened corset has broken in two more places, and my braided hair has loosened, frayed ends poking out every which way. My brow has a sheen of sweat gathered, my feet and hands are throbbing from how much magic poured through them, and my dress has splatters of viscid gold all over it.

"Look at everything you've accomplished," Midas says as he glances around the room. Rather than critical, his expression is almost...awed.

I let my own eyes wander, noting every bit I've adorned, including the pillars and beams and floor, since I have to be careful to keep the integrity of the castle. I don't want it to come crashing down from all the weight like the pillow did to Slade's bed.

But to me, it's just a color. I don't look at it and see wealth, because what freedoms has it ever bought me? Every time I gold-touch something, I just keep paying a price that grows steeper and steeper. Gold is just a four-letter word for greed.

"A single touch, and you can do all this," Midas goes on, glancing down at the buffet in front of us, now laden with golden tableware. He picks up one of the plates, so shiny that it reflects his image. His thumb brushes over it like one would caress a lover. "Gold is the epitome of wealth and power. It's the one constant in this world that will always ensure I can get whatever I want. That people will bow down at my feet. With such unattainable riches as this, I can always have the upper hand." He speaks with reverence, the pious worshipping at his altar, and I'm the tithe.

Midas turns to look at me after he sets the plate back down. "Your magic truly is remarkable, Auren. You are exceptional."

Feeling uncomfortable with his praise, I look away and wipe my hands on the front of my dress. "I'd like to see Digby now."

"Of course," he says without missing a beat. "I gave you my word."

Thank the Divine.

The squeak of a hinge echoes through the huge room, and I turn to see the servant's door at the back of the ballroom open and a maid bustle in.

"Ah, right on time."

The woman comes over and sets down a tray on the table beside us before she curtsies and departs.

"I wanted to ensure you had some refreshments at dusk," he tells me. "I knew you'd be exhausted again, and I wanted to provide for you." With a flourish, he removes the lid on the tray, revealing the food and wine beneath. "Sit down, Precious. Eat and drink, and then I'll take you to your guard."

As annoyed as I am with having to wait even longer, I *am* starved. And he's right, I do feel exhausted again, nearly as drained as I was the night that Slade found me on the staircase and carried me to my room. I can't be collapsing on the floor with the present company, especially not right now when I need to be alert for Digby.

I sit down on the low bench in front of the table and start to eat while Midas pours me a goblet of wine. I quickly devour the cold cuts and cheese, my empty stomach growling in satisfaction while Midas putters with the items on the table like he's cataloguing their combined worth.

Between bites of food, I gulp down the wine too, though it's nearly as thick and sweet as syrup. In the back of my head, on the back of my *tongue*, I'm wishing for a different drink. Because this room-temperature, perfectly aged and sweetened wine is okay, but it doesn't hold a candle to a certain ice-cold, corked, bottom-of-the-barrel wine from Fourth's army. Now *that* was good.

Then again, maybe it was just the company.

Still, I down it all and then finish off a sugared tart too, knowing that my body needs whatever energy I can give it. My body is aching from my power depletion, and the call for sleep comes in the form of a sting against my eyes, but I shove it away and shore myself up.

Feeling anxious, I get to my feet, wiping some crumb remnants off my dress. "I'm finished."

"You sure you had enough?" Midas asks, gaze running over the tray and all the pieces of food I've left behind. Except for the wine. I polished that sucker right off.

"I'm sure," I say with a definitive nod, edginess taking over. "I just want to see Digby."

Shoulders stiff, ribbons coiled, I wait to see if he tries to put me off again, if he's going to try to go back on his word, but Midas nods and says, "Then I'll take you to him now."

My defensive posture loosens with a breath.

I'm coming, Digby.

CHAPTER 41

AUREN

I *follow a step behind* Midas as he leads the way out of the ballroom and into the great hall. His guards are waiting for him, and they peel away from the wall when they see us coming, falling in behind with matching strides.

I'm a pulped mesh of exhaustion, yet corners of anxious anticipation sharpen my edges. Even with the food I've eaten, I can feel my body weakening with every step until I have to look down at my feet to keep them moving.

Midas takes me out of the great hall, down a corridor and to a set of stairs. I try to memorize the path so that I can relay it to Lu later in case she hasn't found the way yet, but it's a struggle to pay attention because of how drained I feel.

I squeeze my stinging eyes shut and then miss a step from my lack of concentration. Luckily, my ribbons help catch my fall.

"Careful, Precious," Midas murmurs.

I take my time down the steps, gripping the railing in a tight hold. When I reach the bottom of the stairs, I blow out a breath of relief.

I'm tired. So tired.

A brisk cold in the air makes me shiver, and I take a second to look around, though aside from the shadowed lighting, the space is unremarkable. Just plain and gray, like a servant's passageway.

Midas keeps walking down the corridor, and I swipe my hand over my forehead to get rid of the sweat gathered against my hairline. "Are we close?" Even my voice sounds weary.

"Yes, we're here," Midas tells me, and I jerk my head up to look as he comes to a stop in front of a plain wooden door.

He nods to one of the guards, and the man steps forward with a key, shoving it into the lock. My heart is pounding in my head, in my temples, in my *veins*.

I feel so sick with worry. Or maybe I'm just plain sick. Too much power use has left me to feel like every drop of gold my skin created was me slowly bleeding out.

I try to push past the feeling, but it just keeps getting worse, my limbs tingling, my vision bending.

When the door swings open, Midas looks at me with a smile and then strides inside, while I gulp in a breath and tell myself to get my shit together. Stumbling forward, I pass through the threshold, because I don't care how sick I feel, nothing is going to keep me from seeing Digby. Not even myself.

As soon as I'm inside, the guards close the door behind me to leave us in privacy.

I take two steps before coming to an abrupt stop.

My mouth opens in a soundless pant, eyes sweeping over the dimly lit room of plain gray floors and walls, a crescent window too high to reach, a cot on the floor.

I blink, trying to register what I'm seeing, though it's difficult past the haze that's descended in my mind.

"Digby?"

The steps I take forward are like slogging through deep sand, each lift of my feet a weighted struggle. My vision has gone tunneled, drops of black ink staining around the edges.

When I reach the bedside and look down, my stomach slants like the steep pitch of a roof, meant to make everything slip off before it can settle. My legs and face both crumple, and the only reason I stay upright is because I manage to catch myself on the wall, palm abraded against the stone as I stare down in horror.

The man lying on the bed is unrecognizable.

It's not skin I'm looking at, it's a map of mottled

bruises showing where each injury travelled, the passages that took them from black and blues to yellows and greens. Swollen cheeks, split lip, fingernails gone black, and gray hair darkened by grime and plastered against his forehead.

My hand slaps over my mouth like I want to stifle the agony that courses through me, but I could never cover that up.

Because Digby is broken.

This is not the man I remember. This isn't my strong, gruff, stoic guard. The person lying on this cot is a mess of injuries and pain, skin too many colors to count. If it weren't for the wheezing from his lungs, I would think he was dead.

My wet eyes begin to drip, tears scalding my cheeks as my world tilts. My hands hesitate over him, hovering over his tattered and filthy uniform, the golden fabric tarnished and torn. I'm too afraid to touch him in case it causes more pain, so I reach out with one ribbon to gently brush against his arm.

"Why is he like this?" I ask, my voice coming out in a hoarse whisper, though it thunders in my chest. When I don't get an answer, I round on Midas, but spinning that fast makes my dizziness worse. *"What did you do?"* I'm able to shout it out this time, the thunder audible as it rents through the air.

Midas leans against the wall with his hands in his

pants pockets, looking back at me with a dispassionate gaze. "Me?" he asks, and then he starts to slowly shake his head. "Oh, I didn't do this, Auren. *You* did. Whenever you broke a rule. Every time you tried to pull away from me, you did this. I warned you."

My mouth drops open, but he pushes off the wall and strides over to me, stopping just an inch away. I lift my chin and glare at him, though the outline of his face has starbursts of fractured light around it, prisms of refracting colors that wobble every time I blink.

"You think I don't know about you sneaking out of your room? You think I don't know about your visit to Mist last night?" he demands, something lurid and callous in his voice. "That was very stupid of you."

Nausea roils in my stomach, beads of strain brining against my brow.

"She sent word to me the moment you left her rooms," he informs me before his hands clamp around my arms, the grip digging in with a painful pinch. "*She's* loyal. Which is what you should've been."

"I *was*!"

And look where that got me.

Midas shakes his head in disgust. "You're lucky you're indispensable to me, Auren," he says, tone warped with a warning that bows between us.

Wrenching out of his hold, I stumble back, my shoulder hitting the wall. My body is suddenly burning hot, my vision murky, bogged down by a fog that isn't there.

"What are you going to do to Mist?" I demand. "Are you going to let your new *betrothed* kill her?" My voice echoes, bounces off the walls—*or is that just happening in my ears?*

He narrows his eyes. "All you need to focus on now is how *your* actions have affected this man."

With acid crawling up my throat, I look back at Digby, my vision swaying. Like walking across a capsizing ship, I try to get to him. I unravel my ribbons so I can drag him out of here, but I trip over them, knees landing on the hard ground as I cry out from the impact. Bursts of color explode in my vision, my limbs zinging with electric pulses.

On my knees, I lean toward my guard, my hands coming up to gently shake his shoulder. "Digby, can you hear me?"

Nothing.

I shake him a little more, but I'm so terrified of hurting him more than he already is. "Digby, wake up!" Panic comes in the lash of my voice and the crack of my jaw.

A horribly hot wave washes over me, making me feel strange, growing worse when the dizziness strikes me again.

And that's when I realize...

"Something's wrong."

Palpitations thrum erratically against my ribs like an off-tempo beat. I can *taste* the flaring light that's prisming my vision, and my body keeps flushing with this uncomfortable heat. This isn't just me feeling power-drained. This isn't just shock from seeing the state of Digby.

Something is very, very *wrong*.

Midas comes around to stand in front of me, his shadow oppressive. "I'm sure you're feeling strange, but you'll get used to it."

"What do you mean?" Slurred words, heavy lids. "What did you do?"

"It's just the effect of the dew. You must be reacting poorly since it's your first time, especially since you're depleted. I made sure you had quite a high dose."

Horror crashes over me.

A gasp tears from my lips, ragged fear leaking out.

I'm choppy and uneven, snatched up in the blades of a water mill, yanked from the depths just to be flipped over and dropped back down again.

I struggle to get to my feet, using the edge of Digby's cot to pull myself up. "You...you *drugged* me?"

I start to gag, like my mind is trying to jumpstart my body into dispelling the dew he slipped into me, but I know it's far too late for that. I feel it everywhere, from my tingling toes to my sparkling vision.

"I've tried everything to get through to you. It's

partly my fault for being too busy to deal with you sooner, but now I'll have things well in hand."

"You fucking bastard!" I lob back, pure fury straightening me up, the ends of my ribbons wobbling as they try to help me stay upright.

Midas comes nearer and places an unyielding grip on my quaking chin. "Just breathe through it, Precious. Stop fighting it. The dew will make you feel good if you just relax."

Make me feel good.

Flashbacks of visiting the saddle wing for the first time come rushing forward. I remember the bloodshot eyes and giggles. The languid bodies and carnal craving.

Oh goddess...

My eyes squeeze shut, prickles of tears crushed in the corners, left to leave me sodden and stuck. That horrible heat flushes across my skin again, and I groan, not in pleasure, but immeasurable dismay, because this can't be happening. I can't let this horrible drug make me feel lust toward him.

I would rather die.

"Shh, it's okay, Precious. I'll take care of you. With the dew, you'll be so much more relaxed from now on." Hands move, squeezing my tense shoulders, bunching the knotted muscle with his unwanted touch.

"No..."

He ignores me, stroking the curve of my arms, petting

up and down, down and up. My body is in a riot, flooded with too much dew, magically drained and exhausted, adrenaline spiked with shock. It's all too much, my senses a chaos of crisscrossed directions that leave me with nowhere to go.

Midas pulls me to him, hitting me with his scent that always carries a hint of metallic sharpness. The dew wants me to give in to him. I can feel its lecherous claws digging in, and he's counting on me to fall under the weight of its inebriated delirium.

"This is going to make you all better, Auren," he soothes in my ear. My stomach churns over the words, wanting to hurl them back up. "It's been too long since I've felt you. You're going to love it."

Bile smashes up my throat, burning the back of my tongue.

Here.

Like this.

He's drugged me, brought me to a beaten man's bedside, and is going to try to take advantage right here, right now, like *this*.

Disgusted anger lashes through the haze of dew and comes hurtling upward. All my limbs and ribbons may be jellied and sluggish, but for a split second, I fight through it.

With a noise I didn't even know I could make, I bring my ribbons up and slam them into him in a sudden burst of strength.

Midas goes crashing back into the wall and falls to the floor, but the move makes *me* fall too. My ribbons crumple as I land hard on my hands and my knees, yet the pain feels like bubbles popping against my skin, even that distorted.

A pained curse flies from his mouth, and my head whips up. "You will *never* touch me again!" I growl, not even recognizing the sound of my voice. "I hate you. I fucking HATE YOU!" I scream, my throat shredding, the room splitting.

Midas sits up, a hand lifting to swipe at the back of his head, fingertips coming back bloody. When he sees the red stain on his fingertips, his eyes flash up to mine with fury. "How dare you harm your king!"

I'm running off pure adrenaline, anger perched on my ribs and fueling my fire. "You're not my king! You're not my anything! I *despise* you," I spit out, my voice like venom expelling out to blind him with my enmity. "I thought you loved me, but you only love yourself. I know what it feels like now to truly be cherished and respected, and those are two things you've *never* done," I pant, each word as sharp as claws. "You're nothing but a false king who uses and manipulates everyone in his life because you secretly loathe yourself."

Something sinister coalesces in his eyes, gathers on his brow, settles in the depths of his darkened eyes. I kneel there shaking and raw, glaring at him through all the bits and pieces of me scraped open.

The energy I expelled has left me weakened, my ribbons flopping on the floor like beached fish. My vision flares as another wave of heat passes through me to instigate some forced thirst of desire that I refuse to have for this man.

I gasp and clutch my head, trying to fight past it, and that's when Midas pounces.

One second, he's across the room, and the next, his fist is in my hair and he's slamming my front to the ground. *Hard.*

I cry out, my cheek cracking with the impact that I'm sure would be worse if it weren't for the drug coursing through my veins.

"You know what it's like to be *cherished and respected?*" he snarls in my ear, his body pressing me down. "So you *did* fuck that grotesque horned commander, didn't you? You let that Fourth filth touch what's *mine.*"

"I'm not yours!" Spittle and fury expels from my mouth as he holds me down. "And that Fourth filth is ten times the male you could *ever* be!"

With gritted teeth, I try to make my ribbons lurch up and shove him away again, but it's like trying to move limbs that have had their circulation cut off for too long. They flop clumsily, too affected by the drug.

Midas snatches them up in his other hand and wraps them around his fist like a leash pulled tight.

"I tried to do this the easy way, Auren. But you've left me no choice."

I'm wrenched up to my feet like a rag doll, my vision tipping, pinpricks scurrying down my skin. I look up just as Midas shouts for the guards to come in, but I don't glance at the door.

No, my attention is on Digby.

Digby, whose swollen eyes are suddenly wide open and latched onto me with recognition. I almost cry out at the sight of them. The brown of tree bark, scalded by the rays of a summer sun.

I see his throat work, how it bobs beneath his messy gray beard, and then his cracked lips move to say, "Miss Auren," and I really do cry out this time.

He's alive.

He's awake.

"I'm going to save you," I vow, the words coming from a stripped and slivered throat, a bleeding tongue of slurring whispers.

But he hears it.

Our moment is cut short when the guards come in, and Midas lifts me up by my ribbons and hair, shoving me face-first against the wall, too fast to stop.

"Hold her."

A collection of firm hands come up, taking over Midas's grip. Prisms of rainbow light stretch across my vision, though the bright rainbows don't fit here in this violent dimness. My bleary eyes take in a profiled face with a thick brown sideburn. Scofield. *When did he get here?*

I'm held against the wall just as Midas ordered, and I want to struggle, I want to *scream*, but I'm floating on a stream of lethargy with no way to cross the current.

"You brought this on yourself, Auren," Midas says, making my heavy lids blink.

"Wha—"

That's when I see the sword in Midas's grip. A golden blade, so sharp it seems to cut through the air as he lifts it right over Digby.

That's when I start to struggle. Only the pure surge of panic makes it possible. I shove at Scofield and the others, but I can't get them off.

"No! Digby!"

With frenzied, wide eyes, I see Midas look at me and lift the sword. My throat closes, cinches tight like the knot of a noose, and I screech at him to leave Digby alone, leave him alone, alone, alone...

But the drug has altered my depth perception, because it's not Digby he brings the sword down on.

It's me.

I was so aware of being held against the wall, solely focused on trying to fight the effects of the drug and get to Digby, that I didn't even realize that the guards still have my ribbons pulled taut. That they're stuck in the mercy of crushing grips.

A split-second warning of terror is all I get.

Then, Midas brings the sword down on them, the edge of the sharp blade slicing into their golden lengths, and my entire sense of self fractures.

All I know is utter agony.

Utter, eclipsing, unmitigated agony.

I don't just scream.

I *rupture*.

There is no dulled pain this time. When that sword hacks through my ribbons, I feel *everything*.

The bite of the blade cleaves into the top where they grow between my shoulder blades, and my vision cleaves with them.

I'm in complete shock, pain exploding beneath the blow of the torture. My ribbons jerk and recoil, screaming a silent scream that fuses into my spine and rattles down every bone.

In speckles of splintered vision, I see three of them flutter to the ground at my feet. Their ends are frayed and uneven, tiny droplets of golden blood weeping from their mangled ends.

I stare at them, mind not quite grasping what this means, and they twitch in response, like the tail of a lizard cut from its body, still spasming where it lies.

A horrible, wailing, guttural bellow tears from my chest. "No, no, no, no! Not my ribbons, *not my ribbons*!"

"You caused this. You will not attack your king,"

Midas hollers back, a manic wildness raving out of the cold determination of his tone.

With desperate panic, I try to steel the rest of my ribbons, try to sharpen their edges and turn them as firm as solid metal, but I can't. Not with the drug, not with the exhaustion, the shock, the pain.

I can't. I can't, I can't, I can't—

My sobs quake and wrench and threaten to topple. "Oh goddess, *please*..."

Midas raises the sword and brings it down again.

And again.

And again.

More ribbons fall at my feet, more screams explode from my throat and rip me in two. At some point, vomit heaves out of my mouth, leaving me to choke on acidic torment. I am nothing but flashing pain as he severs my very soul from my body.

I cry. I scream. I beg.

I spit and flail and fight, and my vision fractures, my body unable to hold myself up beneath the weight of the pain.

None of it matters. The guards still hold my ribbons taut. Midas still brings the sword down and cuts a part of me away, strand by golden strand, another limb lost.

I don't know how long it takes.

Seconds? Minutes? Hours? I black out, become a

convulsing mass of wailing stupor whose only cognizance is misery.

And then...

He cuts off the last one, and I shatter.

Right there on the floor, pieces of me left like bits of useless rags. Like the strings of a harp that can no longer play. Like the strands that once wove me together.

I'm dropped, body left in a heap to lie on the hard stone floor, but I don't feel it. I don't notice the blurred forms of the guards as they start to file out. I only see my ribbons, lifeless and lackluster. Just like me.

"You did this to yourself."

My eyes roll up to Midas's towering figure, to the hard set of his jaw. To the cruelty in his eyes.

He passes off the sword, straightens his tunic. "Disobedience has consequences, Auren. I needed to cut away this disobedient disease I've let fester in you. This was what you led me to do," he tells me, peeling me raw.

The tears that fall down my cheeks cut me open, drip by drip, hot gashes that slice through my face and sting all the way to my essence. Midas's mouth thins, eyes flickering with some unknown emotion that's probably as close to softening as they can get.

"Don't disobey me anymore, Precious. I hate seeing you like this." His gaze shifts over the inert ribbons, down my throbbing spine. "This hurts me a lot more than it hurts you."

Infuriated outrage flares in the mouth of my beast, but I'm far too numb to spew it. He didn't just chop off meaningless streams like trimming off a bit of fabric. My ribbons weren't just attached to my back, they were attached to my fucking *soul*.

The moment he sliced them away, he took something integral. He gouged in and ripped a part of me away, and now...

I'm empty. Mangled. Nothing but a radiation of agony.

The maimed edges along my spine are choppy and blunt, short and twitching with spasms I can't control. Each mutilated end pokes out from my back like snapped wings plucked bare of feathers.

With a shake of his head, Midas straightens himself up, already convinced that his every action was justified. "I'll have a mender tend to you later. Take some time to rest, Precious," he says softly before he turns and walks out, and I flinch when his shoes step on my ribbons, as if I can feel the phantom pain of their massacred lengths as they're crushed under his heel.

When the door slams shut, the sound tips me over the edge, and my consciousness casts me into a cold oblivion.

I fall willingly into the darkness with a plea for escape, while twenty-four pieces of me are left to wilt and wither in gilded grief. I shudder as my back drips and my eyes weep, knowing I'll never be whole again.

CHAPTER 42

AUREN

The pain doesn't let me stay unconscious for very long. I'd gladly lie here on the cold floor where I can dream instead of wake, but I'm not that lucky.

That's the thing about escapism. In whatever form, it always ends, and then we're forced back into a reality that's not nearly as satisfying.

A whimper precedes my vision, lips parting before my lids can. When I blink blearily, I note how dark the room is, the high window showing me a single star.

This too? I ask the goddess in her twinkling watch. *I had to endure this too?*

My eyes blur from a soul-deep pain that stems from the stolen threads of my back. With my cheek pressed against the rough stone floor, an exhale rattles out of me.

Numb. That's how I feel when I stare at the pieces of

me lying listlessly on the ground. Their gold seems duller, long lengths looking like a puddle of fabric, lacking all of their personality and liveliness.

My palm scrapes against the floor, arm stretching to reach for the one closest to me. I manage to drag it toward me, holding it in front of my face. I stare at the jaggedly cut edge, swipe along the curdled blood that's dried like clumps of gold paint.

The ribbon droops between my fingers, a weary vine ripped from its roots. I try to move one of them on instinct, but...nothing. Nothing except an endless throb of pain from each snipped stem.

"Miss Auren."

I jolt from the voice, but it makes my back tighten, which causes a frenzy of sharp pain to run up and down my spine. A curse flies from my mouth before I suck in enough air to breathe through it.

"Steady."

My eyes fly up to him, and it just goes to show my state of mind, because I forgot we were in the same room. "*Digby*." My voice cracks, throat ruined from my screams.

He's still lying on his cot that's attached to the wall, but he's managed to roll over onto his side so that he's facing me. Just seeing him looking at me, alive, makes me crumple all over again, and I'm wracked with emotion too full to contain.

Behind his gray beard, I see his lips tremble, his

eyes holding a sheen of sadness, and it hits me right in the chest. The sight of him like this, beaten and bruised, left in a cold, dark room for who knows how long, it *kills* me.

"Don't cry."

Just hearing his gruff voice makes me cry harder. Teardrops dapple my face, each one a grievance left to splatter on the ground.

I force myself to sit up so I can see him better, gritting my teeth past the pain that shoots down my back, the tattered ends of deadened ribbons spiking with agony.

Digby's lips thin as he watches me curse and pant and wince, but I manage to get into a sitting position, though my stomach is roiling by the time that I do. With my back too tender, I scoot over to the corner, and then let my shoulder and arm slump against the wall so that I don't graze my wounds.

Swiping away the tears on my face, I look at Digby, knowing that if he's not trying to move, then he must really be hurt.

Dragging my eyes over his wrinkled old uniform, I wonder exactly what kind of injuries he's sustained.

"I didn't know you were here," I whisper.

He nods.

"I thought you were dead."

He shakes his head in answer.

The smallest smile tips my lips. "There's my guard of few words," I tease gently, even though it feels forced, even though every breath I pull in shoots pain down my back.

Digby grunts in response, but I can see that his own mouth twitches too. It's a farce—this tiny bit of comfort. But it's the only bit we'll have.

"What happened?" I ask, voice hoarse and twinging. "How did you get here?"

His eyes flicker. "Saw you get taken."

"By the Red Raids?"

Digby nods and says, "Rode straight here to alert the king so he could send help. I've been in this room ever since." His voice is even more grating than mine, and I wonder if it's from disuse. When I calculate how long he must've been in here, hurt and alone...

My stomach clenches between fists, wrung out until I can taste bile on my tongue. "He *never* should've done this to you," I say, the anger in me fighting with the drugged haze in my system.

"I failed you, my lady. He was right to lock me up."

"Stop with the *my lady* shit, and don't you *dare* think that any of this is justified. It's not." None of it.

My eyes fall unbidden to the floor again, to the ribbon I'm still clutching in my hand.

Digby's gaze follows, but he doesn't speak about them. Maybe he can sense that I'm barely holding on by the ruined stubs that hang limp along my spine. For once, I'm grateful for his penchant for few words.

Yet even though he doesn't bring it up, I see his hand curl into a fist, though his pinky doesn't move. From fingernail to second knuckle, it's stained like he dipped it in an inkwell. Claimed by the bite of frost, probably while he rode to Fifth to help save me.

How much more of him has been deadened? What other parts of him are hurt irrevocably because of Midas and me?

I close my eyes and let my head drop against the wall beside me, the cold stone pressing against my tender cheek. "Sail died," I whisper, and even now, I feel my chest constrict at saying those words aloud.

"He was a good soldier."

"He was a good man," I reply. "He died protecting me, and now you..."

"Don't you worry about me," he retorts. "I want you to worry about *you*. I want you to be safe even when I can't stand guard."

Water rushes into my eyes, and my bottom lip trembles. My heart isn't just beating—it's *taken* a beating too.

"I'm so sorry, Dig," I say softly, my throat squeezing shut. When I open my eyes again, he's still looking at me, no blame in his expression, no hate. "I'll do whatever it takes to get you out of here. Strike a deal with Midas to get him to let you go."

But Digby shakes his head. "I'm your guard, Miss

Auren. My place is with you," he declares, as though it should be obvious.

Something sharp and small stabs right through my heart. Who knew loyalty could hurt so much?

"Now isn't the time to be stubborn."

"I'm not." He rolls his neck a bit so he can look up at the ceiling. Maybe it's just as hard for him to look at the tattered remains on the floor as it is for me. "The second I was assigned the post to be your guard, I found my purpose, my lady. All those other shits weren't good enough to watch over you."

I let out a shaky smile. "You really were the only one I could ever trust in Highbell," I tell him. "Even when I was just a snotty girl complaining about being bored, or all those hours of practicing the harp, you were always there. You were my steady."

He swallows hard again like he's digesting my vulnerable words. Then, "You *were* bad at playing that thing. Had to come in with bits of kerchief stuffed in my ears."

A sad laugh creases the tears into my cheeks. "I remember."

We fall into silence for a moment, but there's so much I want to say to him, so much undone in the threads of this raw moment. But I don't know if I'll ever get another chance like this, which is why I clear my throat and say, "You were the closest thing I had to a father," I admit, my voice small, eyes cast down as I twirl the ribbon around my finger. "I knew I drove you nuts sometimes, but you always made me feel safe. And I never thanked you enough."

He makes a noise, like a shaken breath past a graveled throat. "It was always my pleasure to serve you, my lady." Then, in quiet gruffness, he adds, "Any father would be damn lucky to have you for a daughter."

A vapor of melancholy condenses in the air between us. Every breath I take in saturates my soul with its drizzling grief.

After a while, I let the ribbon drop from my fingers, let it land on the floor.

"Look at us now, Dig," I say, trying to smile up at him, though my face pulls into a grimace instead. "I bet you wish you would've played that drinking game with me."

A short, rasped chuckle escapes him. "Aye, my lady," he breathes out with a sigh. "Aye."

My lids droop, shivers covering my skin.

If I can rest for a bit, then hopefully I won't be too drained once dawn comes, and I can fight back. I just need the sun. Once it rises, I will gold-touch every guard in my path if I have to in order to get Digby out of here.

Slade will be worrying. I was supposed to meet him in the library, so he'll know something's wrong since I didn't show up. I just need to rest, to bide my time and pray for the day to come.

After a few quiet minutes tick by, the heaviness of my body drags me into an in-between place where pain doesn't exist. I drift, like a boat without an anchor, lost in a shallow sea.

Yet I'm washed right back up to the rocky shore again, jerking against a collision of awareness when a noise clanks in the hall.

The door suddenly swings open, making me jerk upright, sending my back into snaps of torment again.

I barely have time to react before four guards rush in and grab me. Two of them hoist me up by my arms, another one blocks my feet when I try to kick out, and the last one is Scofield, who steps up and blocks my view of Digby.

I can hear Digby cursing and some kind of scuffle ensuing, but my eyes widen when Scofield holds up familiar white petals, freckled with blood-red dewdrops.

"No!" Through panic and frenzy, I struggle to fight off the guards, but the moment one of them grazes against my back, I cry out in agony, the fight pouring out from the wounds.

"Is that too much?" one of the other guards questions.

"King Midas's orders," Scofield replies, a look of guilt flashing past his eyes for a moment, though it does nothing to placate the hate I feel for him. "Just hold still, my lady," he pleads, as if he wants me to make this easier for him.

"Fuck you!" I heave, vision bursting with circles of black that threaten to stain my consciousness.

"Don't hurt her!" Digby shouts before hissing in a breath.

A snarl rips from my throat when Scofield moves just enough for me to see ginger-headed Lowe holding Digby down.

"Open, my lady."

My gaze is ripped away from Digby as Scofield shoves the petals toward my mouth, but I snap at him, teeth as vicious as a timberwing, hard and quick enough that I draw blood.

He curses and flinches his hand back, looking at me with a flash of anger. Using his other hand, he grips my cheeks and then squeezes *hard* on my jaw, forcing my lips to part. Before I can so much as curse him, he shoves three petals inside my mouth, clamps my jaw shut, and then covers both of his hands over my mouth and nose.

I feel the saccharine liquid coating my tongue, feel the petals dissolving in my mouth. I try to spit, but Scofield presses my lips hard against my teeth, not letting me open. The inside of my lip slices open as I struggle, but I can't breathe with his hand clamped over my face.

My body panics at the lack of air, and then it betrays me by swallowing. The second I do, horror fills my eyes.

Too much. They gave me too damn much.

Scofield lets go, and I cough out huge gasps of torn

breath that rip right from the center of my chest. "Get your fucking hands off her!" Digby growls.

"It's okay, Dig," I gulp, because I can't let him take another beating. I need him to live. Need him to let me go without a fight that will only leave him even worse for wear.

"It's *not* fucking okay!"

The drug hits me instantly, like being pushed into a lake, the slap of the surface jolting me from head to toe. My mind folds in, the pages of a book creased right down the center, jumbling my thoughts, crimping my words.

I can't even think straight. I'm just full body spasms, a shredded tongue, a bowed spine, a spinning stomach. And *heat*. Unbearable heat connected to my core that makes me throb right at the center.

No...

My burning eyes lift to Digby one last time before I'm dragged out of the room. My chin slumps against my chest, body succumbing to unnatural warmth. I fade into unconsciousness, hearing Digby's last shout and the door slamming shut.

But in my head, I'm whispering, *it's okay, it's okay, it's okay*.

CHAPTER 43

AUREN
Ten years ago

I've started sitting beneath the dock of the harbor.

It spans at least a hundred feet, its worn wood roped by boats that bob alongside its straight-laced reach. It's been built right into the sloped shore, so the start of it has an angle of sand right at its base, the perfect size for someone to hide.

So I do.

Inside deep divots of beach sand, I sit with my knees bent in front of me while ocean waves curl and flatten. I lean against the post, watching the ships in the distance. The one with the yellow sun in the middle of bright cerulean sails is practically gleaming, like it's beckoning to me.

But I stay here in my hidden spot, anchored to

Derfort, slumming in the shadows on stolen time. Every breath I take in is the brined air of a sea breeze, tainted with the scent of bogged-down ships and netted fish. And man. I can smell the man I was with like he's saturated my pores, stained every place he touched.

Repressing a shudder that has nothing to do with the cool air, I yank my eyes away from the ship. I can't recall how many times I've come here over the past several weeks, looking out longingly toward the sea.

It's always in the late afternoon that I come, when I've finished with my customer at *The Solitude*. I return to Zakir's under escort and then slip right back out again by sneaking out a window and climbing the rain gutter to the roof.

I've become surprisingly nimble at jumping the waterlogged shingles before climbing down three buildings over where I then slip into the alleyway and head to the beach.

The rampant rainstorms always help me to sneak out here without too much attention. When rain falls, most people look down, face shielded from the onslaught, so they don't notice the golden girl beneath her ratty hood hurrying by, because everyone else is doing the same.

Right now though, there's only a slight drizzle, and the noise of the drops hitting the wooden boards above me is almost soothing.

I let my hands dip into the soft beach sand, watching

it fall between the cracks of my fingers as I pile it up again. Here beneath the dock, it's cool to the touch, little sprinkles of iron peppered in the grains.

I've gotten lucky in this spot, with no one bothering me except for the old beggar woman who sometimes sleeps here, curled around the beam beneath layers of raggedy clothes. But right now, I have the small wedge to myself, mostly hidden by the curve of the hill at my back, while the sounds of the port roar as steadily as the crash of the waves.

At this time of day, the dock is far less busy. The fishermen have all come back in with the tide, the docked ships have lowered their gangways, and the sailors are already in the heart of Derfort Harbor to eat, drink, sleep on a bed that doesn't rock with the waves, or find a saddle to ride.

I've stayed too long today.

The sun is kissing the sea, the clouds in front of the horizon singed around their billowed edges, burning bright orange and pink. Such a pretty sunset in Derfort Harbor is rare.

So here I sit, soaking in the sight, hoping it can heal my weary spirit.

It doesn't.

I clump the soft sand in my palm again, watching the grains pour down while I ignore the shouts from the people and the caws of the gulls. My mind isn't on them.

It's on the small pouch lying heavy against my thigh where it's been sewn beneath my skirt.

Hidden there, tied with twine to ensure it doesn't jingle, lies tips from pleased customers—thirty coins to be exact.

Even there, in a hidden pocket, they feel dirty.

But every time I add another coin to it, I feel the weight of its added presence like a watchful stare. Like it's waiting. For Zakir to find it or for someone on these rabid streets to steal it or...

Or.

It's that *or* that keeps me up at night.

It's that *or* that drags my feet to sit beneath this dock and watch the bobbing ships as they draw anchor and set sail toward the sunset.

Somewhere behind me, there are bodies hanging, fleshly flags of warning to thieves and murderers and stowaways.

But still, I consider that *or*.

Shouts from above draw my eye, and I see the shadows of heavy boots passing over the cracks of the boards, hear the thumps of steps as they walk down the dock.

I envy those people. They get to hop on a boat and leave this place. "Got it all?" a gruff voice asks.

"Yeh," someone else replies, an accent thick on his tongue.

"Good, I wanna get the fuck out of this place."

"Captain's on the way."

I take that as my own cue to get up, since I need to get back before the others start trickling in and return to Zakir's from their daily duties. If I'm gone, they'll rat me out in an instant and be rewarded generously for it.

With my hood drawn up, I crawl out from my wedge and slog through the deep sand, stepping on bits of broken shells and dried seaweed.

I crest the slope and head for the sand-drenched boardwalk that's attached to the dock. It leads to the cobbled street just beyond, the start of the market dividing beach from buildings.

The last of the merchants and workers who stay out on the dock all day to sell wares or shine shoes or braid nets are leaving too. They walk along with slumped backs and chapped fingers, some rolling their carts behind them, causing constant thumps of uneven wheels over the rickety planks.

I stay to the edge, making sure to give them plenty of room to go around me, while avoiding the eyes of the sailors heading back to the boats. Walking with my head down while being aware of everything around me is a necessary skill I've learned.

Which is why it's so jarring when someone suddenly shoves into me from behind, nearly making me topple over. I jolt to a stop, an apology already stuttering past my lips. I've learned the hard way to always apologize, whether it's your fault or not. People have been stabbed here for less.

"I'm sorry—"

A smooth voice cuts me off. "The painted girl of Derfort Harbor."

My head wrenches up, and I look up at an unfamiliar face. Tawny skin, long black hair secured at the nape of his neck, a smooth face with plump cheeks. I'd think the man was friendly if it weren't for the pin secured to his loose blue tunic. A pin of a sundial pointing due East.

He grins, showing a few missing teeth. "Hello, pet. Barden wants you to come see him so you two can talk," the man says, and despite the smoothness of his voice, his words scrape down my spine.

I don't care what he says. Barden East does not want to *talk*.

He wants me in his employ. To take me from Zakir and work me for himself. Barden doesn't appreciate the customers I've been pulling in. I'm competition.

My tongue is stuck to the roof of my mouth as the man moves like he's going to grab my arm, only to stop when he looks over my shoulder. I follow his gaze with a hasty glance, finding two of Zakir's goons cutting their way toward me from the street.

Oh no.

Barden's man curses under his breath and then pins

me with a look. "Come find him, girl. Trust me, you don't want him to come find you." With those parting words, he turns and walks away.

I'm frozen in place, my eyes flying back and forth between the man's retreating form as he heads back to East's territory, and Zakir's goons as they stalk toward me.

The hair on the back of my neck lifts, and my heart pounds. The pouch of coins beneath my skirt weighs my choices.

How long? How long can I keep living like this, sold for a coin day after day? It's just a matter of time before Barden snatches me up, either with a deal struck by Zakir...or something more sinister.

Zakir certainly won't believe me that I had nothing to do with being approached by Barden's man. I'll be punished, since he's grown increasingly paranoid about losing me.

But does it really matter who owns me? Am I really any better off than those bodies swaying on their ropes?

It feels like I stand stuck at a mental crossroads for hours, when really, it's just a second.

I'm afraid. Dreadfully so. My heart is pounding a drumbeat against my muscles, pumped blood shoving at me to *move*. To *try*.

Shove down weakness and strength will rise.

The innkeeper's voice rises up in me, but this time,

I hear it in my own voice, feel it in the pinching of my back.

I could let Zakir West's men take me. I could give in to Barden East.

East and West.

Two directions, both of which will leave me to drift in hopelessness.

Or...

My head turns, gaze latching onto the people walking along the dock, at the boats floating on the water. At the sun on the cerulean sail shining against the sky like my own personal lodestar.

And right now, in this moment, I seize it like it's a sign from the goddesses.

So I turn around and *run*.

I run like I've never run in my entire life. My feet pound against the boardwalk, skirt whipping around my legs, hair flying back with my hood.

I can hear shouts, but it just makes me go faster, my steps avoiding the merchants and sailors that I pass, darting around them when I leap onto the dock.

My too-tight boots punish my toes as my feet pound against the timeworn wood, my lungs burning from the demand of my sprint, but I don't stop.

Not even when my foot catches on a rolling cart, nearly sending it and me toppling over. Not even when the merchant curses me while several others turn to look.

I just keep going, eyes set on the closest boat on the dock
and its rope being untwined from the post.

I can make it...I *have* to make it.

Please let me make it.

The trip up with the cart lost me precious seconds—
precious distance—so I don't dare chance a look over my
shoulder. I can't afford to look. Every second, every step,
counts.

"Stop!" one of Zakir's men shouts.

But I won't stop, not now, when I've finally decided
to *try*.

One more pounded step along the dock, and then, I
jump.

I jump right for the little boat already starting to row
away, for the small open space right at the back of it.

For a moment, both time and my body seem to
suspend.

And then I hit feet-first in a landing that shoots pain
up both legs. I nearly topple overboard, capsizing the boat
with me, but surprised shouts ring out, and the people I've
unceremoniously joined manage to hold it steady before
it can tip.

A man with a weather-worn face and sunspots along
his cheeks snarls at me as he grabs my arm. "What the
fuck do you think you're doing, girl?"

"Just throw her over, Hock!" another man in the
boat says.

"No! Please!"

Hock ignores me, of course, and starts to yank my arm, but he pauses when a voice says, "Stop."

The man and I freeze, both turning to look at the woman sitting at the front of the boat, a pair of oars clasped in her hands. She's tall, and has chin-length brown hair shorn crooked, and a hard face in blotches of pink and peel.

"Why are you all gold?" she questions boldly.

"Oh, um." I fumble for a moment before saying, "Some of the saddles here paint themselves. Drives up customers."

She lets out a scoff but continues to row, as if she's not even bothered that a painted girl just practically leapt in her lap.

Shouts from the dock have me whipping my head back to see Zakir's men skid to a stop, their arms waving as they shout for the boat to turn around and return me. My stomach roils at the look on their faces, and one of them starts to rip off his shirt, like he's going to dive in and get me.

"You trying to escape, gold girl?" the woman asks, drawing my attention back to her.

Her brown eyes are without warmth, but they don't hold cruelty either. She looks like the sort of person who shoots straight.

"Yes, but I can pay," I answer quickly. "Please. Just

take me to your ship, and I'll ask your captain for passage. I'm not a stowaway. I have coin for the trip."

Her shoulders roll, heaving the oars back, continuing to row us along. A splash behind me sends my heart racing, and I know that one of Zakir's goons is swimming toward me.

"Mara..." the other man in the boat cautions.

"Quiet," she barks, still looking at me with a tilt of her head. "How much you got?"

I swallow hard, darting a look at all three of them. "Enough."

I know better than to tell them how much or to reach for my coin pouch in front of anyone.

A smirk creases her face. "Not stupid, then. That's good."

I can hear the steady splashes through the water, and I cut another nervous glance over my shoulder, seeing the man getting closer, though it's clear he's not much of a swimmer.

After another moment, Mara says, "You pay for passage, but you won't be idle, neither. You'll scrub the floorboards every day till we get to Second Kingdom. We need a new scrubber anyway."

My eyes widen and my lips part in surprise.

Second Kingdom.

I've never been to the southernmost part of Orea, but I know that the desert land is scarce on rain and it's an ocean away. Just the thought of the sun and the distance is enough to make my heart leap.

"You'll take me? *You're* a captain?" I've never seen a woman captain before, and I can't help but think that this really *was* divined by the goddesses. That it was meant to be that I should run now, when I could land in her little boat.

Yet that thought is solidified when she nods her head at a ship in the distance. "Aye. She's mine."

My gaze follows hers, only to lock onto cerulean blue sails with a billowing sun.

Hopeful tears flood into my eyes. I'm leaving. I'm actually *leaving*.

Hock sighs and drops hold of my arm. "I'll take care of the fish."

I turn just as Zakir's man reaches the back of the boat. I flinch away as his arms come up and he tries to hoist himself inside, but Hock spins around, grabs an extra oar, and then smashes it into the man's head.

The goon cries out, falling back into the ocean with a splash and sputter. I watch the water nervously, but...he doesn't come back up again.

With a satisfied nod, Hock simply sits back down with the oar, while the third man pulls a pipe from his pocket and starts to smoke.

"Unless you wanna take a swim and go back, I suggest you sit your ass down, girl," Mara says.

Instantly, I jerk down onto the floor of the boat, my movements rocking it slightly. She and Hock row, while I pant with breath that doesn't quite seem to settle in my lungs.

The last of the sunset bleeds away into shades of gray, stealing the sun in a watercolor night. But I stare in disbelief at the dock, at Zakir's second man standing there with his hands on his hips, watching as he gets smaller, watching as Derfort gets further away.

I have to pinch my arm to show myself that this is real. It's taken ten years, but I've used the weight of a coin pouch to draw up like an anchor and let me sail away.

This time, when I turn my face into the ocean breeze, it doesn't hold the stench of Derfort Harbor. It smells like a chance for me to start over somewhere new. A chance where I can be safe, far away from men like Zakir West and Barden East.

Because me, I'm going *south*.

CHAPTER 44

AUREN

Tufts of snow surround me.

This place looks familiar and yet, not. I look around with a frown marring my face, eyes squinting.

For as far as I can see, there's nothing but an expanse of bright white snow blown in, resembling the sand dunes of Second Kingdom. Its curved crests slope up like raised bumps along chilled skin, though I feel no cold.

The sky above me is nearly as bright and colorless as the ground. My fingers dig into the snow, cupping a handful of it and letting it pour back out. When I glance down at my hand, my skin is gleaming, shining with light, though there is no sun to reflect it.

With my frown deepening, I try to get up from this snow that's neither cold nor wet. Yet before I can try to push up, I hear a sound.

My head jerks to the right, and I see Digby lying on his back ten feet away from me. His face is a mess of bruises, lips so swollen I almost miss it when they move. "Guard her," he says.

I blink with confusion. "What?" I ask, though my voice echoes, repeats, like I've shouted down an endless cave.

"Guard her." His voice is solid to my hollow, matte to my gloss.

"Digby, are you ok?"

But he just says, "Guard her," again, the same gruff order, same fierce look in his eye.

And that's when I remember.

That was the last thing he said before he rode off in the Barrens, before the Red Raids attacked. It was the last thing he ordered Sail. To guard me.

"Dig..."

"GUARD HER!"

The shout is so unexpected that I flinch backward in the snow, though this time, instead of having no temperature at all, it's searing hot.

A yelp escapes me as I jerk my hands off the ground, but when I glance up at Digby again, it isn't him.

"*Sail*?" I choke out.

Cerulean blue eyes lock on me. As bright as a different kind of sail.

A pang resonates through my chest, leaving me to

ache. I think it will always hurt, this sense of loss. I don't think that will ever go away.

That's the curse of the survivors. We have to live with our dead.

Lu's earlier words repeat in my head, and I feel a tear drip from the corner of my eye. "I'm sorry," I whisper.

It's okay, he mouths.

A second later, his brow creases, and he drops his head to look down, just as a patch of blood sews into his chest.

I try to scramble to my feet so I can go to him, to get my body to move, but the snow seems to stick me in place. I squeeze my eyes shut tight, limbs flailing over the ground that's heavy and hot, while frustrated tears drip from my eyes when Sail begins to fade away.

"Sail!" I scream, but he just shakes his head. Mouths that, *it's okay.*

Those words are a requiem that will always lament in my ears.

I squeeze my eyes shut, hating this, hating that I still can't save him, can't save Digby. But then, a gasp tears from my throat, and my eyes shoot open again.

I blink heavy lids, realizing there is no snow, no heat, no Digby or Sail. Coming back into consciousness is like clearing smoke, trying to wave it away with my hands, but it doesn't dissipate the haze.

I shove off the layers of blankets piled on top of me

and sit upward in a bed I don't recognize, my back slightly twinging. There's a blazing fire burning in the hearth across from me, making me even hotter than the blankets I'm trapped in. Seconds coalesce, smoke thickening in my head.

Was I dreaming? I can't remember now. My cheeks feel stained with tears, but I don't know why. My head feels like it's been stuffed with downy feathers, and there's a throbbing between my legs, a wetness there.

I try to move, to talk, but I can't.

Worry springs to my consciousness, and a low ache I can feel down my spine. I know there's something important, something significant about all of this, but I'm not sure what it is.

Where am I?

Before my emotions strangle me, the haze beckons to me again, calling with a whisper of a breath. I lie down on my side, embracing the calm, humming at the delicious heat that's clutching my body like a shroud.

I'm in and out.

Noises, voices I can't decipher. Fuzzy images. There's Scofield with his back to me. Another guard I don't know. There's a maid bringing in a tray. There's Polly, sitting on the chair near my bed, holding a familiar little box, a stack of white petals inside.

So warm...

I press my thighs together, a throb at the apex of

them that demands friction I can't seem to give. My stomach is cramping slightly, and my breasts feel heavy, sensitive.

Every time the silk sheets shift against my skin, I feel it like a caress. My nerves are alight with the sensation. I try to drag off my gloves and tug at my nightgown so I can have the air on my bare skin, but my hands don't work right.

Frustrated, my eyes close, and I just *feel*. I feel hands holding me on the railing of a stairwell. A mouth running up the side of my neck, and lips pressing against it with the barest hint of teeth. My body burns, the flames flooding my head with even more smoke.

I need more.

Something drags against my arm, and then I feel a wetness gather there too, like the trail of a tongue. I peel open my eyes and find Midas standing beside my bed. The thing touching me is a fur shawl, the wet sensation is my gold-touch leaking from my arm.

He moves the shawl away, and then there's a dainty looking crown being pressed against my skin. Then, shells gathered along a silver chain necklace. Each thing that grazes me feels so good that I nearly moan aloud, my body hungry for touch.

Brown eyes flick up to me, and lips tilt up. "Ready for the ball, Precious?"

A ball? I envision supple dresses and honeyed wine

and sweet tarts. I picture sensual music and my body being held as I dance.

I nod dazedly. Yes. A ball.

"Good. Sit up so you can dress."

It takes effort to do as he says and push myself up, to slip my legs over the side of the bed. Meanwhile, he carries the items he held against my skin and takes them to the door, passing them to someone outside the room.

When he comes back to the bedside, he's carrying a gown draped over his arm, white in color, looking as soft and smooth as butter.

"Put this on."

I want to feel it against my skin, so I grip the nightgown around my waist and take it off. When I grab the new dress and pull it over my head, my skin washes it in gold, and this time, I *do* let out a moan. The bodice rubs against my bare breasts, peaking my sensitive nipples. The waist cinches like a lover's hands gripping me, and the skirt strokes over my smooth thighs.

Delicious.

There's a pause after the noise my throat rumbles out. "I've made you feel good, haven't I, Precious?" Midas murmurs.

"Yes," I breathe, basking in the feel of the creamy texture hugging my curves.

He lets out a little laugh. "These next."

Stockings, gloves, shoes, I put them all on, one after

another. When I'm finished, I close my eyes, head falling back, because every drag of fabric across my heated body feels so...*sensual*.

I'm vaguely aware of my hand moving, of brushing my hair, though I don't remember when I was handed a comb.

I don't remember standing up either, now facing Midas, comb gone. I don't remember Polly coming into the room, but here she is. Wearing a golden dress, the sheer fabric draping off her body, held together by a clasp at her throat, just like mine. It showcases her every curve, her silhouette a carnal shadow beneath the layers. *I wonder if that's what I look like...*

Midas is speaking with her, and although I can hear him, I can't quite grasp the words.

"—at all times. No one is allowed to touch her. Give her one more before you leave. You know where to go. I'll be expecting you."

"Yes, my king."

"You'll earn a full box tonight," he tells her, petting her head, and she practically purrs.

He strides over to me while I sway on my feet. "I'll see you soon, Precious."

More time must pass, because the next thing I know, I'm standing at the balcony door, staring at the gentle snow falling down. The light is waning gray, a somber sterling to soak the sky.

I'm not sure how long I watch the snow, but my feet twinge, as if I've been standing for a long time. A movement reflected in the glass has me turning around, finding Polly walking over to the door and opening it. She's talking to a guard, but I don't comprehend the words.

Instead, my attention snags onto her blond tresses piled atop her head with a strip of gold silk. Something taps against my fuzzy mind as I stare at her tied bow, at the end of the strand that dangles down the side of her neck.

For reasons lost on me, I feel my hand lift, feel myself reaching behind me.

My fingers bump against the fabric of my closed-back dress, but something seems off. Instead of layers of ribbons beneath, there's just pain.

A frown splits between my brows, drawing a line of confusion. Something is wrong. Something is missing.

But it's like trying to catch the seeds of a dandelion in the wind. Every time I get closer to the blowing puff, it twirls just out of my reach.

I blink, and Polly is suddenly in front of me. Her cheeks are dusted with rouge that matches the red bloodshot of her lined eyes, while the gray daylight casts a gloom against her beauty. "Time to go to the ball," she says, motioning me forward.

The frown doesn't leave my face, but I take a step

forward, and before I know it, I'm following her out and gliding down the hall.

Blinks and steps.

Steps and blinks.

Something is wrong.

Something is missing.

I stumble on the stairs, my gloved hand gripping the railing to catch myself. Polly whirls, though she doesn't look at me. "Don't touch her," she hisses—at the guards I think, though I'm too dazed to look.

"Something's wrong," I mumble, and for a second, memory zings.

Have I said that before?

Polly glances back at me and scoffs with contempt. "You don't deserve dew. It's wasted on you."

Dew?

When she turns to walk again, I'm distracted by that dangling ribbon once more as it sways from her hair.

Ribbon...

A hand plucks a stem. A mouth blows dandelion seeds.

"Up here, miss."

Polly gathers her skirts in her hands, and then we're walking up again, on a different set of stairs this time. Passing through the narrow door, I immediately squint at the barrage I'm hit with.

Music amidst a backdrop of hundreds of voices.

The warmth of bodies, of candlelight dripping from the icicle chandeliers gilt with gold. I step forward, realizing that I'm standing atop the mezzanine of the ballroom, the small indoor balcony overlooking the space below.

"You're supposed to sit in this chair over here and wait," Polly tells me, but her voice goes in one ear and out the other. My senses are caught up in the sway of bodies dancing below, the instruments thickening the air with its melody, perfumes lilting alongside. Yet I'm searching, looking through the crowd before I even can grasp who I'm looking for.

When my search is fruitless, my attention snags at the long drapes of golden tapestry hanging from behind the dais where four throne-like chairs have been brought in.

I stare at the huge strips of fabric, remembering... remembering...

My fist closes at my side, clutching a clump of those slippery dandelion memories.

This time when my hand goes behind me, my fingers feel along my spine.

Something's wrong.

Something's missing.

My fingers touch, pain sprouts, and I'm suddenly flooded with the vision of a sword as it arced down, my spine arcing with it.

A tiny breath flows. "My ribbons..."

"What?" Polly questions.

I slap a palm over my mouth as a confused cry wrests out of me, and I whirl around, dizziness coming over me like an undulating wave.

"What's wrong with you?" Polly asks, her nose wrinkling as she sees me curl over into myself, body trembling as I remember.

I remember.

The vicious cleave of a sword. Petals forced in my mouth. A hacked strip floating to the floor.

My ribbons…

Agony fills my heart that far surpasses what I feel physically. The drug must be numbing some of the pain, because all I feel is a steady throb that follows the curve of my empty back. It's like having missing limbs, trying to wriggle fingers you no longer have. My muscles bunch and strain, trying to move what's no longer there.

Gone.

Gone gone gone gone...

My breaths are coming in quick now—too quick. I'm gulping in heaves of air that don't reach my lungs, suffocating in my own inhales. Awful heat drenches me, holding me under as my stomach cramps, my sex throbbing.

Oh goddess…I'm so high.

My mind scrambles, trying to remember my timeline and how long I must've been gone since I gold-touched things in the ballroom. But I can't grasp it. Not with the way my mind floats. Not when I keep fixating on the way my dress feels against my skin, like a sun-warmed petal dragged across my legs.

"Just relax. The king will be coming up here to do his demonstration soon," Polly snaps at me, drawing my attention. "Why he wants *you* up here, I'll never know."

"I need to go. I need to go." The panicked words are a rasp, but Polly narrows her blue eyes.

"You can't go yet. He specifically wants you up here." She reaches into her cleavage and pulls out a tiny pouch. Dipping her fingers inside, she plucks two petals from it, and proceeds to plop one of them into her mouth. Then she holds the other out for me to take. "Here. It'll make you feel good."

Feel good... My body purrs with decadent promise, but I shake my head, trying to shoo away the haze that threatens to settle around me. "No."

Polly's lips purse. "Listen, you gilt cunt, the king wants you to stay put and be calm. I'm not going to lose out on my reward because you're having a freak out. So you *will* eat this, and you'll be grateful for it!" she hisses.

An angry flutter rustles in my gut, though my mind roils. "*No.*"

Her eyes harden as sharp as glass. "Fine, then I'll make you."

She moves to shove it toward my mouth, but my

gloved hand shoots out, albeit clumsily, and I manage to grab the petal and smash it between our fingers. Her eyes go wild with manic anger as I ruin it, letting the crushed pieces fall to the ground.

"You bitch!" The blaring music drowns out Polly's furious yell, but I hear nothing else except the hate pouring off her tone.

My vision fills with prisms of light as it spins. The dew coursing through me is *strong*, muddling me, making me forget, filling me with a wave of heat again that makes me groan. I just need to lie down. I need to rest. *I need...*

Curses are spewing from Polly's painted lips while she kneels on the floor, trying to collect the little bits of ruined petal. But I barely hear her. My entire body is throbbing, needy, at war with my consciousness trying to fight past it. Goddess, I'm so *hot.*

Why am I so hot? Why am I so dizzy, why is Polly yelling, why is my back hurting, why...

Why, why, why.

Polly's trying to gather crushed pieces of dew, I'm trying to gather *myself*, and then, the door suddenly swings open.

And in walks Midas.

CHAPTER 45

AUREN

Midas's *sudden presence puts a* pin in my panicked confusion.

He's dressed impeccably from head to toe, the stiff fabric ensuring not a single wrinkle exists, buttons shaped like golden bells going from pelvis to throat. He's wearing his favorite six-spired crown upon his honeyed hair, the ends pointed like the tip of a claw.

Behind him, lingering in the doorway, stands Rissa, her blue eyes rapidly taking in the scene before landing on me.

Rissa...

There was something I needed to tell Rissa.

My thoughts contort and bend. I try to remember. I try and *try*...

Midas glares down at Polly, who's frozen on the floor, and his jaw tightens. "*What* are you doing?"

Polly goes pale, her gauzy dress bunched up around her thighs as she freezes with bits of crushed petal in her hand. "My king..."

"I gave you *one* job," he growls. "You were to bring her up here and watch her. The dew was to be given to her *after* the demonstration. Not before."

"I...I'm sorry, my king. The favored was growing anxious, so I thought—"

"You are not employed to *think*," he interrupts. "I'll deal with your punishment later. Gather yourself and leave now."

Polly's blue eyes shine with tears, but mine widen.

Leave now.

My gaze flies over to Rissa. *Leave.* We had a plan to leave.

Thoughts and memories tumble like a weed blown in an errant wind. Bits and pieces break off, letting me gather up the scraggly branches. Every sharp-husked branch I grab onto stabs against my aching consciousness.

I'm at the ball, the dew that's in Polly's hand is coursing through *me*, and I was going to leave with Rissa. That's why she's looking at me like that.

The cloud of confusion tries to settle over me, but I wave it away, focusing, trying to gather broken branches and blowing dandelion seeds.

I was supposed to leave with Rissa. We had a deal. She wanted to get away on the night of the ball. But something is *really* wrong, I know that much. She needs to escape without me. Now might be her only chance.

Polly clutches Midas's pant leg as she starts to beg and cry and apologize. It's the distraction I need.

Leave, I mouth to Rissa. *Go.*

Her eyebrows jump up in surprise, and for the first time, something hesitant crawls over her beautiful face. As if she's unsure. As if she doesn't want to leave me behind.

It makes my heart squeeze in my chest, but I know I'm in no state to escape with her. Rissa is a survivor, though. If anyone can make it out of here, it's her.

Midas knocks Polly away with a jab of his foot, which just makes her cry even harder. He shoots a look over his shoulder at Rissa. "Take her and get out of here. I don't want to see her again. And make sure she doesn't have any more dew."

Polly wails, nearly loud enough to be heard over the music, but another memory sticks to my outstretched grasp. *Take her and get out of here,* Midas said, and I nod at Rissa in agreement. *Take her, and get yourselves out.*

Rissa hurries to pull an inconsolable Polly to her feet, while Midas walks over to the small table along the wall and pours himself a drink, expression rife with irritation.

I slump against the wall, feeling like there are thousands of torn bits of paper all jumbled up in my head, words slowly falling down into place.

Rissa maneuvers Polly, making it seem like they stumble, causing them to draw nearer. "Come with me," she murmurs, and even though it seems like she's talking to Polly, I know she's saying it to me.

Tears fill my eyes. We were reluctant allies at best, and yet here she is, trying to get me to go with her, and I have a feeling it's not just about the gold.

I shake my head, giving her a sad smile. "Go."

I don't dare say more than that, and neither does she, not even with the sound of Polly's choked sobs drowning us out or Midas's inattention.

Rissa gives me one more reluctant look before she turns away, steadying Polly at her side as they go. I let out a shaky breath, praying to the goddesses that she can make it out.

Please let her make it out.

I wish I could remember what I was supposed to tell her, but I lose my chance anyway when the door closes behind her. With a loosened breath, I rub at my temples, yet the music of the ballroom is so loud that it's almost thick enough to taste the ballad on my tongue, to swallow the melody whole.

But even that doesn't distract from this sense of dread wriggling in my gut. What else have I forgotten? What else has happened? There are gaping black holes in my mind that I desperately need filled in.

A bead of sweat drips down my neck. The salt trail

slips down my back until it's soaked up somewhere along the way, landing with a sting from a wound that shouldn't be there.

My heart pounds in my chest.

Wrong. Something's wrong.

A sense of deja vu crashes over me, because *I've said that before.*

More of my coherency starts to filter in drip by drip, like water drops from a cave's roof, each one forming the stalactite of my memories. I rub at my temple again, chewing on another upbeat tempo that blares in my ears, only to realize that Midas is speaking to me.

"What?"

He gives me a careful look. I hadn't even realized he'd come over to stand in front of me.

"It's time for my announcement, and then I'll need to make a demonstration. So I need you to pay attention." He's talking to me slowly, enunciating every word. "I need you to take off your glove and gold-touch the railing when I point to you. The sun is setting, so we don't have much time. Alright?"

I stare at him.

I was leaving with Rissa. I'm at the ball. Someone gave me dew. My back hurts.

When I don't say anything, Midas sighs. "When are you gold-touching the railing, Precious?" he presses.

"When you point."

He gives me a tight smile. "That's right. Don't forget, okay?"

Forget... How much did I forget?

"Okay."

After giving me another long look, Midas then makes his way over to the middle of the mezzanine's curved balcony, a hand raised in a signal. Below, the musicians immediately cease playing, and the noise of the crowd dies down.

Blessed quiet.

"Welcome to our celebratory ball!" he announces, charm thick in his tone. His voice drawls, filtering in and out as my mind continues to drip. To collect. Dandelions and tumbleweeds and paper and stalactites...

Still keeping to the shadowed recesses, my eyes skim the crowd, stomach churning with every sweep as I search for answers, search for something, search for *someone...*

"The prosperity of Sixth Kingdom has bolstered Fifth, and it is my duty to ensure Orea's northern kingdoms are strong and united." Midas's voice booms out, echoes, spins around. He presses a hand against his chest in a humbled gesture. "Even still, I have failed. By coming here to strengthen Fifth, Sixth Kingdom has suffered by my absence under the influence of the cold queen. Although the riots were a tragic, terrible thing, it was also good in a way."

My eyes lift to the windows, to the dying light.

Something twinges in my back.

"It has brought about change," Midas goes on. "I have heard the voices crying up from the people. That their labors deserve more from their monarchs, and I agree." He lets that sink in, a lofty pride carried in the upturn of his chin. "The recent death of Queen Malina shows me that as a king, I must do more. That the people deserve a true queen who is beloved by them. That the kingdoms can be strengthened by unity."

Murmuring spreads through the crowd.

Murmuring goes on inside *me*.

And there—a dark, quiet voice.

Remember.

Midas's palms rest steadily on the balcony. "There is one such beloved queen," he says, gaze passing over the hundreds of people below. "In fact, she is here tonight."

He motions toward the opposite end of the room, and everyone turns to look where Queen Kaila stands up from the throne, hand cupped as she gives a proud wave. She looks striking in a deep blue dress, yet with a glimmering gold crown on her head woven into the loops of her black hair. I squint my eyes, flicking my attention from the familiar crown to the fur shawl around her shoulders, to the shell necklace around her neck. All gilded.

The things Midas touched against my arm.

"I am pleased to announce that Queen Kaila of Third Kingdom and I have decided to wed!"

My brows pull together. Midas is remarrying, but...I knew that. I knew, and I didn't care, because...because...

The crowd gasps and claps, the sound rustling in my head like running through dry leaves, every step another whoosh of air, another crinkle and snap beneath bare feet.

And those feet take me right to Slade.

My heart stops when my gaze lands on his dark presence standing in the middle of the colorful ballroom, like a pitch-black pupil in the middle of a multi-colored iris. He doesn't see me, but I see him, and it's enough.

It's enough.

The wavering, drifting boat of my mind yanks to a stop, suddenly grounded by his anchor. My grip closes around dandelion seeds. The tumbleweed stops its roll. Ripped paper fuses back in place. A last drip of water settles at the tip of a stalactite.

A head of feathers lifts up in my chest, a beast of anger blinking both eyes open. And that's when she turns, spreads her wings, showing me a tail full of feathers that stream down like golden ribbons.

Ribbons.

My breath catches. My back throbs.

I bring my trembling hands to come up and ghost over my back. My aching, *empty* back.

Remember.

I do.

Everything suddenly comes rushing in. It's a barrage

of rain that floods my mind and roars in my ears. Or maybe that's the anger that just awoke, shaking off the groggy drug with a grind of a fang-filled beak.

Midas's voice rises, competing with my own internal noise, and the crowd is eating up his announcement like sheep eating grain right from his hand. They don't see that he's no shepherd. They don't see the predatory teeth. "I will bring the prosperity of my power, not only to Sixth and Fifth Kingdoms, but to Third as well. With the union of Fifth Kingdom and now my betrothal to Queen Kaila, we will take care of our people, and as the Golden King, I will bring Orea into a Golden Age!"

A clamor of applause breaks out, and Midas drops his hand at his side, pointing his finger covertly. His signal. The one for me to put on a demonstration to perfectly end his pretty little golden speech.

But I don't move.

At the lapse of a second, his eyes cut over to me. "Gold-touch the railing," he orders, speaking from the side of his mouth, but I still don't do it.

Maybe it's my fae heritage that allowed me to burn off the dew, or maybe it's something else, but either way, I've cut through the last of the haze with a billowing breath.

Midas's face darkens for a split second before he flicks a look back down at the crowd. He says something to finish the speech, making up for his lack of a flashy presentation of turning the mezzanine gold. They laugh at whatever he said, not noticing anything is amiss, but then, he's always been good at charming a crowd. At charming *me*.

He used a silver tongue against a golden heart, and the glint of his lies dimmed every truth I knew.

Midas steps away from the railing, away from the crowd's eyes. It's only in private that he ever shows his true color, and it sure as hell isn't gold.

The music starts up again, going along with the mingling voices and clinking glasses. There are hundreds of people down there. *Slade* is down there. But up here, in the shadows of the mezzanine, it's just Midas and me.

Creases of anger line his forehead as he bears down on me. "What the hell was that, Auren? I explained what I needed you to do. It was fucking *simple*. You've completely ruined my golden speech!" he exclaims, brown eyes gone as dark as flooded dirt.

Hate is a visceral thing, a bloom unearthed in the background. I see it in his eyes, and maybe he sees it in mine too.

"You drugged me." The accusation falls from a flat tone, as dry as prostrated plains. Even now, I can taste the viscid petal speckled with crimson dewdrops. It bled saccharine sweetness on my tongue. Saturated my mind. Syruped my limbs. Made me forget.

Even though it's water that fills my eyes, it feels like fire.

"You drugged me," I say again, stomach churning with an angry eddy. I want him to get swept up in it, to be pulled under. "You hurt Digby." My second accusation tosses and seethes, like the sea beneath a storm, and I sail right into it with a brutalized back. "You *cut off my ribbons*!"

My voice cracks and crashes, the words grinding like the crush of gravel under a heel. My limbs tremble with rage.

Midas stares at me, and I can see his surprise that I'm so coherent, but my coherency is the least of his problems.

After a second, he crosses his arms and spreads his legs, plants his feet. "Yes, I did," he admits with a terse tone. "You disobeyed me. Every punishment was deserved."

Deserved.

Something prods in my chest, pounds against my ribs. The hammer of a blacksmith against an anvil, red-hot metal ready to be forged.

Midas lifts a shoulder. "Stop fighting me, Auren. This is your life. It's time for you to settle back into it. You will take dew daily, and you will do your duty to your king."

"It terrifies you, doesn't it?" I ask. "Knowing that everything you are, hinges on me."

Something dark flickers across his face.

"You speak about *my* punishment, but how about we consider what *you* deserve?"

I take a step closer to him, leaving just a foot of distance between us. To show him that I'm not afraid. To show him that even though he split me down the middle and stole pieces from my soul, he'll never win.

My golden eyes burn as I look him dead in the eye. "I'm going to leave you, Midas," I declare ruthlessly, enjoying it when his entire body stiffens. "I'm going to go where you can never find me again. You'll search the ends of Orea for me. You'll hear rumors, whispers of where I am, but every single time, I'll slip through your fingers."

At his sides, his hands tighten into fists, as if he's already trying to close up the cracks.

"I'll drag you along to every decrepit corner of the world, but you won't ever find me. You'll go months, years, decades searching in wild desperation."

Chills scatter over my arms, like the goddesses are listening, a shiver of an omen kissed upon my skin.

"Your golden trinkets will dwindle. Your fame will turn to ridicule as your people turn against you. Your betrothed will abandon you, and the laws of this world will force the crown off your head, and *still*, you won't find me. No matter how tirelessly you look. No matter how furious your search. And it will make you go mad."

He can't even blink, he stares so wildly at me, and I revel in it.

"You thought gold and power was your ascension, but it'll be your downfall. You thought you could hoard me forever, but I'll disappear right out from under your nose." That pounding against my ribs hammers louder, shoots sparks off my soul. "You'll be a laughingstock. Hated. *Destitute*."

Midas flinches at that word. Physically jerks back, body rocking with the shock of my speech, and my beast and I preen beneath the delivered threat, celebrate the discovery of his worst fear.

"You will have no one and nothing to comfort you. You'll die alone and poor, ruined by your own greed, and it will be exactly what you *deserve*."

I land the last blow, watch him ring with it. Feel the reverberations as they tremble the air. As *he* trembles with it.

His fists unclench and clench again. His head shakes, like he's trying to argue away my words or rattle them out of his skull.

"*No*," he denies, though it comes out like an order. "You think you'll get away from me? You think your monster commander will help you?"

"The only monster in this castle is *you*."

Midas laughs, a cruel sound to poison the air. "I already have him, you know," he tells me smugly, waiting to see how I take the news. "So if you think Commander Rip is going to come up here and rescue you, you're going to be sorely disappointed."

"I don't need anyone to rescue me."

My foot lifts as I take another step forward, and I enjoy it immensely when I see Midas take a step *back*. Satisfaction purrs from my gut.

"I'll kill him," Midas threatens. "I'll kill that spiked bastard, and your guard too."

Fury catches from the sparks, makes my eyes narrow in a squint. He expects me to falter beneath the threat, but instead, I burn hotter. "Touch them, and I'll touch *you*."

The threat pulls the blood from his face, his tanned skin going pale.

But right then, my skin tingles. A shiver travels down my tormented spine. Dusk hits, setting the sun and stealing my power with it.

Midas must notice, either because I let something show on my face, or his internal clock has become nearly as good as mine, because a cruel smile tips up his lips. "Colorful speech, Auren. Too bad you don't have what it takes to back up those fiery words," he mocks, making my eyes flash. "Be careful with that tongue of yours, hmm? We're safe up here for the time being with the music and crowd, but Queen Kaila has a way of stealing secrets." He glances over me appraisingly. "Though I have to admit, I'm surprised by this outspoken side of you. You've certainly come a long way since being the painted girl from Derfort Harbor."

I blink. Something sharp scrapes my insides, blade angled just right. "What did you say?"

He tilts his head, like a cat considering whether it wants to pounce on a mouse. "Didn't I ever tell you I lived in Third Kingdom for a time?" The question is a taunt pulled tight. A rope at my ankles to yank my feet out from under me.

It succeeds.

Something like gratification pulls at the skin around his eyes. "You never came to see me, pet."

Cold unease scampers up my spine. "What are you talking about, Midas?"

He walks over to the pitcher of wine again, pours himself another glass, indulging in his moment. "You know, it's easier than people think to get ahead in this world. You just need the drive to do it." He takes a long gulp before turning around to face me again, a drip of wine staining his lip. "Even a bastard drifter without two coins to rub together can make a name for himself. A name you've heard of, actually."

Now it's my face that has all the blood draining from it, the gold paling at my cheeks.

"I worked my way up. Was a runner for a thief, but he didn't realize the potential that was brewing in that port city. It only took two years before his territory became mine. Thieving, pirating, flesh trading. I did it all, controlled dozens of workers. It was a perfected operation," he brags, pure pride shining through his voice. "People feared the name I made up. Wouldn't even think of stepping foot on my side of the city without permission, because my name showed that I owned it."

My heart drops, shatters, a million shards of ice left to temper the heat of my anger.

Something unfamiliar lifts behind his kingly mask, something insipid and seedy. I suddenly have the scent of iron and fish stuck in my nose, making my stomach roil as he fixes a glare on me. "You were the painted girl who cut into my profits, and then had the nerve to *run*."

Realization batters my chest and corrupts the air enough to make me choke on it. "Barden East," I whisper in shocked horror. "You were Barden East."

His smile is an accumulation of every sharpened edge piled in my chest. "And you're ten years too late."

CHAPTER 46

AUREN

No.

His declaration quakes beneath my feet. It makes bells of alarm ring in my ears louder than Highbell's ever did.

Midas can't be Barden East. He just *can't*. Because that would mean that I ran right into the arms of the man I tried to escape. I willingly gave myself to someone who *took* others. Who used them, sold them, treated them like a commodity for his own selfish gain.

My head is shaking with denial, even as my gut tells me it's true. "You can't have been."

"I was."

Something tears in my throat, a grievous noise spilling from a gaping mouth—a gaping *soul*.

"*How?*"

Midas swirls his wine around, taps the front of his collar six times. "It wasn't too difficult to earn my place as the crime lord in Derfort. There were small-time criminals there who were in sore need of a true leader— which I became. I saw an opportunity, and I took it," he adds with a shrug. "So many shipments came in and out of that port, and once I took over the territory, I had access to resources from nearly every kingdom. I accumulated a lot of wealth and notoriety, had people at my beck and call."

I'm hearing him, but his words are spoken into a hollow cave of my own emptying emotions. I'm numb, reeling, in too much shock to even react.

"But after years of that, I grew bored. Plus, I was sick and tired of always smelling fish," he admits, the slight lift of his lip belying his distaste. "I wanted more— more power, more wealth, more opportunity, and a more palatable territory."

All those years, all this time... I had confided in him. Told him about Derfort, about what I was made to do. He pretended not to know. Pretended to *care*, and yet all along, he was my owner's competitor. The catalyst to the night I finally fled.

My steps are rooted to the floor. There's no turning away from the truth that he spews like a gloat.

"In a way, you leaving was the offense I needed. I decided to follow you so I could drag you right back to Derfort, rub it in Zakir's face, and set an example to others who'd run."

I stare at him, but I don't even know this man standing in front of me. It's like he's peeled away a layer and exposed the infection within, something that has festered in its own corruption that I somehow overlooked.

"You disappeared for a while, so it took some effort to catch your trail. But eventually, I heard curious talk amongst other vagabonds along the road. Talk of a raid finding a king's fortune in a tiny village called Carnith... and of a girl who shone against the desert sands like a nugget of gold."

My breath gets knotted up like a rope stuck in my throat. "You followed me to Carnith?"

"Of course I did. The gods smiled down on me, too, because that's when your power manifested. That's when it was clear that you weren't just a painted girl perfect for the business of flesh trading. You were *so much more*."

Tears fill my eyes as his verbal jabs stab me through, hollow me out. All a lie. Right from the very beginning.

He played the part of a crime lord, then a rescuer, then a *king*. I shared my body with him, when he used the bodies of others for profit. Just thinking of all the times he touched me and I touched him makes my skin crawl.

"I'm a planner, Auren," Midas says as he watches me drown in the shadows, my fingers snagging at my hair. "You were exactly what I needed to get more. To get ahead. It was fated by the great Divine."

He sets his wine glass down, and I whirl around, my world whirling with me.

"I finally caught up to you when you were in that backwoods village after you'd fled Carnith," he tells me offhandedly. "I made the men I'd brought split up, so some of them could pose as raiders. Half of us attacked, the other protected the villagers. I had them all kill each other after that, instigated in-fighting over the spoils," he adds with a shrug. "Couldn't have any of them speaking of your magic or connecting me to Derfort as Barden East. Not when I intended to shed that name. Not when I realized that Princess Malina was in possession of a throne and yet lacked magic to keep it. Sixth Kingdom was in debt and in need of a king, so I gave it one. It was meant to be. I've always been partial to the number six," he adds with twisted arrogance.

My head swims like I might pass out, but I manage to fall into the chair instead and pull in a choked breath. "You never rescued me." I say it aloud, but it's really just affirmation for myself, a crack that rents down the foundation of my life, splitting my past into something unrecognizable.

Midas looks pleased with himself, and maybe that's what bothers me the most. The smug look on his face. As if he's been waiting ten years to shove it in mine.

That moment of him rescuing me was what made me trust him. It created the base for my shaken footsteps. I viewed him as some sort of savior. But he orchestrated even that. He manipulated me right from the start, before we even spoke face-to-face.

He made me trust him, *love* him. He made me think he was my hero, when all along, he was my villain.

He walks nearer, standing over me like he's relishing in this moment, like he wants to soak it up and wring me back out. "I owned half a shipping port and an incredibly lucrative business. But when I realized you had magic to go with that gold skin, I knew right then that I could own a whole damn kingdom." Midas's eyes gleam with the greed that consumes him. "And now...I don't just own half of a city, I own half of *Orea*."

An ugly, twisting grip tightens around my stomach. "Not yet."

His eyes flash. "You won't be saying that after tonight."

I have no idea what he means by that, and I don't get a chance to ask. Midas leans over, head poised in front of mine as he looks me over with detached assessment. "You know, we could've kept going on as we were, you could've had your semblance of freedom, but you ruined it."

His tone is definitive, full of the authority he's stolen. Full of something cruel, too.

"You won't just be locked in a cage anymore, Auren, I'll lock you up in your own *mind*. I'll keep you on dew and drain your magic forever until the day you die, and even then, I'll pluck every gilded hair from your head and scrape the gold from your skin, because you are mine to use as I will." His exhale condenses against my face, the scent of wine heavy on his breath, and I wonder how I ever thought this evil man loved me.

As if everything he's saying and doing isn't awful enough, Midas then straightens up and slips his hand into his pocket. When he pulls it out again, a thick strip of gold is bunched in his palm.

My entire body freezes in place. A gush of tears well up in my eyes as I take in the sight of my mangled ribbon, at the little beads of golden blood stuck to one end like the cooled drips of candle wax from a jagged wick.

A sob takes the place of my breath while I stare at its length, stare at the piece of *me* now ruined in Midas's grasp. My eyes sting with a burn that seeps straight into my spine, and twinges of pain erupt down the length of my back as if each chopped root there can feel the pain of our separation all over again.

I watch numbly as he wraps it around my wrists like I'm prey caught in his snare, and I can't struggle, because it's...*me*. It's not some meaningless strand he roped me with. It's the ultimate mind game and perversion of control.

He ties it off with a thick knot, the satin-like strand digging into my skin painfully like a penance for losing them in the first place. For not being strong enough to stay whole beneath the might of this man who has hacked away at me, drained me, stole every piece of me.

How much more of me is he going to take?

"Everything, Auren. I'm going to take *everything*."

My wet eyes look up at him, because I hadn't even realized I'd spoken aloud.

Midas straightens up, fixes the crown atop his head so it's perfectly aligned as he gives an impassive inspection over the tears that land on the binds around my wrists.

"Stay here, or I'll drag your lover up from the dungeon and kill him in front of you," he purrs, the threat kept soft in the lurk of his tone. "Now, if you'll excuse me, I have a toast to make. Enjoy the show, Precious."

My gaze stays fixed on the ribbon after Midas leaves the mezzanine. There's a ballad playing below, though I don't hear it. I just stare and stare at the gold that Midas has used to ensnare me. As the truth of who he really is—then *and* now—builds in my head like the squall of a tempestuous force.

When I fled Derfort Harbor and sailed across the

Weywick Sea in the ship with cerulean sails, there was a single storm on the journey.

Just one.

It didn't happen at night. There was no darkness that swallowed the sea and made it look like we were sailing on starlight and storm clouds.

No, this was during the bold noon of day, when the sun shone milky and high, split down the middle with bulbous clouds that came to purge like a blister.

I should've gone to the lower levels when it hit, but I didn't. I'm not sure why. Maybe I couldn't bear the thought of being sequestered below deck, stuck in a stagnant room no bigger than a closet with a hammock for a bed and a bucket for an upturned stomach.

But really, I think the truth is that I wanted to feel the air as it raged.

So I was up there on deck beneath a speckled sky that was neither dark nor light, but somehow both at the same time. With my feet planted beneath crouching knees, I kept my arms wrapped around the rough rail for dear life as my hair whipped at my face.

The ship rocked back and forth like a cradle ready to tip, and waves came up to slap against the deck in the angry hit of a sea god. I could see the shouts being tossed back and forth between the small crew, but their voices were swallowed up. The thrashing wind tore the sounds from where they belonged and seemed to throw them clear across the water.

But even as fear gripped me that I'd be tossed overboard or that the sea would break the ship in half and swallow it whole, I was in awe of the storm that seethed. In awe of the sudden change that took over the clear day and smooth waters and turned it into a violent surge.

Whatever it was that drew me up there that day, it meant that I was there to watch the lightning strike the water. I was there to see what happens when a force of nature unleashes.

The lightning was a jagged arrow shot from the bow of the cloud. It struck the choppy, maelstrom of waves, and a fissure of electric cracks erupted over the surface of the water like it had shattered the sea.

And that's what this is like.

Like I'm hanging on for dear life as bulbous clouds form inside of me, fed by the fumes of Midas's revelations. A heavy barrage has built within the frenzy of my kinetic thoughts, a thunderbolt ready to splinter the tumultuous waves within. Ready to land with a fatal strike.

I've been drowned out by the force of the storm.

My gaze plods over the ribbon one last time before I get to my feet, hands clasped together as if in prayer. I walk over to the balcony of the mezzanine and look below, seeing Midas at the dais with Queen Kaila and Prince Niven, Oreans dotting the floor like confetti.

But there, cutting through the throng like the drive of an iron stake, is Slade.

The moment my eyes latch onto him, he stops in his tracks and looks up, gaze meeting mine, as if he could feel me looking at him.

A sob lodges in my throat. Even though he's *right there*, he feels so very far away.

Even from the distance between us, it's as if he can see me right up close, because something fierce flashes in his face. Something furious on my behalf.

With darkness looming over his brow, he starts stalking forward again, eyes not leaving my face.

He's coming for me.

But his stride is suddenly interrupted when Midas's voice cuts through the din. "Time for the royal toast! King Ravinger, if you would join us?"

Slade stops in his tracks as the people turn to look at him, though they give him a wide berth. For a moment, he hesitates, and the crowd looks from him to Midas and back again.

"King Ravinger?" Midas presses.

Even from up here, I can see Slade grind his jaw. His eyes flash up to me again for a split second, and I give a tiny nod to urge him to go. Only then does he reluctantly turn around and head back.

He comes to a stop with the other three monarchs on the raised dais. Midas stands in the middle with Queen Kaila on his left, Niven on his right, and Slade takes up his spot right beside the prince. A saddle hurries over to serve them each a gold goblet. Movement ripples through the rest of the room as the crowd hurries to grab drinks of their own.

I back up, keeping to the shadowed corner of the mezzanine.

Armed with their various cups, Midas announces, "Raise your glasses!" From up here, I can see everyone lift their arms up, drinks held aloft. "We toast tonight to the unity of our kingdoms!" he calls out with a proud smile. "To Orea!"

"To Orea!" everyone else chants on cue, and then glasses are lifted to lips and wine gulped back before cheers and applause roam through the room.

If it weren't for the fact that my attention has stayed locked on Slade the whole time, I might have missed what happens next. Because of my homed gaze, I see the way Slade's brow furrows right before he turns his head to look at Prince Niven. I follow his gaze, frown gathering between my own brows before I really even register that something is wrong.

One moment, everyone is drinking and cheering, but then, the goblet slips from Niven's hand and crashes to the ground.

The people nearest him startle, but it becomes apparent very quickly that there's more wrong than just a dropped cup.

Prince Niven locks his hands around his throat, eyes gone wide in fear, just as someone in the crowd screams.

The prince stumbles, and purple-cloaked Ranhold guards come rushing forward. With pure panic, his fingers claw down his neck—a neck that's now lined with black veins spreading up toward his cheeks.

"*Oh no...*" My whisper is swallowed up by the eruption of shouts from below, as dark froth starts to bubble out from the young prince's lips.

"Poison! The prince has been poisoned!" someone screeches.

I watch in horror as the prince falls to his knees too quick for the guards to catch him.

"Mender! Where's the royal mender?" Midas booms out.

A gray-haired man in purple robes surges forward and falls to his knees in front of the prince, a red band tied around his arm. From up here, I have the perfect vantage point to see the mender's hands skate shakily over Niven's chest, head tilted against his mouth.

Midas pushes past his own guards to kneel beside the mender too. Queen Kaila hangs back, her brother standing in front of her like a shield, while more men stand behind her.

A frenzy of quieted confusion vibrates in the room, the crowd on edge between wanting to back away and wanting to get a closer look. But I see it the moment that Prince Niven's body goes unnaturally still.

Dismay knots in my shoulders and twists in my gut

as the mender's face goes grim, his head shaking up at Midas from behind the wall of Ranhold guards.

When Midas stands up again, making the huddling guards part, the crowd gasps at the sight of Niven where he lays, and I don't blame them. There's gray skin now where the youth of vibrancy just was, his chest puffed up and unmoving, a foamed mouth like whipped mud. But worst of all are the veins, black as night, bleeding up from the skin of his neck.

My hands shake where they grip the railing, dread filling the air like thick fog, and I know what the mender is going to say before he even gets to his feet.

"The prince is dead!"

CHAPTER 47

AUREN

T*he mender's announcement makes the* entire crowd gasp at the same moment. Ranhold guards hurry to pick up their prince carefully, his prone body gone stiff, his color unnatural, pain still laced through his unblinking eyes.

My stomach heaves, bile rising in my throat.

"Poison!" another person shouts as Niven's body is carried away.

"No, look at him!" a man in a bright purple dress suit calls out, shaky finger pointing. "Look at his veins! This is the work of King Rot!"

Everyone seems to jerk their gazes toward his dark countenance at the same time. Eyes bouncing from the lines on Niven's neck to the lines that always reside on Slade's.

My chest goes tight, breath stolen between the uproar that punches out through the people as their shock quickly turns to blame.

I'm not sure when his Wrath arrived, but aside from an absent Fake Rip, they're all circling Slade, their formation tightening around him. Slade's face is grim, hands hanging down at his sides, the mood in the room gone from celebratory to accusatory in the blink of an eye.

"People, people!" Midas calls out, palms held up to gesture that they listen. "That is a very serious allegation!"

"King Rot killed our prince!" a woman cries in hysterics, making everyone erupt into a frenzy again.

My heart drops right down through my toes as I watch everything unfold, as I remember what he said.

I own half of Orea.

Not yet.

You won't be saying that after tonight.

My mind riots, fury rising up, because this is *him*. This scheme, this *murder*, is Midas's doing. He's orchestrated yet another monarch's death and pinned the blame on someone else.

Midas turns to Slade, as if he's both troubled and repelled at the very thought. "King Ravinger, we will have to detain you for these accusations."

"You can fucking try," Osrik snarls beside him, his voice booming from beneath his helmet.

The entire room bristles with outrage. And I can see it—the secret smirk in Midas's eye.

No.

Like this is a ball of unravelling yarn, I know how the string will roll out. There's no way Slade will go willingly. Even from here, I can feel something building in him, feel that nauseating, deathly power of his coiling in the air.

My feet are moving before I even blink. I'm tugging and pulling at the ribbon, forcing it down, until I can slip one of my hands out from its hold, leaving only my left wrist still bound with its loops.

Midas isn't just here to take over Fifth and marry into Third. It's not enough for him. It's *never* enough. And Slade is the most powerful opponent he's ever faced.

So Midas figured out a way to take him out too.

Didn't Slade tell me himself that he doesn't make a move against Midas because of the people? For the very reason of what I see playing out in the ballroom right now?

They'll hate him, rise up against him. The other monarchs will attack his kingdom. He'll become the scapegoat for everyone to hate.

Slade will have no choice but to retaliate tonight, just to ensure Midas doesn't throw him in a dungeon, leaving him to rot like his name. Since Slade won't let that happen, that means he'll use his power to get out of here and seal his kingdom's fate.

I can't let that happen.

Something in me, that brewing storm held against a sunlit sea, it starts to *crackle*. That creature nesting in the clouds of my electric anger calls out, her screech like thunder.

Like a gust of air catapults me, I rush toward the mezzanine door. I turn the handle and let myself out as the beat of my heart thrashes like pounding waves against my ribs.

Down the stairs, I pass a foursome of guards, two of which are Scofield and Lowe, the other two I recognize from that cold, dim room. I catch them off guard by my sudden appearance, but I don't stop, even though my anger is hurled at them with a lashing tongue.

"My lady!" Scofield calls.

"I am *not* your lady." My tone has no softness, no familiarity. It's spoken from my mouth, and yet, the voice is harder, flatter, carrying hate and betrayal with every press of teeth.

Scofield's steps falter as I rush past, either from the disdain in my voice or the guilt he bears. In fact, none of the guards move to bar me, and I wonder if it's because of the shame they carry for their part in my torture.

Good.

The ribbon tied around my wrist sears against my skin, burning with the same anger that's brewing in my veins.

I hope they're thinking of what they did to me. I hope Scofield is remembering his fingers mashing the petals into my mouth. Or how they all pinned me against the wall while Midas cut off my ribbons. I hope they never stop hearing my screams from that room, because I certainly won't.

The archway of the ballroom is a gaping mouth that I get swallowed into. It's only taken me seconds to get from the mezzanine to down here, but the atmosphere of the crowd has worsened, brewing its own kind of storm. The people have surged forward as close to the dais as they can get, while servants and saddles are pressed against the walls.

I push myself through the gilded room, and for once, everyone is too focused on something else to pay me any notice at all. The guards get lost in the throng, unable to follow my path as I slip past people. My feet take me straight to the side of the dais, where Ranhold guards are now circling Slade and his Wrath.

Even with the anger of the crowd, everyone has enough sense to stay back, and it isn't because of Osrik's, Lu's, and Judd's imposing figures. No, what holds them back is Slade himself.

The capricious lines of his power are coiling around his neck like aggravated snakes writhing on the ground. They move and shift, disappearing beneath the black scruff on his jaw, leading down to sink beneath his collar.

My heart clamps at the sight of Slade as people shout and curse at him. His magic hisses, hitting me with a wave of queasiness, and the ground beneath his feet seems to pucker and rumble.

But I don't fear him. Not even with his threatening power that branches around his skin. Not even with the vicious glint in his eye, or with the twisted wood crown on his head that makes him look every bit the rotten king.

I know what they see, but it isn't what *I* see, and this isn't his fault. He's simply been set up to take the fall so that Midas can continue to rise.

How much more of me are you going to take?

Everything.

It's not just me that Midas is going to take from. Being the king of Sixth isn't enough, and taking Fifth was just the beginning. He's marrying Third, making Fourth the enemy...and what next? Will he move on to Second and First too? Will he stop then?

But I know the answer to that already.

Midas won't *ever* stop.

He may not have magic, but his strength lies in his scheming manipulations, and it's terrifying to realize just how powerful he's truly become.

Slade locks eyes with me, finding me in the middle of the crowd, and maybe he can see the fear in my face, because whatever power was brewing inside of him stutters to an instant stop. The nauseous effect of his magic cuts off at the stem, the furrowing floor ceasing its rooting rumble.

The soldiers take advantage of the pause and close in on him, and dread spikes down my spine. He's going to push and push until Slade snaps. Midas wants him to break the treaty, dissolve the alliance, back Slade into a corner.

"Take him!" Midas shouts, just as Osrik lets out a vicious bellow, a sword held in each hand.

"Stop!" I shove my way past the rest of the people, plowing straight through the line of gilt guards. They balk at my intrusion and then immediately back away, ensuring they don't touch me, though they don't lower their swords.

Within seconds, I'm standing in front of Slade like a shield, chest heaving. "*Don't touch him.*"

My shout is for the crowd, but my words are for Midas.

We've locked eyes, both of us on opposite ends of the dais. There might be hundreds of spectators, but all I see is him.

"What are you doing, Auren?" Midas nearly hisses. "Get away from him right now and come to me."

I give him a slow shake of my head. "Never."

Never again.

A tic appears in Midas's jaw.

"I won't let you take him too."

He's taken everything else from me, just like he promised. He even took our past. But I won't let Midas take Slade.

So caught up in my stare-off with Midas, I almost forgot about the male at my back. A dark, forbidding voice slips out from between his lips and tangles down my spine. "Auren..."

"Don't use your magic," I beg, glancing at Slade over my shoulder. "It's what he wants, to make you even more hated and feared. Don't give that to him."

"He deserves no less."

"No, but you deserve more," I murmur.

A rigid tension fits between my shoulder blades, but it isn't fear as I take a public stand against Midas. We are inherently protective of our lives, to do whatever we have to do to make it through. It's an inner instinct, and one I've always followed. Biologically, we are meant to preserve, to survive. But surviving isn't my intent at this moment. Right now, I want to *fight*.

"Lower your swords away from my favored!" Midas shouts, making the guards flinch, blades drooping.

"I'm not your favored," I declare, not caring that we have a crowd, not caring that Queen Kaila is staring daggers at me or that her brother is looking at me with something like pity. "King Ravinger didn't kill Prince Niven. *You* did." My voice cracks like a whip, ripping out gasps from the onlookers.

Midas's eye twitches, twin patches of red bursting across furious cheeks. "Clear the room!"

There's a shocked pause, and then various soldiers start to push the crowd back to empty the ballroom. But the people are resistant and angry at being ordered away. They're too caught up in the spectacle, wanting to watch this play out, wanting to know who's really at fault.

"Who killed our prince?" someone demands.

"We deserve to know!"

More shouts lift up like a chorus, their voices growing belligerent as the guards start using more force to shove them out.

Midas begins to stalk forward but jerks to a stop again when the Wrath close in around me. Not in threat, but in protection. Slade has stepped closer too, the heat of his chest burning against my back.

That one simple move makes something ugly appear in Midas's eyes. Realization seems to dawn as he looks between Slade and me, and maybe my previous words finally sink in. *I won't let you take him too.*

And I won't, because—

"He's *mine*." My voice is strong, unwavering. Just a vicious growl of protective fury.

A wicked satisfaction purrs in my chest at the hateful shock on Midas's face.

"It was *him*?" he accuses, tone bitten out between his clenched teeth.

"Like I tried to tell your torturer, it sure wasn't me."

Everyone whips their heads around to see Fake Rip walking forward with a stumbling Digby slung at his side.

My eyes widen, heartbeat faltering. Not just at the sight of my guard up and out of that awful room, but for the first time ever, Fake Rip's helmet is nowhere to be seen.

Though he still wears the rest of his spiked armor, his face is finally visible. My gaze runs over him with greedy curiosity, entranced by the pale skin, the scruff of his jaw, the angles of his face, and I'm instantly struck by the familiarity.

Great Divine, Fake Rip is Slade's damned *brother*.

They look so much alike. If it weren't for the slight differences I can pick out like the darker green eyes, the narrower face, the difference in expression, and the lack of an aura, I'd think that he was Slade.

"Stop right there," Midas orders.

Fake Rip and Digby pause short of the dais, two of the soldiers breaking off to detain them, while more shouts rise from the crowd. The people are still fighting as they're herded out, but the guards push and shove, lined up like a human wall to force them out.

"Auren, come here right now," Midas demands, finger pointed to the ground beside him.

"We're leaving," I declare, my determination fortified by the weight of my tone. I let my gaze skip to

Manu—the queen's brother and advisor. "You'd be wise to do the same." A flicker of doubt flashes over his face as he shares a brief look with his husband.

"*Auren*," Midas says threateningly.

"Oh, let her go, Tyndall," Queen Kaila says airily, coming up to stand beside him. "It's clear that her loyalty lies with Fourth Kingdom. Let her lose her favor. It's what she deserves."

Though Kaila's words are meant to bite, they don't leave their mark on me. *Yes*, I want to say. *Let me go*.

Troubled calculations war on Midas's face as he attempts to scheme his way out of this.

"I'm done, Midas," I say quietly. "It's over."

The last fragile string that tied me to him was the fact that I thought he'd saved me all those years ago. It was his one redeeming quality. But that too has been snipped away as the lie came to light.

He thinks he can throw me in a cage again and keep me drugged, but Slade will never let that happen, and neither will I.

I've put him on the spot now. Forced his hand, as he's forced mine so many times. He's out-magicked with Slade, has to keep up appearances with his new bride-to-be, and hopefully, I've cast enough doubt in front of the people that Fourth Kingdom won't suffer for the death of Prince Niven.

It's all there in my face as I watch Midas. The

determination. The refusal. He didn't overplay his hand, he just didn't realize that there was another player at the table.

A long, tense moment passes, with only the shuffling sound of feet being funneled through the ballroom archway.

"You want to leave? To be the whore of King Rot?" Midas spits.

The low growl from Slade behind me sends a shiver down my neck.

My teeth grit at that word, but I don't let it show on my face. "Better the whore to the man at my back than the favored to *you*."

Midas moves forward, maybe to try and strangle me where I stand, but Slade steps in front of me so fast he's just a blur of movement. "You take one more step, and I'll rot you where you stand." Tension roils off Slade's shoulders, billowing black with the blight of his magic, and I know he means every word.

You say the word, and it's done. I'd end him in a breath, in a room full of people who'd run screaming, with monarchs who'd band together against me. If you wanted me to do it, I would.

Slade's words ring in my ears as loud as the croon of my creature.

Gently, I reach up and press a hand against his back, the tense muscles bunching beneath my touch. Slade turns to face me, eyes drawn in like shutters. "Don't," I whisper. "I won't let him make you into the villain."

A gaze as sharp as thorns hooks into me, holds me hostage. "I told you, I'll be the villain for you."

Resolve bolsters my spine. "Yes. But so will I."

CHAPTER 48

AUREN

Maybe Midas is too bold, but he takes another step so he's only a few feet away, gaze moving quickly from the last stragglers of the crowd and then back to me.

"You want to leave, Auren?" he asks, his quiet tone belying something sinister that simmers beneath the surface.

"*Yes.*"

His jaw grinds, mine locks.

Seconds, minutes, hours seem to pass as we stare each other down. The king and the pet, the crime lord and the painted girl, the liar and the fool.

He lifts his chin and jerks it up. "Then go."

It takes a moment for me to comprehend what he said.

He walks over with hate in his eye, looking us up and down. "Let Ravinger's pollution leave this kingdom," he announces with open disdain.

Slade wastes no time turning to me and the others. "Let's go."

I'm stunned for a moment, so surprised that all I can do is stand there and stare at Midas.

He agreed. He actually *agreed*.

I'm going to be able to walk right out the front door, and I won't have to hide or flee. I stopped Slade from unleashing his power and potentially causing the rest of Orea to wage war against him.

But that split second of self-satisfied victory is all I get. Because in the next blink, Midas's guards have shoved at the Wrath, and an eruption of retaliation breaks out between them. Unfortunately, I realize a second too late that it's just a distraction.

Midas grabs me, my back hitting his chest, making a burst of pain erupt down my spine. Before the black dots can leave my vision, I have a blade pressed against my throat.

"Use your magic, and I'll slice her open!"

My hearing wanes as I breathe through the agony of my back, but when I blink enough to clear my eyes, I find Slade two feet away, looking absolutely fucking *murderous*.

"Let her go. *Now*."

His voice is a rupture of violent threat so cold that I actually shiver.

"Hold back your rot and your soldiers, Ravinger," Midas threatens, and I feel the edge of sharpness digging into my skin. I hiss in pain as the blade sinks in, and feel something wet dribble down.

Slade's green eyes bleed black. "You are a fucking dead man."

I can practically feel the satisfaction hum in Midas's chest. Slade showed his hand—showed that he's not willing to chance me getting hurt.

I scrabble against Midas's arm, trying to pull it away from my neck, but his hold is too firm, and one knock against my back makes me arch in pain. The blade digs in with a silent order to hold still, right over a healed scar in the same exact spot.

Automatically, my wide eyes lock onto Digby, and I know we're both remembering when Fulke held me the same way. It was a different blade and a different king, but the threat was the same. Death's promise held against my throat.

But this time, Digby can't save me.

Midas holds me tighter, backing up a step as I look around wildly at the guards that circle him, at the Wrath held at bay, bodies tense, like they're just waiting for Slade's order. At Digby's wide-eyed face, his broken body still held up by Fake Rip.

"Leave now, or I'll slit her throat," Midas threatens.

Fear pounds down my limbs. No one moves a single muscle.

"You won't kill her," Slade snarls. I don't know if it's denial or a promise.

"If I can't have her, no one can." Midas's cold, calculating voice makes my heart drop. Because I can hear the truth binding his words. He would rather kill me than let me leave. He's betting on both of our lives that Slade won't risk it, and he bet *right*.

"Go now, Ravinger. You have thirty seconds, or I *will* kill her."

The Wrath shift on their feet. Fake Rip looks at me, fury flickering over his face.

But Slade's gaze is locked on me. "Use your ribbons," he urges, and a choked sob curdles from my cinched throat.

"I can't."

Midas pulls my body closer, his hold banded around my waist so hard that it's a struggle to breathe, especially as he chuckles against me. "Oh, she didn't tell you? She lost that privilege."

Slade's eyes drop when Midas motions to my left hand where the ribbon is still tied loosely around my limb.

Something like appalled torment flushes over Slade's face as his eyes flash from my ribbon and back to my face. "*Auren...*"

Tears that feel like fire burn down my cheeks, and my chest expands with the cry of rumbling rage that builds like a storm.

"She's helpless and completely at my mercy, and she *will* die at my hand if you force it."

My anger lifts up her head from the billowing clouds, the word *helpless* echoing inside of them, clinking with electric frenzy.

"Ten seconds, Ravinger," Midas barks against my ear, but I don't hear him. I don't hear what Slade says back either, or note the agonized hesitation on his face as my eyes flutter closed.

Because there's thunder in my ears.

The furious, feathered, snapping beast is brooding on a storm, and I'm ready to watch it *rage*. Wings opening, teeth gleaming, her eyes as gold as mine. And her screech, that call that ruptures like lightning, it doesn't shatter a sea. It shatters *me*.

A scorching threat opens up in me like a crack in the earth, and maybe Midas can feel it too, because his steps stumble.

My mouth opens with a decadent inhale, and this anger, it's like a breath of fresh air that I never let myself take before.

But I'm breathing in now, and I find I like the taste.

My eyes wrench open, body unfurling, a roaring of storm-ravaged waves filling my ears. I look down at my hands, at the fire that burns beneath the skin, and I feel nothing but untapped, wild, raw power.

The night may have stolen the sun, and Midas may have stolen my ribbons, but I'm *not* helpless.

And all at once, I'm calling to the magic not under the control of others, not ruled by the sun, but by *me*.

Because every gilded inch, every piece of metallic glint I've wrought is *mine*.

Another inhale sucks into my lungs as I sag against Midas's hold, blade forgotten, time suspended. I open my mouth and tip up my hands, calling to the gold I've made.

And it answers back.

With fire in my eyes and a flap of furious wings in my chest, I bring my gold thrashing to life.

The floor goes molten; the walls bleed; every goblet, drapery, instrument, chair—they all turn viscous and malleable, melted down by the pure fury that burns in my veins.

Highbell guards scream as their armor suddenly liquefies, and with a flick of my wrist, I make it swallow some whole. More dives down their mouths, gurgling their screams. The ones who run get trapped by the gold floor, sticking them in place and refusing to let them go.

Even the gilt blade held at my throat melts in an instant, Midas jerking back, hand opening with a yelp of surprise.

I whirl around, another flick of my wrist making the

gold at his back peel from the walls like thick paint. In an instant, the gluey tendrils reach out and snag him, tearing him off me. His body plasters against the simmering wall as the curtains drip down like gilt molasses and wrap around his torso, tying him in place.

"Auren," he cries out, but his voice is lost to me. My creature is out in full-force, and she doesn't answer to him.

I turn back to the pounding feet of the fleeing armored men. With a twisted smile, I take them without mercy, because mercy was never shown to me.

One after the other, I use whatever is closest, the gold going wherever I direct it.

The chandelier drips piercing needles of gilt rain, stabbing one guard straight through. The sconces on the wall melt like candle wax and drip onto the head of another. The ground swallows three more whole, their struggles going still as statues, bodies half buried into the floor with their screams.

I see the skirts of Queen Kaila's dress as she escapes, her gilded crown, necklace, and shawl left behind in her flee. My creature tenses in irritation, but I turn to the rest of Highbell and Ranhold's soldiers, ending them with relish.

My pulse pulls at my veins, a demanding pace set by my racing heart.

Because it's not enough. This release of revenge, this unleashed power, it's not enough.

An infuriated screech caws in my ear with a thundering boom, every flap of wing making me feel higher and higher, my spirit taken flight on the wind of my storming fury.

I kill every single guard in the room, not stopping until their screams and running steps are trapped in the clammy grip of my gold that crushes and swallows them.

The ballroom has turned into a veritable sea of livid gold waves ready to flood the world.

"Au-Auren..."

My beast and I turn, eyes gleaming as we lock onto Midas, who's stuck against the wall, body half frozen into it, and my mouth tips up into a vicious smile that's not my own.

The second he held that blade to my throat, I knew I didn't just want to escape him. I wanted to *destroy* him.

His eyes are wild as a golden grasp of fingers holds him in place, his body suspended. He's the one who's well and truly *helpless*.

"Let me go, Auren," he pleads, his voice high-pitched as he struggles. "You don't want to do this."

I feel my head tilt, feel my creature blink. "Oh, but I do."

My voice singes, landing against his ear and making him twitch with the burn.

"Auren. Precious..."

A cruel, fiery laugh sears my throat. "I'm not your Precious."

I stand before the man who has done nothing but use me, lie to me, manipulate me, threaten me, and abuse me for over *ten years*. I look at him, and hate looks with me.

He flinches as I lift my hand and place it against his cheek, letting the ruined strip of my ribbon brush against his skin. I lean in close so that my voice can heat his face, so that he can look me in the eye and see the fury searing my vision. "You can't cut off the strings of your puppet and still expect it to move for you."

He balks, the rest of the blood in his face draining away.

I move my palm up and then drag my finger against the crown still resting on his head.

He may wear the crown, but I was the one who made it gold.

With just a thought, I make the sharp ends of each spire curve. The gold crown bends in a bow to me, in a nod of who's truly in power. He thrashes as it clutches him like claws, digging in just enough to make small droplets of blood bead against his forehead.

My gaze bounces between his eyes, soaking up the fear there, soaking up this moment as my gold soaks up everything else.

Then, I lean in and whisper, "Goodbye, Midas." I

place my lips against his cheek, because he defeated me with a kiss, so why shouldn't I do the same to him?

He chokes with a sob, or maybe it's a curse. I don't know and I never will, because the second my lips lift from his skin, a gilt kiss is already there imprinted on the spot. Golden fragments, as fine as powder, that I pulled from the air and left to glint against his cheek.

Then, I pat the spot with my finger.

Tap, tap, tap, tap, tap.

Five times—not six.

With a smirk, I back away as he thrashes, but my magic already has a hold on him. The hooked fingers of the wall clutch him, the gleaming spot I left on his cheek moving, searching, slinking over his face before it wraps down his throat, a hard edge cutting into the spot where he'd held a blade to mine.

He fights it, oh, he fights it.

I make him feel every inch of it as it devours him whole. Because with everything he's revealed, everything he's done, *this* is what he deserves. He let gold consume him a long time ago. I'm just letting it finish the job.

After a handful of breaths, the liquid metal begins to dribble out of his mouth, bleeding from his eyes, more drops falling out of his nose.

The gold he coveted so much, the gold he loved more than anything else, eats him alive.

When it has a hold of his heart, I let it finish him,

stealing his last beat. I watch the last of his fight, the last of his life, leave his body like water draining out, until there's nothing left of him.

He's dead.

Dead, dead, dead.

The gold throughout the castle shudders.

Then, with a sweep of my hand, I encase his body completely, dark satisfaction lifting my lips. I turn away from his shocked, unmoving face, at the chest that no longer rises, at his fused mouth, his silver tongue now swallowed by my gold.

I take a breath, feeling that my beast is gratified.

...Gratified, but not *appeased*.

Because my anger isn't quenched. My power bubbles and twists, slinking like lava, pushing me to keep going, demanding *more*.

The angry monster in me still wants to punish. To kill. To wipe out everyone and anyone who stood by and let me suffer. As I look around at this room that now ebbs and flows by my calling, a destructive temptation ripples across the floor, and I realize something.

Instead of being afraid of the world, I could make the whole damn world afraid of *me*.

With a devilish tilt of my lips, I stride forward, bringing the gold with me like the swell of a sea. But it lugs now, a heavy weight that makes my breath heave, sweat breaking out upon my brow. With great strain, I *pull* at the magic, pushing past the sudden surge of exhaustion as I head for the archway.

I can't stop now. I want to swallow this castle whole, trap everyone in it. Let them be smothered in their own covetous greed. I want to let my power scour the land, clear across the Barrens, right back to Highbell. I'll let it devour everything in our path, and I'll—

Someone steps into my path.

A gilded wave pauses behind me, risen up into the curl of a punishing crest, my hands shaking with the effort to hold it.

The creature in me blinks, snapping at the interruption, but the crackling anger falters, because we recognize him. Recognize the dark aura of power that arcs around him like smoke.

"Goldfinch, can you hear me?" he asks gently.

My head cocks, though I don't answer. Gold weighs down my bones and slouches my shoulders as I struggle to take in a full breath.

The male steps forward, an inky black form against the shine I've wrought. "Auren, you can let go now."

My brow furrows. *Let go?*

I don't want to let go. I want to continue to rage. I want to take my gold that was stolen from me, and punish everyone in my path. I want to be the monster that's been held back for far too long.

The male takes another step, and my beast screeches

at him, though he doesn't seem deterred. He should be running away from us, should be terrified like everyone else, but instead, he keeps coming, closer and closer, until he stands just a foot away. "You need to let go, baby. You're draining yourself."

My mouth drops into a frown.

"Draining?"

Eyes so dark green they look black are locked on my face, caressing over my own gaze. "Yes," he says quietly. "You need to drop the magic before you hurt yourself."

My back bristles. "My gold won't hurt me."

"It already is." He tips his head, and I look down, though I don't see anything amiss.

"Your aura is fading," he tells me. "You can't see it, but I can. I need you to breathe and let go of your power."

Panic surges up in me. If I let go of my power, I'll be weak again. Helpless.

Fury sparks in my eyes, and the gold flexes behind me like fingers clenching into a fist. "No."

"You're alright now. You don't need it," he vows, and despite the anxiety running through me, his voice is deep and soothing, calling to another part of me, a part buried beneath the anger.

But my beast fights against it. She doesn't want to let go, though every second that I hold the gold makes my strength wane, my limbs heavy and numbed.

"I want everyone to hurt like I hurt," I say through gritted teeth.

"You punished the one who mattered."

Something wars inside of me. A weight is dragging me down as my magic demands more. I let some of the gold behind me lope down and seep through the archway. I let more break the windows, yank on the pillars. I let it climb the walls of Ranhold, following the screams and running footsteps, searching to swallow…

More, it whispers. *More*.

But he comes forward in another bold step, interrupting my concentration, distracting my magic's reach. He stands right in front of me, his aura curling around me as he takes up my sight, my hearing, my *smell*. I can't help but breathe him in, the metallic storm clearing from my nostrils, the scent of wood and soil and bitter chocolate filling me instead.

He touches my cheek, lets his rough hand skate over my skin. "Come back to me, Goldfinch."

I shudder, and his touch yanks at my awareness, splitting away from the anger driving me. My eyes widen, vision clearing from the haze. "Slade…?"

He nods. "That's right, baby. Let the magic go."

I swallow hard, suddenly feeling the weight of the power, how it's *crushing* me.

My legs start to give out, but Slade catches me before I fall, though his hands land on my back, making me cry out in pain and yank away from him.

"Oh goddess..." I stagger, but it's not from the raw ache of my ribbons, it's the pressure of the power bearing down on me. "I can't!" My voice cracks out, lands in a heap as my eyes fill with panicked tears. "I don't know how to let go!"

A curse flies from Slade's mouth for a moment before he grabs my arms to hold me. "Breathe, Auren," he commands.

My eyes are wild, bouncing around the ballroom, at the gold that suddenly feels like it's closing in on me. "I can't control it, I can't—"

"You *can*," he growls in my face, the coils of his own power twisting like roots along his jaw. "Try, Auren. It's your power, it answers to you."

But he's wrong. This isn't my power at all. This is something born from inside of me, from the raging anger I held in too long.

My entire body shakes from the crushing weight of it, and all around me, the gold starts to boil and hiss, and it takes everything in me to hold it back. Even still, it slinks forward, creeping, pushing the boundaries. My heart leaps into my throat when I see it inching around Slade and trying to latch onto his feet. I shoot my hand forward to direct it away, a terrified gasp flooding from my surging chest.

I barely have the might to send it back, but more is advancing, a ripple going through the floor, edging nearer. I have no idea where everyone else is, but terror grips my chest. What if I killed the Wrath, or Digby, or innocents? And yet, that's what is going to happen, because my control is fading fast.

"It's going to hurt you!" I cry, hands now scrabbling to push him away. "Go, Slade, I can't...I can't hold it back much longer, and I don't know how to stop it!"

Hands land on my cheeks, cupping my face, and my eyes spring open, though I hadn't realized I'd even closed them.

"Look at me."

Frightened eyes lock onto him. "You have to leave."

But the stubborn male shakes his head. "I already told you. If you think I'm leaving without you, you're out of your damned mind."

The echo of his previous words brings a sob up my throat as exhausted, terrified tears track down my face.

How quickly this astonishing power turned so disastrous. How quickly it overwhelmed me.

I can't do what he's saying. I've never had good control over my magic, and now, it's running rampant, its will trying to buckle my own.

"Auren, your aura is fading fast, you have to let go!" he pleads.

There's alarmed fear in his eyes now, and his aura lurches around me, like it's trying to grasp onto my own to keep it from fading. I've never seen him look afraid before, and the sight of it makes me tremble.

I can *feel* myself draining, but if I let it go like he wants me to, then the tentative tether I have on the gold will give way. It will unleash on him and anyone else in its path before it settles, and I can't let that happen. I made the gold unleash with the heart of a beast, and now, its single-minded will is to destroy.

"Leave. *Please*," I beg.

I shudder with the effect of the drain, of trying to hold onto this power that's overtaken every part of me.

My vision blacks out, and I slump, ears roaring, though I don't know if that's the magic overloading my veins, or my galloping pulse. There's a tug through my gut, like my very life-force is being pulled on, and it tears a ragged breath from my panting chest.

I can hold it. I *will* hold it, until he's out of harm's way, for as long as my exhaustion can stand it.

My eyes are heavy, my breathing labored. Sweat drips down my neck and stings the jagged cuts of my ribbons, and I feel something in me sinking.

I'm dying.

"Dammit, Auren, you don't have time. *Let go!*" Slade roars.

I open my mouth to tell him I can't, but all that comes out is a pitiful whimper.

Then, he suddenly yanks my face forward and presses his lips against mine. The shock of it stuns me for a moment, and my faltering hold on the magic wavers.

Slade pulls back, something pained in his eyes. "Forgive me," he breathes against my mouth.

I want to ask him what he means, but I don't get the chance.

In the next brush of his lips against mine, his power rises up, the cloying, corrupt magic that steals the breath from my chest.

A choked noise catches in my throat as I feel something horrible rake down my insides, like poisoned air. My wet eyes go wide in shock, and I try to flinch away from him, but Slade holds me still, green eyes keeping me hostage.

My lips part on a jagged, rough cry rent from the stutter in my heart. From something insipid and withering that seems to decay the very bones in my body.

"Forgive me," he whispers again.

I couldn't answer him even if I wanted to. My vision decays, and in the next instant, my hold on the magic snaps with the last of my strength, like a dam bursting. All I feel before I black out is a clash of metal and rot, of gold and black colliding together in a rush of heat and dust.

The last thing I hear is Slade's voice from that moment in the library.

We all have our edge, Auren. One day, you're going to find where yours is.

I found it, I want to tell him.

I found my edge.

The question is, did I fall, or did I fly?

EPILOGUE

SLADE

I'm not a male prone to feeling panic.

But when Midas grabs Auren and holds a blade to her throat, panic *becomes* me.

My power rears up so fiercely that I nearly stagger with it, my feet grinding into a rumbling floor.

"Use your magic, and I'll slice her open!" Midas spits, and his shout arrests me in place.

I react instantly, yanking onto my power as I lock it down and signal for my Wrath to halt. Ranhold and Highbell guards stop too, while Queen Kaila's men back her away, pressing her toward the far wall, trying to protect her from the exchange.

The entire ballroom goes still. Or maybe that's just me, but time has paused, my damn heartbeat paused with it.

Auren's body is crushed, held roughly against Midas's chest. Her throat bobs beneath the glinting blade held there, her golden eyes wide with shock and fear. That look makes me lose *my fucking mind.*

I can feel my power reacting to her terror, can feel the remnants of its reach trying to leap right off my skin and strangle Midas where he stands.

My voice punches out between clenched teeth. "Let her go. *Now.*"

Midas only holds her tighter, eyes skimming the room.

"Hold back your rot and your soldiers, Ravinger."

My Wrath are five steps away in their own stare-off with the guards, but they stay where they are, not moving an inch. None of them will give Midas a reason to hurt her. Digby too has frozen in place, his gaze locked on the threat.

Midas shifts his stance and digs the blade in, causing a dribble of gold blood to leak from Auren's sensitive throat. And just the sight of that—of a single drip tracing down her skin—makes something feral open up in me.

My teeth ache with the need to sharpen, spikes threatening to puncture through my back and arms, my vision tunneling as the push for violence rattles my skull.

The tiny noise Auren lets out makes my warring soul splinter, my entire body shaking. She tries to claw his hands away from her, but the bastard has a solid hold.

Furious magic bites at my skin and arches into my feet, but I dig in, holding it back. "You are a fucking dead man," I vow darkly.

Midas has the good sense to look worried. It was only for a blink before he shuttered the expression, but the savage fae in me relishes in it.

Good. He *should* be worried.

"Leave now, or I'll slit her throat," he grits out, steps backing away, dragging her with him.

If he thinks I'd ever leave her, he's not nearly as intelligent as he thinks he is.

"You won't kill her."

It's a fucking promise.

Midas knows it, too. He can see it in my face.

His jaw tightens, a different kind of resolve settling there. "If I can't have her, no one can."

Unease rushes through my veins, diluting my festering ire. I glance from him to her, my body tense, fists clenched at my sides. All I want to do is let my magic lash out, to bleed up through his legs and corrode him from cock to crown.

But I can't.

I fucking *can't*.

Because I can see in the crazed resolve in his eyes that the threat he's laid out isn't a ploy. If he feels even a hint of it, if my magic doesn't react fast enough to kill him first, he will open her throat and I will watch her die right in front of me.

Midas will never let her go, and I will never risk her. He can see the truth of that in every second of my hesitation. The line of blood shimmering on her neck is the only blood I'll allow to be spilled.

"Go now, Ravinger. You have thirty seconds, or I will kill her."

I can feel my Wrath look at me, waiting for an order one way or another, but I'm stuck in this dilemma.

"Use your ribbons," I urge her. They're strong. *She's* strong. She only needs to trust herself and—

A lamenting sob pours out of her mouth, eyes filling as she looks at me with something like regret. "I can't."

I frown, not understanding the look on her face, but Midas's laugh heckles me.

"Oh, she didn't tell you?" he asks smugly, mouth curved up. "She lost that privilege."

My body goes still. Even the roots clawing at my neck seem to pause.

Midas motions down to her hand, and for the first time in all of this madness, I realize what's tied around her wrist.

A single gold ribbon. One I know very well. One I expect to lift up and move.

Except...it doesn't. It's not trying to weave closer to me or shove Midas away in a protective furor. It just hangs there limply, and I know instantly that something is wrong. It's in the lackluster color, the drooping ends. Even at rest, Auren's ribbons are always...*alive*. As vibrant as she is.

And that's when I see the severed end, the curdled drips of blood left behind.

No. *No.*

Something roars in my ears, and my eyes flash up to her misery-laced face, as the realization of what he's taken from her sinks into me like a boulder. "Auren..." I rasp, my voice sounding as gutted as I feel.

As tears drip down her cheeks, my heart feels like it breaks in half.

"She's helpless and completely at my mercy, and she will die at my hand if you force it," Midas says, but I barely even hear it. "Ten seconds, Ravinger."

Wretched, furious grief knocks the breath from my lungs at the reality that I've failed her so thoroughly. I fucking *can't* leave her...but I can't risk Midas killing her either.

But then...something changes in Auren's eyes.

If I weren't so attuned to her, I might've missed it—the flicker of light that crackles in her golden irises. I definitely *wouldn't* have missed the flare of her aura, though. It pulses so brightly for a moment that it stings my eyes.

That's all the warning I get before the entire room seems to erupt with power all at once.

Everywhere around me, the gold that Auren has

created seems to come to life. All I have time to do is suck in a breath as the floor, the walls, the fucking *table*, every inch of metal, melts like magma. It starts to attack like it's taken on a mind of its own, like it heard the call of its mistress, and it's come to do her bidding.

Where there was stillness before, there's now a rupture of movement all throughout the ballroom.

Queen Kaila screams, her people trying to get her out through the back, only to stop short as an unlucky Highbell guard runs through the doorway and is immediately swallowed by a waterfall of gold that drips from the wall, consuming him in a metallic splash.

Guards start fleeing, but my own Wrath come directly to me, tightening around me in a protective circle. Osrik, Judd, and Lu have their swords ready, but what can that do against this? My eyes cut over to my brother Ryatt as he comes to stand beside me too. He's careful to keep Digby propped up at his side, though it's an awkward hold with the spikes attached to his armor.

"What the *fuck*?" Ryatt says, as we all watch the gold strike. In both liquid and solid forms, it plunges people beneath its glossy depths, piercing others through, attacking left and right, while we're left to watch the melee.

"Rip..." Lu cautions, her hold tightening on her hilt.

Through the panic of the room, I watch Auren. Watch her aura flare brightly again and burn my eyes like I'm looking directly at the sun.

"She snapped," Judd murmurs, flinching when the damn ground comes up twenty feet away from us, opening like the mouth of a bird, beak swallowing a Highbell guard whole.

My attention is intent on Auren, on the way she's moving, on her expression. Her power is killing everyone in the ballroom, and now she has Midas pinned to the wall.

The gold isn't attacking us, but the hysteria of her flashing aura worries me.

"Go," I order the others.

Lu gapes at me. "Rip—"

"Auren isn't fully in control right now, and I don't want any of you getting hurt."

"What about you?" she volleys.

I shake my head. "She won't hurt me."

The gold takes that moment to kill a Highbell guard right in front of us, his armor crushing his chest in with an audible crack.

"You sure about that?" Judd asks dubiously.

Osrik curses, drawing my eye back to Auren, and we all go still as we watch her place a kiss on Midas's cheek. I might've gotten jealous if it weren't for the fear in his eyes.

When she pulls back, the press of her lips leaves a mark behind, and my own power surges up. I watch in rapt fascination as Auren's gold slithers and moves, and then, it starts to *devour* him. It's a reveling fiend, shoving in his mouth, binding his limbs, holding him hostage until his struggles go still, his body adhered to the wall.

Shock courses through me at how fast it happened.

Midas is *dead,* trapped in the metal he coveted.

My breath hisses between my teeth as a barrage of emotions crashes over my head like thunder. Surprise, pride, guilt, it all rushes over me, soaking me through.

I've wanted that fucker dead since I found out he kept her in a cage. I've imagined rotting his spine and leaving him paralyzed on the ground for the birds to peck. The moment he laid hands on her, I wanted to lay hands on *him*.

But I didn't need to.

I'm so fucking proud of her. She destroyed him so spectacularly that my chest swells, even as I feel guilt that she was put in this position in the first place.

You did it, Goldfinch.

I knew she could burn brighter than the sun if she only stepped out of his shade. But fuck. Even my faith in her strength didn't match up to just how magnificent she really is.

That's my girl.

"Shit, she killed him," Osrik exclaims, doing nothing to hide the glee in his voice. "She actually *killed* him. Fucking amazing."

"Good," Digby spits, the colors of his bruised face darker with his fierce expression.

Lu snorts. "Alright, how about we make sure she doesn't kill *us* before we start celebrating?"

"Go," I tell them. "Move slowly."

This time, they don't argue. The five of them make a beeline for the archway, their steps cautious as they walk over the rippling floor, Ry and Osrik pulling along Digby between them.

When the gold doesn't immediately attack them, they start going faster, tentative steps gliding across the space. Only when they slip out of the ballroom do I let out a breath of relief.

I turn back toward Auren just as she looks around the now empty room, her expression ecstatic...though not quite her own.

The gold has overtaken the space, moving like a tumultuous sea, churning and lifting, the walls weeping down like rain on a windowpane.

Auren's attention snags onto the archway, and something nefarious warps her face, making her eyes gleam with light.

My chest tightens at the look of Auren's waning aura, at the gold that starts to flicker. The magic is riding her hard—too hard. It's draining her faster than I can blink. Though based on the volatile look on her face, I don't think she even realizes the toll this is taking.

The gold room lives and breathes by her hand, and she's controlling so very much of it—*too* much of it.

She starts striding toward the exit, so I make my way across the room, the soles of my shoes sticking to the floor like I'm walking on syrup. Gold laps at my ankles, the subtle waves of a tide washing up on the shore.

I don't break my pace until I slide in front of her, blocking the archway.

Auren jerks to a stop, a massive crest of gold at her back casting her in a shadow, the wave of a tsunami ready to hit.

She watches me, but it's not just her looking out of her eyes. Something else lurks there too.

I can feel her hunger, her need for revenge, and I have no qualms with her meting it out. I would gladly step aside and let her cast her reckoning on this whole damn kingdom. I'm not blocking her for *them*.

It's her sapping strength that roots me in place. It's fear that has me gently coaxing her, because I can feel the power feeding on her, draining her, *killing* her.

"Goldfinch, can you hear me?" I say softly.

Her head tilts, like she's trying to place me, and my own expression turns grim, my chest going tight.

The magic has taken over.

"Auren," I coax, taking a step forward. "You can let go now."

A frown mars her beautiful face, resistance tightening in the gold behind her. The magic is sparking, making her skin gleam like beams of light reflecting off her skin even as sweat drips from her brow and her breathing grows labored.

Too much. It's taking too fucking much.

I eat up the distance between us, ignoring the floor that pricks through my boots, my sole focus on her, on keeping the panic from my eyes so I can try to calm her down. "You need to let go, baby. You're draining yourself."

"Draining?" she asks, though her voice sounds strangely hollow.

I nod. "Yes. You need to drop the magic before you hurt yourself."

The room seems to pulse.

"My gold won't hurt me," she hisses, something almost animalistic bearing down on me through her eyes.

"It already is. Your aura is fading. You can't see it, but I can. I need you to breathe and let go of your power." There's a plea in my voice.

"*No*." The floor shifts in an angry wave.

My teeth grit when her aura dims, and I know I have to fucking stop this. "You're alright now. You don't need it," I say, trying to assuage her magic.

But then she goes and breaks my damned heart.

"I want everyone to hurt like I hurt."

My lips press together in a hard line, fingers itching to reach out and touch her. "You punished the one who mattered," I promise her.

You punished *him*.

Giving in to the need riding me, I take another step forward and reach out to caress her cheek. "Come back, Goldfinch," I murmur, her bright eyes making mine burn, though I don't look away.

Something shudders through her at my touch, her waning aura trembling, and then she blinks, the strange glow of her eyes receding.

"Slade?"

Hope leaps in my chest. "That's right, baby. Let the magic go."

Just when I think I have my Goldfinch back, Auren's eyes flare with panic as she curses the gods. "I can't. I don't know how to let it go!"

Fuck.

I grab her trembling arms, trying to steady her while my own power beats at me, reacting to her terror. "Breathe, Auren."

The room quakes, gold jumping and jerking in an erratic fit. "I can't control it, I can't—"

"You *can*," I tell her, because I won't accept anything else. She didn't defeat Midas just for her own power to turn on her. "Try, Auren. It's your power, it answers to you."

She winces, her skin gone hot to the touch as she tries, but when the floor ripples again, her anxiety surges back full force.

"It's going to hurt you!" she cries, shoving at me. "Go, Slade, I can't...I can't hold it back much longer, and I don't know how to stop it!"

Refusing to let her push me away, I grab both of her cheeks and say, "Look at me."

Her fearful eyes well up with tears. "You have to leave."

And let her drain herself to death? Never.

"I already told you. If you think I'm leaving without you, you're out of your damned mind," I growl.

The gilded ceiling begins to drip like rain, the walls warping, the floor roiling, and Auren trembles with all of it, her aura so muted that it's nearly snuffed out.

"Auren, your aura is fading fast, you have to let go!" I shout, voice rising to be heard above the groaning gold.

There's a plea in her streaming eyes. "Leave. *Please*," she says, slumping in my arms, her legs failing her.

I barely duck as a stream of gold falls just to the left of me, crashing to the ground. "Dammit, Auren, you don't have time. *Let go!*"

But she either can't anymore, or she won't. My power is going fucking crazy, magic leaking from my feet, cracking the gold beneath me. When her aura nearly winks out, the roots around my chest claw inward like they're trying to burrow straight through my damn heart.

Terror grapples my entire body, severs right down to my soul. She can't die. She fucking *can't*.

I won't let her.

So I do the only thing I can think of before it's too late and she lets the power drain her completely.

Leaning forward, I breathe her scent in, relish in the heat emanating from her skin. "Forgive me," I whisper, because I loathe myself for what I'm about to do—for taking the choice away from her. But when it comes to her life, I can't just sit back and let her sacrifice herself. Not for me.

My lips press against hers, even now, the supple warmth of them enough to take me to my knees. The moment she parts her mouth for me, I breathe out the rotted power within me. I let it sink in past her lips, feel it slip down her throat and root beneath her skin.

Her power wavers at the sudden intrusion, but the look of fear in her eyes nearly kills me.

"Forgive me," I say again, because she's scared of *me*. But she's weak, so fucking weak, and I'm out of time.

With another push of power, I force her body to languish, even as my instincts scream that this is wrong. My own magic wars with me as I force her in a stasis between life and decay, as I make my power rot her from within. But I'm scared, so fucking scared that I could hurt her, that I could somehow do something wrong, push too hard.

"Forgive me," I whisper for a third time, but I know she can no longer hear me. *Please let this work,* I implore silently. *Please let her be okay.*

When her aura is nothing but a wisp, she finally slumps, letting out a single, dusty breath as I catch her in my arms.

Without her consciousness to direct it, the wave of gold comes crashing to the floor. Taking a limp Auren in my arms, I run out of the archway just as a loud smash sounds. But even in the hall, more insipid gold is dropping from the ceiling and solidifying against the floor in uneven waves, nearly making me trip.

I dodge and duck, my spikes digging beneath my skin in a protective surge, wanting to come breaking out, but I grit my teeth and suppress it.

Gold floods the floor, splashing against the stairs, an unsuspecting servant crying out from somewhere behind me.

"Over here!"

I find Osrik waving me forward, and I skid to the right, trying to keep from jostling Auren too much as he leads me out.

The entire castle seems to groan, and I realize that more gold than just what was in the ballroom is rioting without Auren conscious to direct it.

No wonder she fucking drained herself. It's like she brought every piece of gold in the castle to life.

"Out here," Osrik grunts, just before he takes a sharp right, where a doorway is being propped open by Ryatt.

The moment we make it out, Ry lets the door slam

shut, and not three seconds later, something hard slams against the door, splintering the wood. We all back up on instinct, watching as gold curls through the break. But much to my relief, it gives one last shake before it solidifies, its movement stiffening to a stop.

The crashing and crackling of the rest of Ranhold Castle dies down too, until bleak, unnatural silence bleeds through the air.

"Shit," Lu says, letting out a low whistle.

Osrik looks down at Auren. "Is she okay?"

My stomach churns, a tic jumping in my jaw. "I don't know."

Shockwaves go through my Wrath, and then a hobbling Digby comes pushing past them to check on Auren. When he sees the state of her, he brings a pair of glaring eyes up to me. "You'd better fix her. You hear me, boy? *Fix. Her.*"

I blink at the fierceness in his tone. I don't think anyone has ever dared to call me *boy*, even when I was one. Yet I'm too damn terrified to even be bothered. I have no idea if I did more harm than good by using my power to keep her in this paused state, but I need to get her out of here. Far away, where there is no gold to grip her.

I turn and start stalking off, the others hurrying to match my step as I head for my army's camp.

"What do you want to do, Slade?" Ry asks at my side.

My eyes harden with my resolve, only softening when they drop down to Auren's face.

I'm going to fix her. She's going to be alright.

I won't accept anything else. I won't even *consider* it.

Shouting voices from the front of the castle carry across the night air, making my steps quicken.

"We need to leave. Right fucking now," I reply grimly. "Get the army back to Fourth."

As soon as the panic abates, the survivors and witnesses are going to be talking. Accusing. Pointing fingers. They're going to want answers and demand atonement. Because the dead can't say what transpired in that ballroom.

But Queen Kaila can.

She and her group were in there. They saw what happened, and they saw that it was Auren who made it so.

It's just a matter of time before they come for her.

But I'll be fucking ready.

GOLDEN GOLD VINE
PART THREE

Oh, this miser did prize her,
  this golden gold vine.
He couldn't stop now,
  so he sat at her shrine.

He had to cut, to cull, and to bleed.
For her to keep growing, that was the creed.

Whenever he plucked
  her vine until bare,
he'd sit by her stems,
  into skin he would tear.

Losing himself, as he sat and he flayed.
Yielding himself, as he laid in her shade.

He soon gave up his toes, his fingers, mere stumps.
His teeth, he yanked out, in white and red clumps.

Dropped into soil,
like rain for her roots.
Up grew her blossoms,
inedible fruits.

The gold was his blanket,
his prize, and his gloat.
The thorns for his teeth,
the leaves as his coat.

He took what she made,
and reaped what she sowed.
Addicted, entitled, thinking—
wealth he was owed.

But bitter her roots
became as she bloomed.
This golden gold vine,
resented and fumed.

So blinded by gleam,
he just couldn't see
what he became
by demands he decreed.

When he first found her
along that plain road,
he didn't yet know
what he picked when he trode.

For it wasn't just her
that he took on that day.
Greed was the weed
he invited to stay.

In his house the gold took up all of the room.
He thought it a triumph. (But it was a tomb.)

Tangled and knitted,
every corner, leaves spewed.
Still, he wanted more
—Oh! Just a few!

No hair or nails, no eyes or nose.
No fingers or ears, nor any toes.
Yet he'd satisfy himself with his own greedy prose.
He was the richest alive! Anything he could buy!
(Yes, it was true, that wasn't a lie.)
Though he did not realize, no he could not conceive,
that his obsession for gold was what made him unweave.

The old miser lived on,
a sorry state of affairs.
Sacrificing his tongue,
his legs, arms—both in pairs.

He couldn't touch or talk, nor could he see.
But what did that matter, when what mattered was he
was alone with his vine, his treasure sublime.
No need for his senses or to walk or to sign,
when all that he wanted was her opulent shine.

And all the while, this old miser clung to the vine.
His mute mouth empty, but still miming, *"mine."*

The vine did outgrow his little house on the hill.
Winding down to the forest, all twine and twill.

She'd grown so large, while he'd withered
down to a pulp.
Until finally, she took the last of him, in one final gulp.

His stumped and stubbed pieces,
now taken inside her.
This golden gold greed,
like a web from a spider.

And upon his death,
the vine did slowly die back.
It shrunk from forest to yard,
its gold gone to lack.

The only bit that remained,
on that house on the hill
was a flicker of gleam
against a cracked windowsill.

And there right beneath,
under a pile of rubble,
was one golden vine,
its short thorns like stubble.

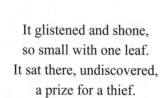

It glistened and shone,
so small with one leaf.
It sat there, undiscovered,
a prize for a thief.

This vine as golden as a small piece of sun,
it waited right there for someone to come.
And when someone did, (for there would always be one)
she perked up and straightened,
she showed off her shine.
And he stole and he smiled,
and whispered greedily, "*mine*."

READ ON FOR A SNEAK PEEK AT THE NEXT BOOK IN THE PLATED PRISONERS SERIES

THE KING IS DEAD, BUT AM I FREE?

GLOW

THE PLATED PRISONER SERIES

RAVEN KENNEDY
INTERNATIONAL BESTSELLING AUTHOR

CHAPTER 1

QUEEN KAILA

The air is full of screams.

The entire front of Ranhold Castle is an ocean shore of people washed up on the courtyard. They ebb and flow, frothy cries making waves as they undulate in a shallow mob.

Behind me, Ranhold guards are trying to push out the subjects through the gate, with frenzied command that barely cuts through the chaos. Half the people are trying to come back in to see what's going on, the other half fleeing for their lives.

Manu and my guards got us outside, but only just. My heartbeat is a hammer, and the breath that I'm sucking in is just as rushed as the adrenaline pumping through my veins. It's the sort of harried vulnerability that makes me feel no better than a cornered animal. One who's frozen in snow, unable to move. And yet, what's really keeping me still are the sounds coming from the castle. Sloshing. Dripping. Clanging. Smashing. *More screaming.*

Another sharp slap of shrieks erupts when liquid gold suddenly bursts through the front doors. Everyone flinches back, gasping bodies caught in the swell of panic, shoving into the mass behind them as they try to get further away.

Manu and Keon stand in front of me, facing Ranhold Castle, and they both push me back protectively while our guards surround us. Not all of my guards made it out, yet I haven't wanted to look around to see just how many I lost.

The gold spews from the doorway and curls around the castle walls, gushing down the front steps. Like outstretched hands, it nearly grabs hold of a man, but he gets yanked out of the way by some guards at the very last second.

The liquid metal slams down from its unsuccessful reach like a petulant child smashing fists in a fit against the ground and sending splatters flying. Mottled gashes of gold streak across the snow-covered steps, marring the stone. More of it drips like blood from the window sills, staining the glass and peeking past the frames.

We're surrounded by the castle's lantern-lit outer walls, and even though it's supposed to make us feel protected, it's only keeping everyone trapped out here together. I'm about to suggest to my brother that we get away in case the gold keeps pouring out and we become trapped with the crowd, but another loud crash happens somewhere inside, cutting me off.

My eyes wildly veer between my brother's and Keon's forms, wondering what else inside has been destroyed, who else has been killed. But then, as if that last noise was a signal for the end, the gold that's gripping the front walls suddenly stops glinting, stops rippling.

It hardens in place as the castle goes suddenly quiet.

The screaming of the crowd cuts off too, everyone waiting with bated breath to see if it's actually over. I'm not sure how long we all stand there, watching and listening, but the splotches of gold along the grayed, frozen stone are no longer moving, and despite the torches casting off firelight, everything seems darker. Colder.

The movement and sounds may have ceased, yet those things instead spring to life inside of me. My body begins to tremble, my mind a funnel of noisy thoughts swirling around.

What in the Divine just happened?

My shoes are soaked through as I stand here in the snow, my skin pebbled from the awful frigid night air. I wasn't meant to be outside in this dress. I should be in the ballroom right now. I should be celebrating my engagement announcement and making plans for my control to now spread to Sixth Kingdom.

At the very least, I should be warmer.

When I look down, I see blotches of gold splashed onto my deep blue dress in a motley of gleaming spots. I don't dare run my finger over it. Not after what I saw in that ballroom.

"Has it stopped?" I ask.

The question is overly simplified for what just happened in there. Has it stopped—*it*. The berserk gold that just rose up with furious motive. I already know my mind is going to be stuck with the memory of tonight for a long time, that I'm going to replay it over and over again.

I won't be able to erase the way the gold moved with violent precision. How it dripped down the walls. How it pooled on the ground. How it splashed, and stabbed, and *consumed*.

"Has it stopped?" I ask again, my voice shriller than I've ever heard it.

I've never been so close to mortal danger before, and my body knows it. Which is why my pulse is still racing, why the tempo of it is pounding in my ears.

Why I can't stop shaking.

"I think so," Manu finally answers as he turns around.

His husband still watches the castle, as if he doesn't trust taking his eyes off it. As if he expects the violence of the liquid metal to lash back to life.

"Damned Divine," I hear him say beneath his breath.

Perhaps his murmured curse has pulled the stopper from the bottled-up crowd, because a flurry of voices starts to pour through the courtyard. Automatically, my power sweeps out, pulling their words to me. My magic sweeps down, catching what they're saying and stringing them up in my mind.

"What's happened?"

"This is King Midas's gold-touch."

"Where's King Midas? Where's King Rot?"

"Our prince is dead."

"Did Midas do this on purpose?"

"But what happened?*"*

The words flow from their mouths to my ears, where they gather like threads in a web for me to spin. Yet soon, I don't even need my power to hear them, because the crowd begins to shout, demanding answers in frenzied cries loud enough for all.

"Shit," Manu hisses, turning toward me. "Maybe you should—"

Someone suddenly shouts, "I know what happened!"

All eyes slam onto the woman, who staggers to the front. She points a shaky finger toward the doors, gold bleeding from their depths like a gaping wound.

"This wasn't King Midas's doing!" she spits out, a long curtain of black hair hanging down her back, her dress looking like part of it melted off. "It was his gold-touched pet! She stole his magic!"

I rear back in surprise, her words tangling up in my head.

"Who is that?" Manu murmurs.

A man from the crowd shoves forward. "What are you talking about, woman?"

She straightens up, sweeping a proud look over the crowd. "I am one of King Midas's royal saddles, and I can tell you all right now that this was all because of Auren. She did this! The gilded whore stole his magic when he gold-touched her, and she figured out she could use it for herself. She lied to him, and now she's attacked him. I saw it with my own eyes when I was running out!"

Shock cuts like an oar through a surf.

"What the fuck?" Manu hisses beneath his breath as he turns to me.

When the woman places a hand on her stomach, it occurs to me who exactly this is.

Mist. The saddle Midas impregnated.

As her words sink in, I start to shake my head in denial at first, and yet, it *must* be true, because what I saw in that room… It was like the gold wasn't in Midas's control at all, like someone else was doing it…

How did I not discover this secret sooner?

"Look!" someone shouts. "Timberwings! Someone's fleeing on timberwings!"

"It's her! The gilded murderer!"

Acknowledgments

I'm just going to jump right in and admit that this book was incredibly difficult to write. I struggled *many* times, wondering if I was getting any of the words right, if I was portraying Auren honestly. Not only is this the longest book I've written to date, but it was also the most complex. I think I had more loose strands to weave than Midas did. I lost hold of them several times, got them all tangled, wanted to give up. If it weren't for the people in my life, I wouldn't have been able to keep hold of the strings.

To my husband, my steady, my home: Thank you for handling everything in the real world, while I dealt with this fictional one. I love you forever and always. Also, you're cute and funny, and you bring me treats, so I like you.

To my daughter who reminds me to breathe and to play: You are my heart.

To my family: Your constant encouragement and pride is what started this all, and I'm so damn lucky to have you guys.

I have so many people in the book world that have made all the difference for me.

Firstly, I'm just blown away by the kindness and support from the Bookstagrammers and BookTokers who have promoted these books. Every single time I get tagged in another gorgeous photo or fun video, it just reminds me how awesome bookish people are. Special shout out to Candice on her Instagram @canxdancexreads because since the moment you read Gild, you have helped to spread the word about this series and been my most epic hype girl. Thank you!

To Sarah Finger Parker: I'm not even sure I can explain how thankful I am. You seriously dragged me over the finish line kicking and screaming (and sometimes bribing) and I love you for it. Thank you for your friendship, and for all the times you woke up at 4 AM in Australia just so you could meet me in the sprint room or help me brainstorm. You're the best sprint partner ever, and this book (and this Raven) would've fallen apart so many times if it weren't for you. 10/10 would recommend.

To Ivy Asher and Ann Denton: How the hell did I get so lucky to land you ladies? This book world would be so lonely and difficult without you. I couldn't ask for more loyal, kind, funny, and just all-around awesome people to have in my squad. Thank you for always beta reading even though you always have a million other things on your plate. And I'm glad we embraced TikTok and now make up entire conversations with videos. I'm here for it.

To Helayna: I'm convinced you're a magical unicorn. This book was rough, and I missed so many deadlines, and still, you worked your magic and stuck with me even though I was a mess. I sent you this book in THIRTEEN different clumps. (I know, I counted.) But somehow, you wrangled me in and polished this beast of a book that just wouldn't end. Thank you for being your magical, patient, understanding self.

To Amy: Thank you for all of your hard work with the formatting of this series. I couldn't ask for an easier person to work with!

To Aubrey: Thank you for all of the gorgeous graphics and designs you make for this series. I'm blown away every single time you send me something.

To Lisa, Cheria, and Reagan: Thank you for moderating my reader group! I never have to worry, because you ladies take care of everything while I'm stuck in the writing cave.

And thank you to my readers.

Every single one of you.

I can't believe how much love I've gotten for this series, or the overall support as an author. I'm so grateful that I get to have this job, because it's all I've ever wanted to do. So thank you for every sentence you read, every review you leave, every post you make. Thank you for taking a chance on a golden girl with ribbons on her back and a fae with spikes on his arms. You guys are pure gold.

—Raven

Raven Kennedy

ABOUT THE AUTHOR

Raven Kennedy is a California girl born and raised, whose love for books pushed her into creating her own worlds.

Her debut series was a romcom fantasy about a cupid looking for love. She has since gone on to write in a range of genres, including the adult dark fantasy romance: The Plated Prisoner Series, which has become a #1 international bestseller with over two million books sold worldwide.

Whether she makes you laugh or cry, or whether the series is about a cupid or a gold-touched woman in a castle, she hopes to create characters that readers can root for.

When Raven isn't writing, she's reading or spending time with her husband and daughters.

You can connect with Raven on her social media, and visit her website: ravenkennedybooks.com